Y0-CKO-675

WHEN LAST SEEN

A JOAN KAHN BOOK

Books by Arthur Maling

SCHROEDER'S GAME
RIPOFF
BENT MAN
DINGDONG
THE SNOWMAN
LOOPHOLE
GO-BETWEEN
DECOY

WHEN LAST SEEN *(Editor)*

WHEN LAST SEEN

Mystery Writers of America
Anthology 1977

EDITED BY
Arthur Maling

HARPER & ROW, PUBLISHERS
New York, Hagerstown, San Francisco, London

Grateful acknowledgment is made for permission to reprint the following:

"Gone Girl" by John Ross Macdonald. Copyright 1953 by Kenneth Millar. First published in *Manhunt.* Reprinted by permission of the author.

"The Crime of Ezechiele Coen" by Stanley Ellin. Copyright © 1963 by Stanley Ellin. First published in *Ellery Queen's Mystery Magazine.* Reprinted by permission of the author.

"That Monday Night" by Pauline C. Smith. Copyright © 1971 by H.S.D. Publications, Inc. First published in *Alfred Hitchcock's Mystery Magazine.* Reprinted by permission of the author.

"The Three Halves" by Joe Gores. Copyright © 1968 by Davis Publications, Inc. First published in *Ellery Queen's Mystery Magazine* under the title "File #3: The Pedretti Case." Reprinted by permission of the author.

"Back in Five Years" by Michael Gilbert. Copyright 1949 by Michael Gilbert. First published in England in *John Bull,* and in the United States in *Ellery Queen's Mystery Magazine.* Reprinted by permission of the author.

(continued)

"The Dog Incident," an original story by Patrick O'Keeffe, copyright © 1977 by Patrick O'Keeffe.

WHEN LAST SEEN. Copyright © 1977 by Arthur Maling. All rights reserved. Printed in the United States of America. No part of this book may be used or reproduced in any manner whatsoever without written permission except in the case of brief quotations embodied in critical articles and reviews. For information address Harper & Row, Publishers, Inc., 10 East 53rd Street, New York, N.Y. 10022. Published simultaneously in Canada by Fitzhenry & Whiteside Limited, Toronto.

FIRST EDITION

Designed by Eve Callahan

Library of Congress Cataloging in Publication Data
Main entry under title:
   When last seen.
   CONTENTS: Introduction.—Macdonald, R. Gone girl.—
   Ellin, S. The crime of Ezechiele Coen.—Smith, P. C.
   That Monday night.—[etc.]
   1. Detective and mystery stories, American.
I. Maling, Arthur. II. Mystery Writers of America.
PZ1.W573   [PS648.D4]   813'.0872   77–3795
ISBN 0–06–012848–8

---

77 78 79 80 10 9 8 7 6 5 4 3 2 1

"The Vanishing of Velma" by Edward D. Hoch. Copyright © 1969 by H.S.D. Publications, Inc. First published in *Alfred Hitchcock's Mystery Magazine*. Reprinted by permission of the author.

"The Perfectionist" by Gerald Tomlinson. Copyright © 1973 by Gerald Tomlinson. First published in *Ellery Queen's Mystery Magazine*. Reprinted by permission of the author.

"The Girl Who Found Things" by Henry Slesar. Copyright © 1976 by Davis Publications Inc. First published in *Alfred Hitchcock's Mystery Magazine*. Reprinted by permission of the author.

"Born Killer" by Dorothy Salisbury Davis. Copyright © 1957 by Dorothy Salisbury Davis. First published in *Ellery Queen's Mystery Magazine*. Reprinted by permission of the author.

"Putting the Pieces Back" by Bill Pronzini. Copyright © 1976 by Davis Publications, Inc. First published in *Alfred Hitchcock's Mystery Magazine,* April 1976. Reprinted by permission of the author.

"The Philippine Key Mystery" by James Holding, Jr. Copyright © 1976 by Davis Publications, Inc. First published in *Ellery Queen's Mystery Magazine*. Reprinted by permission of the author and the author's agents, Scott Meredith Literary Agency, Inc., 845 Third Avenue, New York, N.Y. 10022.

"The Lost Heir" by Lillian de la Torre. Copyright © 1974 by Lillian de la Torre. First published in *Ellery Queen's Mystery Magazine*. Reprinted by permission of the author.

"Nadigo" by Stanley Cohen. Copyright © 1976 by Stanley Cohen. First published in *Mystery Monthly*. Reprinted by permission of the author.

"The Blue Door" by Vincent Starrett. Copyright © 1976 Michael Murphy as literary executor for Vincent Starrett. First published in *Real Detective Tales*. Reprinted by permission of the author.

"All the Way Home" by Dan J. Marlowe. Copyright © 1965 by Davis Publications, Inc. First published in *Ellery Queen's Mystery Magazine* as "By Jaime Sandaval." Reprinted by permission of the author.

For all those who love to read—and all those who try to write—mystery stories

CONTENTS

Introduction	ix
GONE GIRL *by Ross Macdonald*	1
THE CRIME OF EZECHIELE COEN *by Stanley Ellin*	37
THAT MONDAY NIGHT *by Pauline C. Smith*	65
THE THREE HALVES *by Joe Gores*	93
BACK IN FIVE YEARS *by Michael Gilbert*	111
THE VANISHING OF VELMA *by Edward D. Hoch*	123
THE PERFECTIONIST *by Gerald Tomlinson*	145
THE GIRL WHO FOUND THINGS *by Henry Slesar*	157
BORN KILLER *by Dorothy Salisbury Davis*	185
PUTTING THE PIECES BACK *by Bill Pronzini*	203
THE PHILIPPINE KEY MYSTERY *by James Holding*	211
THE LOST HEIR *by Lillian de la Torre*	229
NADIGO *by Stanley Cohen*	249
THE DOG INCIDENT *by Patrick O'Keeffe*	269
THE BLUE DOOR *by Vincent Starrett*	279
ALL THE WAY HOME *by Dan J. Marlowe*	325

INTRODUCTION

"SHE WENT OUT—AND INTO NOWHERE."

So ran the headline of the Chicago *Sun-Times* on Monday, August 30, 1976.

The story below the headline was written by Bob Greene, and described the events preceding the disappearance of fourteen-year-old Barbara Glueckert, who had attended a rock concert with a girlfriend and a new acquaintance who called himself Tom Edwards, had become separated from them—and had not been seen or heard from since.

Edwards had subsequently been identified as Thomas Urlacher, a twenty-four-year-old with a long record of arrests, but no convictions, for rape and other crimes of violence, and a warrant had been issued for him. But he too had disappeared.

The case wasn't new: Barbara Glueckert had already been missing for nine days. Nor was it unusual. Thousands of teenagers vanish every year. Thousands of adults too. Some are found, some are not. And every now and then a partly decomposed body is discovered buried in some wooded area or floating in a river.

Yet Greene's story had been given the entire front page of a large metropolitan newspaper. It had been placed ahead of stories of much greater national and international importance.

Why?

Because of the skill of the man who wrote it. Greene has the rare talent of being able to take a small news item and turn it into a moving and exciting prose piece that you remember long after you have discarded the pages on which it was printed. It is this talent that has earned him a coast-to-coast reputation.

A forerunner of Greene's had a similar talent. And became interested in a case that was not too different from the Glueckert case.

One hundred and thirty-five years ago, a young New York woman named Mary Cecilia Rogers disappeared, and not long afterward her body was found floating in the Hudson River. She had been murdered. The newspapers of the time—the New York *Journal of Commerce,* the New York *Commercial Advertiser*—devoted a considerable amount of space to the crime. And their articles stirred the imagination of Greene's forerunner, who decided to turn the facts of the Rogers case into a short story.

The story appeared in 1842. Its title was "The Mystery of Marie Rogêt." The man who wrote it was Edgar Allan Poe. And it is still, after six generations, being read and enjoyed.

The Chevalier C. Auguste Dupin, who in Poe's story solved the crime, was the first fictional detective to appear in literature, and the prototype of all that followed, from Sherlock Holmes to Hercule Poirot. But while Poe invented the fictional detective, he did not invent the missing-person story. That goes back to the beginning of storytelling itself. It has flourished throughout the ages.

And in this volume, sixteen authors demonstrate that it is still flourishing. All of them are members of Mystery Writers of America. All of them have the uncommon ability to devise tales that surprise, puzzle, alarm and, ultimately, satisfy legions of readers.

Each of the stories they have contributed deals, in some way, with a missing person. But each story has a different approach, a different feel. Which is only natural, since each of them sprang from a different imagination.

Socially, I have found, mystery writers are pleasant, mild-mannered people. Yet when they sit down at their typewriters something seems to happen to them. They become bloodthirsty. They concoct evil.

Every one of those whose work is represented here must, at some point, have begun to speculate about someone like Barbara Glueckert or Mary Cecilia Rogers—someone who went out and didn't come back. Where such speculation took them you will see for yourself. My only comments are that it took them into some very dark corners.

And that the following pages show how sixteen pleasant, mild-mannered men and women can concoct evil, and do it cleverly.

ARTHUR MALING

GONE GIRL

Ross Macdonald

Ross Macdonald

William Goldman has called Ross Macdonald "one of the best American novelists now operating."

Dick Adler has said of him, "I know of no other writer who catches the spectrum of California life so succinctly, or old sadness in such an immediate way."

And Walter Clemens has written that Macdonald "is a deviser of plots of infernal intricacy," adding that "these plots aren't merely ingenious contraptions; they yield illuminations that outlast our engrossed first reading to find out what will happen, and they retain their power on rereading."

Macdonald's principal creation is Lew Archer, a private detective. And Archer has become not only one of the enduring figures of American detective fiction but also one of its major influences. A man in the mold of Sam Spade and Philip Marlowe—but more compassionate than Spade, less detached than Marlowe—he is essentially a loner, but a loner with deep feelings and ready empathy.

Macdonald himself was born in Los Gatos, California, and was raised in Canada. He is an alumnus of the University of Western Ontario, the University of Toronto and the University of Michigan. After service in the U.S. Navy during World War II, he taught English before becoming a full-time writer. He now lives with his wife, mystery novelist Margaret Millar, in Santa Barbara, California.

Describing Archer, Macdonald says, he "is not so much a knight of romance as an observer, a socially mobile man who knows all levels of Southern California life and takes a peculiar wry pleasure in exploring its secret passages. Archer tends to live through other people, as a novelist lives through his characters."

In "Gone Girl" Archer observes, and becomes involved in, the lives of some very troubled people. Blood is spilled, some of it his. But he solves a murder case, satisfactorily, credibly. "Gone Girl" is Archer at his best.

A. M.

GONE GIRL

It was a Friday night. I was tooling home from the Mexican border in a light blue convertible and a dark blue mood. I had followed a man from Fresno to San Diego and lost him in the maze of streets in Old Town. When I picked up his trail again, it was cold. He had crossed the border, and my instructions went no further than the United States.

Halfway home, just above Emerald Bay, I overtook the worst driver in the world. He was driving a black fishtail Cadillac as if he were tacking a sailboat. The heavy car wove back and forth across the freeway, using two of its four lanes, and sometimes three. It was late, and I was in a hurry to get some sleep. I started to pass it on the right, at a time when it was riding the double line. The Cadillac drifted towards me like an unguided missile, and forced me off the road in a screeching skid.

I speeded up to pass on the left. Simultaneously, the driver of the Cadillac accelerated. My acceleration couldn't match his. We raced neck and neck down the middle of the road. I wondered if he was drunk or crazy or afraid of me. Then the freeway ended. I was doing eighty on the wrong side of a two-lane highway, and a truck came over a rise ahead like a blazing double comet. I floorboarded the gas pedal and cut over sharply to the right, threatening the Cadillac's fenders and its driver's life. In the approaching headlights, his face was as blank and white as a piece of paper, with charred black holes for eyes. His shoulders were naked.

At the last possible second he slowed enough to let me get by. The truck went off onto the shoulder, honking angrily. I braked gradually, hoping to force the Cadillac to stop. It looped past me in an insane arc, tires skittering, and was sucked away into darkness.

When I finally came to a full stop, I had to pry my fingers off the wheel. My knees were remote and watery. After smoking part of a cigarette, I U-turned and drove very cautiously back to Emerald Bay. I was long past the hot-rod age, and I needed rest.

The first motel I came to, the Siesta, was decorated with a vacancy sign and a neon Mexican sleeping luminously under a sombrero. Envying him, I parked on the gravel apron in front of the motel office. There was a light inside. The glass-paned door was standing open, and I went in. The little room was pleasantly furnished with rattan and chintz. I jangled the bell on the desk a few times. No one appeared, so I sat down to wait and lit a cigarette. An electric clock on the wall said a quarter to one.

I must have dozed for a few minutes. A dream rushed by the threshold of my consciousness, making a gentle noise. Death was in the dream. He drove a black Cadillac loaded with flowers. When I woke up, the cigarette was starting to burn my fingers. A thin man in a gray flannel shirt was standing over me with a doubtful look on his face.

He was big-nosed and small-chinned, and he wasn't as young as he gave the impression of being. His teeth were bad, the sandy hair was thinning and receding. He was the typical old youth who scrounged and wheedled his living around motor courts and restaurants and hotels, and hung on desperately to the frayed edge of other people's lives.

"What do you want?" he said. "Who are you? What do you want?" His voice was reedy and changeable like an adolescent's.

"A room."

"Is that all you want?"

From where I sat, it sounded like an accusation. I let it pass. "What else is there? Circassian dancing girls? Free popcorn?"

He tried to smile without showing his bad teeth. The smile was a dismal failure, like my joke. "I'm sorry, sir," he said. "You woke me up. I never make much sense right after I just wake up."

"Have a nightmare?"

His vague eyes expanded like blue bubblegum bubbles. "Why did you ask me that?"

"Because I just had one. But skip it. Do you have a vacancy or don't you?"

"Yessir. Sorry, sir." He swallowed whatever bitter taste he had in his mouth, and assumed an impersonal obsequious manner. "You got any luggage, sir?"

"No luggage."

Moving silently in tennis sneakers like a frail ghost of the boy he once had been, he went behind the counter, and took my name, address, license number, and five dollars. In return, he gave me a key numbered fourteen and told me where to use it. Apparently he despaired of a tip.

Room fourteen was like any other middle-class motel room touched with the California-Spanish mania. Artificially roughened plaster painted adobe color, poinsettia-red curtains, imitation parchment lampshade on a twisted black iron stand. A Rivera reproduction of a sleeping Mexican hung on the wall over the bed. I succumbed to its suggestion right away, and dreamed about Circassian dancing girls.

Along towards morning one of them got frightened, through no fault of mine, and began to scream her little Circassian lungs out. I sat up in bed, making soothing noises, and woke up. It was nearly nine by my wristwatch. The screaming ceased and began again, spoiling the morning like a fire siren outside the window. I pulled on my trousers over the underwear I'd been sleeping in, and went outside.

A young woman was standing on the walk outside the next room. She had a key in one hand and a handful of blood in the other. She wore a wide multicolored skirt and a low-cut gypsy sort of blouse. The blouse was distended and her mouth was open, and she was yelling her head off. It was a fine dark head, but I hated her for spoiling my morning sleep.

I took her by the shoulders and said, "Stop it."

The screaming stopped. She looked down sleepily at the blood on her hand. It was as thick as axle grease, and almost as dark in color.

"Where did you get that?"

"I slipped and fell in it. I didn't see it."

Dropping the key on the walk, she pulled her skirt to one side with her clean hand. Her legs were bare and brown. Her skirt was stained at the back with the same thick fluid.

"Where? In this room?"

She faltered. "Yes."

Doors were opening up and down the drive. Half a dozen people began to converge on us. A dark-faced man about four and a half feet high came scampering from the direction of the office, his little pointed shoes dancing in the gravel.

"Come inside and show me," I said to the girl.

"I can't. I won't." Her eyes were very heavy, and surrounded by the bluish pallor of shock.

The little man slid to a stop between us, reached up and gripped the upper part of her arm. "What is the matter, Ella? Are you crazy, disturbing the guests?"

She said, "Blood," and leaned against me with her eyes closed.

His sharp glance probed the situation. He turned to the other guests, who had formed a murmuring semicircle around us.

"It is perfectly hokay. Do not be concerned, ladies and gentlemen. My daughter cut herself a little bit. It is perfectly all right."

Circling her waist with one long arm, he hustled her through the open door and slammed it behind him. I caught it on my foot and followed them in.

The room was a duplicate of mine, including the reproduction over the unmade bed, but everything was reversed as in a mirror image. The girl took a few weak steps by herself and sat on the edge of the bed. Then she noticed the blood spots on the sheets. She stood up quickly. Her mouth opened, rimmed with white teeth.

"Don't do it," I said. "We know you have a very fine pair of lungs."

The little man turned on me. "Who do you think you are?"

"The name is Archer. I have the next room."

"Get out of this one, please."

"I don't think I will."

He lowered his greased black head as if he were going to butt me. Under his sharkskin jacket, a hunch protruded from his back like a displaced elbow. He seemed to reconsider the butting gambit, and decided in favor of diplomacy.

"You are jumping to conclusions, mister. It is not so serious as it looks. We had a little accident here last night."

"Sure, your daughter cut herself. She heals remarkably fast."

"Nothing like that." He fluttered one long hand. "I said to the people outside the first thing that came to my mind. Actually, it was a little scuffle. One of the guests suffered a nosebleed."

The girl moved like a sleepwalker to the bathroom door and switched on the light. There was a pool of blood coagulating on the black and white checkerboard linoleum, streaked where she had slipped and fallen in it.

"Some nosebleed," I said to the little man. "Do you run this joint?"

"I am the proprietor of the Siesta motor hotel, yes. My name is Salanda. The gentleman is susceptible to nosebleed. He told me so himself."

"Where is he now?"

"He checked out early this morning."

"In good health?"

"Certainly in good health."

I looked around the room. Apart from the unmade bed with the brown spots on the sheets, it contained no signs of occupancy. Someone had spilled a pint of blood and vanished.

The little man opened the door wide and invited me with a sweep of his arm to leave. "If you will excuse me, sir, I wish to have this cleaned up as quickly as possible. Ella, will you tell Lorraine to get to work on it right away pronto? Then maybe you better lie down for a little while, eh?"

"I'm all right now, Father. Don't worry about me."

When I checked out a few minutes later, she was sitting behind the desk in the front office, looking pale but composed. I dropped my key on the desk in front of her.

"Feeling better, Ella?"

"Oh. I didn't recognize you with all your clothes on."

"That's a good line. May I use it?"

She lowered her eyes and blushed. "You're making fun of me. I know I acted foolishly this morning."

"I'm not so sure. What do *you* think happened in thirteen last night?"

"My father told you, didn't he?"

"He gave me a version, two of them in fact. I doubt that they're the final shooting script."

Her hand went to the central hollow in her blouse. Her arms and shoulders were slender and brown, the tips of her fingers carmine. "Shooting?"

"A cinema term," I said. "But there might have been a real shooting at that. Don't you think so?"

Her front teeth pinched her lower lip. She looked like somebody's pet rabbit. I restrained an impulse to pat her sleek brown head.

"That's ridiculous. This is a respectable motel. Anyway, father asked me not to discuss it with anybody."

"Why would he do that?"

"He loves this place, that's why. He doesn't want any scandal made out of nothing. If we lost our good reputation here, it would break my father's heart."

"He doesn't strike me as the sentimental type."

She stood up, smoothing her skirt. I saw that she'd changed it. "You leave him alone. He's a dear little man. I don't know what you think you're doing, trying to stir up trouble where there isn't any."

I backed away from her righteous indignation—female indignation is always righteous—and went out to my car. The early spring sun was dazzling. Beyond the freeway and the drifted sugary dunes, the bay was Prussian blue. The road cut inland across the base of the peninsula and returned to the sea a few miles north of the town. Here a wide blacktop parking space shelved off to the left of the highway, overlooking the white beach and whiter breakers. Signs at each end of the turnout stated that this was a County Park, No Beach Fires.

The beach and the blacktop expanse above it were deserted except for a single car, which looked very lonely. It was a long black Cadillac nosed into the cable fence at the edge of the beach. I braked and turned off the highway and got out. The man in the driver's seat of the Cadillac didn't turn his head as I approached him. His chin was propped on the steering wheel, and he was gazing out across the endless blue sea.

I opened the door and looked into his face. It was paper white. The dark brown eyes were sightless. The body was unclothed except for the thick hair matted on the chest, and a clumsy bandage tied around the waist. The bandage was composed of several blood-stained towels, held in place by a knotted piece of nylon fabric whose nature I didn't recognize immediately. Examining it more closely, I saw that it was a woman's slip. The left breast of the garment was embroidered in purple with a heart containing the name "Fern" in slanting script. I wondered who Fern was.

The man who was wearing her purple heart had dark curly hair, heavy black eyebrows, a heavy chin sprouting black beard. He was rough-looking in spite of his anemia and the lipstick smudged on his mouth.

There was no registration on the steeringpost, and nothing in the glove compartment but a half-empty box of shells for a .38 automatic. The ignition was still turned on. So were the dash and headlights, but they were dim. The gas gauge registered empty. Curlyhead must have pulled off the highway soon after he passed me, and driven all the rest of the night in one place.

I untied the slip, which didn't look as if it would take fingerprints, and went over it for a label. It had one: Gretchen, Palm Springs. It occurred to me that it was Saturday morning and that I'd gone all winter without a weekend in the desert. I retied the slip the way I'd found it, and drove back to the Siesta Motel.

Ella's welcome was a few degrees colder than absolute zero. "Well!" She glared down her pretty rabbit nose at me. "I thought we were rid of you."

"So did I. But I just couldn't tear myself away."

She gave me a peculiar look, neither hard nor soft, but mixed. Her hand went to her hair, then reached for a registration card. "I suppose if you want to rent a room, I can't stop you. Only please don't imagine you're making an impression on me. You're not. You leave me cold, mister."

"Archer," I said. "Lew Archer. Don't bother with the card. I came back to use your phone."

"Aren't there any other phones?" She pushed the telephone across the desk. "I guess it's all right, long as it isn't a toll call."

"I'm calling the Highway Patrol. Do you know their local number?"

"I don't remember." She handed me the telephone directory.

"There's been an accident," I said as I dialed.

"A highway accident? Where did it happen?"

"Right here, sister. Right here in room thirteen."

But I didn't tell that to the Highway Patrol. I told them I had found a dead man in a car on the parking lot above the county beach. The girl listened with widening eyes and nostrils. Before I finished she rose in a flurry and left the office by the rear door.

She came back with the proprietor. His eyes were black and bright like nailheads in leather, and the scampering dance of his feet was almost frenzied. "What is this?"

"I came across a dead man up the road a piece."

"So why do you come back here to telephone?" His head was in butting position, his hands outspread and gripping the corners of the desk. "Has it got anything to do with us?"

"He's wearing a couple of your towels."

"What?"

"And he was bleeding heavily before he died. I think somebody shot him in the stomach. Maybe you did."

"You're loco," he said, but not very emphatically. "Crazy accusations like that, they will get you into trouble. What is your business?"

"I'm a private detective."

"You followed him here, is that it? You were going to arrest him, so he shot himself?"

"Wrong on both accounts," I said. "I came here to sleep. And they don't shoot themselves in the stomach. It's too uncertain, and slow. No suicide wants to die of peritonitis."

"So what are you doing now, trying to make scandal for my business?"

"If your business includes trying to cover for murder."

"He shot himself," the little man insisted.

"How do you know?"

"Donny. I spoke to him just now."

"And how does Donny know?"

"The man told him."

"Is Donny your night keyboy?"

"He was. I think I will fire him, for stupidity. He didn't even tell me about this mess. I had to find it out for myself. The hard way."

"Donny means well," the girl said at his shoulder. "I'm sure he didn't realize what happened."

"Who does?" I said. "I want to talk to Donny. But first let's have a look at the register."

He took a pile of cards from a drawer and riffled through them. His large hands, hairy-backed, were calm and expert, like animals that lived a serene life of their own, independent of their emotional owner. They dealt me one of the cards across the desk. It was inscribed in block capitals: Richard Rowe, Detroit, Mich.

I said: "There was a woman with him."

"Impossible."

"Or he was a transvestite."

He surveyed me blankly, thinking of something else. "The HP, did you tell them to come here? They know it happened here?"

"Not yet. But they'll find your towels. He used them for bandages."

"I see. Yes. Of course." He struck himself with a clenched fist on the temple. It made a noise like someone maltreating a pumpkin. "You are a private detective, you say. Now if you informed the police that you were on the trail of a fugitive, a fugitive from justice. . . . He shot himself rather than face arrest. . . . For five hundred dollars?"

"I'm not that private," I said. "I have some public responsibility. Besides, the cops would do a little checking and catch me out."

"Not necessarily. He *was* a fugitive from justice, you know."

"I hear you telling me."

"Give me a little time, and I can even present you with his record."

The girl was leaning back away from her father, her eyes starred with broken illusions. "Daddy," she said weakly.

He didn't hear her. All of his bright black attention was fixed on me. "Seven hundred dollars?"

"No sale. The higher you raise it, the guiltier you look. Were you here last night?"

"You are being absurd," he said. "I spent the entire evening with my wife. We drove up to Los Angeles to attend the ballet." By way of supporting evidence, he hummed a couple of bars from Tchaikovsky. "We didn't arrive back here in Emerald Bay until nearly two o'clock."

"Alibis can be fixed."

"By criminals, yes," he said. "I am not a criminal."

The girl put a hand on his shoulder. He cringed away, his face creased by monkey fury, but his face was hidden from her.

"Daddy," she said. "Was he murdered, do you think?"

"How do I know?" His voice was wild and high, as if she had touched the spring of his emotion. "I wasn't here. I only know what Donny told me."

The girl was examining me with narrowed eyes, as if I were a new kind of animal she had discovered and was trying to think of a use for.

"This gentleman is a detective," she said, "or claims to be."

I pulled out my photostat and slapped it down on the desk. The little man picked it up and looked from it to my face. "Will you go to work for me?"

"Doing what, telling little white lies?"

The girl answered for him: "See what you can find out about this —this death. On my word of honor, Father had nothing to do with it."

I made a snap decision, the kind you live to regret. "All right. I'll take a fifty-dollar advance. Which is a good deal less than five hundred. My first advice to you is to tell the police everything you know. Provided that you're innocent."

"You insult me," he said.

But he flicked a fifty-dollar bill from the cash drawer and pressed it into my hand fervently, like a love token. I had a queasy feeling that I had been conned into taking his money, not much of it but enough. The feeling deepened when he still refused to talk. I had to use all the arts of persuasion even to get Donny's address out of him.

The keyboy lived in a shack on the edge of a desolate stretch of dunes. I guessed that it had once been somebody's beach house, before sand had drifted like unthawing snow in the angles of the walls and winter storms had broken the tiles and cracked the concrete foundations. Huge chunks of concrete were piled haphazardly on what had been a terrace overlooking the sea.

On one of the tilted slabs, Donny was stretched like a long albino lizard in the sun. The onshore wind carried the sound of my motor to his ears. He sat up blinking, recognized me when I stopped the car, and ran into the house.

I descended flagstone steps and knocked on the warped door. "Open up, Donny."

"Go away," he answered huskily. His eye gleamed like a snail through a crack in the wood.

"I'm working for Mr. Salanda. He wants us to have a talk."

"You can go and take a running jump at yourself, you and Mr. Salanda both."

"Open it or I'll break it down."

I waited for a while. He shot back the bolt. The door creaked reluctantly open. He leaned against the doorpost, searching my face with his eyes, his hairless body shivering from an internal chill. I pushed past him, through a kitchenette that was indescribably filthy, littered with the remnants of old meals, and gaseous with their odors. He followed me silently on bare soles into a larger room whose sprung floorboards undulated under my feet. The picture window had been broken and patched with cardboard. The stone fireplace was choked with garbage. The only furniture was an army cot in one corner where Donny apparently slept.

"Nice homey place you have here. It has that lived-in quality."

He seemed to take it as a compliment, and I wondered if I was dealing with a moron. "It suits me. I never was much of a one for fancy quarters. I like it here, where I can hear the ocean at night."

"What else do you hear at night, Donny?"

He missed the point of the question, or pretended to. "All different things. Big trucks going past on the highway. I like to hear those night sounds. Now I guess I can't go on living here. Mr. Salanda owns it, he lets me live here for nothing. Now he'll be kicking me out of here, I guess."

"On account of what happened last night?"

"Uh-huh." He subsided onto the cot, his doleful head supported by his hands.

I stood over him. "Just what did happen last night, Donny?"

"A bad thing," he said. "This fella checked in about ten o'clock—"

"The man with the dark curly hair?"

"That's the one. He checked in about ten, and I gave him room thirteen. Around about midnight I thought I heard a gun go off from there. It took me a little while to get my nerve up, then I went back to see what was going on. This fella came out of the room, without no clothes on. Just some kind of a bandage around his waist. He looked like some kind of a crazy Indian or something. He had a gun in his hand, and he was staggering, and I could see that he was bleeding some. He come right up to me and pushed the gun in my gut and told me to keep my trap shut. He said I wasn't to tell anybody I saw him, now or later. He said if I opened my mouth about it to anybody, that he would come back and kill me. But now he's dead, isn't he?"

"He's dead."

I could smell the fear on Donny: there's an unexplained trace of canine in my chromosomes. The hairs were prickling on the back of my neck, and I wondered if Donny's fear was of the past or for the future. The pimples stood out in bas-relief against his pale lugubrious face.

"I think he was murdered, Donny. You're lying, aren't you?"

"Me lying?" But his reaction was slow and feeble.

"The dead man didn't check in alone. He had a woman with him."

"What woman?" he said in elaborate surprise.

"You tell me. Her name was Fern. I think she did the shooting, and you caught her red-handed. The wounded man got out of the room and into his car and away. The woman stayed behind to talk to you. She probably paid you to dispose of his clothes and fake a new registration card for the room. But you both overlooked the blood on the floor of the bathroom. Am I right?"

"You couldn't be wronger, mister. Are you a cop?"

"A private detective. You're in deep trouble, Donny. You'd better talk yourself out of it if you can, before the cops start on you."

"I didn't do anything." His voice broke like a boy's. It went strangely with the glints of gray in his hair.

"Faking the register is a serious rap, even if they don't hang accessory to murder on you."

He began to expostulate in formless sentences that ran together. At the same time his hand was moving across the dirty gray blanket. It burrowed under the pillow and came out holding a crumpled card. He tried to stuff it into his mouth and chew it. I tore it away from between his discolored teeth.

It was a registration card from the motel, signed in a boyish scrawl: Mr. and Mrs. Richard Rowe, Detroit, Mich.

Donny was trembling violently. Below his cheap cotton shorts, his bony knees vibrated like tuning forks. "It wasn't my fault," he cried. "She held a gun on me."

"What did you do with the man's clothes?"

"Nothing. She didn't even let me into the room. She bundled them up and took them away herself."

"Where did she go?"

"Down the highway towards town. She walked away on the shoulder of the road and that was the last I saw of her."

"How much did she pay you, Donny?"

"Nothing, not a cent. I already told you, she held a gun on me."

"And you were so scared you kept quiet until this morning?"

"That's right. I was scared. Who wouldn't be scared?"

"She's gone now," I said. "You can give me a description of her."

"Yeah." He made a visible effort to pull his vague thoughts together. One of his eyes was a little off center, lending his face a stunned, amorphous appearance. "She was a big tall dame with blondy hair."

"Dyed?"

"I guess so, I dunno. She wore it in a braid like, on top of her head. She was kind of fat, built like a lady wrestler, great big watermelons on her. Big legs."

"How was she dressed?"

"I didn't hardly notice, I was so scared. I think she had some kind of a purple coat on, with black fur around the neck. Plenty of rings on her fingers and stuff."

"How old?"

"Pretty old, I'd say. Older than me, and I'm going on thirty-nine."

"And she did the shooting?"

"I guess so. She told me to say if anybody asked me, I was to say that Mr. Rowe shot himself."

"You're very suggestible, aren't you, Donny? It's a dangerous way to be, with people pushing each other around the way they do."

"I didn't get that, mister. Come again." He batted his pale blue eyes at me, smiling expectantly.

"Skip it," I said and left him.

A few hundred yards up the highway I passed an HP car with two uniformed men in the front seat looking grim. Donny was in for it now. I pushed him out of my mind and drove across country to Palm Springs.

Palm Springs is still a one-horse town, but the horse is a Palomino with silver trappings. Most of the girls were Palomino too. The main street was a cross-section of Hollywood and Vine transported across the desert by some unnatural force and disguised in western costumes which fooled nobody. Not even me.

I found Gretchen's lingerie shop in an expensive-looking arcade built around an imitation flagstone patio. In the patio's center a little fountain gurgled pleasantly, flinging small lariats of spray against the heat. It was late in March, and the season was ending. Most of the shops, including the one I entered, were deserted except for the hired help.

It was a small shop, faintly perfumed by a legion of vanished dolls. Stockings and robes and other garments were coiled on the glass counters or hung like brilliant treesnakes on display stands along the narrow walls. A henna-headed woman emerged from rustling recesses at the rear and came tripping towards me on her toes.

"You are looking for a gift, sir?" she cried with a wilted kind of gaiety. Behind her painted mask, she was tired and aging and it was Saturday afternoon and the lucky ones were dunking themselves in kidney-shaped swimming pools behind walls she couldn't climb.

"Not exactly. In fact, not at all. A peculiar thing happened to me last night. I'd like to tell you about it, but it's kind of a complicated story."

She looked me over quizzically and decided that I worked for a living too. The phony smile faded away. Another smile took its place, which I liked better. "You look as if you'd had a fairly rough night. And you could do with a shave."

"I met a girl," I said. "Actually she was a mature woman, a

statuesque blonde to be exact. I picked her up on the beach at Laguna, if you want me to be brutally frank."

"I couldn't bear it if you weren't. What kind of a pitch is this, brother?"

"Wait. You're spoiling my story. Something clicked when we met, in that sunset light, on the edge of the warm summer sea."

"It's always bloody cold when I go in."

"It wasn't last night. We swam in the moonlight and had a gay time and all. Then she went away. I didn't realize until she was gone that I didn't know her telephone number, or even her last name."

"Married woman, eh? What do you think I am, a lonely hearts club?" Still, she was interested, though she probably didn't believe me. "She mentioned me, is that it? What was her first name?"

"Fern."

"Unusual name. You say she was a big blonde?"

"Magnificently proportioned," I said. "If I had a classical education I'd call her Junoesque."

"You're kidding me, aren't you?"

"A little."

"I thought so. Personally I don't mind a little kidding. What did she say about me?"

"Nothing but good. As a matter of fact, I was complimenting her on her—er—garments."

"I see." She was long past blushing. "We had a customer last fall sometime by the name of Fern. Fern Dee. She had some kind of a job at the Joshua Club, I think. But she doesn't fit the description at all. This one was a brunette, a middle-sized brunette, quite young. I remember the name Fern because she wanted it embroidered on all the things she bought. A corny idea if you ask me, but that was her girlish desire and who am I to argue with girlish desires."

"Is she still in town?"

"I haven't seen her lately, not for months. But it couldn't be the woman you're looking for. Or could it?"

"How long ago was she in here?"

She pondered. "Early last fall, around the start of the season. She only came in that once, and made a big purchase, stockings and nightwear and underthings. The works. I remember thinking at the time, here was a girlie who suddenly hit the chips but heavily."

"She might have put on weight since then, and dyed her hair. Strange things can happen to the female form."

"You're telling me," she said. "How old was—your friend?"

"About forty, I'd say, give or take a little."

"It couldn't be the same one then. The girl I'm talking about was twenty-five at the outside, and I don't make mistakes about women's ages. I've seen too many of them in all stages, from Quentin quail to hags, and I certainly do mean hags."

"I bet you have."

She studied me with eyes shadowed by mascara and experience. "You a policeman?"

"I have been."

"You want to tell mother what it's all about?"

"Another time. Where's the Joshua Club?"

"It won't be open yet."

"I'll try it anyway."

She shrugged her thin shoulders and gave me directions. I thanked her.

It occupied a plain-faced one-story building half a block off the main street. The padded leather door swung inward when I pushed it. I passed through a lobby with a retractable roof, which contained a jungle growth of banana trees. The big main room was decorated with tinted desert photomurals. Behind a rattan bar with a fishnet canopy, a white-coated Caribbean type was drying shot-glasses with a dirty towel. His face looked uncommunicative.

On the orchestra dais beyond the piled chairs in the dining area, a young man in shirt sleeves was playing bop piano. His fingers shadowed the tune, ran circles around it, played leapfrog with it, and managed never to hit it on the nose. I stood beside him for a while and listened to him work. He looked up finally, still strumming with his left hand in the bass. He had soft-centered eyes and frozen-looking nostrils and a whistling mouth.

"Nice piano," I said.

"I think so."

"Fifty-second Street?"

"It's the street with the beat and I'm not effete." His left hand struck the same chord three times and dropped away from the keys. "Looking for somebody, friend?"

"Fern Dee. She asked me to drop by some time."

"Too bad. Another wasted trip. She left here end of last year, the dear. She wasn't a bad little nightingale but she was no pro, Joe, you know? She had it but she couldn't project it. When she warbled the evening died, no matter how hard she tried, I don't wanna be snide."

"Where did she lam, Sam, or don't you give a damn?"

He smiled like a corpse in a deft mortician's hands. "I heard the boss retired her to private life. Took her home to live with him. That is what I heard. But I don't mix with the big boy socially, so I couldn't say for sure that she's impure. Is it anything to you?"

"Something, but she's over twenty-one."

"Not more than a couple of years over twenty-one." His eyes darkened, and his thin mouth twisted sideways angrily. "I hate to see it happen to a pretty little twist like Fern. Not that I yearn—"

I broke in on his nonsense rhymes: "Who's the big boss you mentioned, the one Fern went to live with?"

"Angel. Who else?"

"What heaven does he inhabit?"

"You must be new in these parts—" His eyes swiveled and focused on something over my shoulder. His mouth opened and closed.

A grating tenor said behind me, "Got a question you want answered, bud?"

The pianist went back to the piano as if the ugly tenor had wiped me out, annulled my very existence. I turned to its source. He was standing in a narrow doorway behind the drums, a man in his thirties with thick black curly hair and a heavy jaw blue-shadowed by closely shaven beard. He was almost the living image of the dead man in the Cadillac. The likeness gave me a jolt. The heavy black gun in his hand gave me another.

He came around the drums and approached me, bull-shouldered in a fuzzy tweed jacket, holding the gun in front of him like a dangerous gift. The pianist was doing wry things in quickened tempo with the dead march from *Saul.* A wit.

The dead man's almost-double waved his cruel chin and the crueler gun in unison. "Come inside, unless you're a government man. If you are, I'll have a look at your credentials."

"I'm a freelance."

"Inside then."

The muzzle of the automatic came into my solar plexus like a pointing iron finger. Obeying its injunction, I made my way between empty music stands and through the narrow door behind the drums. The iron finger, probing my back, directed me down a lightless corridor to a small square office containing a metal desk, a safe, a filing cabinet. It was windowless, lit by fluorescent tubes in the ceiling. Under their pitiless glare, the face above the gun looked more than ever like the dead man's face. I wondered if I had been mistaken about his deadness, or if the desert heat had addled my brain.

"I'm the manager here," he said, standing so close that I could smell the piney stuff he used on his crisp dark hair. "You got anything to ask about the members of the staff, you ask me."

"Will I get an answer?"

"Try me, bud."

"The name is Archer," I said. "I'm a private detective."

"Working for who?"

"You wouldn't be interested."

"I am, though, very much interested." The gun hopped forward like a toad into my stomach again, with the weight of his shoulder behind it. "Working for who did you say?"

I swallowed anger and nausea, estimating my chances of knocking the gun to one side and taking him bare-handed. The chances seemed pretty slim. He was heavier than I was, and he held the automatic as if it had grown out of the end of his arm. You've seen too many movies, I told myself. I told him, "A motel owner on the coast. A man was shot in one of his rooms last night. I happened to check in there a few minutes later. The old boy hired me to look into the shooting."

"Who was it got himself ventilated?"

"He could be your brother," I said. "Do you have a brother?"

He lost his color. The center of his attention shifted from the gun to my face. The gun nodded. I knocked it up and sideways with a hard left uppercut. Its discharge burned the side of my face and drilled a hole in the wall. My right sank into his neck. The gun thumped the cork floor.

He went down but not out, his spread hand scrabbling for the gun, then closing on it. I kicked his wrist. He grunted but wouldn't let go of it. I threw a punch at the short hairs on the back of his neck. He took it and came up under it with the gun, shaking his head from side to side.

"Up with the hands now," he murmured. He was one of those men whose voices go soft and mild when they are in killing mood. He had the glassy impervious eyes of a killer. "Is Bart dead? My brother?"

"Very dead. He was shot in the belly."

"Who shot him?"

"That's the question."

"Who shot him?" he said in a quiet white-faced rage. The single eye of the gun stared emptily at my midriff. "It could happen to you, bud, here and now."

"A woman was with him. She took a quick powder after it happened."

"I heard you say a name to Alfie, the piano player. Was it Fern?"

"It could have been."

"What do you mean, it could have been?"

"She was there in the room, apparently. If you can give me a description of her?"

His hard brown eyes looked past me. "I can do better than that. There's a picture of her on the wall behind you. Take a look at it. Keep those hands up high."

I shifted my feet and turned uneasily. The wall was blank. I heard him draw a breath and move, and tried to evade his blow. No use. It caught the back of my head. I pitched forward against the blank wall and slid down it into three dimensions of blankness.

The blankness coagulated into colored shapes. The shapes were half human and half beast and they dissolved and reformed. A dead man with a hairy breast climbed out of a hole and doubled and quadrupled. I ran away from them through a twisting tunnel which led to an echo chamber.

Under the roaring surge of the nightmare music, a rasping tenor was saying, "I figure it like this. Vario's tip was good. Bart found her in Acapulco, and he was bringing her back from there. She conned him into stopping off at this motel for the night. Bart always went for her."

"I didn't know that," a dry old voice put in. "This is very interesting news about Bart and Fern. You should have told me before about this. Then I would not have sent him for her and this would not have happened. Would it, Gino?"

My mind was still partly absent, wandering underground in the echoing caves. I couldn't recall the voices, or who they were talking about. I had barely sense enough to keep my eyes closed and go on listening. I was lying on my back on a hard surface. The voices were above me.

The tenor said, "You can't blame Bartolomeo. She's the one, the dirty treacherous lying little bitch."

"Calm yourself, Gino. I blame nobody. But more than ever now, we want her back, isn't that right?"

"I'll kill her," he said softly, almost wistfully.

"Perhaps. It may not be necessary now. I dislike promiscuous killing—"

"Since when, Angel?"

"Don't interrupt, it's not polite. I learned to put first things first. Now what is the most important thing? Why did we want her back in the first place? I will tell you: to shut her mouth. The government heard she left me, they wanted her to testify about my income. We wanted to find her first and shut her mouth, isn't that right?"

"I know how to shut her mouth," the younger man said very quietly.

"First we try a better way, my way. You learn when you're as old as I am there is a use for everything, and not to be wasteful. Not even wasteful with somebody else's blood. She shot your brother, right? So now we have something on her, strong enough to keep her mouth shut for good. She'd get off with second degree, with what she's got, but even that is five to ten in Tehachapi. I think all I need to do is tell her that. First we have to find her, eh?"

"I'll find her. Bart didn't have any trouble finding her."

"With Vario's tip to help him, no. But I think I'll keep you here with me, Gino. You're too hot-blooded, you and your brother both. I want her alive. Then I can talk to her, and then we'll see."

"You're going soft in your old age, Angel."

"Am I?" There was a light slapping sound, of a blow on flesh. "I have killed many men, for good reasons. So I think you will take that back."

"I take it back."

"And call me Mr. Funk. If I am so old, you will treat my gray hairs with respect. Call me Mr. Funk."

"Mr. Funk."

"All right, your friend here, does he know where Fern is?"

"I don't think so."

"Mr. Funk."

"Mr. Funk." Gino's voice was a whining snarl.

"I think he's coming to. His eyelids fluttered."

The toe of a shoe prodded my side. Somebody slapped my face a number of times. I opened my eyes and sat up. The back of my head was throbbing like an engine fueled by pain. Gino rose from a squatting position and stood over me.

"Stand up."

I rose shakily to my feet. I was in a stone-walled room with a high beamed ceiling, sparsely furnished with stiff old black oak chairs and tables. The room and the furniture seemed to have been built for a race of giants.

The man behind Gino was small and old and weary. He might have been an unsuccessful grocer or a superannuated barkeep who had come to California for his health. Clearly his health was poor. Even in the stifling heat he looked pale and chilly, as if he had caught chronic death from one of his victims. He moved closer to me, his legs shuffling feebly in wrinkled blue trousers that bagged at the knees. His shrunken torso was swathed in a heavy blue turtleneck sweater. He had two days' beard on his chin, like moth-eaten gray plush.

"Gino informs me that you are investigating a shooting." His accent was Middle-European and very faint, as if he had forgotten his origins. "Where did this happen, exactly?"

"I don't think I'll tell you that. You can read it in the papers tomorrow night if you are interested."

"I am not prepared to wait. I am impatient. Do you know where Fern is?"

"I wouldn't be here if I did."

"But you know where she was last night."

"I couldn't be sure."

"Tell me anyway to the best of your knowledge."

"I don't think I will."

"He doesn't think he will," the old man said to Gino.

"I think you better let me out of here. Kidnaping is a tough rap. You don't want to die in the pen."

He smiled at me, with a tolerance more terrible than anger. His eyes were like thin stab-wounds filled with watery blood. Shuffling unhurriedly to the head of the mahogany table behind him, he pressed a spot in the rug with the toe of one felt slipper. Two men in blue serge suits entered the room and stepped towards me briskly. They belonged to the race of giants it had been built for.

Gino moved behind me and reached to pin my arms. I pivoted, landed one short punch, and took a very hard counter below the belt. Something behind me slammed my kidneys with the heft of a trailer truck bumper. I turned on weakening legs and caught a chin with my elbow. Gino's fist, or one of the beams from the ceiling, landed on my neck. My head rang like a gong.

Under its clangor, Angel was saying pleasantly, "Where was Fern last night?"

I didn't say.

The men in blue serge held me upright by the arms while Gino used my head as a punching bag. I rolled with his lefts and rights as well as I could, but his timing improved and mine deteriorated. His face wavered and receded. At intervals Angel inquired politely if I was willing to assist him now. I asked myself confusedly in the hail of fists what I was holding out for or who I was protecting. Probably I was holding out for myself. It seemed important to me not to give in to violence. But my identity was dissolving and receding like the face in front of me.

I concentrated on hating Gino's face. That kept it clear and steady for a while: a stupid square-jawed face barred by a single black brow, two close-set brown eyes staring glassily. His fists continued to rock me like an air hammer.

Finally Angel placed a clawed hand on his shoulder, and nodded to my handlers. They deposited me in a chair. It swung on an invisible wire from the ceiling in great circles. It swung out wide over the desert, across a bleak horizon, into darkness.

I came to, cursing. Gino was standing over me again. There was an empty water glass in his hand, and my face was dripping.

Angel spoke up beside him, with a trace of irritation in his voice: "You stand up good under punishment. Why go to all the trouble, though? I want a little information, that is all. My friend, my little girlfriend, ran away. I'm impatient to get her back."

"You're going about it the wrong way."

Gino leaned close and laughed harshly. He shattered the glass on the arm of my chair, held the jagged base up to my eyes. Fear ran through me, cold and light in my veins. My eyes were my connection with everything. Blindness would be the end of me. I closed my eyes, shutting out the cruel edges of the broken thing in his hand.

"Nix, Gino," the old man said. "I have a better idea, as usual. There is heat on, remember."

They retreated to the far side of the table and conferred there in low voices. The young man left the room. The old man came back to me. His storm troopers stood one on each side of me, looking down at him in ignorant awe.

"What is your name, young fellow?"

I told him. My mouth was puffed and lisping, tongue tangled in ropes of blood.

"I like a young fellow who can take it, Mr. Archer. You say that you're a detective. You find people for a living, is that right?"

"I have a client," I said.

"Now you have another. Whoever he is, I can buy and sell him, believe me. Fifty times over." His thin blue hands scoured each other. They made a sound like two dry sticks rubbing together on a dead tree.

"Narcotics?" I said. "Are you the wheel in the heroin racket? I've heard of you."

His watery eyes veiled themselves like a bird's. "Now don't ask foolish questions, or I will lose my respect for you entirely."

"That would break my heart."

"Then comfort yourself with this." He brought an old-fashioned purse out of his hip pocket, abstracted a crumpled bill and smoothed it out on my knee. It was a five-hundred-dollar bill.

"This girl of mine you are going to find for me, she is young and foolish. I am old and foolish, to have trusted her. No matter. Find her for me and bring her back and I will give you another bill like this one. Take it."

"Take it," one of my guards repeated. "Mr. Funk said for you to take it."

I took it. "You're wasting your money. I don't even know what she looks like. I don't know anything about her."

"Gino is bringing a picture. He came across her last fall at a recording studio in Hollywood where Alfie had a date. He gave her an audition and took her on at the club, more for her looks than for the talent she had. As a singer she flopped. But she is a pretty little thing, about five foot four, nice figure, dark brown hair, big hazel eyes. I found a use for her." Lechery flickered briefly in his eyes and went out.

"You find a use for everything."

"That is good economics. I often think if I wasn't what I am, I would make a good economist. Nothing would go to waste." He paused and dragged his dying old mind back to the subject: "She was here for a couple of months, then she ran out on me, silly girl. I heard last week that she was in Acapulco, and the federal Grand Jury was going to subpoena her. I have tax troubles, Mr. Archer, all my life I have tax troubles. Unfortunately I let Fern help with my books a little bit. She could do me great harm. So I sent Bart to Mexico to bring her back. But I meant no harm to her. I still intend her no harm, even now. A little talk, a little realistic discussion with Fern, that is all that will be necessary. So even the shooting of my good friend Bart serves its purpose. Where did it happen, by the way?"

The question flicked out like a hook on the end of a long line.

"In San Diego," I said, "at a place near the airport: the Mission Motel."

He smiled paternally. "Now you are showing good sense."

Gino came back with a silver-framed photograph in his hand. He handed it to Angel, who passed it on to me. It was a studio portrait, of the kind intended for publicity cheesecake. On a black velvet divan, against an artificial night sky, a young woman reclined in a gossamer robe that was split to show one bent leg. Shadows accentuated the lines of her body and the fine bones in her face. Under the heavy makeup which widened the mouth and darkened the half-closed eyes, I recognized Ella Salanda. The picture was signed in white, in the lower right-hand corner: "To my Angel, with all my love, Fern."

A sickness assailed me, worse than the sickness induced by Gino's fists. Angel breathed into my face: "Fern Dee is a stage name. Her real name I never learned. She told me one time that if her family knew where she was they would die of shame." He chuckled dryly. "She will not want them to know that she killed a man."

I drew away from his charnel-house breath. My guards escorted me out. Gino started to follow, but Angel called him back.

"Don't wait to hear from me," the old man said after me. "I expect to hear from you."

The building stood on a rise in the open desert. It was huge and turreted, like somebody's idea of a castle in Spain. The last rays of the sun washed its walls in purple light and cast long shadows across its barren acreage. It was surrounded by a ten-foot hurricane fence topped with three strands of barbed wire.

Palm Springs was a clutter of white stones in the distance, diamonded by an occasional light. The dull red sun was balanced like a glowing cigar butt on the rim of the hills above the town. A man with a bulky shoulder harness under his brown suede windbreaker drove me towards it. The sun fell out of sight, and darkness gathered like an impalpable ash on the desert, like a column of blue-gray smoke towering into the sky.

The sky was blue-black and swarming with stars when I got back to Emerald Bay. A black Cadillac followed me out of Palm Springs. I lost it in the winding streets of Pasadena. So far as I could see, I had lost it for good.

The neon Mexican lay peaceful under the stars. A smaller sign at his feet asserted that there was No Vacancy. The lights in the long low stucco buildings behind him shone brightly. The office door was open behind a screen, throwing a barred rectangle of light on the gravel. I stepped into it, and froze.

Behind the registration desk in the office, a woman was avidly reading a magazine. Her shoulders and bosom were massive. Her hair was blond, piled on her head in coroneted braids. There were rings on her fingers, a triple strand of cultured pearls around her thick white throat. She was the woman Donny had described to me.

I pulled the screen door open and said rudely, "Who are you?"

She glanced up, twisting her mouth in a sour grimace. "Well! I'll thank you to keep a civil tongue in your head."

"Sorry. I thought I'd seen you before somewhere."

"Well, you haven't." She looked me over coldly. "What happened to your face, anyway?"

"I had a little plastic surgery done. By an amateur surgeon."

She clucked disapprovingly. "If you're looking for a room, we're full up for the night. I don't believe I'd rent you a room even if we weren't. Look at your clothes."

"Uh-huh. Where's Mr. Salanda?"

"Is it any business of yours?"

"He wants to see me. I'm doing a job for him."

"What kind of a job?"

I mimicked her: "Is it any business of yours?" I was irritated. Under her mounds of flesh she had a personality as thin and hard and abrasive as a rasp.

"Watch who you're getting flip with, sonny boy." She rose, and her shadow loomed immense across the back door of the room. The magazine fell closed on the desk: it was *Teen-age Confessions*. "I am Mrs. Salanda. Are you a handyman?"

"A sort of one," I said. "I'm a garbage collector in the moral field. You look as if you could use me."

The crack went over her head. "Well, you're wrong. And I don't think my husband hired you, either. This is a respectable motel."

"Uh-huh. Are you Ella's mother?"

"I should say not. That little snip is no daughter of mine."

"Her stepmother?"

"Mind your own business. You better get out of here. The police are keeping a close watch on this place tonight, if you're planning any tricks."

"Where's Ella now?"

"I don't know and I don't care. She's probably gallivanting off around the countryside. It's all she's good for. One day at home in the last six months, that's a fine record for a young unmarried girl." Her face was thick and bloated with anger against her stepdaughter. She went on talking blindly, as if she had forgotten me entirely: "I told her father he was an old fool to take her back. How does he know what she's been up to? I say let the ungrateful filly go and fend for herself."

"Is that what you say, Mabel?" Salanda had softly opened the door behind her. He came forward into the room, doubly dwarfed by her blond magnitude. "I say if it wasn't for you, my dear, Ella wouldn't have been driven away from home in the first place."

She turned on him in a blubbering rage. He drew himself up tall and reached to snap his fingers under her nose. "Go back into the house. You are a disgrace to women, a disgrace to motherhood."

"I'm not *her* mother, thank God."

"Thank God," he echoed, shaking his fist at her. She retreated like a schooner under full sail, menaced by a gunboat. The door closed on her.

Salanda turned to me. "I'm sorry, Mr. Archer. I have difficulties with my wife, I am ashamed to say it. I was an imbecile to marry again. I gained a senseless hulk of flesh, and lost my daughter. Old imbecile!" he denounced himself, wagging his great head sadly. "I married in hot blood. Sexual passion has always been my downfall. It runs in my family, this insane hunger for blondeness and stupidity and size." He spread his arms in a wide and futile embrace on emptiness.

"Forget it."

"If I could." He came closer to examine my face. "You are injured, Mr. Archer. Your mouth is damaged. There is blood on your chin."

"I was in a slight brawl."

"On my account?"

"On my own. But I think it's time you leveled with me."

"Leveled with you?"

"Told me the truth. You knew who was shot last night, and who shot him, and why."

He touched my arm, with a quick, tentative grace. "I have only one daughter, Mr. Archer, only the one child. It was my duty to defend her, as best as I could."

"Defend her from what?"

"From shame, from the police, from prison." He flung one arm out, indicating the whole range of human disaster. "I am a man of honor, Mr. Archer. But private honor stands higher with me than public honor. The man was abducting my daughter. She brought him here in the hope of being rescued. Her last hope."

"I think that's true. You should have told me this before."

"I was alarmed, upset. I feared your intentions. Any minute the police were due to arrive."

"But you had a right to shoot him. It wasn't even a crime. The crime was his."

"I didn't know that then. The truth came out to me gradually. I feared that Ella was involved with him." His flat black gaze sought my face and rested on it. "However, I did not shoot him, Mr. Archer. I was not even here at the time. I told you that this morning, and you may take my word for it."

"Was Mrs. Salanda here?"

"No sir, she was not. Why should you ask me that?"

"Donny described the woman who checked in with the dead man. The description fits your wife."

"Donny was lying. I told him to give a false description of the woman. Apparently he was unequal to the task of inventing one."

"Can you prove that she was with you?"

"Certainly I can. We had reserved seats at the theatre. Those who sat around us can testify that the seats were not empty. Mrs. Salanda and I, we are not an inconspicuous couple." He smiled wryly.

"Ella killed him then."

He neither assented, nor denied it. "I was hoping that you were on my side, my side and Ella's. Am I wrong?"

"I'll have to talk to her, before I know myself. Where is she?"

"I do not know, Mr. Archer, sincerely I do not know. She went away this afternoon, after the policemen questioned her. They were suspicious, but we managed to soothe their suspicions. They did not know that she had just come home, from another life, and I did not tell them. Mabel wanted to tell them. I silenced her." His white teeth clicked together.

"What about Donny?"

"They took him down to the station for questioning. He told them nothing damaging. Donny can appear very stupid when he wishes. He has the reputation of an idiot, but he is not so dumb. Donny has been with me for many years. He has a deep devotion for my daughter. I got him released tonight."

"You should have taken my advice," I said, "taken the police into your confidence. Nothing would have happened to you. The dead man was a mobster, and what he was doing amounts to kidnaping. Your daughter was a witness against his boss."

"She told me that. I am glad that it is true. Ella has not always told me the truth. She has been a hard girl to bring up, without a good mother to set her an example. Where has she been these last six months, Mr. Archer?"

"Singing in a night club in Palm Springs. Her boss was a racketeer."

"A racketeer?" His mouth and nose screwed up, as if he sniffed the odor of corruption.

"Where she was isn't important, compared with where she is now. The boss is still after her. He hired me to look for her."

Salanda regarded me with fear and dislike, as if the odor originated in me. "You let him hire you?"

"It was my best chance of getting out of his place alive. I'm not his boy, if that's what you mean."

"You ask me to believe you?"

"I'm telling you. Ella is in danger. As a matter of fact, we all are." I didn't tell him about the second black Cadillac. Gino would be driving it, wandering the night roads with a ready gun in his armpit and revenge corroding his heart.

"My daughter is aware of the danger," he said. "She warned me of it."

"She must have told you where she was going."

"No. But she may be at the beach house. The house where Donny lives. I will come with you."

"You stay here. Keep your doors locked. If any strangers show and start prowling the place, call the police."

He bolted the door behind me as I went out. Yellow traffic lights cast wan reflections on the asphalt. Streams of cars went by to the north, to the south. To the west, where the sea lay, a great black emptiness opened under the stars. The beach house sat on its white margin, a little over a mile from the motel.

For the second time that day, I knocked on the warped kitchen door. There was light behind it, shining through the cracks. A shadow obscured the light.

"Who is it?" Donny said. Fear or some other emotion had filled his mouth with pebbles.

"You know me, Donny."

The door groaned on its hinges. He gestured dumbly to me to come in, his face a white blur. When he turned his head, and the light from the living room caught his face, I saw that grief was the emotion that marked it. His eyes were swollen as if he had been crying. More than ever he resembled a dilapidated boy whose growing pains had never paid off in manhood.

"Anybody with you?"

Sounds of movement in the living room answered my question. I brushed him aside and went in. Ella Salanda was bent over an open suitcase on the camp cot. She straightened, her mouth thin, eyes wide and dark. The .38 automatic in her hand gleamed dully under the naked bulb suspended from the ceiling.

"I'm getting out of here," she said, "and you're not going to stop me."

"I'm not sure I want to try. Where are you going, Fern?"

Donny spoke behind me, in his grief-thickened voice: "She's going away from me. She promised to stay here if I did what she told me. She promised to be my girl—"

"Shut up, stupid." Her voice cut like a lash, and Donny gasped as if the lash had been laid across his back.

"What did she tell you to do, Donny? Tell me just what you did."

"When she checked in last night with the fella from Detroit, she made a sign I wasn't to let on I knew her. Later on she left me a note. She wrote it with a lipstick on a piece of paper towel. I still got it hidden, in the kitchen."

"What did she write in the note?"

He lingered behind me, fearful of the gun in the girl's hand, more fearful of her anger.

She said, "Don't be crazy, Donny. He doesn't know a thing, not a thing. He can't do anything to either of us."

"I don't care what happens, to me or anybody else," the anguished voice said behind me. "You're running out on me, breaking your promise to me. I always knew it was too good to be true. Now I just don't care any more."

"I care," she said. "I care what happens to me." Her eyes shifted to me, above the unwavering gun. "I won't stay here. I'll shoot you if I have to."

"It shouldn't be necessary. Put it down, Fern. It's Bartolomeo's gun, isn't it? I found the shells to fit it in his glove compartment."

"How do you know so much?"

"I talked to Angel."

"Is he here?" Panic whined in her voice.

"No. I came alone."

"You better leave the same way then, while you can go under your own power."

"I'm staying. You need protection, whether you know it or not. And I need information. Donny, go in the kitchen and bring me that note."

"Don't do it, Donny. I'm warning you."

His sneakered feet made soft indecisive sounds. I advanced on the girl, talking quietly and steadily: "You conspired to kill a man, but you don't have to be afraid. He had it coming. Tell the whole story to the cops, and my guess is they won't even book you. Hell, you can even become famous. The government wants you as a witness in a tax case."

"What kind of a case?"

"A tax case against Angel. It's probably the only kind of rap they can pin on him. You can send him up for the rest of his life like Capone. You'll be a heroine, Fern."

"Don't call me Fern. I hate that name." There were sudden tears in her eyes. "I hate everything connected with that name. I hate myself."

"You'll hate yourself more if you don't put down that gun. Shoot me and it all starts over again. The cops will be on your trail, Angel's troopers will be gunning for you."

Now only the cot was between us, the cot and the unsteady gun facing me above it.

"This is the turning point," I said. "You've made a lot of bum decisions and almost ruined yourself, playing footsie with the evilest men there are. You can go on the way you have been, getting in deeper until you end up in a refrigerated drawer, or you can come back out of it now, into a decent life."

"A decent life? Here? With my father married to Mabel?"

"I don't think Mabel will last much longer. Anyway, I'm not Mabel. I'm on your side."

I waited. She dropped the gun on the blanket. I scooped it up and turned to Donny. "Let me see that note."

He disappeared through the kitchen door, head and shoulders drooping on the long stalk of his body.

"What could I do?" the girl said. "I was caught. It was Bart or me. All the way up from Acapulco I planned how I could get away. He held a gun in my side when we crossed the border; the same way when we stopped for gas or to eat at the drive-ins. I realized he had to be killed. My father's motel looked like my only chance. So I talked Bart into staying there with me overnight. He had no idea who the place belonged to. I didn't know what I was going to do. I only knew it had to be something drastic. Once I was back with Angel in the desert, that was the end of me. Even if he didn't kill me, it meant I'd have to go on living with him. Anything was better than that. So I wrote a note to Donny in the bathroom, and dropped it out the window. He was always crazy about me."

Her mouth had grown softer. She looked remarkably young and virginal. The faint blue hollows under her eyes were dewy. "Donny shot Bart with Bart's own gun. He had more nerve than I had. I lost my nerve when I went back into the room this morning. I didn't know about the blood in the bathroom. It was the last straw."

She was wrong. Something crashed in the kitchen. A cool draft swept the living room. A gun spoke twice, out of sight. Donny fell backwards through the doorway, a piece of brownish paper clutched in his hand. Blood gleamed on his shoulder like a red badge.

I stepped behind the cot and pulled the girl down to the floor with me. Gino came through the door, his two-colored sports shoe stepping on Donny's laboring chest. I shot the gun out of his hand. He floundered back against the wall, clutching at his wrist.

I sighted carefully for my second shot, until the black bar of his eyebrows was steady in the sights of the .38. The hole it made was invisible. Gino fell loosely forward, prone on the floor beside the man he had killed.

Ella Salanda ran across the room. She knelt, and cradled Donny's head in her lap.

Incredibly, he spoke, in a loud sighing voice: "You won't go away again, Ella? I did what you told me. You promised."

"Sure I promised. I won't leave you, Donny. Crazy man. Crazy fool."

"You like me better than you used to? Now?"

"I like you, Donny. You're the most man there is."

She held the poor insignificant head in her hands. He sighed, and his life came out bright-colored at the mouth. It was Donny who went away.

His hand relaxed, and I read the lipstick note she had written him on a piece of porous tissue:

"Donny: This man will kill me unless you kill him first. His gun will be in his clothes on the chair beside the bed. Come in and get it at midnight and shoot to kill. Good luck. I'll stay and be your girl if you do this, just like you always wished. Love. Ella."

I looked at the pair on the floor. She was rocking his lifeless head against her breast. Beside them, Gino looked very small and lonely, a dummy leaking darkness from his brow.

Donny had his wish and I had mine. I wondered what Ella's was.

THE CRIME OF EZECHIELE COEN

Stanley Ellin

Stanley Ellin

Stanley Ellin says, "William Carlos Williams, that distinguished poet, on being asked for the umpteenth-million time why he insisted on living his life in Paterson, New Jersey, of all places, said in effect that, however stony the ground, a man is wise to put down deep roots into it. For the same reason perhaps, having been born and raised in Brooklyn, New York, I continue my life there, fleeing south to my Florida apartment only when the first snowflake falls each winter. I have come to be wary of that first snowflake. At the age of sixty, I have learned that too many others are sure to follow.

"On the other hand, I am not, like W. C. Williams, a writer who came early to his trade. I held various life-preserving jobs until I served time in the army during World War II, then, after discharge, supported by a wife who has been my spinal column since our youthful elopement—she still is after thirty-nine years of almost alarmingly happy marriage—I tried writing full-time. Through a story titled 'The Specialty of the House' I found myself a Writer for better or worse and have since produced a dozen novels and three dozen short stories to substantiate the claim.

" 'The Crime of Ezechiele Coen' was born out of two experiences far apart from each other. Rambling through Rome, my wife and I found ourselves in the midst of the ancient Roman ghetto and fell into the hands of a self-appointed guide who instantly became a self-appointed member of the family. And long before that I had served as a juror on a case where a young policeman was being tried on charges of taking graft. What with one thing and another, I suppose the story of Ezechiele Coen was inevitable."

And a splendid story it is. Of a crime committed more than a generation before, now questioned and re-explored. Told with the vast skill that has made Stanley Ellin one of the most highly regarded writers in the field of mystery fiction.

A.M.

THE CRIME OF EZECHIELE COEN

Before the disenchantment set in, Noah Freeman lived in a whirl of impressions. The chaotic traffic. The muddy Tiber. The Via Veneto out of Italian movies about *la dolce vita*. The Fountain of Trevi out of Hollywood. Castel Sant' Angelo out of *Tosca*. Rome.

"Rome?" Pop had said. "But why Rome? Such a foreign place. And so far away."

True. But to old Pop Freeman, even Rockland County, an hour from New York, was far away, and his two weeks of vacation there every summer an adventure. And, in fact, it was unlikely that Pop had been too much surprised at his son's decision to go journeying afar. After all, this was the son who was going to be a doctor—at the very least a teacher—and who had become, of all things, a policeman.

"A policeman in the family," Pop would muse aloud now and then. "A detective with a gun in the family like on TV. My own son. What would Mama say if she ever knew, may she rest in peace?"

But, Noah had to admit, the old man had been right about one thing. Rome was far, far away, not only from New York, but also from the blood-quickening image of it instilled in young Noah Freeman when he was a schoolboy soaking himself in gaudy literature about Spartacus and Caesar and Nero. And the Pensione Alfiara, hidden away in an alley off Via Arenula, was hardly a place to quicken anyone's blood. It took an ill wind to blow an occasional American tourist there. In Noah's case, the ill wind was the cab driver who had picked him up at Fiumicino airport and who happened to be Signora Alfiara's brother-in-law.

It was made to order for disenchantment, the Pensione Alfiara. Granting that it offered bargain rates, its cuisine was monotonous, its service indifferent, its plumbing capricious, and its clientele, at least in early March, seemed to consist entirely of elderly sad-eyed Italian villagers come to Rome to attend the deathbed of a dear friend. Aside from Signora Alfiara herself and the girl at the portiere's desk, no one on the scene spoke English, so communication between Noah and his fellow boarders was restricted to nods and shrugs, well meant, but useless in relieving loneliness.

Its one marked asset was the girl at the portiere's desk. She was tall and exquisite, one of the few really beautiful women Noah had yet encountered in Rome, because among other disillusionments was the discovery that Roman women are not the women one sees in Italian movies. And she lived behind her desk from early morning to late at night as if in a sad self-contained world of her own, skillful at her accounts, polite, but remote and disinterested.

She intrigued him for more than the obvious reasons. The English she spoke was almost unaccented. If anything, it was of the clipped British variety, which led him to wonder whether she might not be a Briton somehow washed up on this Roman shore. And at her throat on a fine gold chain was a Mogen David, a Star of David, announcing plainly enough that she was Jewish. The sight of that small familiar ornament had startled him at first, then had emboldened him to make a friendly overture.

"As a fellow Jew," he had said smilingly, "I was wondering if you —" and she had cut in with chilling politeness, "Yes, you'll find the synagogue on Lungotevere dei Cenci, a few blocks south. One of the landmarks of this part of Rome. Most interesting, of course"—which was enough to send him off defeated.

After that, he regretfully put aside hopes of making her acquaintance and dutifully went his tourist way alone, the guide book to Rome in his hand, the Italian phrase book in his pocket, trying to work up a sense of excitement at what he saw, and failing dismally at it. Partly, the weather was to blame—the damp gray March weather which promised no break in the clouds overhead. And partly, he knew, it was loneliness—the kind of feeling that made him painfully envious of the few groups of tourists he saw here and there, shepherded by an officious guide, but, at least, chattering happily to each other.

But most of all—and this was something he had to force himself to acknowledge—he was not a tourist, but a fugitive. And what he was trying to flee was Detective Noah Freeman, who, unfortunately, was always with him and always would be. To be one of those plump, self-satisfied retired businessmen gaping at the dome of St. Peter's, that was one thing; to be Noah Freeman was quite another.

It was possible that Signora Alfiara, who had a pair of bright, knowing eyes buried in her pudding face, comprehended his state of mind and decided with maternal spirit to do something about it. Or it was possible that, having learned his occupation, she was honestly curious about him. Whatever the reason, Noah was deeply grateful the morning she sat down at the table where he was having the usual breakfast of hard roll, acid coffee, and watery marmalade, and explained that she had seen at the cinema stories about American detectives, but that he was the first she had ever met. Very interesting. And was life in America as the cinema showed it? So much shooting and beating and danger? Had he ever been shot at? Wounded, perhaps? What a way of life! It made her blood run cold to think of it.

The Signora was unprepossessing enough in her bloated shapelessness, her shabby dress and worn bedroom slippers; but, at least, she was someone to talk to, and they were a long time at breakfast settling the question of life in America. Before they left the table Noah asked about the girl at the portiere's desk. Was she Italian? She didn't sound like it when she spoke English.

"Rosanna?" said the Signora. "Oh, yes, yes, Italian. But when she was a little one—you know, when the Germans were here—she was sent to people in England. She was there many years. Oh, Italian, but *una Ebrea,* a Jew, poor sad little thing."

The note of pity rankled. "So am I," Noah said.

"Yes, she has told me," the Signora remarked, and he saw that her pity was not at all for the girl's being *una Ebrea.* More than that, he was warmed by the knowledge that the beautiful and unapproachable Rosanna had taken note of him after all.

"What makes her sad?" he asked. "The war's been over a long time."

"For some, yes. But her people will not let her forget what her father did when the Germans were here. There was the Resistance here, the partisans, you know, and her father sold them to the Germans. So they believe. Now they hate her and her brother because they are the children of a Judas."

"What do you mean, so they believe? Are they wrong about her father?"

"She says they are. To her, you understand, the father was like a saint. A man of honor and very brave. That might be. But when the Germans were here, even brave men were not so brave sometimes. Yet, who am I to say this about him? He was the doctor who saved my life and the life of my first son when I gave birth to him. That is why when the girl needed work I paid back a little of my debt by helping her this way. A good bargain, too. She's honest, she works hard, she speaks other languages, so I lose nothing by a little kindness."

"And what about her brother? Is he still around?"

"You see him every day. Giorgio. You know Giorgio?"

"The cleaning man?"

"He cleans, he carries, he gets drunk whenever he can, that's Giorgio. Useless, really, but what can I do? For the girl's sake I make as much use of him as I can. You see the trouble with kindness? I wish to repay a debt, so now the windows are forever dirty. When you need that one he is always drunk somewhere. And always with a bad temper. His father had a bad temper, too, but at least he had great skill. As for the girl, she is an angel. But sad. That loneliness, you know, it can kill you." The Signora leaned forward inquiringly, her bosom overflowing the table. "Maybe if you would talk to her—"

"I tried to," said Noah. "She didn't seem very much interested."

"Because you are a stranger. But I have seen her watch you when you pass by. If you were a friend, perhaps. If the three of us dined together tonight—"

Signora Alfiara was someone who had her own way when she

wanted to. The three of them dined together that night, but in an atmosphere of constraint, the conversation moving only under the impetus of questions the Signora aimed at Noah, Rosanna sitting silent and withdrawn as he answered.

When, while they were at their fruit and cheese, the Signora took abrupt and smiling leave of them with transparent motive, Noah said with some resentment to the girl, "I'm sorry about all this. I hope you know I wasn't the one to suggest this little party. It was the lady's idea."

"I do know that."

"Then why take out your mood on me?"

Rosanna's lips parted in surprise. "Mood? But I had no intention —believe me, it has nothing to do with you."

"What does it have to do with? Your father?" And seeing from her reaction that he had hit the mark, he said, "Yes, I heard about that."

"Heard what?"

"A little. Now you can tell me the rest. Or do you enjoy having it stuck in your throat where you can't swallow it and can't bring it up, one way or the other?"

"You must have a strange idea of enjoyment. And if you want the story, go to the synagogue, go to the ghetto or Via Catalana. You'll hear it there quick enough. Everyone knows it."

"I might do that. First I'd like to hear your side of it."

"As a policeman? You're too late, Mr. Freeman. The case against Ezechiele Coen was decided long ago without policemen or judges."

"What case?"

"He was said to have betrayed leaders of the Resistance. That was a lie, but partisans killed him for it. They shot him and left him lying with a sign on him saying *Betrayer*. Yes, Mr. Freeman, Ezechiele Coen who preached honor to his children as the one meaningful thing in life died in dishonor. He lay there in the dirt of the Teatro Marcello a long time that day, because his own people—our people—would not give him burial. When they remember him now, they spit on the ground. I know," the girl said in a brittle voice, "because when I walk past them, they remember him."

"Then why do you stay here?"

"Because he is here. Because here is where his blackened memory

—his spirit—remains, waiting for the truth to be known."

"Twenty years after the event?"

"Twenty or a hundred or a thousand. Does time change the truth, Mr. Freeman? Isn't it as important for the dead to get justice as the living?"

"Maybe it is. But how do you know that justice wasn't done in this case? What evidence is there to disprove the verdict? You were a child when all this happened, weren't you?"

"And not even in Rome. I was in England then, living with a doctor who knew my father since their school days. Yes, England is far away and I was a child then, but I knew my father."

If faith could really move mountains, Noah thought. "And what about your brother? Does he feel the way you do?"

"Giorgio tries to feel as little as he can about it. When he was a boy everyone said that some day he would be as fine a man and a doctor as his father. Now he's a drunkard. A bottle of wine makes it easy not to feel pain."

"Would he mind if I talked to him about this?"

"Why would you want to? What could Ezechiele Coen mean to you anyhow? Is Rome so boring that you must play detective here to pass the time? I don't understand you, Mr. Freeman."

"No, you don't," Noah said harshly. "But you might if you listen to what I'm going to tell you. Do you know where I got the time and money to come on a trip like this, a plain ordinary underpaid cop like me? Well, last year there was quite a scandal about some policemen in New York who were charged with taking graft from a gambler. I was one of them under charges. I had no part of that mess, but I was suspended from my job and when they got around to it, I was put on trial. The verdict was not guilty, I got all my back pay in one lump, and I was told to return to duty. Things must have looked fine for me, wouldn't you think?"

"Because you did get justice," Rosanna said.

"From the court. Only from the court. Afterward, I found that no one else really believed I was innocent. No one. Even my own father sometimes wonders about it. And if I went back on the Force, the grafters there would count me as one of them, and the honest men wouldn't trust me. That's why I'm here. Because I don't know whether to go back or not, and I need time to think, I need to get away from them all. So I did get justice, and now you tell me what good it did."

The girl shook her head somberly. "Then my father isn't the only one, is he? But you see, Mr. Freeman, you can defend your own good name. Tell me, how is he to defend his?"

That was the question which remained in his mind afterward, angry and challenging. He tried to put it aside, to fix on his own immediate problem, but there it was. It led him the next morning away from proper destinations, the ruins and remains italicized in his guide book, and on a walk southward along the Tiber.

Despite gray skies overhead and the dismally brown turbid river sullenly locked between the stone embankments below, Noah felt a quickening pleasure in the scene. In a few days he had had his fill of sightseeing. Brick and marble and Latin inscriptions were not really the stuff of life, and pictures and statuary only dim representations of it. It was people he was hungry to meet, and now that he had an objective in meeting them he felt more alive than he had since his first day in Rome. More alive, in fact, than in all those past months in New York, working alongside his father in the old man's tailor shop. Not that this small effort to investigate the case of Ezechiele Coen would amount to anything, he knew. A matter of dredging up old and bitter memories, that was about what it came to. But the important thing was that he was Noah Freeman again, alive and functioning.

Along Lungotevere dei Cenci, construction work was going on. The shells of new buildings towered over slums battered by centuries of hard wear. Midstream in the Tiber was a long narrow island with several institutional buildings on it. Then, facing it from the embankment, the synagogue came into view, a huge Romanesque marble pile.

There was a railing before the synagogue. A young man leaned at his ease against the railing. Despite the chill in the air he was in shirt sleeves, his tanned muscular arms folded on his chest, his penetrating eyes watching Noah's approach with the light of interest in them. As Noah passed, the man came to attention.

"*Shalom.*"

"*Shalom,*" Noah said, and the young man's face brightened. In his hand magically appeared a deck of picture post cards.

"Post cards, hey? See, all different of Rome. Also, the synagogue, showing the inside and the outside. You an *Americano Ebreo,* no? A *landsman?*"

"Yes," said Noah, wondering if only *Americano Ebreos* came this way. "But you can put away the pictures. I don't want any."

"Maybe a guide book? The best. Or you want a guide? The ghetto, Isola Tiberina, Teatro Marcello? Anywhere you want to go, I can show you. Two thousand lire. Ask anybody. For two thousand lire nobody is a better guide than Carlo Piperno. That's me."

"Noah Freeman, that's me. And the only place I want to go to is the rabbi's. Can I find him in the synagogue?"

"No, but I will take you to his house. Afterwards we see the ghetto, Tiberina—"

The rabbi proved to be a man of good will, of understanding; but, he explained in precise English, perhaps he could afford to be objective about the case of Ezechiele Coen because he himself was not a Roman. He had come to this congregation from Milan, an outsider. Yet, even as an outsider he could appreciate the depth of his congregation's hatred for their betrayer. A sad situation, but could they be blamed for that? Could it not be the sternest warning to all such betrayers if evil times ever came again?

"He's been dead a long time," said Noah.

"So are those whose lives he sold. Worse than that." The rabbi gestured at the shuttered window beyond which lay the Tiber. "He sold the lives of friends who were not of our faith. Those who lived in Trastevere across the river, working people, priests, who gave some of us hiding places when we needed them. Did the daughter of Ezechiele Coen tell you how, when she was a child, they helped remove her from the city at night in a cart of wine barrels, risking their lives to do it? Does she think it is easy to forget how her father rewarded them for that?"

"But why here?" Noah protested. "Why should your congregation make her an outcast? She and her brother aren't the guilty ones. Do you really believe that the sins of the fathers must be visited on the children?"

The rabbi shook his head. "There are sins, Signor Freeman, which make a horror that takes generations to wipe away. I welcome the girl and her brother to the synagogue, but I cannot wipe away the horror in the people they would meet there. If I wished to, I could not work such a miracle.

"Only a little while ago there was a great and flourishing congregation here, signore, a congregation almost as ancient as Rome itself. Do you know what is left of it now? A handful. A handful who cannot forget. The Jews of Rome do not forget easily. To this day they curse the name of Titus, who destroyed the Temple in Jerusalem, as they remember kindly the name of Julius Caesar, who was their friend, and for whose body they mourned seven days in the Forum. And the day they forgive Titus will be the same day they forgive Ezechiele Coen and his children and their children to come. Do you know what I mean, Signor Freeman?"

"Yes," said Noah. "I know what you mean."

He went out into the bleak cobblestoned street, oppressed by a sense of antiquity weighing him down, of two thousand years of unrelenting history heavy on his shoulders, and not even the racketing of motor traffic along the river embankment, the spectacle of the living present, could dispel it. Carlo Piperno, the post-card vendor, was waiting there.

"You have seen the rabbi? Good. Now I show you Isola Tiberina."

"Forget Isola Tiberina. There's something else I want you to show me?"

"For two thousand lire, anything."

"All right." Noah extracted the banknotes from his wallet. "Does the name Ezechiele Coen mean anything to you?"

Carlo Piperno had the hard, capable look of a man impervious to surprise. Nevertheless, he was visibly surprised. Then he recovered himself. "That one? *Mi dispiace, signore.* Sorry, but he is dead, that one." He pointed to the ground at his feet. "You want him, you have to look there for him."

"I don't want him. I want someone who knew him well. Someone who can tell me what he did and what happened to him."

"Everybody knows. I can tell you."

"No, it must be someone who wasn't a child when it happened. *Capisce?*"

"*Capisco.* But why?"

"If I answer that, it will cost you these two thousand lire. Shall I answer?"

"No, no." Carlo reached out and dexterously took possession of the money. He shrugged. "But first the rabbi, now Ezechiele Coen, who is in hell long ago. Well, I am a guide, no? So now I am your guide."

He led the way through a labyrinth of narrow streets to an area not far from the synagogue, a paved area with the remains of a stone wall girdling it. Beyond the wall were tenements worn by time to the color of the clay that had gone into their brick. Yet their tenants seemed to have pride of possession. In almost every window were boxes of flowers and greenery. On steps and in stony courtyards, housewives with brushes and buckets scrubbed the stone and brick. In surrounding alleys were small stores buzzing with activity.

With shock Noah suddenly realized that here was the ghetto, that he was standing before a vestige of the past which thus far in his life had been only an ugly word to him. It was the presence of the wall that provided the shock, he knew. It had no gate, there was no one to prevent you from departing through it, but if it were up to him he would have had it torn down on the spot.

A strange place, Rome. Wherever you turned were the reminders of the cruel past. Memorials to man, the persecuted. This wall, the catacombs, the churches built to martyrs, the Colosseum. There was no escaping their insistent presence.

Carlo's destination turned out to be a butcher shop—the shop of Vito Levi, according to the sign over it. The butcher, a burly gray-haired man, stood behind his chest-high marble counter hacking at a piece of meat, exchanging loud repartee with a shriveled old woman, a shawl over her head, a string bag in her hand, waiting for her order. While Carlo was addressing him he continued to chop away with the cleaver, then suddenly placed it on the counter and came around to meet Noah in the street, wiping his hands on his apron as he came. The old woman followed, peering at Noah with beady-eyed interest, and in another minute others from the street were gathering around getting the news from her. Ezechiele Coen may have been dead twenty years, Noah thought, but his name was still very much alive in these quarters.

He was not sorry that the matter was going to be discussed in public this way. As a young patrolman on the beat he had learned not to be too quick to break up a crowd around an accident or crime; there might be someone in the crowd who had something to say worth hearing. Now he gathered from the heat of discussion around him that everyone here had something to say about Ezechiele Coen.

With Carlo serving as interpreter, he put his questions first to Levi the butcher, and then to anyone else who volunteered information. Slowly, piece by piece, the picture of Ezechiele Coen and his crime took shape. It was Levi who supplied most of the information—the time, the place, the event.

The butcher had known Ezechiele Coen well. Like all others he had trusted him, because no man had a greater reputation for honesty than the doctor. He was a great doctor, a man of science; yet he was a man of God, too, devout, each morning binding on his phylacteries and saying his prayers, each sabbath attending the synagogue. Not that there was any gentleness in him. He was a proud man, an arrogant man, a man who would insult you to your face for the least offense. After all, it was one thing to be honest, but it was something else again to behave as if you were the only honest man in the world. The only one on earth who would never compromise with truth. That was Ezechiele Coen. You might trust him, but you could not like him. He was too good for that.

Then the trust was betrayed. Over the years one had learned to live with Il Duce, but when the Germans came to Rome, the Resistance of a generation ago reawoke. Sabotage, spying, a hidden press turning out leaflets which told the truth about Il Duce and his ally. Many said it was useless, but Vito Levi, the butcher, and a few others continued their secret efforts, knowing they had nothing to lose. Jews were being deported now, were being shipped to the Nazi slaughter pens in carloads. What else to do then but join some of their Gentile neighbors in the Resistance?

"Ask him," said Noah to Carlo, "if Ezechiele Coen was one of the Resistance," and when Carlo translated this, the butcher shook his head.

Only once was the doctor called on to help. Three leaders of the Resistance had managed to get into Rome from the mountains—to help organize the movement here, to give it leadership. They were hidden in a cellar in Trastevere, across the river, one of them badly wounded. The doctor's son, only a boy then, no more than fifteen years of age, was a courier for the partisans. He had brought his father to attend the wounded man, and then, soon after, the three men together were captured in their hiding place by the Germans. They had been betrayed by the honest, the noble, the righteous Ezechiele Coen.

"Ask him how he knows this?" Noah demanded of Carlo. "Was there a confession?"

There was no need for one, as it happened. There was no need for any more evidence than the money case of Major von Grubbner.

Noah silently cursed the tedious process of translation. Carlo Piperno was the kind of interpreter who richly enjoys and intends to get the maximum effect from his role. It took him a long time to make clear who and what Major von Grubbner was.

The Major was one of the men assigned to the Panzer division quartered along the Tiber. But unlike the German officers around him, Major von Grubbner was cunning as a fox, smooth in his manner, ingratiating in his approach. Others came with a gun in their hands. He came with an attaché case, a black leather case with a handsome gold ornament on it, a doubleheaded eagle which was a reminder of the great name of his family. And in the case was money. Bundles of money. Packages of lire, fresh and crisp, a fortune by any estimate.

Give the devil his due. This von Grubbner was a brave man as well as a cunning one. He walked alone, contemptuous of those who needed guards to attend them, the money case in his hand, a smile on his lips, and he invited confidences.

"After all," he would say, "we are businessmen, you and I. We are practical people who dislike trouble. Remove the troublemakers and all is peaceful, no? Well, here I am to do business. Look at this money. Beautiful, isn't it? And all you have to do is name your own price, expose the troublemakers, and we are all happy. Name your own price, that's all you have to do."

And he would open the case under your nose, showing you the money, fondling it, offering it to you. It was more than money. It was life itself. It could buy the few scraps of food remaining to be bought, it could buy you a refuge for your wife and children, it could buy you safety for another day. Life itself. Everyone wants life, and there it was in that little black leather case with the doubleheaded eagle in gold marking it.

Only one man was tempted. The day after the three partisans were taken, Ezechiele Coen was seen fleeing with that case through the alleys, running like a rabbit before the hounds of vengeance he knew would soon be on him. Only Ezechiele Coen, the devout, the honorable, the arrogant, fell, and died soon for his treachery.

Vito Levi's words needed translation, but not the emotion behind them. And the crowd around Noah, now staring at him in silence, did not need its feelings explained. Yet, the story seemed incomplete to him, to Detective Noah Freeman, who had learned at his job not to live by generalities. The evidence, that was what had meaning.

"Ask them," he said to Carlo, "who saw Ezechiele Coen with that case in his possession," and when Carlo translated this, Levi drove a thumb hard into his own chest. Then he looked around the crowd and pointed, and a man on its outskirts raised his hand, a woman nearby raised hers, someone else raised a hand.

Three witnesses, four, five. Enough, Noah thought, to hang any man. With difficulty, prompting Carlo question by question, he drew their story from them. They lived in houses along Via del Portico. It was hot that night, a suffocating heat that made sleep impossible. One and all, they were at their windows. One and all, they saw the doctor running down the street toward the Teatro Marcello, the leather case under his arm. His medical bag? No, no. Not with the golden eagle on it. It was the doctor with his blood money. This they swore on the lives of their children.

During siesta time that afternoon, Noah, with the connivance of Signora Alfiara, drew Rosanna out of doors for a walk to a café in the Piazza Navona. Over glasses of Campari he told her the results of his investigation.

"Witnesses," she said scathingly. "Have you found that witnesses always tell the truth?"

"These people do. But sometimes there can be a difference between what you imagine is the truth and the truth itself."

"And how do you discover that difference?"

"By asking more questions. For example, did your father live in the ghetto?"

"During the war, yes."

"And according to my street map the Teatro Marcello is outside it. Why would he be running there with the money instead of keeping it safe at home? Even more curious, why would he carry the money in that case, instead of transferring it to something that couldn't be identified? And why would he be given that case, a personal possession, along with the money? You can see how many unanswered questions come up, if you look at all this without prejudice."

"Then you think—"

"I don't think anything yet. First, I want to try to get answers to those questions. I want to establish a rational pattern for what seems to be a whole irrational set of events. And there is one person who can help me do this."

"Who?"

"Major von Grubbner himself."

"But how would you ever find him? It was so long ago. He may be dead."

"Or he may not be. If he is not, there are ways of finding him."

"But it would mean so much trouble. So much time and effort."

The way she was looking at him then, Noah thought, was more than sufficient payment for the time and effort. And the way she flushed when he returned her look told him that she knew his thought.

"I'm used to this kind of effort," he said. "Anyhow, it may be the last chance I'll have to practice my profession."

"Then you're not going back to your work with the police? But you're a very good detective. You are, aren't you?"

"Oh, very good. And," he said, "honest, too, despite the popular opinion."

"Don't say it like that," she flashed out angrily. "You are honest. I know you are."

"Do you? Well, that makes two of us at least. Anyhow, the vital thing is for me to locate von Grubbner if he's still somewhere to be found. After that, we'll see. By the way, do you know the date when all this happened? When your father was seen with that case?"

"Yes. It was the fifth of July in 1943. I couldn't very well forget that date, Mr. Freeman."

"Noah."

"Of course," said Rosanna. "Noah."

After returning her to her desk at the pensione, Noah went directly to police headquarters. There he found his credentials an open sesame. In the end he was closeted with Commissioner Ponziani, a handsome urbane man, who listened to the story of Ezechiele Coen with fascination. At its conclusion he raised quizzical eyebrows at Noah.

"And your interest in this affair?"

"Purely unofficial. I don't even know if I have the right to bother you with it at all." Noah shrugged. "But when I thought of all the red tape to cut if I went to the military or consular authorities—"

The Commissioner made a gesture which dismissed as beneath contempt the clumsy workings of the military and consular authorities. "No, no, you did right to come here. We are partners in our profession, are we not, signore? We are of a brotherhood, you and I. So now if you give me all possible information about this Major von Grubbner, I will communicate with the German police. We shall soon learn if there is anything they can tell us about him."

Soon meant days of waiting, and, Noah saw, they were bad days for Rosanna. Each one that passed left her more tense, more dependent on him for reassurance. How could anyone ever find this German, one man in millions, a man who might have his own reasons for not wanting to be found? And if by some miracle they could confront him, what would he have to say? Was it possible that he would say her father had been guilty?

"It is," said Noah. He reached out and took her hand comfortingly. "You have to be prepared for that."

"I will not be! No, I will not be," she said fiercely. Then her assurance crumpled. "He would be lying, wouldn't he? You know he would." The passage left Noah shaken. Rosanna's intensity, the way she had clutched his hand like a lost child—these left him wondering if he had not dangerously overreached himself in trying to exorcise the ghost of Ezechiele Coen. If he failed, it would leave things worse than ever. Worse for himself, too, because now he realized with delight and misery that he was falling hopelessly in love with the girl. And so much seemed to depend on clearing her father's reputation. Could it be, as Rosanna felt, that Ezechiele Coen's spirit really waited here on the banks of the Tiber to be set at rest? And what if there were no way of doing that?

When Signora Alfiara called him to the phone to take a message from the police, Noah picked up the phone almost prayerfully.

"Pronto," he said, and Commissioner Ponziani said without preliminary, "Ah, Signor Freeman. This affair of Major von Grubbner becomes stranger and stranger. Will you meet with me in my office so that we may discuss it?"

At the office the Commissioner came directly to the point.

"The date of the unhappy event we are concerned with," he said, "was the fifth of July in 1943. Is that correct?"

"It is," said Noah.

"And here," said the Commissioner, tapping a finger on the sheet of paper before him, "is the report of the German authorities on a Major Alois von Grubbner, attached to the Panzer division stationed in Rome at that time. According to the report he deserted the army, absconding with a large amount of military funds, on the sixth of July in 1943. No trace of him has been discovered since."

The Commissioner leaned back in his chair and smiled at Noah. "Interesting, no? Very interesting. What do you make of it?"

"He didn't desert," said Noah. "He didn't abscond. That was the money seen in Ezechiele Coen's possession."

"So I believe, too. I strongly suspect that this officer was murdered —assassinated may be a more judicious word, considering the circumstances—and the money taken from him."

"But his body," Noah said. "Wouldn't the authorities have allowed for possible murder and made a search for it?"

"A search was made. But Major von Grubbner, it seems, had a somewhat"—the Commissioner twirled a finger in the air, seeking the right word—"a somewhat shady record in his civilian life. A little embezzling here, a little forgery there—enough to make his superiors quickly suspect his integrity when he disappeared. I imagine their search was a brief one. But I say that if they had been able to peer beneath the Tiber—"

"Is that where you think he ended up?"

"There, or beneath some cellar, or in a hole dug in a dark corner. Yes, I know what you are thinking, Signor Freeman. A man like this Doctor Ezechiele Coen hardly seems capable of assassination, robbery, the disposal of a body. Still, that is not much of an argument to present to people violently antagonistic to his memory. It is, at best, a supposition. Fevered emotions are not to be cooled by suppositions. I very much fear that your investigation has come to an abrupt and unhappy ending."

Noah shook his head. "That attaché case and the money in it," he said. "It was never found. I was told that when Ezechiele Coen was found shot by partisans and left lying in the Teatro Marcello, the case was nowhere to be seen. What happened to it?"

The Commissioner shrugged. "Removed by those who did the shooting, of course."

"If it was there to be removed. But no one ever reported seeing it then or afterward. No one ever made a remark—even after the war when it would be safe to—that money intended to be used against the Resistance was used by it. But don't you think that this is the sort of thing that would be a standing joke—a folk story—among these people?"

"Perhaps. Again it is no more than a supposition."

"And since it's all I have to go on, I'll continue from there."

"You are a stubborn man, Signor Freeman." The Commissioner shook his head with grudging admiration. "Well, if you need further assistance, come to me directly. Very stubborn. I wish some of my associates had your persistence."

When Rosanna had been told what occurred in the Commissioner's office she was prepared that instant to make the story public.

"It is proof, isn't it?" she demanded. "Whatever did happen, we know my father had no part in it. Isn't that true?"

"You and I know. But remember one thing: your father was seen with that attaché case. Until that can be explained, nothing else will stand as proof of his innocence."

"He may have found the case. That's possible, isn't it?"

"Hardly possible," Noah said. "And why would he be carrying it toward the Teatro Marcello? What is this Teatro Marcello anyhow?"

"Haven't you seen it yet? It's one of the ruins like the Colosseum, but smaller."

"Can you take me there now?"

"Not now. I can't leave the desk until Signora Alfiara returns. But it's not far from here. A little distance past the synagogue on the Via del Portico. Look for number 39. You'll find it easily."

Outside the pensione Noah saw Giorgio Coen unloading a delivery of food from a truck. He was, at a guess, ten years older than his sister, a big, shambling man with good features that had gone slack with dissipation, and a perpetual stubble of beard on his jowls. Despite the flabby look of him, he hoisted a side of meat to his shoulder and bore it into the building with ease. In passing, he looked at Noah with a hangdog beaten expression, and Noah could feel for him. Rosanna had been cruelly wounded by the hatred vented against her father, but Giorgio had been destroyed by it. However this affair turned out, there was small hope of salvaging anything from those remains.

Noah walked past the synagogue, found the Via del Portico readily enough, and then before the building marked 39 he stood looking around in bewilderment. There was no vestige of any ruin resembling the Colosseum here—no ruin at all, in fact. Number 39 itself was only an old apartment house, the kind of apartment house so familiar to rundown sections of Manhattan back home.

He studied the names under the doorbells outside as if expecting to find the answer to the mystery there, then peered into its tiled hallway. A buxom girl, a baby over her shoulder, came along the hallway, and Noah smiled at her.

"Teatro Marcello?" he said doubtfully. *"Dove?"*

She smiled back and said something incomprehensible to him, and when he shook his head she made a circling gesture with her hand.

"Oh, in back," Noah said. "Thank you. *Grazie.*"

It was in back. And it was, Noah decided, one of the more incredible spectacles of this whole incredible city. The Teatro Marcello fitted Rosanna's description: it was the grim gray ruin of a lesser Colosseum. But into it had been built the apartment house, so that only the semicircle of ruins visible from the rear remained in their original form.

The tiers of stone blocks, of columns, of arches towering overhead were Roman remains, and the apartment house was a façade for them, concealing them from anyone standing before the house. Even the top tier of this ancient structure had been put to use, Noah saw. It had been bricked and windowed, and behind some of the windows shone electric lights. People lived there. They walked through the tiled hallway leading from the street, climbed flights of stairs, and entered kitchens and bedrooms whose walls had been built by Imperial slaves two thousand years ago. Incredible, but there it was before him.

An immense barren field encircled the building, a wasteland of pebbly earth and weeds. Boys were playing football there, deftly booting the ball back and forth. On the trunks of marble columns half sunk into the ground, women sat and tended baby carriages. Nearby, a withered crone spread out scraps of meat on a piece of newspaper, and cats—the tough-looking pampered cats of Rome—circled the paper hungrily, waiting for the signal to begin lunch.

Noah tried to visualize the scene twenty years before when Ezechiele Coen had fled here in the darkness bearing an attaché case marked with a doubleheaded eagle. He must have had business here, for here was where he lingered until an avenging partisan had searched him out and killed him. But what business? Business with whom? No one in the apartment house; there seemed to be no entrance to it from this side.

At its ground level, the Teatro Marcello was a series of archways, the original entrances to the arena within. Noah walked slowly along them. Each archway was barred by a massive iron gate beyond which was a small cavern solidly bricked, impenetrable at any point. Behind each gate could be seen fragments of columns, broken statuary of heads and arms and robed bodies, a litter of filthy paper blown in by the winds of time. Only in one of those musty caverns could be seen signs of life going on. Piled on a slab of marble were schoolbooks, coats, and sweaters, evidently the property of the boys playing football, placed here for safety's sake.

For safety's sake. With a sense of mounting excitement, Noah studied the gate closely. It extended from the floor almost to the top of the archway. Its iron bars were too close together to allow even a boy to slip between them, its lock massive and solidly caked with rust, the chain holding it as heavy as a small anchor chain. Impossible to get under, over, or through it—yet the boys had. Magic. Could someone else have used that magic on a July night twenty years ago?

When Noah called to them, the boys took their time about stopping their game, and then came over to the gate warily. By dint of elaborate gestures, Noah managed to make his questions clear, but it took a package of cigarettes and a handful of coins to get the required demonstration.

One of the boys, grinning, locked his hands around a bar of the gate and with an effort raised it clear of its socket in the horizontal rod supporting it near the ground. Now it was held only by the cross rod overhead. The boy drew it aside at an angle and slipped through the space left. He returned, dropped the bar back into place, and held out a hand for another cigarette.

With the help of the Italian phrase book, Noah questioned the group around him. How long had these locked gates been here? The boys scratched their heads and looked at each other. A long time. Before they could remember. Before their fathers could remember. A very long time.

And how long had that one bar been loose, so that you could go in and out if you knew the secret? The same. All the *ragazzi* around here knew about it as their fathers had before them.

Could any other of these gates be entered this way? No, this was the only one. The good one.

When he had dismissed them by showing empty hands—no more cigarettes, no more coins—Noah sat down on one of the sunken marble columns near the women and their baby carriages, and waited. It took a while for the boys to finish their game and depart, taking their gear with them, but finally they were gone. Then Noah entered the gate, using his newfound secret, and started a slow, methodical investigation of what lay in the shadowy reaches beyond it.

He gave no thought to the condition of his hands or clothes, but carefully pushed aside the litter of paper, probed under and between the chunks of marble, all the broken statuary around him. At the far end of the cavern he found that once he had swept the litter aside there was a clear space underfoot. Starting at the wall, he inched forward on his knees, sweeping his fingers lightly back and forth over the ground. Then his fingertips hit a slight depression in the flinty earth, an almost imperceptible concavity. Despite the chill in the air, he was sweating now, and had to pull out a handkerchief to mop his brow.

He traced the depression, his fingertips moving along it, following it to its length, turning where it turned, marking a rectangle the length and width of a man's body. Once before, in the course of his official duties, Detective Noah Freeman had marked a rectangle like this in the weed-grown yard of a Bronx shanty, and had found beneath it what he had expected to find. He knew he would not be disappointed in what would be dug up from this hole beneath the Teatro Marcello. He was tempted to get a tool and do the digging himself, but that, of course, must be the job of the police. And before they would be notified, the pieces of the puzzle, all at hand now, must be placed together before a proper witness.

When Noah returned to the Pensione Alfiara, he brought with him as witness the rabbi, bewildered by the unexplained urgency of this mission, out of breath at the quick pace Noah had set through the streets. Rosanna was at her desk. She looked with alarm at Noah's grimy hands, at the streaks of dirt and sweat on his face. For the rabbi she had no greeting. This was the enemy, an unbeliever in the cause of Ezechiele Coen. She had eyes only for Noah.

"What happened?" she said. "What's wrong? Are you hurt?"

"No. Listen, Rosanna, have you told Giorgio anything about von Grubbner? About my meeting with the police commissioner?"

"No."

"Good. Where is he now?"

"Giorgio? In the kitchen, I think. But why? What—?"

"If you come along, you'll see why. But you're not to say anything. Not a word, do you understand. Let me do all the talking."

Giorgio was in the kitchen listlessly moving a mop back and forth over the floor. He stopped when he saw his visitors, and regarded them with bleary bewilderment. Now is the time, Noah thought. It must be done quickly and surely now, or it will never be done at all.

"Giorgio," he said, "I have news for you. Good news. Your father did not betray anyone."

Resentment flickered in the bleary eyes. "I have always known that, signore. But why is it your concern?"

"He never betrayed anyone, Giorgio. But you did."

Rosanna gasped. Giorgio shook his head pityingly. "Listen to him! *Basta, signore. Basta.* I have work to do."

"You did your work a long time ago," Noah said relentlessly. "And when your father took away the money paid to you for it, you followed him and killed him to get it back."

He was pleased to see that Giorgio did not reel under this wholly false accusation. Instead, he seemed to draw strength from it. This is the way, Noah thought, that the unsuspecting animal is lured closer and closer to the trap. What hurt was that Rosanna, looking back and forth from inquisitor to accused, seemed ready to collapse. The rabbi watched with the same numb horror.

Giorgio turned to them. "Do you hear this?" he demanded, and there was a distinct mockery in his voice. "Now I am a murderer. Now I killed my own father."

"Before a witness," Noah said softly.

"Oh, of course, before a witness. And who was that witness, signore?"

"Someone who has just told the police everything. They'll bring him here very soon, so that he can point you out to them. A Major von Grubbner."

"And that is the worst lie of all!" said Giorgio triumphantly. "He's dead, that one! Dead and buried, do you hear? So all your talk—!"

There are animals which, when trapped, will fight to the death for their freedom, will gnaw away one of their own legs to release themselves. There are others which go to pieces the instant the jaws of the trap have snapped on them, become quivering lumps of flesh waiting only for the end. Giorgio, Noah saw, was one of the latter breed. His voice choked off, his jaw went slack, his face ashen. The mop, released from his nerveless grip, fell with a clatter. Rosanna took a step toward him, but Noah caught her wrist, holding her back.

"How do you know he's dead, Giorgio?" he demanded. "Yes, he's dead and buried—but how did you know that? No one else knew. How do you happen to be the only one?"

The man swayed, fell back against the wall.

"You killed von Grubbner and took that money," Noah said. "When your father tried to get rid of it, the partisans held him guilty of informing and shot him while you stood by, refusing to tell them the truth. In a way, you did help kill him, didn't you? That's what you've been carrying around in you since the day he died, isn't it?"

"Giorgio!" Rosanna cried out. "But why didn't you tell them? Why? Why?"

"Because," said Noah, "then they would have known the real informer. That money was a price paid to you for information, wasn't it. Giorgio?"

The word emerged like a groan. "Yes."

"You?" Rosanna said wonderingly, her eyes fixed on her brother. "It was you?"

"But what could I do? What could I do? He came to me, the German. He said he knew I was of the Resistance. He said if I did not tell him where the men were hidden I would be put to death. If I told, I would be saved. I would be rewarded."

The broken hulk lurched toward Rosanna, arms held wide in appeal, but Noah barred the way. "Why did you kill von Grubbner?"

"Because he cheated me. After the men were taken, I went to him for the money, and he laughed at me. He said I must tell him about others, too. I must tell everything, and then he would pay. So I killed him. When he turned away, I picked up a stone and struck him on the head and then again and again until he was dead. And I buried him behind the gate there because only the *ragazzi* knew how to get through it, and no one would find him there."

"But you took that case full of money with you."

"Yes, but only to give to my father. And I told him everything. Everything. I swear it. I wanted him to beat me. I wanted him to kill me if that would make it all right. But he would not. All he knew was that the money must be returned. He had too much honor! That was what he died for. He was mad with honor! Who else on this earth would try to return money to a dead man?"

Giorgio's legs gave way. He fell to his knees and remained there, striking the floor blow after blow with his fist. "Who else?" he moaned "Who else?"

The rabbi looked helplessly at Noah. "He was a boy then," he said in a voice of anguish. "Only a boy. Can we hold children guilty of the crimes we inflict on them?" And then he said with bewilderment,

"But what of the blood money? What did Ezechiele Coen do with it? What became of it?"

"I think we'll soon find out," said Noah.

They were all there at the gates of the Teatro Marcello when Commissioner Ponziani arrived with his men. All of them and more. The rabbi and Carlo Piperno, the post-card vender, and Vito Levi, the butcher, and a host of others whose names were inscribed on the rolls of the synagogue. And tenants of the Teatro Marcello, curious as to what was going on below them, and schoolboys and passersby with time to spare.

The Commissioner knew his job, Noah saw. Not only had he brought a couple of strong young *carabinieri* to perform the exhumation, but other men as well to hold back the excited crowd.

Only Giorgio was not there. Giorgio was in a bed of the hospital on Isola Tiberina, his face turned to the wall. He was willing himself to die, the doctor had said, but he would not die. He would live, and, with help, make use of the years ahead. It was possible that employment in the hospital itself, work which helped the unfortunate, might restore to him a sense of his own worth. The doctor would see to that when the time came.

Noah watched as the police shattered the lock on the gates and drew them apart, their hinges groaning rustily. He put an arm around Rosanna's waist and drew her to him as the crowd pressed close behind them. This was all her doing, he thought. Her faith had moved mountains, and with someone like this at his side, someone whose faith in him would never waver, it would not be hard to return home and face down the cynics there. It didn't take a majority vote of confidence to sustain you; it needed only one person's granite faith.

The police strung up lights in the vaulted area behind the gate. They studied the ground, then carefully plied shovels as the Commissioner hovered around them.

"*Faccia attenzione,*" he said. "*Adagio. Adagio.*"

The mound of dirt against the wall grew larger. The men put aside their shovels. Kneeling, they carefully scooped earth from the hole, handful by handful. Then the form of a body showed, fleshless bones, a grinning shattered skull. A body clad in the moldering tatters of a military uniform.

And, as Noah saw under the glare of droplights, this was not the first time these remains had been uncovered. On the chest of the skeletal form rested a small leather case fallen to rot, marked by the blackened image of a double headed eagle. The case had come apart at all its seams, the money in it seemed to have melted together in lumps, more like clay than money, yet it was clearly recognizable for what it was. Twenty years ago Ezechiele Coen had scraped aside the earth over the freshly buried Major Alois von Grubbner and returned his money to him. There it was and there he was, together as they had been since that time.

Noah became aware of the rabbi's voice behind him. Then another voice and another, all merging into a litany recited in deep-toned chorus. A litany, Noah thought, older than the oldest ruins of Rome. It was the *kaddish,* the Hebrew prayer for the dead, raised to heaven for Ezechiele Coen, now at rest.

THAT MONDAY NIGHT

Pauline C. Smith

Pauline C. Smith

Stories that leave you knowing that something terrible is about to happen are especially chilling. And rare. "That Monday Night" is such a story.

Murder has been committed. Lives have been wrecked. And now . . .

Not everyone can write that kind of story. But Pauline C. Smith has the special ability it takes. She can tell a good tale and she can make you shiver.

Often, tiny grains of fact are to the writer of fiction what grains of sand are to the oyster. And in the case of "That Monday Night," its author says: "That I live in the town I write about and the jacked-up car was discovered in a local shopping center is factual. That the girl's body was found, the family destroyed, a neighbor dissolved in the juice of her own hangup and a co-worker's life broken apart through the tragedy is fictional."

About herself, she adds: "I live on a hillside with a gentle dachshund, a fierce Siamese, my typewriter and a glorious view of the Pacific Ocean. During the twenty-five years I've been fabricating fiction from fact, I have had five books published and some eight hundred stories."

"That Monday Night" is a beautiful sample of how a locale and an incident, the discovery of a jacked-up car, can be catalysts for a memorable story that builds to an unexpected, frightening climax.

A.M.

THAT MONDAY NIGHT

That Monday night at nine o'clock, as soon as *Laugh-In* was over, Jim Copeland remembered to get up and turn on the porch light. His daughter, Michele, should be home from the store by nine-thirty. She always was.

He yawned, stretched and looked at the TV news. Discarding the movie on 4 that would take too long, he switched to Channel 2. Then he went into the kitchen, opened a can of beer, returned, settled down to the television set and was sound asleep by nine-fifteen.

The screen finished its Mayberry problems and began a Doris Day entanglement, continuing then with Carol Burnett's comedic exaggerations.

Jim Copeland slept on.

Mrs. Carrie Mason, the middle-aged widow next door, was also watching television, from her bed. Her bedroom window looked out upon the Copeland porch, so that she saw the light when it went on at nine o'clock. *For Michele,* she thought, knowing that the girl worked on Monday nights at Harper's Department Store in the Plaza Shopping Center. She would be home at nine-thirty right on the dot, because she always was, then the light would go off.

Carrie became absorbed in the movie, not noticing that the porch light remained on, not until after the movie was over at eleven. Her first thought, then, was that Jim Copeland had forgotten to turn it off after Michele's arrival home. "Just like a man," she muttered, knowing that Mrs. Copeland, Sue, was in Tremont, baby-sitting for that married daughter of hers, the one with three children. With Sue gone, wouldn't Jim Copeland keep the porch light on until all hours!

Carrie switched off her TV set, went to the kitchen, swallowed a jigger of bourbon to help her sleep, returned to the bedroom, turned off her light and opened the window a scant three inches. Just before she slanted the blind slats enough so that the morning sun would not awaken her with the terrible start of remembering that she was alone and a widow, she looked out upon the Copeland driveway where Michele always parked her car and found it empty!

Her heart squeezed and her mind formulated four thoughts in rapid succession. The first: *That eighteen-year-old child who had seemed so dependable, so studious and conscientious was, perhaps, like the rest of this young college generation, out whooping it up heaven-knows-where.* The second: *That father, who seemed so nice for a man, was letting her whoop it up while he sat goggle-eyed in front of his television set, which she could see grayly flickering in the Copeland living room.* Her third thought was that there was some kind of trouble: *Michele never stayed out after her evening at the store and her father never stayed up on a week night.* Fourth: *She would go over and find out, being a woman and with Sue gone.* Then she remembered that she was a forty-year-old widow . . . well, all right, forty-five, and her act of Samaritanism might be misinterpreted, especially with a jigger of liquor on her breath.

She lay down, but uneasily, and slept restlessly, the empty space in the Copeland driveway on her mind.

It was one o'clock when she was awakened by the rumble of Jim Copeland's car as it backed with noisy abandon from the garage.

She peeked out between the slats of the blind. The Copeland driveway was empty and fog-washed. The Copeland garage was open and dark. The porch light still shone, as did a lamp dimly from the living room.

Something was wrong.

The town lay between the ocean and the mountains, quietly serene. With a sprawling megalopolis to the south and a tightly aloof city to the north, it was left out by the AP and the UPI news reports and ignored during the television weather forecast—a forgotten town.

At nine-thirty that Monday night, a co-worker, Linda Fischer ("I'm in jewelry, but Michele moved around from department to department because she went to college, you see, and only worked two nights a week plus Saturday . . ."), saw Michele in the brightly lighted parking lot. "Of course I know it was Michele Copeland. She was standing there by her car, that little green bug she drives, and she waved when my husband and I drove by. My husband picks me up about nine-twenty. He parks in the A section, and when I'm through we drive down to the D section, which is near the coffee shop, and we go in there for coffee and a snack."

The coffee shop, Linda Fischer explained to the police on Tuesday when they questioned her, stayed open until ten. She and her husband left just before it closed. There was only one car in the D section when they left, probably the coffee shop owner's car, and the owner explained to the police when questioned that, yes, he took off five minutes after the last customers, but he drove out the other side. Out through D, he meticulously explained, to the turnoff on Sargent and, as far as he could remember, there wasn't a car in the parking lot. As far as he could *see* there wasn't a car; but then, of course, he hadn't looked back toward A, the Harper parking lot. Why should he? He was going the other way.

Linda Fischer and her husband drove from D section, after coffee and a sandwich, about nine fifty-five, she thought, out through A again, and they saw Michele's car still there, jacked up. They supposed she had gone off with the friend who had been helping her because the friend's car was gone.

"A friend?" asked the police.

How could Linda know that? She and her husband had seen this man there at nine-thirty or thereabouts. No, they couldn't see him very well, he'd been tall and thin and had dark hair, she thought. He seemed to be fooling around with the jack, and his car—at least they assumed it was his car—had been parked next to Michele's, so they supposed she had come out from the store, found a flat and called him, a friend.

What kind of car? Linda was asked. She didn't know; light, probably white—at least a pale color.

Anyway, Michele waved to Linda, and she wouldn't wave if anything were wrong, would she?

Linda did not add that her husband had wanted to stop. "Maybe I can help," he had said in his involved way. "Don't be silly," Linda had answered. "She's got help." Anyway, Michele was pretty, and it was Linda's mission in life to keep her husband away from pretty girls.

Just the same, ever since that Tuesday morning when the police had questioned her, Linda was nagged by the guilty suspicion that maybe it wasn't a happy hand greeting Michele had waved at nine-thirty Monday night, but a frantic wigwag of terror.

Well, she couldn't tell the police that, could she? And what would be the use now?

On Tuesday morning Sue Copeland, Michele's mother, prepared to leave her daughter Dorrie's home in Tremont immediately after breakfast.

"But Mom, why so early? It's only a couple of hours' drive and, anyway, by the time you get there, Dad'll be at work and Michele at school. Why not wait and leave this afternoon?"

Sue did not know why, unless being unaccustomed to the demands of three small children during a long weekend, she felt the abrupt need of the quiet of her home. "Oh, I don't know, Dorrie," she said. "I guess I just want to get the house straightened up." A limp excuse, since Michele was neat as a pin and Jim never got anything out of place.

Dorrie firmed her lips and spoke precisely. "Well," she said, "if you don't want to hear about the trip and the speech Hal gave at the convention," a snappish attempt to cover up and superimpose the selfish guilt of a married daughter who would call a mother out on the freeway two hours away to go through a three-day brat-race just because it was cheaper and more convenient than hiring a baby-sitter who would baby-sit only, and not clean and wash and cook and rock. "If you don't want to have a *visit* and just *enjoy*. I thought you'd stay a little while, at least, after we got home and Hal had gone off to work. So we could talk *alone*. I thought you wouldn't leave until afternoon. At least noon."

"I know, honey," said Sue vaguely, gathering her bags together and picking up her car keys. "I know," she said, feeling a compulsion to get home without knowing why.

She kissed the three grandchildren, and Dorrie walked with her out to the car.

"I wanted to talk about the trip, Mom," said Dorrie, leaning inside the car, the guilt, now that her mother did not allow her to assuage it with hospitality, melting into tears. "I wanted to have a little while with you. I mean, after you'd taken care of the kids and all, it seems kind of awful that you should pick up and run without a visit with me."

Sue, starting the motor, said, "I know, honey, but another time," unable to explain her obsession that she must hit the freeway and hurry home.

She worked her way through the early morning traffic, away from the city, into the fast lane north through the coastside fog and the overhanging clouds of winter. She made the trip in less than two hours, leaving the freeway and turning onto Sargent, where she drove past the Plaza Shopping Center's morning-filled parking lot without noticing the little green car jacked up in the A section directly behind Harper's Department Store.

She crossed the back residential streets toward the old suburban area and turned onto Rio Mesa. From the end of the block, the moment she turned, Sue routinely observed that Michele's car was gone from the driveway, which was as it should be at ten o'clock on a Tuesday morning. She drove up the quiet street, made the sharp turn required to enter the open garage and braked with startled surprise.

What was Jim's car doing home at this hour of the day?

She eased her car in beside it, then hurried from the garage up the steps of the porch. She noticed the forgotten porch light glowing faintly in the gloom of a cloudy day.

Now alarmed, Sue turned the key and flung open the door.

There sat Jim, sunk in the big chair, his head in his hands.

Before she could speak, he lifted his head and said, "Michele is gone."

"Gone?" Sue's voice rose on the word and reached a shrill note. "What do you mean, gone?"

He told her then about dropping off to sleep, and awakening to discover that it was one o'clock in the morning, with Michele not in her bed and her car not in the driveway.

Sue backed against the door so that it closed with her weight. *Is this what she had been hurrying home to?*

Jim told her, in a dead voice Sue had never before heard, how he got out his car and raced through sleeping streets to the Plaza Shopping Center and found Michele's little green car there, the only car in the entire parking lot, jacked up, with the spare lying on the pavement; not Michele—only Michele's car.

He went on to explain, in this freshly dead voice, his hurried search for a phone booth in among the fog-wet planters and the darkened shops of the mall and how he finally found one and called the police.

The police had it all wrong from the beginning. At first, over the phone, they thought Jim Copeland had wanted them to fix a flat or get someone to fix a flat. Then they thought he was reporting a daughter's stolen car. Finally they got it straight. Well, not really straight because, even after meeting him out there at the lighted parking lot and seeing the jacked-up car and hearing his garbled account, the two patrol officers still confused Michele with the usual teen-ager encountered during the course of their varied, colorful night duty.

"You know who she might have run away with?" asked one.

The other mentioned drugs and possible pregnancy.

However, they did not press charges when Jim Copeland took a poke at one of the officers, even though they did tell him that was no way to find his daughter.

At headquarters, the man at the desk recorded the necessary descriptive information: Name, Michele Copeland. Age, 18. Height, 5'1". Weight, 98 pounds. Brown eyes. Blond hair. Occupation, full-time college student, part-time department store employee. It was not a complete description since Michele's dependable character and her reserved personality had been left out, but the man at the desk said that information was unnecessary.

Because Michele was eighteen and legally an adult, the police could not get out an all-points bulletin on her disappearance for seventy-two hours, and by that time, through interviews with students and faculty members of the college as well as co-workers at the store, it had been well established that she was indeed a good, dependable, conscientious and reserved girl; therefore not the type to take off willingly with some strange man.

This left the police with two theories. Either the tall, thin, dark-haired stranger described by Mrs. Linda Fischer had used physical violence to force Michele into his car, necessitating a search of the hillside arroyos and deserted rocky points of the beach for a body; or the tall, thin, dark-haired stranger was a friend with whom Michele had gone willingly, and the highway patrol was alerted to cover the brushlands and cliffsides for a wrecked, probably white, car and possibly two bodies.

"Can't you describe the guy's car any better than that?" the police asked the Fischers. "You just say a light-colored car, probably white. How about make? Was it a late model? Sedan, convertible, station wagon, compact maybe?"

Linda said she didn't know one car from another, and anyway she hadn't looked at the car. She had just waved back at Michele as they drove on.

At that, her husband glared at her. He would never forgive her for talking him out of stopping on Monday night. He had wanted to stop. He had slowed down even, but know-it-all Linda, who acted like she owned even the breaths he took, hurried him on as she turned and waved and smiled as if butter wouldn't melt in her mouth at that poor girl who was God-knows-where now.

"I'm sorry, officer," said Linda Fischer's husband. "I didn't notice much about the car either, except that it was light—white, probably—and stuck out farther than her little green job in the diagonal parking space right in front of it. What I was noticing was that her trunk was open and it looked as if the guy was getting out the jack, so everything seemed to be under control, with him there and all." He ended his excuse for noninvolvement with a sigh, feeling only partial absolution and none at all for his wife.

Again he glared at her. "Is it true the tire was slashed?" he asked.

Jim Copeland was sure the tire had been slashed. "The sidewall was punctured with a sharp instrument," he declared for the press. The crime-lab report offered the more conservative view that the tire could have been damaged accidentally and routinely by a sharp rock or a piece of glass.

Carrie Mason didn't know what to do.

She had seen Jim Copeland arrive home on Tuesday morning at seven o'clock, just about the time it was beginning to be winter-light. Watching from her bedroom window with the blind slats carefully slanted, she had seen the car pull into the garage and Jim Copeland walk heavily up the porch steps.

The porch light remained on and the driveway remained empty, and she didn't know what to do. She should go over there, shouldn't she? After all, they were neighbors and she was a good friend of Sue's. But then, being a widow and with Sue gone, it might look . . . Well, it might look *funny,* like she was trying to . . . well, trying to promote something.

At eight-thirty she saw the patrol car pull up to the curb and two officers walk up to the Copeland front porch. They went inside the house.

What in the world?

At nine o'clock they left the house and drove the patrol car away, and Carrie Mason was again faced with the question of what to do? Offer her services, her condolence, her sympathy, whatever it was that she should offer? She felt a nagging anxiety that the offer might be coming too late, but she couldn't just stay here in her house with a neighbor in trouble. My goodness, daughter gone, up till all hours, out all night and then the police. It was time, certainly, to throw caution to the winds. Even if she was an attractive forty-five-year-old widow —well, almost fifty—still, this was a duty; but first she must do something about her jumping nerves after seeing the patrol car and the policemen, so she tottered to the kitchen and swallowed a jigger of bourbon, which calmed her but also caused her to realize that she could not possibly, being a nice widow and all, visit a man alone with liquor on her breath.

An hour later she saw Sue Copeland's car turn into the garage.

With Jim's shocking announcement, Sue's reaction was immediate. She went into his comforting arms to comfort him. From that moment on, until he drove Michele's little green car home on Thursday—or perhaps it was with Dorrie's arrival, which also occurred on Thursday—Sue leaned upon Jim and encouraged him. She was his hope as he was hers, with never a thought of recrimination for this accidental tragedy.

They were interviewed together by a young reporter that Tuesday noon, and together they described their daughter—a good, responsible girl, not the type to go off with a stranger, so it had to be foul play. They described the dress she wore, a brown wool with matching coat, and her quiet, orderly habits which would never allow her to act heedlessly. Her grades were excellent. She had no problems. Yes, she dated upon occasion, but seldom, what with her studies and part-time clerking job, and no one steadily.

At the reporter's request, Sue offered him Michele's latest pictures—the year-old graduation photograph, careful to point out that her hair had been long then, but now was cut short, as shown in the more recent snapshots. She broke down and wept, feeling bereft and frightened as if, by relinquishing the pictures of Michele, she were giving up her daughter for lost.

Sue got through that first day by drinking coffee and keeping the pot ready for Jim when he arrived home from either an anxiety-filled trip to the police station or a fearful cruise along lonely roads. She paced the floor and phoned those of Michele's friends who were available and might know something. No one knew anything, or so they said.

She looked with aversion at the plate of cookies Carrie Mason brought apologetically over about two o'clock in the afternoon, smelled Mrs. Mason's mouthwash-spiked breath, and listened with an edge of surprise as Mrs. Mason groped through a perplexing maze of nonintervention excuses for not arriving earlier. Then Sue roused to realize that Mrs. Mason, widowed and somewhat humiliated by it, had probably been on target behind her venetian blind since last night when the pattern of the Copelands had been smashed, wanting to know, to be a part of it, wanting to help but unable to because she was a widow and envious of the non-widowed.

Sue told her all that she knew and they wept together.

The paper, with the front-page item and picture of Michele, was delivered at five, when the winter day began to be night. Sue read about her daughter and looked at the darkening sky, knowing that she was out there someplace.

Through the night, Sue made frequent trips to the front porch to test the black, cold dampness, ashamed of being warm and safe. She stood on the porch in terror of the night and what it might be doing to her child, until Jim urged her back into shamed warmth and safety.

It was during those times that Sue and Jim were close, with the compassion of mother for father and father for mother, not thinking of blame or self-blame, of guilt or self-guilt—not until Thursday, after the seventy-two-hour lapse, when flyers would be distributed to 250 law-enforcement agencies within the state and extending into adjoining states, when the case would reach the television newscast and be released to the press through the AP and the UPI services, when the little green car would be returned to the driveway, and Dorrie would arrive.

Wednesday morning, Carrie Mason divided her time between the venetian blinds of her bedroom and the kitchen stove, cooking up food the Copelands could not possibly eat.

She anguished as she watched the television people haul out their equipment from the truck in front and drag it up the porch steps and into the Copeland house. She castigated herself for her Monday-night-eleven-o'clock-bourbon-breath when she identified the reporter returning to the Copeland house for a second interview. She cooked and watched, flagellating herself for her anxious-widow sins of omission, for had she awakened Jim Copeland from his sleep, his daughter might be home now.

The Wednesday evening article in the local newspaper covered the lower section of the front page, displaying another picture of Michele —one of the snapshots showing her hair cut short and with a smile on her face—that broke Sue's heart. The picture looked back at Sue now under the heading:

HAVE YOU SEEN THIS GIRL?

It was then that Sue phoned her married daughter, knowing that she could put it off no longer in the hope it would not be necessary at all, because now, if she were not warned, Dorrie would have the shock of finding out from her own newspaper or through her television set.

Dorrie became immediately emotional. "When did it happen?" she cried. "On Monday night? When you were *here?*" She was silent for a time, interrupting her mother at last with "But if you had been home, it might not have happened," and quickly adding, "What was Daddy *doing* all that time? *Sleeping?*" and she had the hook upon which to hang her guilt. "You mean he didn't *do* anything? Mom, I'll be there," making the immediate decision to transfer her fault of needlessly needing her mother to her father, so that he could be the sinner and not she. "Mom, I'll drive up tomorrow as soon as I can arrange about Hal and the kids."

"No, honey," protested Sue, knowing Dorrie's tendency to dominate, to push like a bulldozer and whack away like a pile driver. Sue did not want to be pushed or whacked at this point, but wanted only to wait and worry and hope so that she didn't go to pieces, with all the pieces flying out into limbo.

"Absolutely, Mom," said Dorrie. "This is awful! Why, it's awful! I'll be there. You don't have to do a thing. I'll take care of everything."

Just as Michele could not legally be presumed a missing person until seventy-two hours had passed, so could her car not be legally presumed to be abandoned for the same length of time, and it stood there in the parking lot just as she had left it. No fingerprints had been found and none had been expected, due to the heavy fog of Monday night and early Tuesday.

Thursday afternoon the sun came out with brief and pale promise as Jim Copeland changed the tire on his daughter's car.

The shoppers who had parked in A section, most of whom had read the front page of the local paper, and many having heard a number of the news spots from the local radio station, walked an arc of sympathetic self-consciousness around Jim Copeland and his daughter's car. All were hurried and embarrassed except for one, the man who drove into A section in a light gray compact and stepped out of it with an offer to help Jim Copeland change the tire.

The man, youngish, about 35, decided Jim, squinting up at him, really wanted to help. He was slim, personable, conservatively dressed, of medium height and with medium brown hair—unless, of course, he might have been seen at night in the deceptive light of the floods with their elongated shadows, making any man tall, especially if standing next to a girl of 5'1", just as night light colors all brown hair dark, particularly when contrasted with blond.

With the spare in place, the damaged tire, jack and lug wrench back in the trunk, the young man leaned against his car to talk about Monday night.

Grateful for his interest, Jim Copeland listened to ideas that were neither as objective as those of the police nor as emotional as Jim's own, but a combination of emotional objectivity that could be trusted.

"I read about it in last night's paper," said the man, "and I've been hearing radio reports all day. I'm a salesman and in my car a lot and have the radio on. I wonder if the police are going about it in the right way."

"I wonder, too," said Jim Copeland. "They say they aren't even sure if the man with whom those people saw Michele had anything to do with it. They say it's possible he might have driven away and Michele walked off to find a phone, and whatever happened, happened then."

The man shook his head. "He had everything to do with it," he said with certainty. "I'd bet on it. The one with the white car."

"I think so, too," said Jim. "I think he slashed the tire and waited for her."

The man gave the damaged tire a token glance. "No. In the first place, how would he know the driver was a girl? Even if he looked in and saw the registration on the steering-wheel post, how would he know the girl would be alone? Whoever it was didn't plan the thing. It just happened."

Jim closed the trunk and leaned against it. "You think the tire was flat and he saw it and just waited and when it turned out to be a girl, especially a pretty girl, he went through all the motions, and then as soon as there wasn't anyone around, he forced her into his car? She sure as hell wouldn't go with him willingly."

"What if he seemed like a nice sort of fellow? Clean-cut, pleasant, helpful, not a long-haired hoodlum kid or old enough to be a dirty old man, but somewhere in between, and he says he'd be glad to help and he gets out the jack and gets to work. What can happen under the lights? Then he hauls out the spare and bounces it up and down on the pavement and says it needs air—"

"But it had plenty of air," interrupted Jim, kicking the tire.

"Okay," said the man, "but would your girl have known any different if somebody'd told her it hadn't?"

No, thought Jim Copeland. All Michele had known about a car was how to start, drive and stop it. It could have happened the way the man had said.

"So he says he guesses she'd better ride with him down to the filling station to get some air in the tire. The filling station's down on the corner. You can see it from here."

Obediently, Jim Copeland, who was a regular customer of that filling station, shaded his eyes toward the corner of Sargent and Oak, where he could see the top of the station sign.

"What's she going to do? Even a girl like yours, who wouldn't willingly get into a car with a stranger, this time she's going to think nothing of it. After all, the guy's knocking himself out for her, and he's honest enough not to want to take off with her tire, leaving her to stand there all alone, scared he might steal it and not come back." The man smiled, curving the smile into a combination of arrogant pity for the father and pompous regret for the daughter.

"You mean you think she might have been tricked into this weirdo's car?" asked Jim Copeland.

"Not tricked, exactly," said the man, "and the guy wasn't necessarily a weirdo. He might have been sick."

"*Sick?*"

"Look, I'm basing this hypothesis on the psychology I have learned. You see, I set out to be a consulting psychologist and then my wife got sick and I had to drop out of school and make money to take care of her. That was years ago. Haven't had any married life since and no career either. Just work at a sales job to give an invalid wife the things she needs and wants. . . ." He shook his head with self-pity. "That's what I was doing here Monday night, getting her one of the things she's always after me to get—a prescription, ice cream, a heating pad or an ice bag, anything, something—"

"You mean you were here at the shopping center that night?" Jim Copeland leaned forth from the trunk of the little green car to grab the jacket lapels of the man. "You were here that night? Did you see something? Did you see any of that stuff you've been talking about?"

The man shook loose. "I told you," he said, "everything I told you is theoretical. I think about it. The police in a case like this want fingerprints or a hair or something before they're satisfied, and the relatives keep saying, 'My daughter wouldn't,' and all I'm doing is showing how your daughter *might*, because I have studied those things and understand them. And I think he's sick, but a kind of a nice guy, so your girl got into his car . . ."

Jim Copeland smoothed the man's lapels with apologetic pats. He was only trying to help and, God knows, this theory he'd come up with was a lot more believable than those of the police—talking about drugs and pregnancy and running away—none of which could apply to *Michele!*

"So we assume the guy was sick," explained the man. "Oh, not ordinarily, but just when the pressures build up. Let's say he's a nice guy. Your girl wouldn't go with anybody but a nice guy . . ."

Jim Copeland nodded.

"He doesn't plan anything. It gets planned for him."

"Gets planned?" asked Jim.

"That's the psychology of an impulse crime and I think it was a crime of impulse; nothing premeditated, but an extemporaneous impulse triggered by a series of circumstances. The guy's under a lot of pressure, he's at the exploding point. He drives into the parking lot late, just before closing time. He's in a hurry, probably doesn't even notice the little green car with its flat, at first. When he gets ready to leave, he notices but he doesn't think too much about it. The parking lot's thinned out, customers have taken off for their homes filled with loving, healthy, undemanding wives. He starts his motor. Then the girl comes, your girl, and she sees the flat and the guy turns off his motor and gets out."

Jim Copeland swallowed. It could have been exactly like that.

"He's a nice guy," repeated the man. "He really wants to help, so he helps. He gets the jack out. Then the people drive by, those people who saw your girl and the guy. They slow down. They wave. And the guy wonders if your girl might be signaling, might be rejecting him and his help, signaling to her friends.

"But they go on and he jacks up the car and starts to reach for the lug wrench, still helping. Then the explosion comes, the pressures blow sky-high, and he reaches for the spare instead and bounces it on the pavement. The whole thing's set up for him. He's sick and can't help what happens."

Jim Copeland looked away, feeling ill.

The pale sun hid behind the clouds that were rising on the horizon. It would rain again; sure enough, it would rain again tonight.

"He gives her the filling-station pitch. She goes for it because there's not much else she can do. He helps her around his car and opens the door, then goes around to his side, leaving the spare on the pavement. He jumps in and they're off before she can even yell."

Jim Copeland felt as if he were swimming in the filtered light of the winter day. "You think," he said faintly, "that's the way it happened? That anyone could just—"

"That's the way it could have happened," said the man. "There were no signs of struggle. The police pointed that out. You said your girl wouldn't go off with a stranger willingly, so what other way could there be? It's a psychologically sound theory that a sick man, but a nice guy, found a setup just made for him to act on at a time that his pressures exploded."

Jim Copeland looked away.

Then the man gave him hope. "A sick mind like that, though," he said, "knows he's sick and wants to be stopped."

Jim Copeland jerked his head back, and listened with intent.

"He'll cover—self-preservation, you know, being the first law—but at the same time he'll drop clues, just hoping someone will find them and stop him from doing again what he has already done."

The man opened his car door and stepped inside. "I'm sorry, Mr. Copeland," he said, genuinely sorry.

He turned on his motor and the radio sounds came on immediately, faintly at first, to grow stronger into the on-the-hour news broadcast ... "Nothing yet on the Michele Copeland disappearance," came the voice of the announcer. "If you know of anything, or think you might know, or suspect . . ." The man turned down the volume to a whisper and started to back his car from its parking slot.

Jim Copeland straightened from the trunk of the little green car. "What do you think he did with her?" he asked the man.

"What do *you* think?"

Jim Copeland swallowed again.

The man turned the wheel, straightened out, and started down the A section of the parking lot.

"Hey," called Jim Copeland, "I didn't get your name."

The man shouted it out the window, but the sound was lost in the rising wind of the early evening and the growl of the motor as he turned to make the off-ramp onto Sargent.

The police didn't think much of Jim Copeland's theoretical story as told to him by the stranger in the parking lot when he immediately drove the little green car to headquarters and related it.

"A crackpot," they stated. "We get them all the time. A mother who's had it up to here with this rotten kid of hers thinks he did it and wants us to lock him up and throw away the key. Some dame says it's the kind of trick her ex-boyfriend would pull. You been in this work as long as we have, you expect all kinds of trumped-up stories."

"But this was a theory," argued Jim. "This man seemed to know a lot about psychology, and he was basing this theory on his psychological knowledge."

"Every crackpot is a psychologist," said the officer. "They know everything about nothing and are eager to talk about it."

"But it sounded," said Jim with hesitation, "as if it could have really happened. It sounded right, somehow. If you could talk to him . . ."

"Sure," and the officer poised a pencil over a scratchpad. "Sure, we'll talk to him. We talk to all of 'em. Just give us his name and address."

Jim didn't know his name or where he lived. That bit of information had been snatched away in the wind, and maybe he *was* a crackpot, like the officer said. What had the man offered, after all? Just a theory.

Dorrie arrived late that Thursday afternoon, at the beginning of the storm that had been brewing and slacking off, allowing the sun to peek through, then closing in again. The storm broke, dark and vicious, and Dorrie walked in about the same time her father drove the little green car home and parked it, once again, in the driveway.

From then on, every time Sue looked out the window she saw that little green car and shuddered, and every time she turned from the window, Dorrie told her it was Jim's fault that Michele was gone, until she believed it.

"Your own daughter," she denounced him, "and you slept through it all."

"What could I have done?" he asked. "She was gone by ten. That's what those people at the parking lot said."

"With you home here, asleep," accused Sue, appalled at her own vindictiveness, but relieved to have a victim at last.

Jim was confused. "If I'd been awake, I wouldn't have gone after her by ten. Why would I? I'd have thought she'd stopped to have coffee with somebody."

"But not Mom," Dorrie broke in. "If Mom had been here, she'd have known Michele is never late. She'd have been out of here like a flash."

"But she wasn't here," said Jim, seeing his opportunity to fix blame, knowing that if the blame were to be circumvented it must be fixed upon someone else. "She was at your house, baby-sitting. That's why she wasn't here."

Ready for him, Dorrie answered in triumph, "Because she trusted you, that's why she wasn't here. She trusted you to take care of things and protect Michele so this awful thing wouldn't happen."

Thursday evening the story in the paper was more compact and without a photograph, headlined simply HUNT CONTINUES, with a quick synopsis and the usual vague promise of an expected break.

The taped television interview had been cut to the bone to allow newscast pictures and commentary on the storm in progress, with accounts of sliding hillsides in the city to the north and stories of boiling rivers within the sprawling megalopolis to the south. The town in between lay ignored, as usual, except for the tape-cut interview with the parents of Michele Copeland.

However, it, too, was having its storm troubles, with minor erosion of the hills and overflowing river banks, its greatest problem being the flooded streets and, more particularly, that corner at the intersection of Sexton and Sargent where the new tract of houses was under construction. There the water rose and flowed down the grade, bringing with it mud and debris, clogging the curbing outlets and flooding the Plaza Shopping Center parking area so that the water swirled into the mall and threatened the shops.

The storm lasted three days.

During that time, Sue could not sleep, her fearful nights being filled with terror thoughts of her baby, out there someplace, out there alone or with a monster in the cold and the rain, out there dead or dying. Sue could not eat, her frightful days being consumed by horror pictures of ravishment and death. She lived on coffee and the wakefulness it engendered. She lashed out at Jim as an object for her emotion. She worked him over, discovering after all their peaceful years together that she had a talent for it.

Dorrie, having shifted the weight of her own guilt, now carried a new burden. Her parents, always friends, were now enemies, and was that her fault?

"Mom," she cried, "I never heard you talk to Dad like that before."

"He never killed my daughter before," said Sue.

Periodically, Jim drove through the storm to the police station to find the officers engaged with traffic problems and slick-street accidents.

"About my daughter . . ." Jim Copeland asked anxiously, apologetic with this new deep guilt his wife had thrust upon him.

"We're working on it, Mr. Copeland," said the officer. "We've got those flyers out, you know. We wish we had more information, like a better description of the man and what kind of car he drove. We did the best we could with what we have. A picture of your daughter is on the flyer, and anything suspicious—well, we'll hear about it. I know how you feel, Mr. Copeland."

Jim Copeland looked at him blankly. This officer, too young yet for guilt, too young for teen-age daughters, could not possibly know how he felt. Jim turned and left the police station, knowing that he would return shortly, to learn nothing again; but he had to come, a telephone call would not suffice. He had to come through storm-filled streets and climb the stairs and open the heavy doors and ask whichever officer was on the desk at the time, "Have you heard anything about my daughter?" He had to. There was nothing else he could do now.

The storm hampered the search, but it did not hamper Mrs. Carrie Mason. Daily, she made a tent of her late husband's raincoat and crouched under it, a platter of baked, fried, grilled or broiled food covered and clutched, and scampered from her house to the Copelands'.

There she made her offering, always hoping it would be only Sue she might encounter in the kitchen. Even Sue, who had changed so drastically during the last of these few days from a soft and warm anxiety to being anxiously hard and cold, was better than her daughter Dorrie; Dorrie, who looked down her nose from the enviable heights of her youthful husband-filled life and caused within Carrie Mason great pangs of guilt for her own manless old age of almost fifty—no, actually fifty-two, almost fifty-three—and sometimes looked it.

So, guiltily, when it was Dorrie in the kitchen, she handed out the covered plate of whatever she had prepared and asked softly if there had been any news, any news at all.

Dorrie, taking the covered plate without even glancing under the cover, looked down from her pinnacle of security and said there was no news but, "We thank you for your kindness."

"No kindness!" protested Carrie. "It was Monday night when I should have been kind, the night I was sure something was wrong. At eleven o'clock I saw the porch light on and the driveway empty. I should have come then, and I didn't."

"Then it would have been too late," said Dorrie.

It might *not* have been too late, worried Carrie. On a Monday night this town was in bed by eleven and so, with the few cars on the streets at that time of night, they might have found Michele.

Carrie could not easily shift her burden of guilt, being neither young enough nor egotistical enough. Her guilt caused her to make a firm resolve: from now on she would be warmly friendly—instantly. She would not hesitate or vacillate, distrustful of her breath, apprehensive as to appearances, but she would, so help her, aid, assist, succor and befriend anyone who might need her, and she would be watchful for the need.

By Sunday the storm was over.

On Monday, a week after Michele's disappearance, the street maintenance crews were out in full force and got to work to find out what was wrong in the area extending from the hills into the Plaza Shopping Center, which was a mess. The trouble was found to be at the intersection where the new tract of houses was under construction and now a sea of mud. The storm drain there seemed to be clogged, allowing an overflow of water and muck down Sargent, where it spread into the side streets and filled up the parking lot.

A work crew was called, and when they opened up the storm drain they found Michele's body doubled up and stuffed into it, plugging up the opening.

Linda Fischer heard it on the radio.

This was her late day at Harper's Department Store, starting at one and extending to nine o'clock closing time, so she was, that Monday morning, cleaning her apartment with the radio on when the newscast broke in to announce the discovery of Michele Copeland's body. She cringed, thinking, what if, oh my goodness, what if she had allowed her husband to stop that night! He, too, might have been killed. Thus she absolved herself of any guilt, and turned her act of remission into one of nobility.

Her husband heard it during his lunch hour. "That girl," said the man on the stool next to him, "they found her. You know, the girl who disappeared a week ago."

Linda's husband swallowed the bite he had already taken from his sandwich and carefully laid the sandwich back on the plate.

"They found her in the storm drain up on Sargent and Sexton. Awful!"

Mrs. Fischer's husband pushed back his plate, got off his stool and walked woodenly from the drugstore. He walked down the street to the parking lot next to the business-machine office where he worked, got into his car, drove carefully down Main Street, past all the Caution signs to protect the street workers, entered the on-ramp to the freeway at the edge of town and sped north.

He never wanted to see his wife, Linda, again. He would lose himself somewhere, in some city far away, and try to forget that if Linda had not stopped him a week ago, Michele would be alive now.

On that second Monday morning, Carrie Mason was busy preparing a hearty vegetable soup for the Copeland family. The radio in the kitchen, as always, was turned to the local station, but she knew, even before the newscast told her so, that Michele had been found. She knew it when the police car drove up and the two police officers, their faces blankly reluctant, slowly climbed the steps to the Copeland front porch. So Carrie Mason knew, and as soon as the news was announced, remembering her always-be-friendly, help-in-time-of-need resolution, she knew that she would take the bowl of soup over, even though by the time the soup was ready her breath would be redolent of bourbon, that she would look every minute of her almost fifty-three years, and wouldn't know what to say.

Jim Copeland took the news like a doomed man, dully aware of the fact that he was, indeed, doomed.

Sue turned on him with a final "This is your fault," knowing that she would never speak to him again.

Dorrie, in the depths of her new guilt, wished that she could have the old one back, realizing at last that the guilt she had bequeathed herself would be lasting and difficult to endure.

By Monday night the body, having been properly identified, was properly resting in the funeral home.

Monday night, at nine-ten, Linda Fischer emerged from Harper's Department Store into the parking lot of the Plaza Shopping Center. She walked out with a part-time co-worker, a college girl from the notions department in which Michele had worked the week before. The girl hadn't known Michele, but claimed acquaintanceship because they went to the same college and worked in the same store and it was all terribly exciting.

"We actually saw him that night," Linda said, and the girl hung on to her words. "It was just a good thing my husband didn't stop. He might have been killed, too."

There were few cars left in Section A. The two walked carefully on the dry caked mud. "Well, here's my car," said the girl. "Isn't your husband here? Do you want a lift?"

"No, thank you. You go ahead." Linda consulted her watch. "He'll be along," she said. "I'm out a little early. He'll be here by nine-twenty for sure. He always is."

She didn't begin to worry until nine-forty, and the last car was gone from Section A. Then she became frightened and ran past the now-darkened shops to the coffee shop, still light, but empty of customers. The proprietor was just closing up.

"Would you drive me home?" Linda asked him breathlessly. "Would you please drive me home? I'm scared to wait for my husband out there all alone because of what happened . . ."

He would be glad to. He closed up the doughnut case, covered the cakes, turned off the lights and locked the door. He was very kind and solicitous. He helped her into his car and headed toward the apartment section of town where Mrs. Linda Fischer said she lived.

It was not until they reached the turn-off into Sargent that Linda realized she was in exactly the same situation Michele Copeland had been at this very same time last Monday night.

She froze on her side of the seat and her voice, as she gave directions, emerged as a thin thread of sound, stitching together the man's earnest talk of the dangers that lurked for a woman alone in the night. She lived only a few blocks from the Plaza Shopping Center, and she was sure she would never arrive there, but the man drove her directly to her destination and she was startled when he stopped and she looked out at her very own apartment building. She leaned on the door and staggered from the car, too voiceless from her moments of terror to thank the man. Her strength returned with her relief as she ran toward the apartment door, banged it open and stumbled up the stairs.

The moment she opened her own door upon darkness, she realized what an awful thing she had done when she prevented her husband from stopping to help Michele Copeland a week ago. It was the next moment that Mrs. Linda Fischer realized that her husband had left her and would not be back, because the awful thing she did to Michele she had also done to him.

Wednesday was the morning of the funeral. In the curtained-off mourners' section of the chapel, Dorrie sat between Michele's father and Michele's mother so that each parent wept alone through the ceremony.

Wednesday afternoon, Carrie Mason took over a pumpkin pie, and Dorrie had to push aside a mountain of dishes and a stack of pans to find room for it.

The kitchen looked as if a tornado had torn through, and there was Sue, dragging out linens and piling them up, making lists, dashing from one task to another. Carrie Mason wondered what in the world was going on and thought perhaps now that Jim and Sue Copeland were to be alone and with diminished needs, they had decided to reward Dorrie for all her self-sacrificing help by sending her home with extra household goods.

"You will probably be leaving now," Carrie said to Dorrie.

"Tomorrow," said Dorrie.

"I am going with her," said Sue without interrupting the even rhythm of her activity.

"Well," said Carrie, doubtfully supposing that maybe it was all right for a bereaved mother to go off and grieve with her daughter and grandchildren instead of staying home to grieve with the bereaved father, but she wasn't sure. "Well," she said, "that's nice. Now you go right ahead and have a wonderful vacation . . ." and halted midsentence, appalled at her poor choice of words, and unaware of the conversation going on around her until she heard the last part of Sue's amazing announcement, ". . . and I am not coming back. Not ever. I am going to live with Dorrie and her family."

"Yes," said Dorrie. "Mom will live with us."

The minute she said it, Sue knew that she didn't want to go. The minute she said she was never coming back she turned sick at the thought of leaving Jim. The minute she declared, "I am going to live with Dorrie and her family," she wondered how she would be able to bear her daughter's domination and the tyranny of three spoiled grandchildren.

When Dorrie added, to make it stick, "Yes, Mom will live with us," she knew she had saddled herself with a live-in mother, Hal with an unwanted mother-in-law, and the children with a grandmother who would not be good for them and to whom they would not be good. She had done this to herself and hers, and now she would have to live with it.

The two loaded cars, Dorrie's and Sue's, departed on Thursday, leaving Jim Copeland alone. Carrie Mason certainly wanted to take him some food, wanted to be warm and friendly as she had so firmly resolved, but she could not find him! He had gone back to work, of course, but he came home quietly and late. The porch light never went on anymore, nor the light in the living room. Carrie Mason could not see even the flicker of the TV screen.

He was home only twice during the weekends; once when a long-haul moving van carted away certain pieces of furniture, and another time when a local van carted away the rest of it.

Three weeks after the funeral, Michele's little green car had been driven away and the house had been dismantled and a FOR SALE sign went up in the front yard.

Then Jim Copeland came over to see Mrs. Carrie Mason.

She offered him coffee, which he refused, explaining that he was busy and in a hurry. She noticed how thin he had become and she fluttered over him, not caring that she had bourbon on her breath, only wishing to be warm and friendly.

He told her he was living in a small apartment in town and was in the process of selling the house, which was why he was here; he wanted to leave one of the house keys with her, "Just in case," he said, and she wasn't sure whether he meant just in case Sue returned or just in case a prospective buyer wanted to take a look at the house.

The rest of the keys, he explained, were in the hands of the real estate agent who would be showing the house, but he wanted her to have one of them, "just in case."

Then he left and Mrs. Mason had nothing more to look at through the venetian blinds of her bedroom; nothing except the closed drapes of the living room next door, and a corner of the FOR SALE sign out in front.

Money being tight and interest rates up, not many people came to look at the house, but enough so that Carrie learned to recognize the real estate agent's car and to know it wasn't his when the light gray compact drew up to the curb in front of the Copeland house. It drove on again, but returned a few days later.

The third time she saw it, she was out in her front yard planting the last of her spring bulbs and hopeful that she could finish before the twilight turned to darkness. She rose from her knees when the car pulled up out in front, dropped her trowel and walked from her yard to the next and down to the curbing.

"If you are interested in the house," she said to the young man in the car, "I have a key and I can take you through. But we'll have to hurry because the electricity has been turned off and it's getting dark. There won't be much time."

"Oh. Oh, yes," he said, momentarily startled, as if he were so fascinated by the house that he had been totally unaware of her approach. "Didn't the Copelands used to live here?"

"Yes. Such a tragedy." Mrs. Carrie Mason could not see the young man very well in the shadows of the car. He seemed nice, though, and personable. "Did you know them?" she asked.

"I met the girl just once," said the man.

"Michele? The one who was killed?"

"Yes. That one. And I talked to her father once." Abruptly, as if suddenly conscious of her existence, the man leaned across the car seat and looked directly at Carrie Mason in the now-purple twilight. "I have a wife, you see," he said, "who is an invalid . . ."

Carrie clucked with sympathy.

"We live in an apartment now, and I thought if we had a house, she could be outdoors more."

"Oh, she could, and that would be wonderful," enthused Carrie.

"I'm a salesman and out a lot and I would insist upon a good neighborhood, one I wouldn't have to worry about leaving her alone. Nice and quiet. Decent."

Carrie started to describe the utter niceness, the restful, quiet and the pure decency of the neighborhood when he broke in with, "I would like to see the house very much, but as you warned me, it is getting a little dark for that, but if I could look around the neighborhood, Mrs. . . . ?" his voice rising in inquiry.

"Mrs. Carrie Mason," she said.

"Mrs. Mason, I think this might be just the house I have been wanting. I can come back tomorrow, of course, to go through it, but I do want to get a look at the neighborhood first. It's still light enough for that. I wonder if you would show me . . ."

Carrie moved back a step.

"Just a short drive around the block. Only to point out the market and the nearest drugstore." He chuckled in a half-sorrowful, half-rueful fashion. "My wife needs and wants so many things at all hours—a prescription, ice cream, a heating pad or an ice bag, anything, something—"

Carrie remembered her firm resolve to aid and abet in a warm and friendly fashion.

"And if I had someone to show me around so I could describe the neighborhood to my wife tonight, perhaps rouse her interest, then tomorrow . . ."

Carrie gave one backward glance at her lawn, almost dark now, where the trowel and the remaining bulbs lay on the ground, and at her dark and unlocked house. "It will be only a few minutes?" she asked.

"Only a few minutes," he assured her.

She stepped inside the car, and the gray compact moved down the street.

THE THREE HALVES

Joe Gores

Joe Gores

The term "procedural" applies to stories in which the day-to-day routine and procedures of a law-enforcement agency play an important part. They are among the most popular types of mystery fiction in the world today. John Creasey, Maj Sjöwall and Per Wahlöö, Ed McBain—the procedural has attracted some of the most skilled writers of crime fiction that the twentieth century has produced. And none of them is more qualified to work in this particular field than Joe Gores, for, along with the late Dashiell Hammett, he is one of the very few mystery writers who actually was a detective. The short stories and novels he has written around the San Francisco–based private detective agency Daniel Kearny Associates are based on the knowledge he acquired during the years he spent as a private eye, and "The Three Halves" is a fine example of his talent.

From Fairfax, California, where he lives, he reports: "Over twenty years ago, when I was striving desperately to be a writer but couldn't find an editor to admit I was one, I spent a summer as a 'roughie' with a tent carnival making the Midwest county-fair circuit. A year later I wrote a rambling little tale with no point at all about preparing the carnival for the summer tour. This unreadable slice-of-life lay around for many years until, while working on the DKA File stories for EQMM, I realized it made a perfect background for this present yarn. So that scrap of poor fiction, amended and shaped and jigsawed into place, made me a few bucks after all. The moral? Never throw away anything you've written. Sometime you can find a place for it."

A.M.

THE THREE HALVES

FRIDAY, February 28, 6:06 P.M. —— Field agents at Daniel Kearny Associates of San Francisco, who had been working fifteen-hour days as they did at the end of every month, could now begin to relax.

Patrick Michael O'Bannon had come with Kearny from Walters Auto Detectives seven years before; now he was reminiscing, his feet propped on the edge of Kearny's desk, a glass of bourbon in hand, his freckles magnificent, hair blazing, blue eyes bubbling.

"Dan, remember that time we spotted that Lincoln Continen—"

Kearny's intercom buzzed; he winked at O'B and picked up. Even relaxed over a drink he looked aggressively tough, a little older than O'Bannon's forty-one, with a slightly flattened nose, a massive jaw, and gray eyes cold enough to chill bone marrow. In a fair imitation of O'Bannon's voice he said, "Kearny left five minutes ago."

Kathy Onoda, upstairs in clerical, just snorted. She was the DKA office manager, had formerly been Kearny's secretary: a Japanese girl in her late twenties with classically Oriental features.

"You're a scream, Dan. I'm sending a Nate Bemel down; he wants to hire us, contingent basis, on a small lithography firm embezzlement."

Kearny snubbed out his cigarette, suddenly getting serious. "*Contingent* basis? Kathy, you know better than that."

"He's on his way down," she repeated musically. " 'Bye."

Kearny cursed and swiveled back to his desk. His office was in the basement of the converted Victorian ex-bawdy house which now was DKA, tucked away among the field agents' cubbyholes and equipped with a one-way plate-glass door. He waved O'Bannon back to his seat.

"Sit in, O'B. Man wants to hire us on a contingent basis."

"Why'd Kathy even bother to send him down? No payee, no workee."

"That's what I want to find out."

Nate Bemel proved to be a beefy man in his mid-fifties with luxuriant curling black hair, a gentle face, and a huge nose.

"I'd better tell you right away, Mr. Bemel, that we normally take contingent assignments only from large financial institutions," said Kearny. "Frankly, I'm a little puzzled *why* Miss Onoda sent you—"

"Down to see you?" Bemel's voice was so guttural that his English sounded almost like a foreign language. "You see, I own North Beach Litho and I got a very special sort of problem on this embezzlement."

"How much was taken?"

"Sixteen thousand, four hundred and seventy-two dollars."

O'B gave a silent whistle. "The embezzler was your bookkeeper?"

"Yes. Arnaldo Pedretti. But how do *you* know that?"

"By the size of the embezzlement," said Kearny, "he probably was coffee-canning it for months. Unless the bookkeeper was involved, he would have caught the shortages on routine audit."

Bemel nodded. "Arnaldo doesn't come to work one Monday; then I find that for six months he's been depositing only enough clients' checks to cover running expenses. The Friday before, he'd cashed all those other checks he'd been holding out and left with the money."

"When did this happen?" asked O'Bannon.

"May thirtieth. A Friday, like I said. Just nine months ago."

Kearny jerked as if a cigarette had been laid against his spine. "Nine *months* ago and you're just coming around now? The bonding comp—"

"I ain't moved against his bond." Bemel's voice saddened. "I told you—special problem. Arnaldo Pedretti is my brother-in-law."

All was suddenly clear to O'Bannon: his wife, too, was Italian. Italian wives meant Italian families. "Your mother-in-law, Mr. Bemel?"

His sadness deepened. "Seventy-four years old, gentlemen; in the Chinese New Year parade she should be the dragon, already. My Rosa says, 'Listen to Mama.' For nine months I listen." He sat up sternly. "He doesn't come back. All that money he steals, it isn't right. I want you should find him. For this, you keep half of what you recover."

Kearny lit another cigarette. Finding Pedretti would be something all right, as would half of sixteen thousand—if any of it was left. He said, "You want this undercover? Even from the family?"

Bemel bounced in his chair. "Especially from the family. Not even my wife Rosa should know. No charges against him—just my money back I want."

"We'll give it one week without retainer, Mr. Bemel. Miss Onoda will have questions and a paper for you to sign—"

"A paper I don't sign!" he exclaimed. "If my wife Rosa—"

But five minutes later, assured his wife would never find out, Bemel departed for the clerical offices overhead. Kearny smeared out his cigarette. O'B, catching his eye, suddenly held up a hand palm out, like a traffic cop.

"Not *me*, Dan! I've got two flooring checks and that skip—"

"Just until next weekend, O'B," he said airily. "You're always slow the first part of the month anyway."

"That's because I'm so fast the *end* of the month," O'B said.

MONDAY. —— O'B parked on Vallejo Street in North Beach, two blocks from the apartments where the client and Rosa had the upper, Mama Pedretti—and formerly the subject—the lower. O'B reflected sourly on the two pitchers of martinis he'd downed the night before; and now *this* mickey-mouse.

Arnaldo Pedretti, thirty-eight, white, single, last known R/A, 784 Vallejo; last known B/A, North Beach Litho, 652 Vallejo. Period. No further given information. Automobile? None. Driver's license? Yes. O'B wrote *renewal date?* behind that item on the case sheet. Booze? Bemel hadn't known if, where, or with whom. O'B brightened: at least he could get a drink on expense account. Women? Only one known was Agnese Versaggi, daughter of an old friend of Mama Pedretti's, who worked at the bank where Bemel kept his account. Probably carried a rosary when she went out on a date.

There was a snapshot of Pedretti, too. Five feet seven, sallow, with his belly over his belt. Black curly, badly receding hair, heavy horn-rim glasses. A magnificently unhappy-looking man.

O'B locked his car, walked down to Emery Lane, and cut through to the back entrance of Bank of America, Columbus Branch. He sauntered about until he found Agnese Versaggi's Paying and Receiving window. Unlike Pedretti, she had Anglicized her given name to Agnes. A big girl about thirty, nearly voluptuous under a no-nonsense wool suit. Heavy-boned face, wide mouth that smiled easily, big teeth, black hair pulled back carelessly on either side of her face, dark expressive eyes.

O'B returned through the alley to Vallejo Street and selected a small mid-block tavern. A few old Italian gents were drinking red wine at the bar. O'Bannon ordered a beer.

"At least *this* neighborhood hasn't changed much," he remarked.

"You seen the joint down the block? Poetry readings every Tuesday, crazy designs all over the windows, every color you can think of?"

O'Bannon shrugged. "That's just the beats."

"They call themselves hippies now. How long you been away?"

"Since sixty-one—engineering job overseas." He paused. "Say, you know a guy named Arnie Pedretti used to live around here?"

"Pedretti? Sure. But he ain't been around for—oh, hell, must be almost a year now. Took a job out of state, his sister said."

"He used to do his drinking here?"

"You kidding? Some joint down on Bay where old Mama Pedretti wouldn't have no spies—Devlin's Dublin Pub. Member of Roma Athletic Club of Stockton, too, but that's just a gymnasium."

In succession O'B hit three more bars, a hotel, a garage, a wine company, and a dry cleaner. He got one vaguely interesting item at the garage: the subject had been hung up on sports cars.

Driving down to Devlin's, he stopped at the Roma Athletic Club to learn only that the subject had played handball, very badly, and had pitched softball, quite well, for a team sponsored by a local Italian mortician. Devlin's, however, while producing only that the subject and a black-haired gal half a foot taller than he had dropped in occasionally, proved so interesting that O'B remained until five o'clock.

At 5:12, quite tipsy, he was waiting when Agnes Versaggi emerged from the bank and crossed with the light in long strides. Like many big women, she had very shapely legs.

"Miss Versaggi? I'd like to talk to you about Arnaldo Pedretti."

She flashed an unexpected smile and said, "I know a good place on Union that won't be crowded yet. If you're buying."

Making an instant decision, O'B said, "I'm on expense account."

"I thought you were."

She downed her first martini with such ease that O'B abandoned all thought that she carried a rosary on dates.

"I've been expecting someone from the bonding company," she said, "ever since Arnie cashed those checks." Which explained who she thought O'B was. "Mama Pedretti always hoped we'd get married, but me, I knew that what I got, Arnie doesn't need. If you've lived here long—"

"Born in the Mission district."

"So you know about Italian mamas, eh? Mama Pedretti ran Arnie's life. They lived in the same apartment, went to Peter and Paul's together on Sunday—even, she insisted, 'Arnaldo' instead of Arnold. Thirty-eight years old and afraid to drink in a neighborhood bar."

"Devlin's Dublin Pub?" prompted O'Bannon.

"I used to go there with him sometimes; he went for big women, like me. Then that Friday, at the bank, he goes to another window. Always he comes to my window; so after he leaves I check up on him. Sixteen thousand dollars worth of checks he cashed—and didn't deposit. I know what he's doing, but—what's to say? He's got power of attorney, eh? And it is maybe his last chance to get away from Mama."

Then she added darkly, "Maybe he *never* gets away from the family, eh? Even now, seven-thirty at night each first Friday of the month when Mama's away at Stations of the Cross in the cathedral—he calls his sister."

"He calls Mrs. Bemel?" O'B asked sharply.

"Sure. Rosie." She gave a sudden martini giggle. "But you don't tell her I said so, eh? She doesn't know that I know."

"Our little secret," agreed O'B gravely.

It came out so much like "sheecret" that he decided he'd better get something to eat. But he got this excellent idea much too late. He woke up at 6:30 the next morning parked in front of the DKA office, with a mouth like a millhand's undershirt and no recollection of how he had got there. Probably ate some gnocchi at that Italian place that disagreed with him, he decided sagely; then he spent two hours in a Turkish bath and returned at a virtuous nine o'clock.

TUESDAY. —— Giselle Mark was a long, lean, morally upright but wicked-looking blonde in her early twenties. She had started with DKA as a part-time file girl while in college, and had gone in mortal terror of O'Bannon's winks, leers, and blatant propositions until she had realized that his weakness was liquor. Now they were close friends; and she knew that he was the firm's best investigator apart from Kearny himself.

As O'B dialed Searching Registration Service in Sacramento, Giselle said lumpily into her own phone, "My name is Mrs. Angelo Pedretti and I want the service representative for phone number 363-9810."

"Yes, Mrs. Pedretti, may we help you?"

Giselle explained in the limping accent she'd chosen for Mama Pedretti that her income tax consultant needed all available information on her long-distance calls since the previous June. The voice went icy in contemplation of the possible work involved, but finally said, "If you would hold the line, please, I'll try and get that information for you."

O'B hung up, and Giselle covered her mouthpiece. "She's buying it. Anything from S.R.S. on his license or a possible car purchase?"

"They'll check Department of Motor Vehicle files and call us."

Giselle removed her hand quickly. "Yes? I see." She began writing. "Just the one each month and . . . yes. Thank you. That should be all the accountant needs." She said to O'B, "Collect calls came from an Arnold Payne—bound to be Arnaldo Pedretti—in June, July, August, September, and October, each from a different city—"

"And from October on, all calls from Santa Rosa." O'B was reading over her shoulder. "Each from a different phone." He hid a yawn with a freckled fist. "Confirm that they'll all be pay phones, will you, doll? Also check Santa Rosa for a phone listing in either name—though I doubt he's that dumb—and find out if the calls came on the first Friday of each month. I've got a couple of hot field leads—"

"Sure you do. Have a good sleep, you fink," said Giselle.

WEDNESDAY. —— O'Bannon screwed up his leathery face and began reading Giselle's memo. If he hadn't got loaded Monday night and had to spend yesterday recuperating—but to hell with it. O'B was not introspective; few detectives are. Soul searchers are not good at raking over the rubbish heaps in other human lives.

As O'B had expected, all the calls had come from pay phones, and all the calls had been made on the first Friday of the month.

>June 5: Eureka, up in the north coast redwood country.
>July 3: Marysville, moving south.
>August 7: Napa, in the wine country.
>September 4: Vallejo, 40 miles northeast of the city across the Carquinez Straights.
>October 2: the jump to Santa Rosa, due north of San Francisco in Sonoma County.

Where was the pattern? If Payne *were* Pedretti, wouldn't he find better places to live it up on his stolen sixteen thou than a series of small towns?

He buzzed Giselle. "Anything from S.R.S. in Sacramento yet?"

"Negative on a driver's license renewal. They'll call back on the auto registration file check as soon as they complete it."

He then called the client at North Beach Litho. When Nate Bemel's thick accent was in his ear he said, "This is O'Bannon at DKA. I've got a couple of questions. How late do you work on Fridays?"

"Fridays? Home for supper, back here until eight o'clock."

That checked. He said, "I know the phone in your apartment is in Mama Pedretti's name, but who actually pays the bill?"

"You investigating me or—you know who? *I* pay the bill."

"But who *physically* pays it? Writes the check, say?"

"Well, Rosa pays all the household bills. I think she takes the phone bill down to Bank of America and then pays it in cash."

O'B thanked him and hung up. The collect calls made sense now. Only Rosa saw the items on the phone bill. When the call came, she could refuse it if someone else was in the apartment with her. Being sociable, she would go to Agnes Versaggi's window at the bank; Agnes would not have been fooled by Arnold Payne/Arnaldo Pedretti for a minute. But O'B was still no closer to the subject, since it was obvious that Rosa didn't know how to reach him.

Giselle buzzed on the intercom. "S.R.S. just called, O'B. Last September an Arnold Payne bought an XKE-120 Jaguar from a Vallejo dealer. The title slip was mailed in October to—" Her voice fell. "Mailed to Post Office Box 281 in Redwood City. Which is on the Peninsula thirty miles *south* of here, while the phone calls put our—"

"—our Arnold Payne in Santa Rosa, forty miles *north*. Right. How about this, Giselle: he's got a traveling sales job and the box number is his home office address?"

"Selling from a *Jaguar*, O'B? And what about Social Security, Federal withholding taxes, bonding, employment references—"

"Yeah." O'B arched an eyebrow; an idea had come to him. He said, "I'll try to pop that P.O. box, doll. There's *one* possibility—"

The telephone is the skiptracer's most potent tool. O'Bannon in person, without elaborate disguises, was a red-headed Irishman with a hard-bitten face. But O'B on the phone could be anyone from a teen-ager to an octogenarian. For this call he was a truck driver.

"Ah, yeah, say, I'm out here off the Bayshore Freeway on Marsh Road. Got twelve thousand board feet of redwood one-by-six addressed to an Arnold Payne at P.O. Box 281." He paused for dramatic effect. *"Where do you want 'em?"* he asked the post office employee.

"Listen," the clerk squeaked, "that isn't mail! You can't bring—"

"Look, mister," said O'Bannon's truck-driver voice, "I picked up this load from the Sequoia Mills in Eureka last night; you're silly as hell if you think I'm just gonna dead-haul it back up there again."

"Just a minute." The postal clerk went away. This was the crucial moment, since by law the addresses of box holders are not to be given out. The man returned. "Yeah. Haney's Combined Shows, 3951 Edison Way, Redwood City."

O'B had guessed right—a traveling road show. Few carny laborers paid Social Security or even filed W-2 forms. And the little carnivals worked a swing of small-town fairs, livestock shows, and rodeos.

Giselle had an objection. "That's great, but it looks like he left it back in October to stay in Santa Rosa, doesn't it?"

"There's only one way to find out."

Forty minutes later O'B parked his car alongside a small brick building on Edison Way in Redwood City. It was a hot clear day on the Peninsula, very different from the city's March bluster. He locked his topcoat in the car and entered a door marked *C. V. Baggett, General Agent*. Behind a counter was a well-corseted woman with ruthlessly peroxided hair and a face from which time had wrung the milk of human kindness.

O'B gestured at the empty inner office. "Mr. Baggett?"

"Lunch!" The word exploded like a bullet. "I'm Madame George."

"Mr. Baggett *does* represent Haney's Combined Shows?"

"Also Phantasy Phun Phairs." She indicated a garish poster. "I was with Phantasy for twenty years before Haney took over, and twenty after that. Finally told C.V. that I wanted to sleep in a house without wheels on it, so he had me take over running the office here."

"I saw one of your carnivals in Vallejo last year, and—"

"August. Phantasy One. I was managing it then. The Phantasys are truck shows, and Haney's Combined is a railroad show."

"As president of the Erin Auld Sods of San Francisco, I—"

"—want to hire Phantasy One? We put Haney's Combined into the city usually; all the shows are *quite* similar, and they all close the third week in October for the wet months. Haney's reopens in mid-June, and Phantasy Two opened the middle of last month. Phantasy One stays in winter quarters until the fifteenth of this month. End of next week."

"Haney's is fine for us. Ah, where *are* winter quarters?"

"Santa Rosa," said Madame George.

FRIDAY, March 7, 6:50 A.M. —— Under dawn sunlight the Santa Rosa street looked dusty and disheveled, like a man who had drunk too much the night before. A lone mongrel trotted across the narrow blacktop without a thought for cars. O'B, also looking like a man who had drunk too much the night before—which he had—skittered an empty whiskey bottle across the sidewalk. His hands were deep in his faded dungaree pockets.

"It's cold," he complained, hunching his shoulders.

The dog didn't answer. It merely kept on moving, with a reproachful look as if O'B had thrown a beer can at it. O'B crossed the street toward a lot crowded with strange shapes—metal braces, odd-shaped canvas frames, long round iron poles bright with new paint.

The door of an aluminum house trailer on one side of the lot creaked open and a short, almost dapper man stepped out. His thick curly hair was grizzled at the temples, his mustache was neatly trimmed; even in T-shirt and underpants he bore the stamp of authority. A tousled blond head appeared above his shoulder, and he turned to curse in a surprisingly deep voice. The girl disappeared abruptly with a flash of pale nude flesh like the turn of a fish deep in muddy water.

"Jug Butt!" the man roared. "Get 'em up! Gotta hump it today!"

A fat but powerful young man, barefoot, came out of the corrugated iron shed that backed the lot and stood blinking in the sunlight, scratching a remarkable expanse of gut with a grimy paw. He hawked and spat into the oil-soaked dirt, swore, and returned to the shed. From within came loud voices, curses, a thud, heavy laughter.

O'B walked up to the trailer. "You hiring here, mister?"

The stocky straw boss took in his worn clothes, lean drinker's face, red-rimmed eyes. "Yeah. Ten a day, sleep in the shed if you ain't got nowhere else. You ever been a carnival roughie before?"

"No. But I'm not green."

"God knows you ain't. I'm Carlos Ryan."

"Patrick Michael O'Bannon."

Ryan returned his grin. "Okay, Red, once the boys start in you can help Jug Butt load those Tilt-a-Whirl baskets onto a truck."

From the shed came an abnormally skinny man in his mid-twenties with a motorcycle cap pushed sideways on the back of his head. The teen-ager with him, called Billy the Kid, addressed the skinny man as Curly. Next was a lanky, powerful, rawboned man with mean eyes, whose accent identified him as Tex; a quizzical-faced man with a loud voice and a weak chin, named Garrison; and a toothless old duffer called, for obvious reasons, Hairless Hans. Last was Jug Butt.

No Arnaldo Pedretti. It probably had been a nutty hunch anyway, that a man with sixteen thousand would work for sixty a week, sleep-where-you-can. Still, O'B decided he'd give it a day; Payne/Pedretti, he felt sure, had spent some time with this carnival the previous season.

They worked under a sun so hot that O'B wondered if he'd collapse before he even asked a question. He lugged Tilt-a-Whirl baskets with Jug Butt; since gloves were considered cowardly, his hands soon were leaving red smears on the sharp-edged aluminum buckets. Damn Kearny!

At ten o'clock Carlos Ryan emerged, paint-spattered, from the shed. "Hell," he said, "ain't no use dyin' for a sawbuck a day."

They crossed the street to Carter's Joynt, a long narrow neighborhood bar with worn hardwood floors, boiled eggs in glass bowls, and three pinball machines. Tex bought two bucks' worth of dimes; all had beer except Carlos Ryan, who had a shot of bourbon.

Carter, the owner, looked them over, took a deep breath, and said to Billy the Kid, "Say, listen, how old are you, anyway?"

"He's a carny," growled Tex. "He don't have to be of age."

"Yeah? Try telling that to the Alcoholic Beverage Control." Looking at Tex, he subsided suddenly, drew another beer. "Aw, hell."

From 10:30 to noon they worked. Lifting, hauling, sweating, swearing, grunting, O'B learned only that Hairless Hans and Ryan had been with Phantasy One the previous season. Ryan wouldn't talk, but Hans might. O'B would try after lunch, he decided, which was sandwiches at Carter's Joynt. Ryan had another shot. O'B understood the hemannish gesture: with a tough crew like this, the big uninhibited blonde would be honey to the bees unless Ryan were more than mere nominal boss.

At two o'clock Tex, Jug Butt, and Billy the Kid left in one of the ancient trucks to pick up some jenny horses across town. Ryan and Curly were in the paint shed doping fabric wings for the airplane ride, and Garrison was buried in the innards of the antique truck which bore the words POPCORN, PEANUTS, SUGAR CANDY. But as O'B sidled toward Hairless Hans, a new car pulled up and a young man with long hair got out. The pretty girl with him, who wore a Mia Farrow cut, stayed in the car.

"Hey, is there a fellow around here named Billy Weston? About my age, maybe seventeen? They call him Billy the Kid sometimes."

"Billy theh Kid?" Hans scratched where his hair should have been. "Don't recall any sech feller round here."

Curly brought the water jug. "Why'd you say that, Hans?"

The old man drank noisily, Adam's apple popping, water drooling from his nearly toothless mouth. He winked slyly at O'B.

"Now, Curly, say theh Kid had planted his seed in thet there orchard. An' say thet there was thet girl's brother. See? You ain't traveled wit' theh carny yit. Carny takes care of ets own. Carny don't ask questions. Why you figger ain't no tax taken outen y'r pay?" He cackled toothlessly. "Think my mother wouldda know'd me by Hans?"

So much for trying to pump *you,* O'B thought to himself.

Tex's semi grunted around the corner, struck the curb, and blew a tire with a sound like a mortar being fired, then to stop smashed into a tree. Tex jumped from the doorless cab and strode to the shed.

"Hey, you, Carlos Ryan!" When the dapper boss emerged, Tex bellowed, "I thought you said that there truck was fixed up!"

"I did. Garrison's a mechanic and he did it yesterday. He—"

"Who the hell told him?"

"Told him what?"

"That he was a mechanic. Brakes went out on the way over and the clutch on the way back; hadda drive it by ear. He may a' been a mechanic somewhere else, but he ain't but a big mouth around here."

At six o'clock they lined up outside the trailer for their pay. A week before, O'B had been drinking bourbon with Dan Kearny; now he was hot, flushed, sunburned, and tired. He stank. His hands were cut, and where they weren't cut they were blistered. And he was no closer to Arnaldo Pedretti than he'd been that morning. Or was he?

Some nagging thing made him go over to Carter's Joynt to drink beer, listen to the ping of Tex's pinball machine, and talk with Carlos Ryan.

"You must have seen 'em come and go, Carlos," he opened.

"Yeah, Red, been with it long enough to know better." Ryan grinned. "Y'see, I'm half Irish, half Spanish, and half carny."

"That makes three halves," objected O'Bannon.

"You better believe it," said Ryan.

A large laborer with his yellow safety helmet on the stick beside him, the bar's only other customer, gave a snort. "Did you say *carny?*"

Tex said suddenly, "One hundred free games! An' I'm buyin'!"

"Mark 'em off." Carter disgustedly jabbed NO SALE on the register.

"I ain't drinking with no carnies," said the laborer.

"Your privilege," said Ryan quickly; but Tex already had set down his glass of beer and was staring at the construction worker.

"You ain't drinking with us, buddy-buddy? Down in Texas a man don't refuse to drink with another man unless he's meanin' to—"

"Texas?" The laborer leaned back against the bar with his elbows on it. "Feller tole me once that the way to find Texas was to go east far enough to smell it, and south far enough to step in it, and I'd—"

The heel of Tex's hand, swung by a strap-steel right arm, exploded on the other's jaw, upsetting man and stool. The laborer's head rebounded from the hardwood floor with a great ka-thunk as Tex surged forward, giving his battle cry: "YAHOO! SAN ANTON'!"

Ryan flicked O'B's half-full beer off the bar in an underhand arc. The spinning bottle caught Tex just above the right temple; he went over sideways against a dark-varnished plywood booth. He lay still for a time, then sat up rubbing his temple with a horny callused palm.

"Aw, hell, Carlos," he said plaintively, "what'd you have to go an' do that for?"

"We don't want law trouble. C'mon; I gotta make a phone call anyway." He dropped a twenty on the bar and jerked a thumb at the fallen warrior. "You never saw us before, right, Carter?"

Carter grinned. "Total strangers to me, Carlos."

Outside, O'B checked his watch: 7:30. Night had fallen and it was chilly again. He hobbled around the block twice on work-stiffened legs, cursing but glad to be using his head instead of his back once more.

The missing Jaguar bothered him, but there would be an explanation. In the dark he crossed to the aluminum house trailer where, he hoped, Carlos Ryan would supply the answers he needed.

The blonde peered at him with incurious eyes. She was dressed in a sweater and such impossibly tight jeans that she reminded him of Little Annie Fanny in the *Playboy* cartoon satires; nobody could be that dumb, but somebody was. Ryan was working at the small fold-down kitchen table; through the doorway was a narrow living room with a television set, and beyond that the bedroom with an unmade bed.

O'B jerked his head. "Could she go change the sheets or something, Carlos?"

"I'll watch TV," pouted the blonde, pausing at the miniature refrigerator to get a can of beer and wiggle a petulant behind.

"That's a good girl." As *Hogan's Heroes* blasted from the set, O'B flopped his identification open on the table in front of Ryan.

"About your embezzlement last May thirtieth from North Beach Litho—"

Ryan leaped erect, crashing his chair back against the stove. His powerful fingers were clawed for throat gripping, but O'B managed to retain his carefully careless pose.

"Sit down, Pedretti. You're not a killer, just a cheap carny straw boss. God, I never knew roughies worked so hard. Sit down, man."

Carlos Ryan, tough little dude, gave the sort of sob that Arnaldo Pedretti, mama's boy, thief, and sometime bookkeeper might have given, and all the starch went out of him. O'B had seen it a thousand times: you hit the subject with the inevitability of your presence and he reacted blindly, with panic. That was the dangerous time. Then his mind began to function, he made a mental adjustment to the new situation, and you could begin to deal with him on a rational basis again.

"I—how did you find—?"

"It's our business to find people. Your sister didn't mention us when you called her an hour ago because she didn't know about us. What happened to the Jaguar, by the way?"

Pedretti's color was returning. "Gladys totaled it three months ago." He considered for a moment. "She's too dumb to live."

"Agreed." O'B laid down the snapshot. "I almost missed you because I was after an overweight, mousy guy with soft hands, horn-rims, and not much hair. But five months as a roughie toughened you up and slimmed you down. Add a mustache and a good hairpiece and contact lenses—and *presto,* Carlos Ryan."

Pedretti was looking at his picture. "God, that *is* me?"

O'B, busy pouring two bourbons, nodded. "Little things gave you away. I'm enough of a boozer to know you were playing a role with those straight shots. Then the phone call tonight, seven-thirty—on the first Friday of the month. You threw that bottle at Tex underhand—like a softball pitcher. Finally, your woman is six inches taller than you—like Agnes Versaggi. She said you liked 'em big."

"I've found I also prefer 'em like Gladys," he said dryly. "With their brains in their backsides. I should have just left, you know? But without taking the money I never would have made the break. I *had* to take it, so I couldn't ever go back."

"How'd you get your job here?"

"Just chance. I've always been sort of a romantic, so when I ran across Phantasy One up by the Oregon border, I got a job as a roughie. An old gal named Madame George was running it then." His grin was a fleeting Carlos Ryan grin. "Used to be in a skin show; when she got fat she worked a mentalist act. She got the whole story out of me and decided to help me. She set it up for me to run the section this season." He swallowed suddenly. "What happens now, Red?"

Funny: while Pedretti had thought of himself as Carlos Ryan, he had *been* Carlos Ryan—tough, jaunty, uncomplicated. Now he was mush. O'B had preferred Ryan to Pedretti.

"How much money is left?" O'B asked briskly.

"Something over ten thousand. The rest went for the Jag, the contact lenses, the wig. Now—"

"Now we have a drink." O'B fitted actions to words. "And a talk."

Forty minutes later he was on the horn with Dan Kearny.

"Ten thousand is in a Santa Rosa safe-deposit box. He'll turn that over to me on Monday, along with a promissory note for the rest, bank terms at two hundred a month."

"Any chance he's planning a skip, or some rough stuff?"

"He's just damned grateful to get out from under. Besides, there's this other guy, a real old carny type—"

"Dammit, O'Bannon," Kearny bellowed in sudden comprehension, "if you think you're going to run up a big expense account on booze—"

"I'm telling you, Dan," said O'B virtuously, "this other guy will make us a *great* carny contact. His name is Carlos Ryan and he says he's half Irish, half Spanish, and half carny—"

"Wait a minute," objected Dan Kearny, "that makes three halves."

"Why, so it does," said O'Bannon.

BACK IN FIVE YEARS

Michael Gilbert

Michael Gilbert

Most writers start out in careers other than writing, but when they become successful as writers they abandon them. Michael Gilbert is an exception. He began as a lawyer, became successful as a writer—and equally successful in the legal profession. He is a partner in a London law firm as well as the author of an ever-lengthening list of highly regarded novels, short stories, plays and radio and television scripts. He still pursues both careers, writing two and a half pages each morning at his home in Kent before leaving for his London law office.

"Back in Five Years" is the story of a counterfeiter who disappeared; a sleight-of-hand story in the best tradition of British mystery fiction. It originated, Gilbert says, as follows:

"In the years which followed the end of the war, I was living with my wife and the beginnings of my family (two small daughters) in North London. I was also trying to write stories to meet the exacting requirements of *John Bull*, at that period a well-produced and excellently illustrated weekly; now, alas, defunct but at that time a top market for short stories. They had, I think, accepted one of mine. It was whilst I was walking down one of the many rather seedy side-streets near our house that I saw the paper pinned to the gate post and fluttering in the wind: 'Back in five minutes.' It was at that point that the plot of the story, complete and ready-made, dropped into my lap."

A.M.

BACK IN FIVE YEARS

1

When I was a junior inspector attached to the uniformed branch in a North London Division [said Hazlerigg] there was a notice pinned to the door of one of the shops in Malpas Road. Written in a copperplate hand on a neat square of white card (yellowing now with age and weather), it said:

BACK IN FIVE YEARS.

I remember the occasion of this notice being put up, and I remember it coming down again.

There were a number of known counterfeiters at work in London. I don't mean that we knew their names and addresses, for they tend to be shy gentry, but a surprising number of facts about them and their products were filed and tabulated at the Criminal Records Office and in the M.O. file.

There were forgers of Post Office savings books, and there were the gentlemen who specialized in passports and share certificates. But the kings of the trade were the forgers and utterers of bank notes. And the king of kings was a certain shy, unobtrusive genius who manufactured the "Beauties."

His identity was, of course, a mystery. Like the fig tree in the Bible he was known only by his fruits—which were one-pound notes, finely etched and most scrupulously printed.

Really, you know, in a lot of ways they were a better product than the stuff that was being turned out by H. M. Mint. That young lady who sits up in an insert on the back (on the genuine pound notes she looks rather a pudding-faced young person)—well, in his productions she was a miracle of dignified beauty. That's what gave them their name "Beautiful Britannias" or "Beauties." And you can take it from me that there wasn't a policeman in the Metropolis who wouldn't have given his belt and buttons for a chance to lay hands on the artist.

However, as it happened—and as it happens in most police work in my experience—it wasn't one man or even a few men who got on the track of the forger. When this happy event finally came to pass, it was the result of a combination of luck and instinct backed up by the hard slogging work of a great number of people.

The forger usually comes unstuck through his distributors. You know the sort of thing I mean. Mr. A, who makes the stuff, sells it to Mr. B and Mr. C at about seven and sixpence per pound note, and Mr. B and Mr. C take it in wads and get rid of it on the race courses, to the mutual profit of all concerned. Then, in the course of a routine check-up—nothing to do with forgery—Mr. B is found to be in possession of fifty brand-new pound notes, all, curiously enough, bearing the same serial number. Being unable to explain where he got them from, he is taken into custody and as often as not he decides that he will make things a bit easier for himself by "coming clean" to the police. The police then pay a visit to Mr. A, who goes down for seven years, and never knows what hit him.

Well, where the Beauties were concerned, we had regretfully decided that we were up against one of those rarities in the field of crime —an entirely solitary and single-handed operator. A man with at least one Godlike attribute, the strength which comes from loneliness. He must have made his own plate. It may have taken him a year or more of patient trial and error, cutting smoothing, and sizing. He even had a rotation system which enabled him to change the numbering.

But it was his method of distribution that put him at the top of the class.

Having printed a number of very excellent pound notes, he rationed himself to about twenty a week. These he would take and cash personally, going to shops, stores, and post offices all over Greater London, never to the same one twice. He would purchase some small object costing not more than a few pence or a shilling, pay with a pound note, and pocket the change. The system was laborious but almost foolproof. And but for one small thing, I really have my doubts whether we should have got onto him.

The thing was, he had a weakness for pawnbrokers.

I don't know why. It may have been quite unconscious. I suppose pawnbrokers' shops are places which have a wide variety of things which you can pick up for a small sum; and they are usually rather dark and not very crowded and don't make difficulties about change. I don't know what it was. Anyway it proved his undoing.

The pawnbrokers, as you may know, are people who like to work in very closely with the police. There's nothing underhand about it. It just happens to pay both sides that it should be so. There's a *Pawn Brokers List of Stolen Articles* which we publish at Scotland Yard, and most pawnbrokers make a practice of reporting anything suspicious to the local station; and the local police, in return, keep a special eye on their shops, which are a tempting target to the light-fingered fraternity.

Well, over the months and years reports piled up of these pound notes being received by pawnbrokers. So, just on the chance (that's a phrase which features pretty prominently in police work), a letter was sent round to all pawnbrokers saying that if they should happen to notice a man or woman coming into their shop who wasn't a regular customer, and who wanted to make a small purchase and proffered a brand-new pound for it, then would they please make a careful note of his description, etc., etc.

And after a time these descriptions started to add up. It was extraordinarily fascinating, sitting back in an office watching a living person being built up out of fractions, watching his features limn themselves in, and his identity declare itself, like an actor on a television screen which is being brought into focus. We got a picture of a man, middle-sized to small, plump, soft-spoken, with small white hands, strong black hair, and weak, rather peering eyes. His clothes naturally varied from time to time and from place to place, but the essentials were the same.

A very wide and elaborate net was then spread. I won't bore you with all the details, but you can gather the scope of it when I tell you it meant stationing a policeman within call of almost every pawnshop which had not yet been visited and arranging a simple system of signals with the pawnbrokers themselves.

And that was how, at the beginning of June 193–, the police at last caught sight of Mr. Mountjoy and followed him discreetly home to Malpas Road.

Number 14 Malpas Road proved to be a small shop, a sort not uncommon in that district, with living quarters attached and an independent flat over it. Some further facts now came to light; all seemed to point to the one conclusion.

To start with, Mr. Mountjoy's business was that of a one-man printer and type maker, very suitable, we felt, allowing its owner to possess and operate various small machines and lathes without exciting suspicion. Then again, he was a solitary man, who, according to Mr. Crump, of Number 12, his nearest neighbor, spent much of his time out of his shop, apparently on journeys round London, "looking for commissions, I expect," said Mr. Crump. "Not that he seems to get much work. Manages to do very well for himself, none the less."

I was in charge of these local enquiries, and sensing a certain amount of rancor in that last remark, I guessed that there might be some trade rivalry. Mr. Crump was a newsagent and printer himself. However, though I expect I was right, Mr. Crump was unable to help me much, because he didn't know very much. He did say, however, that Mr. Mountjoy seemed to do a lot of work at night.

And in some trepidation, because we didn't want to expose our hand too soon, I tried Mrs. Ireland, who lived in the flat over Mr. Mountjoy's shop. She was a middle-aged party, intensely respectable and slightly deaf. I visited her one morning in the well-worn guise of an inspector of gas meters and found her surprisingly willing to talk. She, unlike Mr. Crump, had the very highest opinion of Mr. Mountjoy. Possibly he *was* one who kept himself to himself but there was no harm that she could see in that. Better than clumping about sticking your nose into what didn't concern you. This, I gathered, was a backhander at Mr. Crump, whom she didn't like. Unfortunately, her deafness prevented her from being able to corroborate the story of night work.

Well, there it was. You now know all that we knew at that point and you can see how we were fixed. I had no doubt in my mind. The description fitted. The set-up was exactly what we had imagined. The printer's shop, the night work, the journeys round London.

There was only one thing to do—take a search warrant and chance the odds.

Accordingly, on Midsummer Day, June 24 just after four o'clock in the afternoon, I took Sergeant Husband with me and walked over to Malpas Road to put the matter to the test. And as I turned into the road the first thing that struck my eye was that damned notice, and I realized that we had missed our man. How narrowly we had missed him became apparent as we pursued our enquiries.

Number 14 was the end house of a block of seven. It had the shop entrance in front and an independent entrance at the side, which led up to Mrs. Ireland's flat.

Now the curious thing was this. Five minutes before we had arrived, several people had seen Mr. Mountjoy come out and pin that notice on his door. But after that no one could say which way he had gone. This didn't all come out at once, but enquiries up and down the street, then and later, only deepened the mystery.

For instance, Mrs. Ireland had been sitting at her window which overlooked the point where the side street joined the main. Although she might be deaf, she certainly wasn't short-sighted, and she happened to have been keeping her eyes open for the postman; and she was prepared to swear that Mr. Mountjoy had neither passed the end of the side road nor gone down it. Suppose, therefore, he had turned to the left outside his front door. But Mr. Crump in Number 12 and the barber in Number 8 had both been in their shops the whole time and were positive that he had not gone past them.

Had he gone back into his shop or the living room behind it? But these were most undeniably empty and had, besides, the sort of "packed-up" appearance of rooms whose owner has left them deliberately. The gas and the electricity in the shop were both turned off, the larder was empty, and tools and kit were stacked neatly.

There was a door leading into the garden, and this was locked. That, by itself, didn't prove anything, of course, but the garden was a dead end. There was a very high glass-bottle-topped wall on the street side, the blank elevation of another house at the end, and a garden full of little Crumps on the right.

Mr. Mountjoy, in fact, had walked into the street, pinned up his famous notice, and then dematerialized.

But unlike the conjurer's lady assistant, he not only disappeared, he stayed disappeared. And that is not such an easy thing to do—not in this country, anyway.

It's difficult enough for a private person who has only got his relatives and friends and the B.B.C. to contend with. But when the police are after you, and when they want you very badly indeed, having narrowly missed laying hands on you last time, and when, to top it all up, they have got a very full and accurate description of you, including such unchangeable items as strong black hair and white pudgy hands—then to remain in the limbo for any length of time is, I should have said, next to impossible.

However, like everything else, Mr. Mountjoy managed it competently enough.

2

The Police Force, like the Army, believes in moving its executives around, and it isn't very often that you retrace your steps. In this case, it was well over four years later—nearly five—that I found myself back at the same North London police station, attached this time to the plain clothes branch, seconded to my old division to help them cope with an outburst of shop breaking.

One of the first places I visited was Malpas Road, and there, sure enough, was the notice.

"Back in five years."

In a district like that you'd have imagined that it would have been torn down or defaced long ago. But it hadn't been. And I gathered, in fact, that it had become a sort of local tradition. Mr. Mountjoy had always been a mystery man to the neighborhood, and his reputation had been nowise diminished by his dramatic disappearance, and the obvious interest of the police in his whereabouts.

There was a strong local feeling, amounting almost to a mass obsession, that five years after his disappearance (on the very day and at the very hour) Mr. Mountjoy would reappear and take that notice down again.

What would happen then no one could suggest.

When I got back I asked the station sergeant about the place. For instance, why hadn't it been relet or taken over by the authorities. Mr. Mountjoy, I gathered, owned the building, but the taxes must be mounting up and there was ground rent to pay and so on, and anyway it was a nice little shop and living quarters. We didn't talk about requisitioning in those days, but we had some powers. Apparently, however, all this had been foreseen by Mr. Mountjoy.

The day before he disappeared he had handed to Mrs. Ireland a sum in notes (genuine ones this time) sufficient to deal with all outgoings *for exactly five years.* At the end of that time, he said, if he hadn't come back she could sell the house and keep the proceeds. And he had even executed a legal document enabling her to do this.

In short, she was to wait for him for five years, and at the end of that time, like the frog in the fairy story, she was to have her reward —unless the fairy prince had reappeared to claim his own.

It sounded pretty fantastic to me.

The next thing that happened, about three weeks later, was the arrival at the station of a badly worried Mr. Crump with a tale that Number 14 was haunted.

He was so clear and circumstantial about it that we gave more attention to his story than the police usually accord to psychic manifestations. Also, of course, we were predisposed to be interested in that particular house.

"Scraping, cutting, and emery-papering," said Mr. Crump, his great red face moist but earnest. "Every night—about midnight or one o'clock. Just like he used to. I don't like it. Nor the wife don't like it. She's talking of moving if it isn't stopped."

"Did you go down and look in?" I asked. "Was there a light on in the shop?"

"Of course there wasn't no light on," said Mr. Crump. "Hasn't the electricity been cut off? I've told you, it's not yooman, this noise isn't."

When I suggested that it might be rats, I thought Mr. Crump was going to detonate, so I hurriedly promised him that we'd look into it and he departed.

We had the keys of the shop, so I let myself in that evening, going after dark to avoid causing any undue stir. I took a torch and made a thorough investigation. It was obvious no one had been there. The dust was inches thick over everything, and the place—well, it *smelled* deserted, if you know what I mean.

When I came out I found half Malpas Road gathered outside armed with sticks and bottles. Apparently a small boy had seen my torch flashing and the crowd were just summoning up courage to break in and lay the ghost when I opened the door and stepped out.

After that, of course, there was no stopping the stories.

Mr. Crump appeared about a month later with an ultimatum.

Either the police "did something" or he was going to clear out himself. He couldn't stand it any longer. His wife had already gone on an indefinite visit to her married sister, and trade was beginning to fall off. The sinister reputation of Number 14 was beginning to corrupt Number 12.

"All right," I said at last. "I'll come along myself tonight and we'll both listen."

When I came off duty at about half past ten that evening, I went along to Malpas Road and Mr. Crump let me in. We sat in his parlor, which was the front room on the first floor overlooking the street, and we drank some beer and talked for a bit, and at midnight, at my suggestion, we turned the lights out and made ourselves comfortable in chairs near the window.

After a bit I must have dozed, because I woke up to feel Mr. Crump gripping my arm.

He said nothing, but I gathered from his breathing, which he was trying to control, that something had happened.

Then, in the stuffy blackness of the room, I heard it too. It was a thin intermittent burr, which sounded like a very sharp edge cutting across some tough substance, and then a scraping, and then the cutting again.

I jumped up, leaped at the door, nearly broke my neck on the stairs, and three seconds later I was out in the street. I had my key at the ready and I snapped open the door of Number 14 and switched on my torch.

There was no one there. Nothing had been disturbed at all. There wasn't even the trace of a rat or mouse paw in the dust. I hadn't thought that there would be. There had been something indefinably human about that sound.

When I got back to Mr. Crump, I found he had turned on the light and poured out some more beer. He seemed much more cheerful. I think that half his trouble had been that no one believed his story.

Also, as we were finishing our beer, he said something which surprised me.

"Thanks," he said. "I've only to put up with it for one more week."

"What do you mean?" I asked.

"Work it out for yourself," he said. "It's the seventeenth of June. Four years and fifty-one weeks ago he left. Said he'd be back in five years. Very methodical man was Mr. Mountjoy."

I could find no comment to make.

3

It was quite illogical and fantastic and I felt that we were making fools of ourselves, but in the end I agreed, weakly, to post two sergeants to watch the back of the house while I kept an unobtrusive eye on the front.

If Mr. Mountjoy was going to maintain his reputation for punctuality, he was due in the street at four o'clock in the afternoon; accordingly, at five to four I turned the corner at the far end of the road and started strolling nonchalantly towards Number 14, stopping every now and then to look in at the various shop windows.

It was a true Midsummer Day, warm and windless, and the children were still in school, so that by Malpas Road standards it was almost quiet.

I looked at my watch and saw that it was just short of four o'clock.

And Malpas Road was still most definitely empty.

At that moment, in the warm summer silence, I heard it again.

I want to be quite clear about this. It was exactly and undeniably the same sound that I had heard that night when I sat up over Mr. Crump's shop. But it did not come from Number 14.

It was from the same side of the street but much lower down.

I moved cautiously along until I could locate it. It came from the barber's shop at Number 8, where Tony Etrillo, the barber, was shaving one of his swarthy compatriots.

The burr and the rasp as the cut-throat razor passed across the strong black stubble—it was unmistakable.

And in that moment the secret of Mr. Mountjoy's disappearance became as abundantly clear to me as it has probably already done to you.

4

The first thing I did was purely symbolic. I took out my knife and levered out the tack which held up that notice. I was about to tear it up but thought better of it and dropped it in my pocket.

Conscious that a dozen pairs of eyes were watching from curtained windows, I went round into the side street and rang Mrs. Ireland's doorbell.

When she opened the door, I didn't do anything dramatic. I just beckoned her out into the street and signaled to one of the sergeants to accompany us, and we all three walked back to the police station together.

For the greater part of the way we were silent, but I felt, in justice, that one thing had to be said.

"A marvelously well-kept-up impersonation, Mr. Mountjoy. It's nothing new for a man to dress as a woman, and I have even heard of cases before where a landlord became his own lodger. But . . . it's a great mistake for any man to do his shaving last thing at night."

THE VANISHING OF VELMA

Edward D. Hoch

Edward D. Hoch

"I published my first story in 1955, at the age of twenty-five," Edward D. Hoch writes, "and through perhaps the first fifteen years of my writing there runs a recurring fascination with the tawdry glitter of amusement parks as a setting for crime.

" 'The Vanishing of Velma' was written as something of a sequel to an earlier Captain Leopold story, 'The House by the Ferris,' about a witch named Stella Gaze who lived at an amusement park called Sportland. The first story turned out quite well and was published in the May 1966 issue of *The Saint Mystery Magazine*. But it was not till a few years later, while reading a story published by a university press, that the idea for a sequel came to me. The story, by an author long forgotten, tells of a man whose child vanishes while on a ferris wheel at an amusement park. It was something of a symbolic fantasy, without solution, but it was enough to bring Leopold back to Sportland and the same ferris wheel that had figured in the earlier story."

Hoch, a resident of Rochester, New York, is an anthologist of short stories as well as a writer of them; and in "The Vanishing of Velma" he sets forth a bizarre problem and has Captain Leopold solve it. After all, how *could* anyone disappear from a ferris wheel in mid-air? Well, Hoch shows us not only how, but why.

A.M.

THE VANISHING OF VELMA

"Remember Stella Gaze?" Sergeant Fletcher asked, coming into Captain Leopold's office with the morning coffee.

"Stella Gaze? How could I forget her?" It had been one of Leopold's oddest cases, some three years back, involving a middle-aged woman who'd committed suicide after having been accused of practicing witchcraft. He thought of Stella Gaze often, wondering what he could have done to handle things differently. "What about her?" he asked Fletcher.

The sergeant slipped into his favorite chair opposite Leopold's desk and carefully worked the plastic top off his cup of coffee. "Well, you remember that her house was directly adjacent to Sportland Amusement Park—in fact, when they couldn't buy her land they built the ferris wheel right next to the house, with only a wire fence separating them."

"I remember," Leopold said. Stella Gaze—no witch, certainly—but only a neurotic woman whom no one understood. She'd tried suicide before, and in the end had been successful.

"Well, listen to this! Last night about ten o'clock, a girl vanished from the top of that same ferris wheel! What do you think the newspapers will do with that when they get it?"

"Vanished?" Leopold scratched his head. "How could she vanish from the top of a ferris wheel?"

"She couldn't, but she did. It wasn't reported to the police till later

—too late for the morning editions, but the papers will be on to it any minute."

As if in answer to Fletcher's prediction, the telephone buzzed, but it was not a curious newsman. It was Leopold's direct superior, the chief of detectives. "Captain, I hate to ask you this, because it doesn't involve a homicide—not yet, anyway. But you worked on the Stella Gaze case out at Sportland three years back, didn't you?"

"That's right," Leopold answered with a sigh, already sure of what was coming.

"We've got a disappearance out there. A girl missing from the ferris wheel. I know you're not working on anything right now, and I thought you might help us out by handling the case with Sergeant Fletcher. The papers are already trying to tie it in somewhat with the Gaze thing, and you'll know what to tell them."

"I always know what to tell them," Leopold said. "What's the girl's name?"

"Velma Kelty. She was there with a boyfriend, and he's pretty shook about it."

"I'll talk to him," Leopold said. "Any special reason for your interest?" He'd known the chief of detectives long enough to ask.

"Not really. The boy is Tom Williams, the councilman's son."

"And?"

A long sigh over the phone. "It might turn out to be sort of messy, Captain, if anything's happened to her. She's only fifteen years old."

So Leopold drove out to visit Tom Williams at his home. He'd never met the boy, and knew his father only slightly, in the vague manner that detectives knew councilmen. The house was large and expensive, with a gently curving driveway and a swimming pool barely visible in the back area.

"You must be the police," the boy said, answering the door himself. "Come in."

"Captain Leopold. You're Tom Williams?"

"That's right, sir." He was about twenty, with sandy hair cropped short and a lanky look that was typical of college boys these days. "Have they found her yet?"

"No, I guess not. Suppose you tell me about it." Leopold had followed him onto a rear terrace that overlooked the pool. It was empty now, with only a rubber animal of some sort floating near the far corner.

"She went up in the ferris wheel and she didn't come down," the young man said simply. "That's all there is to it."

"Not quite all," Leopold corrected. "Why don't you start at the beginning. How old are you, Tom?"

The young man hesitated, running a nervous hand through his sandy close-cropped hair. "I'll be twenty-one in two weeks. What's that got to do with anything?"

"I understand Velma Kelty is only fifteen. I was just wondering how you two happened to get together, that's all."

"I met her through my kid sister," he mumbled. "The thing wasn't really a date. I just took her to Sportland, that's all."

"How many times had you been out with her this summer?"

He shrugged. "Two or three. I took her to a movie, a ball game. Anything wrong with that?"

"Nothing," Leopold said. "Now suppose you tell it like it was, in detail this time."

He sighed and settled a bit deeper into the canvas deck chair. "I took her out for a pizza earlier, and she suggested we play some miniature golf. Sportland was the closest place, so we went there. I parked my car in the lot by the golf course and driving range, but when we'd finished she suggested going on some of the rides. We went on a couple, but the rides right after the pizza upset my stomach a bit. When she suggested the ferris wheel I told her I'd watch."

"And you did watch?"

"Sure. I paid for her ticket and watched her get into one of those little wire cages they have. It was dark by that time, around ten o'clock. You know how they light the wheel at night?"

"I haven't seen it in a few years," Leopold admitted.

"Well, they have colored neon running out on the spokes of the wheel. It looks great from a distance, but close up it's a little overwhelming. Anyway, I didn't remember exactly which of the colored cages she was in, and by the time it had reached the top of the wheel, I'd lost it in the lights."

"Was she alone in her cage?"

"Yeah. The guy tried to get me in at the last minute, but my stomach wasn't up to it. The wheel was almost empty by that time."

"What happened then?"

"Well, I waited for her to come down, and she didn't."

"Didn't?"

"That's right. I watched each cage being unloaded. She wasn't in any of them. After a while I got sorta frantic and had the operator empty them all out. But she wasn't in any of them."

"Who did get out while you were standing there?"

"Let's see—the ones I remember were a father and two little kids, a fellow and girl who'd been necking—they were right ahead of us in line—and a couple of college girls who seemed to be alone. I suppose there were others, but I don't remember them."

"Could she have gotten off on the other side of the wheel?"

"No. I was watching each car when it was unloaded. I was interested in the way the guy was doing it, giving the good-looking girls a quick feel as he helped them to the ground."

"Why did you wait a couple of hours before calling the police?"

"I didn't believe my eyes, that's why! She couldn't have just vanished like that, not while I was watching. The guy operating it told me I was nuts."

"Didn't he remember her?"

"No."

"Even though he wanted you to join her?"

"He said he was busy. He couldn't remember everybody."

Leopold glanced at the official report of the patrolman who'd been summoned. "That would be Rudy Magee?"

"I guess that's his name. Anyway, he dismissed the whole thing and I guess for a minute I just thought I was cracking up. I walked around for a half hour, just looking for her, and then went back to the car and waited. When she didn't come, I walked over to the ferris wheel again and told the guy—Magee—I was going to call the police."

"I see," Leopold said, but he didn't really see very much.

"So I called them. That's it."

Leopold lit a cigarette. "Was she pregnant, Tom?"

"*What?*"

"You understand it's my job to ask all the questions, and that's one of them. You wouldn't be the first boy who wanted a fifteen-year-old pregnant girlfriend to disappear."

"I never touched her. I told you she was a friend of my sister's."

"All right." He stood up. "Is your sister around now?" he persisted.

"She's out."

"For how long?"

He shrugged. "Who knows? She's sorta loose."

"I'll be back," Leopold told him. "What's your sister's name?"

"Cindy. They call her Cin."

"Who does?"

"Her crowd."

"Is she fifteen, too?"

"Sixteen."

Leopold nodded. As he walked around the side of the house, he looked a bit longingly at the swimming pool. The day was warming up, and a dip in the clear blue water would have felt good.

He got back in the car and drove out to Sportland.

Sportland was still big, but it had perhaps retreated a little into itself since Leopold's last visit. The lower portion, once given over to kiddies' rides, had been sold off to a drive-in movie, and the rides in the upper part now seemed a little closer together. The ferris wheel was still in the same place, of course, but Stella Gaze's house had been torn down for parking.

"You Rudy Magee?" Leopold asked a kid at the ferris wheel.

"He's on his break. Over there at the hot-dog stand."

Magee was a type—the sport-shirted racetrack tout, the small-time gambler, the part-time pimp. Leopold had known them through all of his professional life. "I want to talk about last night," he told the thin pale man, showing his identification.

"You mean that kid—the one who lost his girl?"

"That's right."

"Hell, I don't know a thing about it. I think he dreamed the whole bit."

Leopold grunted. "You worked here long? I don't remember you."

"Just since the place opened for the season in May. Why? I gotta be an old-time employee to know people don't disappear from ferris wheels?"

Leopold was about to answer, but a third man had joined them—a stocky thirsty-looking fellow who looked vaguely familiar. "Well, Captain Leopold, isn't it? You working on this Velma Kelty case?"

Leopold looked him up and down. "I don't believe I caught the name."

"Fane. Walter Fane from the *Globe*. You've seen me around headquarters." He pulled an afternoon paper from under his arm. "See? We've got it on page one."

They had indeed. GIRL VANISHES AT AMUSEMENT PARK; COUNCILMAN'S SON QUIZZED.

"Is that the way it is, Captain? Or have you found the body?"

"What body?" Leopold asked.

"You're a homicide captain, right? If you're on the case, there's a body."

"Not this time. I'm just helping out."

"Give me a break, Captain. I can still phone in a new lead for the late sports edition."

Leopold gazed over at the ferris wheel, and at the new parking lot beyond. "Are you superstitious, Fane?"

"Huh?"

"Three years ago, a woman named Stella Gaze was accused of witchcraft."

"Yeah." His eyes brightened a bit. "She lived out here somewhere."

"Right next to the ferris wheel. The house was torn down after she killed herself. But if a girl really did vanish from that ferris wheel, who's to say Stella Gaze's spirit isn't still around?"

"You believe that bunk, Captain?"

"You wanted a new lead. I'm giving you one."

The reporter thought about it for a moment, and then nodded. "Thanks," he said, heading off toward a telephone.

"We can go back to your wheel," Leopold told Rudy Magee. "I want you to tell me how it happened."

"Nothing happened. Nothing at all," Rudy insisted vehemently.

"Well then, tell me what *didn't* happen."

They reached the wheel and Rudy took over from the kid, standing on a raised platform where the cars came to a stop, helping people in and out over the foot-high metal sill. "Watch your step," he told two teen-age girls as he accepted their tickets and shut the wire cage on them. Though Leopold could see only their knees and upper bodies from the ground, he knew Magee was getting a good view from his position.

Rudy let a few cars go by with empty seats before he stopped the wheel again to load the next passengers. "When there aren't many customers, I balance the load," he explained to Leopold.

A young hippie type with sideburns and beads came by. "Is Hazel here?" he asked Magee.

"Not now," the pale man answered. "Maybe later."

Leopold watched the wheel turning against the sky, noting a tree too far away, a lamppost just out of reach. He tried to imagine a fifteen-year-old girl swinging like a monkey against the night sky, trying to reach one of them, and then decided it was impossible. If Velma had gone up—and that was the big *if*—then she'd surely come down as well.

"Satisfied?" Rudy asked curtly.

"Not quite. I understand you've got an easy hand with the girls when you're helping them in and out. You must have seen Velma."

"I told you, and I'm telling you. It was busy. I didn't notice anybody."

But his eyes shifted as he spoke. He was a poor liar. "All right," Leopold said. "Let's try it another way. Lying to me is one thing, lying before a grand jury is something else. The girl is missing and we want to find her. If she turns up dead and you've been lying, that's big trouble for you." He took a chance and added, "They know about your record here, Rudy?"

"What record? A couple of gambling arrests?"

Leopold shrugged. "Why make more trouble for yourself?"

The thin man seemed to sag a little. "All right. I was just trying to stay outa trouble. Understand?"

"Everybody wants to stay outa trouble, Rudy. Now suppose you tell me about it."

"Well, the guy shows up just before ten o'clock with his broad. She's got long black hair and looks about eighteen. They argue for a couple of minutes, because she wants him to go up with her and he doesn't want to. Finally he buys her a ticket and she goes up alone. All alone—nobody sharing the seat with her—just the girl alone."

"And?"

"And she never comes down. Just like he said. Damnedest thing I ever seen."

"You're sure?"

"I'm sure. I was sorta watching for her. You know."

"I know, Rudy. What did you think happened?"

"Hell, I was scared. I thought she opened the cage and jumped. I figured we'd find her body over in the parking lot somewhere."

"But you didn't."

"No. Besides, somebody would have seen her, you know. But I just couldn't figure anything else. Say, do you believe that stuff about the witch and all? Do you think she put a curse on this place before she died?"

Leopold shrugged. "It'll make a good story for a few days, keep them off the kid's back. Maybe by that time we'll find out what really happened to Velma Kelty."

The missing girl had lived with an aunt and uncle in the East Bay region of town, ever since her parents had died in the crash of a private plane some eight years earlier. Captain Leopold drove over to the house, knowing that he was only retracing the steps covered earlier by the missing persons people.

The uncle was a lawyer named Frank Prosper. He was a bulging, balding man whom Leopold had seen occasionally around City Hall. "You mean you've only come to ask more questions?" he challenged, "and not to give us any word of her?"

"There is no word," Leopold said. "I wanted to ask you a few things about her. And about Tom Williams. He seems a little mature to have been dating her."

"We've always had trouble with that girl," Prosper said, biting off the tip of a cigar. "My wife's brother was a wild sort and she takes right after him."

"What do you think about Williams? Do you think he might have harmed her?"

"I don't know. He's not a bad kid. Only thing wrong with him is that he thinks his father's God's gift to politics. Old man Williams is the last of the old cigar chompers." Leopold thought this last was a somewhat odd comment from a man who himself was smoking a cigar at the moment.

"You mean he's crooked?"

"Nothing of the sort! He's just a man who believes in political power at the ward level, the way it was practiced a couple of generations ago. The country has passed men like Williams by, but he doesn't seem to realize it."

"I'd like to know more about your niece. Do you have a picture of her? A snapshot would be fine."

"I gave one to the missing persons people. Here's another." He held out a framed photograph of a shyly smiling girl in a short red dress. She wore her black hair long, half covering a pretty, if unexceptional, face. She seemed several years older than fifteen. Leopold would have taken her for a college girl.

"She doesn't look like the wild sort. What was the trouble?"

"She hung around with a fast crowd. Hippies. That type."

"Tom Williams, a hippie?" Somehow the scene didn't ring true to Leopold.

"Not Williams. His sister. Talk to his sister."

Leopold nodded. "I was thinking of doing just that."

She was in the pool when he returned to the Williams house, splashing around in a brief two-piece suit that stopped just short of being a true bikini. When Leopold called to her from the water's edge, she left the rubber animal to float by itself and kicked out with energy toward where he stood.

"You're Cindy Williams?" Leopold asked, stretching out a hand to help her from the water.

"Just call me Cin," she replied.

He shook the dampness from his cuffs and took a good look at her. Yes, he supposed even in the bathing suit she could have been called a hippie—especially by a paunchy lawyer like Frank Prosper. Her hair was long and stringy, not unlike the missing girl's, except that it was blond. She had the same sort of pretty but unremarkable face. He'd seen her type many times before, downtown, wearing tight jeans and laughing a bit too loudly on a street corner. He wondered what her father, the councilman, thought about it all.

"Velma Kelty," Leopold said. "She was your friend."

Cin Williams nodded. "A year younger than me, but we're in the same class at school."

"I'm investigating her disappearance. Any idea what might have happened to her?"

Cin shrugged her loose, bony shoulders. "Maybe it was the witch." She gestured toward the final edition of the newspaper, where the headline now read: GIRL VANISHES AT AMUSEMENT PARK; WITCHCRAFT HINTED. Walter Fane had phoned in his story on time, and Leopold supposed it was a slight improvement over the earlier headline.

"Were there any other boys beside your brother?" he asked the girl in the bathing suit. "Someone else she might have dated?"

"Gee, I don't know." She was starting to dry off her long suntanned legs with a towel.

"I hear she hung around some with hippies."

"I don't know."

"We'll find out," Leopold said.

A voice called from the terrace at the back of the house. "Cindy, who's that you're talking to?"

"A detective, Daddy. About Velma."

Councilman Williams, whose first name was also Tom, came down the flagstone walk. His son looked a great deal like him, as did the daughter to a lesser extent. There was not a cigar in sight, and despite what Prosper had said, Leopold doubted that he smoked them. "You're Leopold? The chief said he'd put his best man on this thing."

"Captain Leopold, yes."

"Any clues yet, Captain?"

"No clues. It's not the sort of case where you look for clues."

"But the girl disappeared from the ferris wheel."

"Perhaps."

"If there's any way I can help out, down at City Hall . . ."

"Do you know the girl's uncle? Frank Prosper?"

"Yes. He's a lawyer, active in politics. I know him."

The tone was one of prompt dismissal. Perhaps they only belonged to different parties. Leopold looked back to where Cin had finished drying herself. "I was asking your daughter about hippies. I understand Velma traveled with a pretty wild crowd."

"What gave you that idea?" Williams asked. "She was with my daughter a great deal. And with my son recently, of course."

Young Tom Williams came out then, to join them and stand beside his father. He seemed very young, still a boy. "Is there any news about Velma?"

"No news."

"She'll turn up," the father decided. "It's probably just some gag."

Leopold didn't have an answer for that. Standing there with the three of them beside the pool, he didn't have an answer for anything.

Fletcher came in with coffee the next morning. "Anything on the girl, Captain?" he asked, settling into his usual chair.

"Nothing."

"You going to turn it back to missing persons?"

Leopold sighed. "The chief wants me to stay on it another day. He promised Councilman Williams we'd do our best."

"What do you think happened to her?"

Leopold leaned back in his chair. "What do I think happened? I think somebody's trying to pull a neat trick. I think the ferris wheel was chosen because of Stella Gaze and all that talk of witchcraft. But I don't know who's behind it, or what they're trying to accomplish."

"Young Williams?"

"Yes. He has to be in on it. You see, whatever the plan was, it called for witnesses at the wheel to verify the boy's story. Unfortunately for him, Rudy Magee wasn't about to verify anything. That threw him into such confusion that he walked around for an hour or two before even calling the police. That tells us something very interesting, if just a little bit sinister."

"Sinister?"

"Look at it this way. Young Williams and the girl are going to fake a disappearance for some reason—publicity, a joke, anything. She goes up in the ferris wheel, after a big scene with him to draw attention—and then does her vanishing act. Big witchcraft thing, Stella Gaze and all that. Except that it doesn't work because Magee gets scared and denies everything. So what happens? Williams goes away for a while, *but then he comes back and calls the police.* Why? There were two other courses open to him. He could have forgotten the whole thing, or the two of them could have tried it again some other night. Why did he call the police with the weak story he had?"

"You said it was something sinister."

"It is." Leopold swiveled in his chair to stare out the window. The headquarters parking lot was damp and misty, its asphalt surface dark with water from a morning shower. The view wasn't much.

"Sinister how? Like witchcraft?"

"Like murder," Leopold said.

There were other crimes that day, the usual assortment of a city's troubles, and it was not until late in the day that Leopold's mind went back to the vanishing of the fifteen-year-old girl. It was yanked back suddenly by a telephone call.

"Captain Leopold?" A girl's voice, soft.

"Yes."

"This is Velma Kelty."

"Who? You'll have to speak louder." Already he was signaling Fletcher to trace it.

"Velma Kelty. The girl on the ferris wheel."

"Oh yes. I'm glad to hear from you, Velma. Are you all right?"

"I'm all right."

"Where are you, Velma?"

"At Sportland. I'd like to meet you here, later, after dark."

"Couldn't I come out now?"

"No . . . Not yet. After dark."

"All right, Velma. Where should I meet you?"

"Ten o'clock. By the ferris wheel."

"Yes. Of course. I'll be there, Velma."

He hung up and called to Fletcher, but there'd been no time to trace it. There was nothing to do but wait till ten o'clock.

The rain came again about eight, but it lasted only a few minutes. It left behind a summer dampness, though, and a light mist that clung to the road as Leopold drove. Approaching the Sound, he might have been driving toward the end of the earth, were it not for the bright neon of Sportland that told him some sort of civilization still existed out there at the water's edge.

It was five minutes to ten when he reached the ferris wheel. Rudy Magee was on duty again. "You must work all the time," Leopold observed. "You're always here."

"Every other night, alternating with the afternoons," Magee said. "What's up?"

"I thought I might ask you. Seen anybody familiar tonight?"

"Yeah. Now that you mention it, that reporter Fane was nosing around."

"Oh?" Leopold lit a cigarette. "Anybody else?"

"Like who?"

Leopold glanced at his watch. It was just ten o'clock. "Like Velma Kelty, the missing girl."

"Never laid eyes on her. I'd know her from the picture the papers published."

"She's not on the wheel now?"

"I told you I'd know her. There's nobody but a middle-aged couple and a few strays."

He slowed the wheel to a stop and released a young man from his cage. Then he slowed it a few cages on and opened it for a young lady. Leopold saw the hair first, and knew. Rudy Magee saw her too, and let out a muffled gasp.

Velma Kelty had come back.

Leopold beckoned to her and they walked away from the shaken Magee.

"I suppose you're going to tell me you were riding around on that ferris wheel for the last forty-eight hours," Leopold said.

"Sure. Why not?"

He peered at her in the uncertain light. "All right, young lady. You nearly scared that feerris wheel operator to death. I'm taking you home to your uncle."

"I can find my way," she told him. "I just wanted to see you, to show you I wasn't really missing."

"Sure." They were in better light now, crossing to the parking lot. He glanced sideways at her and reached out to touch her long black hair. Then he twisted and gave a sudden tug. It came away in his hand.

"You creep!" Cindy Williams shouted at him, clutching for the wig.

"Now, now. You're playing the big girls' game, Cindy. You have to expect these little setbacks."

"How'd you know it was me?"

"I guess because it looked like you. That's a pretty old trick, to start out a blonde and then change to a brunette. You fooled Rudy Magee, anyway. Of course you had the wig hidden in your purse when you got on the wheel a while ago."

"I just wanted to show you it could be done," she said. "Velma could have worked it just the opposite—gotten on the ferris wheel as a brunette and gotten off as a blonde."

"But you didn't show me anything of the sort, because it didn't work, did it? I recognized you as soon as I got you in the good light, and Tom would have recognized Velma a lot sooner than that, wig or no wig, because he was watching for her." He sighed with exasperation. "All right, get in the car. I'm still taking you home."

She slid into the front seat, pouting for several minutes as he turned the car out of the Sportland parking lot. Presently the garish neon of the amusement park subsided into the background as they drove toward town.

"You think I'm involved, don't you?" she asked.

"I didn't, until tonight. That was a pretty foolish trick."

"Why was it?"

"I might have told Prosper she was alive, gotten his hopes up."

"You think she's dead?"

Leopold kept his eyes on the road. "I think Tom was playing a stunt of some sort and it didn't come off. He waited two hours before calling the police. Why? Because he was trying to decide what he should do. But then he called them after all, even though Magee didn't back up his story. Why again? Because he couldn't come back and try his stunt the next night. Because Velma Kelty really had vanished, only not in the way he made it appear."

"How, then?"

"I wish I knew." He pushed in the cigarette lighter that rarely worked and reached for his crumpled pack. In the light from passing cars her face was tense and drawn. She looked older than her age.

"You must have some idea."

"Sure I do, lots of them. Want to hear one? Velma Kelty died somehow at your house, maybe in the swimming pool, and your father the councilman is implicated. To protect him, you and Tom cook up this disappearance, with you using that black wig. How does that sound to you?"

"Fantastic!"

"Maybe."

They drove the rest of the way in near silence, until they were almost to her house. "By the way," he asked, "how'd you get out to Sportland tonight?"

"Tom drove me," she mumbled. "He dropped me off."

He pulled up in front of her house. 'Want me to come in with you, have a few words with your father?"

"N-no."

"All right. This time."

He watched till she reached the door and then drove on. He was thinking that if his own marriage had worked out he might have had a daughter just about her age—fifteen or sixteen—but that was a heck of a thing for a cop to have on his mind. Velma Kelty might have been his daughter too, and now she was gone.

He went home to his apartment and turned on the air-conditioner. He fell asleep to its humming, and when the telephone awakened him he wondered for an instant what the sound was.

"Leopold here," he managed to mumble into the instrument.

"It's Fletcher, Captain. Sorry to disturb you, but I thought you'd want to know. We found her."

"Who?" he asked through bleary cobwebs.

"The missing girl. Velma Kelty."

"Is she all right?"

"She's dead, Captain. They just fished her body out of the Sound near Sportland."

He cursed silently and turned on the bedside lamp. Why did they always have to end like this?

"Any chance of suicide?"

Fletcher cleared his throat. "Pretty doubtful, Captain. Somebody weighted down the body with fifty pounds of scrap iron."

Leopold went back to the house with the swimming pool, rousing

Tom Williams from his bed just as dawn was breaking over the city. "You'll wake my father," young Williams said. "What do you want?"

"The truth. No more stories about ferris wheels, just the truth."

"I don't know what you're talking about."

"They just fished Velma's body from the Sound. Now do you know what I'm talking about?"

"Oh no!" He seemed truly staggered by the news, as if he refused to comprehend the truth of it.

"That trick with your sister was a bit of foolishness. Is that the way you worked it the other night, with a wig?"

"I swear, Captain, Velma Kelty got on that ferris wheel. She got on and she never got off. I can't imagine what happened to her, or how she ended up in the Sound. What killed her?"

"They're doing the autopsy now. Her body was weighted to keep it at the bottom, but not heavily enough, apparently. It wasn't any accident."

"I . . . I can't imagine what happened to her."

"You'd better start imagining, because you're in big trouble. You and your sister both. Someone killed the girl and threw her body in the Sound. Maybe she was raped first."

"You don't know that!"

"I don't know much of anything at this point, but I can speculate. Did you do it, Tom? Or maybe your father? Or maybe some of the hippie crowd she hung around with? Anyway, the body had to be disposed of, and Velma's disappearance had to take place somewhere else. The ferris wheel seemed logical to you, because of the witch stories, so Cindy put on her wig and you pulled it off. Except that the wheel operator was ready to deny everything. That threw you for a loss, and you spent a couple of hours wondering what to do next."

"No!"

"Then why did you wait all that time before reporting her disappearance? Why, Tom?"

"I . . . I . . ."

Leopold turned away. "You'd better think up a good story. You'll need it in court."

Fletcher looked up from his desk as Leopold entered the squad room and crossed to his private office. "Did you bring the Williams kid in, Captain?"

"Not yet, soon." His lips were drawn into a tight line.

"Crazy story for him to make up, about that damned ferris wheel."

"Yeah." Leopold shuffled the papers on his desk, seeing nothing. "How's the autopsy report?"

"Nothing yet."

"I'm going down there," he decided suddenly.

The medical examiner was a tall red-faced man whom Leopold had known for years. He had just finished the autopsy and was sitting at his desk writing the report. "How are you, Captain?" he mumbled.

"Finish with the Kelty girl?"

"Just about. I have to submit the report. Her things are over there."

Leopold glanced at the clothes, still soggy with water. Dark blue slacks and sweater, sneakers, bra and panties. A heavy piece of cast iron, entwined with damp cord, rested nearby. He looked back at the doctor. "Was she raped, Gus?"

"No. I wish it were that easy. Something like that I could understand." His face was suddenly old.

"What was it, Gus?"

"Fifteen. Only fifteen years old . . ."

"Gus . . ."

The doctor stood up and handed over his report. "There it is, Captain. She died of a massive overdose of heroin, mainlined into a vein near her elbow . . ."

It was late afternoon when Leopold returned to Sportland. He could see the ferris wheel from a long way off, outlined against the blue of a cloudless sky. For the first time he wondered if Stella Gaze really had been a witch, if she really had put a curse on the place. Maybe that was some sort of an explanation.

"You're back!" Rudy Magee said, strolling over to meet him. "I hear they found the girl."

"They found her."

"Not far from here, huh!"

"Close, Rudy. Very close."

"The kid was lying, then?"

"Let's go for a ride, Rudy, on your ferris wheel. I'll tell you all about it."

"Huh? All right, if you really want to. I don't usually go on the thing myself." The kid took over the controls, and he preceded Leopold into one of the wire cages. As the wheel turned and they started their climb, he added, "Great view from up here, huh?"

"I imagine with all this neon lit up at night it's quite a ride."

Rudy chuckled. "Yeah, the kids like it."

"I know how Velma disappeared," Leopold said suddenly.

"You do? Boy, I'd like to know myself. It was a weird thing. The kid played some trick on me, huh?"

"No trick, Rudy. You were the one with the tricks."

The pale man stiffened in the seat beside him. "What do you mean?" The caged seat swayed gently as it reached the peak of its ascent and started slowly down.

"I mean that you've been selling drugs to these kids—hippies, college kids, fifteen-year-old girls. I suppose it was a big kick to go up on this wheel at night with all the colored neon and stuff while you were high on LSD."

"You'd have a tough time proving that," Rudy said.

"Maybe not. Maybe Tom Williams has decided it's time to talk. That was the key question, after all—why he waited so long to report Velma's disappearance to the police. The reason, of course, was that he was high on drugs at the time, probably on an LSD trip. He had to wait till it wore off a little. Maybe you even had him convinced that Velma never did get on your ferris wheel."

"I told you she got on," Magee mumbled. "But she never got off."

"She never got off alive." Leopold watched the scene shifting beneath them as they reached bottom and started up once more. "LSD had become too tame for Velma and her hippie friends. So you maybe sold her some marijuana. Anyway, before long you had her on heroin."

"No."

"I say yes."

He rubbed his palms together. "Maybe I sold the kids a little LSD, but never anything stronger. Never horse."

"Some people call it *horse,* Rudy. Others call it *Hazel.* I heard the kid ask you for Hazel the other day, but it didn't register with me then. Velma Kelty bought the heroin from you, and mainlined it into her vein as she was going up in the ferris wheel. It's a pretty safe place, when you consider it. Only she was fairly new at it, or the stuff was a bad batch, or she just took too much. She crumpled off the seat, into this space at our feet—and she rode around on your ferris wheel for the rest of the night, until the park closed and you could weight the body and toss it in the Sound."

"Somebody would have seen her there."

"No, not from ground level. This metal sill is a foot high, and I noticed that from the ground you couldn't see below girls' knees. A small fifteen-year-old girl could easily crumple into that space, seen by you on that platform every time the wheel turned, but invisible from the ground. The seat just looked empty and of course you were careful to skip it when loading passengers."

"The people in the seat above would have seen her there," Magee argued.

"So you kept that seat empty too. Williams said you weren't busy that night. There were only a few others on the wheel. Besides, Velma was wearing dark blue slacks and sweater, and she had black hair. In the dark no one would have seen her there, especially with all this neon blinding them."

"So you're going to arrest me for disposing of a body?"

"For more than that, Rudy. The narcotics charge alone will keep you behind bars a good long time. But you know the effects of an overdose as well as I do. Velma Kelty was still alive after she collapsed —physically incapacitated, stuporous, with slow respiration, but still alive. She could probably have been saved with quick treatment, but you were too afraid for your own skin. So you let her slowly die here, crumpled into this little space, until the park closed and you could get rid of the body."

"The policeman came, he looked."

"Sure. He came and looked two hours later. Naturally he didn't check each individual seat, because no one would believe she could still be there unseen. Perhaps by that time you had stopped the wheel anyway, with her body near the top. Or maybe you'd even managed to remove it, if business was bad enough to give you a few minutes' break."

Rudy Magee's hand came out of his pocket. It was holding a hypodermic syringe. "You're a smart cop, but not smart enough. I'm not going back inside on any murder rap, or even manslaughter."

Leopold sighed. The wire cage was nearing the ground again. "Do you see that man watching us from the ground? His name is Sergeant Fletcher, and he's awfully good with a gun. I wouldn't try to jab me with that, or yourself either."

As he spoke, Leopold's hand closed around the syringe, taking it from Rudy's uncertain fingers.

"How did you know it all?" he asked quietly, staring into Leopold's eyes.

"I didn't, until I saw the autopsy report. Velma died of an overdose of heroin, and she was last seen alive getting onto your ferris wheel. I put those two facts together and tried to determine if she could have died on your wheel, and just kept going around, without being seen. I decided she could have, and that she did."

The wheel stopped finally, and they got off. There was a bit of a breeze blowing in off the Sound, and it reminded Leopold somehow of Velma Kelty—the living girl, not the body in the morgue. He wished that he had known her. Maybe, just maybe, he could have saved her from Rudy Magee—and from herself.

THE PERFECTIONIST

Gerald Tomlinson

Gerald Tomlinson

"Sometime around the age of forty," Gerald Tomlinson says, "it occurred to me that any writer, or would-be writer, who was born and raised in Elmira, New York, should devote his attention to the mystery field. After all, Frederic Dannay had spent much of his boyhood there *(The Golden Summer);* George Harmon Coxe *(The Groom Lay Dead)* attended high school there; and Mark Twain *(Tom Sawyer, Detective)* was married and buried there. Perhaps, I thought, there is something in the upstate air . . ."

Graduating from Marietta College, Tomlinson went on to "a year at Columbia Law School, two years in Army Intelligence, two years of teaching junior high school, and, ah, how many years of editing elementary and high school textbooks. Along the way I ghostwrote a self-improvement book that year by year has helped furnish the house in Lake Hopatcong, New Jersey, where I live with my wife Alexis and our two sons Eli and Matthew."

In "The Perfectionist" he demonstrates how a man can be undone in spite of all the precautions he has taken. The protagonist is shocked, and so is the reader. And Tomlinson also shows how, when skillfully handled, the most unlikely coincidence can be made to seem plausible.

A.M.

THE PERFECTIONIST

"Let's go, Deutsch. Forty minutes to Grand Central. Get a move on."

Ray Deutsch bent respectfully from the waist and closed the rear door of the black Cadillac limousine. Inside, Frank Prescott, the New Jersey construction magnate, syndicate boss, and multimillionaire, leaned back to read his *Daily News*. On the seat beside Prescott rested the small brown suitcase that Deutsch had been waiting for. Today was the day.

Deutsch, pale and rigid, watched the double row of poplars streak by for the last time. No more Jersey roads, he thought. No more "Pretty Boy" Prescott. No more playing the cowed chauffeur to a loud-mouthed mobster. He smiled tightly.

Prescott's Cadillac, hearse-quiet at 60 miles an hour, flashed south on the Palisades Parkway. Deutsch took pride in his driving. He was quick, alert, canny, a perfectionist behind the wheel. In seven years of driving for Frank Prescott he had never so much as scratched a fender.

The day was sunny, crisp, and bright with promise. Two miles south of the Alpine exit, with the road clear in both directions, Deutsch made the decisive move of his life, the culminating act of his fifty-three years. Bracing himself under the shoulder safety belt, he slammed his foot down hard on the brake pedal. The tires screamed.

Prescott, unbelted as always, rose from his seat like an Apollo at liftoff. His head ricocheted off the ceiling, smashed into the plastic partition that separated him from Deutsch, and the boss of northern New Jersey, unconscious, sagged to the floor like a strand of boiled spaghetti.

Deutsch, nervously humming an old tune, resumed his normal driving. At the Englewood Cliffs exit he left the Parkway and headed south on Hudson Terrace. He passed a dozen large apartment buildings before turning in at the entrance to the Quebec. He drove to the back of the building, where an 800-car parking lot, whose spaces were unnumbered and unreserved, stood half empty at this hour on a Tuesday morning.

Pulling in beside a new dusty dark-green Plymouth, Deutsch opened the rear door of the Cadillac, removed Prescott's suitcase, smiled again at the motionless form, nodded quietly and triumphantly, and closed the door on his past life.

Unlocking a new door, he slid behind the wheel of the Plymouth.

Ray Deutsch's drive to a tiny A-frame house at the northern edge of the Catskills took less than two hours. He owned the A-frame. He had bought it, along with the ten wooded acres surrounding it, six months before in the name of Alfred A. Stocker. The green Plymouth also belonged to Alfred A. Stocker. So did Deutsch's new driver's license, a small checking account balance at the Hancock National Bank, and an oil-company credit card.

The A-frame offered ideal seclusion. The nearest town, Roscoe, was eight miles away and had about 900 people. The nearest house, half a mile away, was occupied by a retired couple in their seventies.

Deutsch carried the suitcase into the living room and set it down before the brick fireplace. He ran his hand through his thinning gray hair, reached tentatively toward the lock on the suitcase, then turned away. Too much of his future rested on the contents of that bag for him to be hasty. He could take a whole year, if he wanted to, before looking into the suitcase, a whole year to sit by the fire and read the hundreds of paperbacks that lined the walls of the living room.

Why hurry? Besides, there were things to get rid of. The chauffeur's uniform had to go. All those identifying cards and papers, all the bureaucratic biography of Ray Deutsch had to go. All fifty-three years of Ray Deutsch had to disappear up the chimney, dissolve into the blue September sky.

He moved the suitcase to the one chair in the room, a lush leather easy chair that a chrome Kovacs reading lamp pointed down on. A year of one's life deserved such a luxurious throne, Deutsch had decided when he was furnishing the house. The chair and lamp were the only extravagant items he had bought in years.

Except for the driver's license in Deutsch's name, he had packed his identifying possessions two weeks earlier in the trunk compartment of the Plymouth. In the days prior to that a number of unmistakable signs had told him that a Prescott payoff was in the offing.

After starting a fire in the fireplace, Deutsch removed the cards and papers of his lifetime from the Plymouth and piled them in a neat stack on the floor. He then crossed to the kitchen, stepped outside, and removed a bottle of Moët from under the wooden step. Its temperature seemed correct.

Back in the living room, as he was about to pop the cork, a thought crossed his mind. He paused, his foot on the stone hearth. Had the hour arrived? Should he really destroy Ray Deutsch, destroy him totally, before he learned how much Alfred A. Stocker was worth? (The genuine Alfred A. Stocker had died at the age of two and was buried in Newburgh, New York—an element that he had picked up from Frederick Forsyth's *The Day of the Jackal*.)

Deutsch considered the matter. He decided that his timing made little difference. Ray Deutsch was dead anyway—the sooner he was completely eliminated the better.

Memories of a radio commercial passed through his head. The commercial advertised a movie designed to leech on the success of *The Godfather*. It said something about not stealing the syndicate's money—"Stealing the mob's money isn't robbery, it's suicide." Deutsch shuddered. He knew it could be suicide. He had taken that into account. He had taken everything into account.

He released the cork. The bubbling champagne flowed from the bottle in a golden fountain. He stood facing the fireplace, the remnants of his old life at his feet. The only thing he regretted losing was the last photograph of his wife, taken a year before she had died. But the image of Flora Alvarez Deutsch had to go too. Stocker intended to be a bachelor.

Picking up the pile of computer-pulp and paper nostalgia, he flung it into the blazing fire, blowing a final kiss to his wife's picture. Then he clinked his glass gently against the bluestone mantelpiece. "Ray Deutsch is dead. Long live Al Stocker." He said the words aloud, in a low hollow voice. They sounded more like a benediction than an invocation, but the somber tone was wrong. Deutsch was giddy with anticipation.

Alfred A. Stocker knew he was rich. He had no idea of the exact amount of money, but he did know that Frank Prescott's personal payoffs were big. Lieutenants and sergeants handled the small change. When Prescott took a trip with his small brown suitcase the balance of payments in the underworld was notably affected.

The Moët was brut and glorious. Deutsch—no, Stocker—poured himself another. This time he toasted the unopened suitcase. "To Pretty Boy Prescott. May he take his loss like a man."

Alfred A. Stocker giggled. He seldom giggled, but at this moment he had reason to be cheerful. Prescott could hardly report the incident to the police. The money that he handled he handled in secrecy. Income-tax evasion was a concept well known to him. More than that, more than the origin of the money, the intended purpose of the money should stop any publicity. It was payoff money, bribe money. It was almost certainly headed for a big-time official. "Why were you carrying X-thousands of dollars in your car, Mr. Prescott?" . . . "Well, er, you see . . ." No, it was not going to be reported to the police.

But it was going to be reported to somebody. There would be clever men, resourceful and dangerous men, looking for Ray Deutsch. And they would look hard, if the suitcase contained what it must contain. There would probably be Lou "Sonny" Visconti, an ex-longshoreman who was now a small-arms expert and Prescott's bodyguard. There might be Arnold "Hatchet Man" Fein, a recent favorite whose methods were messy but effective. Others came to mind. Lars "The Lip" Swenson. Mike "Teddy O" O'Brien. Others.

Alfred A. Stocker. Yes, it was Alfred A. Stocker, no one else, who poured a third glass from the bottle. He toasted Visconti. "Good luck, you stupid—no, make it bad luck." And he sat down at the side of the hearth to preview his future.

One year in the A-frame house. He was safe—he was sure of it. They could never find him here. He was untraceable. He had laid his plans with utter precision, had confided in no one. He was a perfectionist, and he had overlooked nothing.

The suitcase was an unimpressive piece of luggage, the kind a college student might take on an overnight trip to his parents' home. But Ray Deutsch—no, not Ray Deutsch, Alfred A. Stocker—had wagered his life on it. And he had done it with style, not like Deutsch at all, who for fifty-three years had never gambled. One big gamble now—the only one he would ever make.

He had to see the contents of the suitcase. Would there be $100,000? Please, yes. Make it at least $100,000. That was enough. Not a fortune. No big dent in the Prescott bankroll. Not enough to make Lou Visconti, that longshoreman who looked like a croupier, give up his important assignments and devote full attention to the missing chauffeur and the stolen suitcase.

It was time for the opening. Swaying slightly, on his feet now, relaxed and tense at once, he knew he was not going to wait a year, not an hour, to find out what he had. Even if he had gained nothing —even if all he found was a change of underwear—he was committed to the scheme. He was going to spend a year in the Catskills whether he had a fortune or a dirty T-shirt. He had to. He could not circulate until he had become a different person—not just a different person on a driver's license, but a different person in fact, a man who could safely venture out among the Viscontis, the Feins, the Swensons, the O'Briens, and still be unrecognized. And that would take time.

The suitcase was unlocked. He lifted one side. Bright light from the Kovacs lamp shone on the exposed contents. He was right, of course. He knew he would be right. Perfection in all things. It had been his stepmother's watchword.

He kept his excitement suppressed. Deutsch's emotions were always suppressed. But he did feel a slight tremor, a flutter in his chest, as he looked down on the greenbacks. His hand went to his heart. A slight shortness of breath. But no wonder.

Rows and rows of twenty-dollar bills filled the suitcase. They were banded with the amounts marked, but Alfred A. Stocker, wealthy bachelor recluse with time on his hands, counted them all, counted them down to the last bill. $180,000.

What had they been intended to do? What would they have bought at Grand Central, at City Hall, in Albany, in Trenton? Stocker poured another glass of Moët and settled back on the hearth. The books on the shelves looked down on him hazily now, invitingly. Six hundred books, purchased five or ten at a time in Brentano's on Fifth Avenue at 47th Street, while Deutsch—*Stocker*—had waited for Prescott to complete his business in the city.

Deutsch finished the champagne, laid the closed suitcase carefully on the floor, chose a book at random—it was a mystery novel—adjusted his elegant lamp, and began to read.

Six months later he was still reading. No unexpected event had broken the routine of his days. Each morning he went to the small shopping center in Roscoe, picked up the *Daily News* at the drug store, then a bag of groceries at the supermarket. He spoke to no one and never ventured farther away than Hancock.

Every day he read a mystery book from ten until one and in the afternoons he read nonfiction, mainly true crime or American history, with emphasis on the Second World War. In the evenings he watched cable television.

Deutsch altered his physical appearance with grotesque efficiency. At the outset of his stay he went on a 6000-calorie-a-day diet. Always before that a light eater and an active man, he began to expand, to soften, to balloon. Fat surrounded him like a shield of blubber.

The diet made him ill at first, but he kept at it. Eventually he came to like eating mountains upon mountains of food at each sitting. From ascetic sparrow to gluttonous hippo in a year. An effective disguise. Effective, too, was the full gray beard that soon wreathed his face.

It was during the seventh month of exile that he received his only scare. He had just returned from the shopping center, a few minutes before nine on a chilly March morning. As he eased out of the car he saw a metallic-gray Cadillac with New Jersey plates round a bend in the road and slow down in front of his A-frame house. It came to a stop. A squat man with enormous shoulders emerged from the driver's seat and approached.

Watch out! Visconti? But was it? The man came closer. Deutsch, ex-chauffeur and open target, stood transfixed, his eyes glazed. No, it wasn't Visconti. Still—but no, definitely not. The burly man gave him a gap-toothed smile and growled, "Hi, pop. Which way to Roscoe?"

Stocker's breath escaped slowly from between his whitened lips and gray beard. "Straight down the road eight miles. You can't miss it. There's a sign that says, 'Welcome to Roscoe.'"

And that was it. The rest of the time ticked away. There were a couple of references to Frank Prescott in the *Daily News*. The first of these relieved Stocker. It let him know that the boss of northern New Jersey had not been killed by a blow on the head; and while Stocker was pretty sure of that anyway, he could not be absolutely sure. The first three weeks after coming to the A-frame house he had not gone out to buy a newspaper. However, he had watched TV, and he assumed that Pretty Boy was important enough to rate an evening news obituary.

So Prescott was alive, testifying before a Congressional committee, winning construction contracts in Teaneck and Fort Lee, and, best of all, failing to find, maybe even forgetting about, his former chauffeur.

Stocker's plan called for him to leave the A-frame on Monday, August 30, three days short of one year from the date of his "inheritance." Prescott knew Deutsch's mania for exactness, and Alfred A. Stocker accordingly wanted to avoid the anniversary.

On the morning of August 30, a clear day similar to the one on which he had become rich, Stocker packed two suitcases into the Plymouth and set out for Kennedy Airport. He took a roundabout route to avoid any travel on too-familiar roads. By now, however, his disguise was total. He weighed 253 pounds and his full beard was almost white.

To his meager collection of identifying cards and papers he had added a New York State voter-registration card. He was heading for three days in Nassau, the Bahamas. Actually, it would be forever in Nassau if he liked it as well as he expected to. But three days were all he intended to declare. For that short a stay he would need only superficial identification.

He left the Plymouth on upper Broadway, near Yonkers, a parking lot for abandoned and quickly stripped cars, as he knew from past observation. He hailed a cab for JFK. The driver, mercifully, was one of the silent ones. Stocker had no wish to talk about his past, present, or future. All he wanted was to be safely chauffeured toward paradise.

But as he approached the airport he began to get nervous. It was the first time in months he had felt any fear. There was no reason to, of course. He knew it. The plan was perfect. Every track had been covered. There was no way on earth that Prescott and his men could have traced Alfred A. Stocker. The old name—what was it?—was gone; the old appearance was gone; Stocker was a short plane hop away from retirement in the sun.

He tipped the cab driver handsomely, the way a prosperous man should tip his driver. Still, he wished the inner trembling would stop. This should be the happiest time of his life, not one of the most fearful. He fought down the chill.

He went straight to the BOAC counter to check his bags. His ticket, purchased by mail a month earlier, was in order, and Stocker received nonsmoker's seat 9A. It was two hours until takeoff, and he intended to spend it reading Ladislas Farago's *The Game of the Foxes*.

He approached a molded plastic chair in the center of the waiting room. As he was about to sit down, a tall blond man strode toward him, a quizzical expression on his face. Stocker hesitated for a moment and stared at the stranger. Visconti? Dyed hair? Fear began to rise. Silly. Stupid. It wasn't Visconti. Take it easy. Stay calm, he told himself. Stay calm.

The blond man nodded toward him and said in a low pleasant voice, "Deutsch?"

Stocker's hand shot to his chest. He staggered backward, a look of horror shattering his broad face. He tried to scream "No!" but nothing came out but a whimper. Pain crisscrossed his upper torso as he fell to the floor, writhing, face up. His breath exploded into the void, once, twice, three times.

He saw someone in uniform. The blond man appeared shocked. Sunlight streamed through the plate glass, striking Deutsch's distorted face. Within seconds the solar light went out; all the lights in the world went out.

A policeman kneeling beside him said, "Please move away, folks. The gentleman is dead." Then the officer, a young sergeant who seemed unconcerned by the hubbub, got up and turned to the blond man. "Could you tell me what happened, sir? You were talking to him, I think."

The blond man stared at the policeman, stunned. He spoke in a low voice: *"Es ist schrecklich. Ich wollte Ihn nur fragen ob er Deutsch spricht."*

The policeman asked, "Can't you speak English?"

The blond man shuddered. "Sorry. In my shock . . . What I just said was, 'It's terrible. I only wanted to ask him if he speaks German.'"

THE GIRL WHO FOUND THINGS

Henry Slesar

Henry Slesar

In the attempt to solve real-life crimes, clairvoyants—men like Peter Hourkas—are sometimes called in to give their opinions. Also, on occasion, in fictional crimes.

"The Girl Who Found Things" deals with the use of a clairvoyant to solve a fictional crime. With surprising results.

Its author, Henry Slesar, is a New Yorker whose expertise extends to many forms of storytelling. In addition to short stories, he has written novels, screenplays and scores of scripts for radio and television plays. For the past nine years he has been head writer of the daytime suspense serial *The Edge of Night*.

The very first story he ever sold was called "The Brat," he says, adding that this may account for his interest in writing about bratty young people, like "The Girl Who Found Things." And the clash between innocence and evil has been a recurring theme in his fiction.

Indeed, innocence, evil and a bratty young girl are the main elements of this tale that does not turn out quite the way any of its characters thought it would.

A.M.

THE GIRL WHO FOUND THINGS

It was dark by the time Lucas stopped his taxi in the driveway of the Wheeler home and lumbered up the path to the front entrance. He still wore his heavy boots, despite the spring thaw; his mackinaw and knitted cap were reminders of the hard winter that had come and gone.

When Geraldine Wheeler opened the door, wearing her lightweight traveling suit, she shivered at the sight of him. "Come in," she said crisply. "My trunk is inside."

Lucas went through the foyer to the stairway, knowing his way around the house, accustomed to its rich dark textures and somber furnishings; he was Medvale's only taxi driver. He found the heavy black trunk at the foot of the stairs, and hoisted it on his back. "That all the luggage, Miss Wheeler?"

"That's all. I've sent the rest ahead to the ship. Good heavens, Lucas, aren't you *hot* in that outfit?" She opened a drawer and rummaged through it. "I've probably forgotten a million things. Gas, electricity, phone . . . Fireplace! Lucas, would you check it for me, please?"

"Yes, miss," Lucas said. He went into the living room, past the white-shrouded furniture. There were some glowing embers among the blackened stumps, and he snuffed them out with a poker.

A moment later the woman entered, pulling on long silken gloves. "All right," she said breathlessly. "I guess that's all. We can go now."

"Yes, miss," Lucas said.

She turned her back and he came up behind her, still holding the poker. He made a noise, either a sob or a grunt, as he raised the ash-coated iron and struck her squarely in the back of the head. Her knees buckled, and she sank to the carpet in an ungraceful fall. Lucas never doubted that she had died instantly, because he had once killed an ailing shorthorn bull with a blow no greater. He tried to act as calmly now. He put the poker back into the fireplace, purifying it among the hot ashes. Then he went to his victim and examined her wound. It was ugly, but there was no blood.

He picked up the light body without effort and went through the screen door of the kitchen and out into the back yard, straight to the thickly wooded acreage that surrounded the Wheeler estate. When he found an appropriate place for Geraldine Wheeler's grave, he went to the toolshed for a spade and shovel.

It was spring, but the ground was hard. He was stripped of mackinaw and cap when he was finished. For the first time in months, since the icy winter began, Lucas was warm.

April had lived up to its moist reputation; there was mud on the roads and pools of black water in the driveway. When the big white car came to a halt, its metal skirt was clotted with Medvale's red clay. Rowena, David Wheeler's wife, didn't leave the car, but waited with an impatient frown until her husband helped her out. She put her high heels into the mud, and clucked in vexation.

David smiled, smiled charmingly, forgiving the mud, the rain, and his wife's bad temper. "Come on, it's not so bad," he said. "Only a few steps." He heard the front door open, and saw his Aunt Faith waving to them. "There's the old gypsy now," he said happily. "Now remember what I told you, darling, when she starts talking about spooks and séances, you just keep a straight face."

"I'll try," Rowena said dryly.

There was affectionate collision between David and his aunt at the doorway; he put his arms around her sizable circumference and pressed his patrician nose to her plump cheek.

"David, my handsome boy! I'm so glad to see you!"

"It's wonderful seeing you, Aunt Faith!"

They were inside before David introduced the two women. David and Rowena had been married in Virginia two years ago, but Aunt Faith never stirred beyond the borders of Medvale County.

The old woman gave Rowena a glowing look of inspection. "Oh, my dear, you're beautiful," she said. "David, you beast, how could you keep her all to yourself?"

He laughed, and coats were shed, and they went into the living room together. There, the cheerfulness of the moment was dissipated. A man was standing by the fireplace smoking a cigarette in nervous puffs, and David was reminded of the grim purpose of the reunion.

"Lieutenant Reese," Aunt Faith said, "this is my nephew, David, and his wife."

Reese was a balding man with blurred and melancholy features. He shook David's hands solemnly. "Sorry we have to meet this way," he said. "But then, I always seem to meet people when they're in trouble. Of course, I've known Mrs. Demerest for some time."

"Lieutenant Reese has been a wonderful help with my charity work," Aunt Faith said. "And he's been such a comfort since . . . this awful thing happened."

David looked around the room. "It's been years since I was here. Wonder if I remember where the liquor's kept?"

"I'm afraid there is none," Reese said. "There wasn't any when we came in to search the place some weeks ago, when Miss Wheeler first disappeared."

There was a moment's silence. David broke it with, "Well, I've got a bottle in the car."

"Not now, Mr. Wheeler. As a matter of fact, I'd appreciate it if you and I could have a word alone."

Aunt Faith went to Rowena's side. "I'll tell you what. Why don't you and I go upstairs, and I'll show you your room?"

"That would be fine," Rowena said.

"I can even show you the room where David was born, and his old nursery. Wouldn't you like that?"

"That would be lovely," Rowena said flatly.

When they were alone, Reese said, "How long have you been away from Medvale, Mr. Wheeler?"

"Oh, maybe ten years. I've been back here on visits, of course. Once when my father died, four years ago. As you know, our family's business is down south."

"Yes, I knew. You and your sister—"

"My half sister."

"Yes," Reese said. "You and your half sister, you were the only proprietors of the mill, weren't you?"

"That's right."

"But you did most of the managing, I gather. When your parents died, Miss Wheeler kept the estate, and you went to Virginia to manage the mill. That's how it was, right?"

"That's how it was," David said.

"Successfully, would you say?"

David sat in a wing chair, and stretched his long legs. "Lieutenant, I'm going to save you a great deal of time. Geraldine and I didn't get along. We saw as little of each other as both could arrange, and that was *very* little."

Reese cleared his throat. "Thank you for being frank."

"I can even guess your next question, Lieutenant. You'd like to know when I saw Geraldine last."

"When did you?"

"Three months ago, in Virginia. On her semiannual visit to the mill."

"But you were in Medvale after that, weren't you?"

"Yes. I came up to see Geraldine in March on a matter of some importance. As my aunt probably told you, Geraldine refused to see me at that time."

"What was the purpose of that visit?"

"Purely business. I wanted Geraldine to approve a bank loan I wished to make to purchase new equipment. She was against it, wouldn't even discuss it. So I left and returned to Virginia."

"And you never saw her again?"

"Never," David said. He smiled, smiled engagingly, and got to his feet. "I don't care if you're a teetotaler like my aunt, Lieutenant, I've *got* to have that drink."

He went toward the front hall, but paused at the doorway. "In case you're wondering," he said lightly, "I have no idea where Geraldine is, Lieutenant. No idea at all."

Rowena and Aunt Faith didn't come downstairs until an hour later, after the lieutenant had left. Aunt Faith looked like she had been sleeping; Rowena had changed into a sweater and gray skirt. In the living room they found David, a half-empty bottle of Scotch, and a dying fire.

"Well?" Aunt Faith said. "Was he very bothersome?"

"Not at all," David said. "You look lovely, Rowena."

"I'd like a drink, David."

"Yes, of course." He made one for her, and teased Aunt Faith about her abstinence. She didn't seem to mind. She wanted to talk, about Geraldine.

"I just can't understand it," she said. "Nobody can, not the police, not anybody. She was all set for that Caribbean trip, some of her bags were already on the ship. You remember Lucas, the cab driver? He came out here to pick her up and take her to the station, but she wasn't here. She wasn't anywhere."

"I suppose the police have checked the usual sources?"

"Everything. Hospitals, morgues, everywhere. Lieutenant Reese says almost anything could have happened to her. She might have been robbed and murdered; she might have lost her memory; she might even have—" Aunt Faith blushed. "Well, this I'd *never* believe, but Lieutenant Reese says she might have disappeared deliberately— with some *man*."

Rowena had been at the window, drinking quietly. "I know what happened," she said.

David looked at her sharply.

"She just left. She just walked out of this gloomy old house and this crawly little town. She was sick of living alone. Sick of a whole town waiting for her to get married. She was tired of worrying about looms and loans and debentures. She was sick of being herself. That's how a woman can get."

She reached for the bottle, and David held her wrist. "Don't," he said. "You haven't eaten all day."

"Let me go," Rowena said softly.

He smiled, and let her go.

"I think the lieutenant was right," Rowena said. "I think there was a man, Auntie. Some vulgar type. Maybe a coal digger or a truck driver, somebody without any *charm* at all." She raised her glass in David's direction. "No charm at all."

Aunt Faith stood up, her plump cheeks mottled. "David, I have an idea—about how we can find Geraldine, I mean. I'm certain of it."

"Really?"

"But you're not going to agree with me. You're going to give me that nice smile of yours and you're going to humor me. But whether you approve or not, David, I'm going to ask Iris Lloyd where Geraldine is."

David's eyebrows made an arc. "Ask who?"

"Iris Lloyd," Aunt Faith said firmly. "Now don't tell me you've never heard of that child. There was a story in the papers about her only two months ago, and heaven knows I've mentioned her in my letters a dozen times."

"I remember," Rowena said, coming forward. "She's the one who's . . . psychic or something. Some sort of orphan?"

"Iris is a ward of the state, a resident at the Medvale Home for Girls. I've been vice-chairman of the place for donkey's years, so I know all about it. She's sixteen and amazing, David, absolutely uncanny!"

"I see." He hid an amused smile behind his glass. "And what makes Iris such a phenomenon?"

"She's a seer, David, a genuine clairvoyant. I've told you about this Count Louis Hamon, the one who called himself Cheiro the Great? Of course, he's dead now, he died in 1936, but he was gifted in the same way Iris is. He could just *look* at a person's mark and know the most astounding things—"

"Wait a minute. You really think this foundling can tell us where Geraldine is? Through some kind of séance?"

"She's not a medium. I suppose you could call her a *finder*. She seems to have the ability to *find* things that are lost. People, too."

"How does she do it, Mrs. Demerest?" Rowena asked.

"I can't say. I'm not sure Iris can either. The gift hasn't made her happy, poor child—such talents rarely do. For a while, it seemed like nothing more than a parlor trick. There was a Sister Theresa at the Home, a rather befuddled old lady who was always misplacing her thimble or what-have-you, and each time Iris was able to find it—even in the unlikeliest places."

David chuckled. "Sometimes kids *hide* things in the unlikeliest places. Couldn't she be some sort of prankster?"

"But there was more," Aunt Faith said gravely. "One day, the Home had a picnic at Crompton Lake. They discovered that an eight-year-old girl named Dorothea was missing. They couldn't find her, until Iris Lloyd began screaming."

"Screaming . . . ?" Rowena said.

"These insights cause her great pain. But she was able to describe the place where they would find Dorothea: a small natural cave, where Dorothea was found only half alive from a bad fall she had taken."

Rowena shivered.

"You were right," David said pleasantly. "I can't agree with you, Auntie. I don't go along with this spirit business; let's leave it up to the police."

Aunt Faith sighed. "I knew you'd feel that way. But I have to do this, David. I've arranged with the Home to have Iris spend some time with us, to become acquainted with the . . . aura of Geraldine that's still in the house."

"Are you serious? You've asked that girl *here?*"

"I knew you wouldn't be pleased. But the police can't find Geraldine, they haven't turned up a clue. Iris can."

"I won't have it," he said tightly. "I'm sorry, Auntie, but the whole thing is ridiculous."

"You can't stop me. I was only hoping that you would cooperate." She looked at Rowena, her eyes softening. "You understand me, my dear. I know you do."

Rowena hesitated, then touched the old woman's hands. "I do, Mrs. Demerest." She looked at David with a curious smile. "And I'd like nothing better than to meet Iris."

Ivy failed to soften the Medvale Home's cold stone substance and ugly lines. It had been built in an era that equated orphanages with penal institutions, and its effect upon David was depressing.

The head of the institution, Sister Clothilde, entered her office, sat down briskly, and folded her hands. "I don't have to tell you that I'm against this, Mrs. Demerest," she said. "I think it's completely wrong to encourage Iris in these delusions of hers."

Aunt Faith seemed cowed by the woman; her reply was timid. "Delusions, Sister? It's a gift of God."

"If this . . . ability of Iris' has any spiritual origin, I'm afraid it's from quite another place. Not that I admit there *is* a gift."

David turned on his most charming smile, but Sister Clothilde seemed immune to it.

"I'm glad to see I have an ally," he said. "I've been telling my aunt that it's all nonsense—"

Sister Clothilde bristled. "It's true that Iris has done some remarkable things which we're at a loss to explain. But I'm hoping she'll outgrow this—whatever it is, and be just a normal, happy girl. As she is now—"

"Is she very unhappy?" Aunt Faith asked sadly.

"She's undisciplined, you might even say wild. In less than two years, when she's of legal age, we'll be forced to release her from the Home, and we'd very much like to send her away a better person than she is now."

"But you *are* letting us have her, Sister? She can come home with us?"

"Did you think my poor objections carried any weight, Mrs. Demerest?"

A moment later, Iris Lloyd was brought in.

She was a girl in the pony stage, long gawky arms and legs protruding from a smock dress that had been washed out of all color and starched out of all shape. Her stringy hair was either dirty blond or just dirty; David guessed the latter. She had a flatfooted walk, and kept twisting her arms. She kept her eyes lowered as Sister Bertha brought her forward.

"Iris," Sister Clothilde said, "you know Mrs. Demerest. And this is her nephew, Mr. Wheeler."

Iris nodded. Then, in a flash almost too sudden to be observed, her eyes came up and stabbed them with such an intensity of either hostility or malice that David almost made his surprise audible. No one else, however, seemed to have noticed.

"You remember me, Iris," Aunt Faith said. "I've been coming here at least once a year to see all you girls."

"Yes, Mrs. Demerest," Iris whispered.

"The directors have been good enough to let us take you home with us for a while. We need your help, Iris. We want you to see if you can help us find someone who is lost."

"Yes, Mrs. Demerest," she answered serenely. "I'd like to come home with you. I'd like to help you find Miss Wheeler."

"Then you know about my poor niece, Iris?"

Sister Clothilde clucked. "The Secret Service couldn't have secrets here, Mrs. Demerest. You know how girls are."

David cleared his throat, and stood up. "I guess we can get started any time. If Miss Lloyd has her bags ready . . ."

Iris gave him a quick smile at that, but Sister Clothilde wiped it off with, "Please call her Iris, Mr. Wheeler. Remember that you're still dealing with a child."

When Iris' bags were in the trunk compartment, she climbed between David and his aunt in the front seat, and watched with interest as David turned the key in the ignition.

"Say," she said, "You wouldn't have a cigarette, would you?"

"Why, Iris!" Aunt Faith gasped.

She grinned. "Never mind," she said lightly. "Just never mind." Then she closed her eyes, and began to hum. She hummed to herself all the way to the Wheeler house.

David drove into town that afternoon, carrying a long list of groceries and sundries that Aunt Faith deemed necessary for the care and feeding of a sixteen-year-old girl.

He was coming out of the Medvale Supermarket when he saw Lucas Mitchell's battered black taxicab rolling slowly down the back slope of the parking lot. He frowned and walked quickly to his own car, but as he put the groceries in the rear, he saw Lucas' cab stop beside him.

"Hello, Mr. Wheeler," Lucas said, leaning out the window.

"Hello, Lucas. How's business?"

"Could I talk to you a minute, Mr. Wheeler?"

"No," David said. He went around front and climbed into the

driver's seat. He fumbled in his pocket for the key, and the sight of Lucas leaving his cab made it seem much more difficult to find.

"I've got to talk to you, Mr. Wheeler."

"Not here," David said. "Not here and not now, Lucas."

"It's important. I want to ask you something."

"For the love of Mike," David said, gritting his teeth. He found the key at last, and shoved it into the slit on the dashboard. "Get out of the way, Lucas. I can't stop now."

"That girl, Mr. Wheeler. Is it true about the girl?"

"What girl?"

"That Iris Lloyd. She does funny things, that one. I'm afraid of her, Mr. Wheeler. I'm afraid she'll find out what we did."

"Get out of the way!" David shouted. He turned the key, and stomped the accelerator to make the engine roar a threat. Lucas moved away, bewildered, and David backed the car out sharply and drove off.

He got home to find Rowena pacing the living room. Her agitation served to quiet his own. "What's wrong?" he said.

"I wouldn't know for sure. Better ask your aunt."

"Where is she?"

"In her room, lying down. All I know is she went up to see if dear little Iris was awake, and they had some kind of scene. I caught only a few of the words, but I'll tell you one thing, that girl has the vocabulary of a longshoreman."

David grunted. "Well, maybe it'll knock some sense into Aunt Faith. I'll go up to see her, and tell her I'll take that little psychic delinquent back where she came from—"

"I wouldn't bother her now; she's not feeling well."

"Then I'll see the little monster. Where is she?"

"Next door to us, in Geraldine's room."

At the door, he lifted his hand to knock, but the door was flung open before his knuckles touched wood.

Iris looked out, her hair tumbled over one eye. Her mouth went from petulant to sultry, and she put her hands on the shapeless uniform where her hips should be.

"Hello, handsome," she said. "Auntie says you went shopping for me."

"What have you been up to?" He walked in and closed the door. "My aunt isn't a well woman, Iris, and we won't put up with any bad behavior. Now, what happened here?"

She shrugged and walked back to the bed. "Nothing," she said sullenly. "I found a butt in an ash tray and was taking a drag when she walked in. You'd think I was burning the house down the way she yelled."

"I heard you did some fancy yelling yourself. Is that what the Sisters taught you?"

"They didn't teach me anything worthwhile."

Suddenly Iris changed; face, posture, everything. In an astonishing transformation, she was a child again.

"I'm sorry," she whimpered. "I'm awfully sorry, Mr. Wheeler. I didn't mean to do anything wrong."

He stared at her, baffled, not knowing how to take the alteration of personality. Then he realized that the door had opened behind him, and that Aunt Faith had entered.

Iris fell on the bed and began to sob, and with four long strides, Aunt Faith crossed the room and put her plump arms around her in maternal sympathy.

"There, there," she crooned, "it's all right, Iris. I know you didn't mean what you said, it's the Gift that makes you this way. And don't worry about what I asked you to do. You take your time about Geraldine, take as long as you like."

"Oh, but I *want* to help!" Iris said fervently. "I really do, Aunt Faith." She stood up, her face animated. "I can *feel* your niece in this house. I can almost hear her—whispering to me—telling me where she is!"

"You can?" Aunt Faith said in awe. "Really and truly?"

"Almost, almost!" Iris said, spinning in an awkward dance. She twirled in front of a closet, and opened the door; there were still half a dozen hangers of clothing inside. "These are *her* clothes. Oh, they're so beautiful! She must have looked beautiful in them!"

David snorted. "Has Iris ever seen a photo of Geraldine?"

The girl took out a gold lamé evening gown and held it in her arms. "Oh, it's so lovely! I can *feel* her in this dress, I can just *feel* her!" She looked at Aunt Faith with wild happiness. "I just know I'm going to be able to help you!"

"Bless you," Aunt Faith said. Her eyes were damp.

Iris was on her best behavior for the rest of the day; her mood extended all the way through dinner. It was an uncomfortable meal for everyone except the girl. She asked to leave the table before coffee was served, and went upstairs.

When the maid cleared the dinner table, they went to the living room, and David said, "Aunt Faith, I think this is a terrible mistake."

"Mistake, David? Explain that."

"This polite act of Iris'. Can't you see it's a pose?"

The woman stiffened. "You're wrong. You don't understand psychic personalities. It wasn't *her* swearing at me, David, it was this demon that possesses her. The same spirit that gives her the gift of insight."

Rowena laughed. "It's probably the spirit of an old sailor, judging from the language. Frankly, Aunt Faith, to me she seems like an ordinary little girl."

"You'll see," Aunt Faith said stubbornly. "You just wait and see how ordinary she is."

As if to prove Aunt Faith's contention, Iris came downstairs twenty minutes later wearing Geraldine Wheeler's gold lamé gown. Her face had been smeared with an overdose of makeup, and her stringy hair clumsily tied in an upsweep that refused to stay up. David and Rowena gawked at the spectacle, but Aunt Faith was only mildly perturbed.

"Iris, dear," she said, "what have you done?"

She minced into the center of the room. She hadn't changed her flat-heeled shoes, and the effect of her attempted gracefulness was almost comic; but David didn't laugh.

"Get upstairs and change," he said tightly. "You've no right to wear my sister's clothes."

Her face fell in disappointment and she looked at Aunt Faith. "Oh, Aunt Faith!" she wailed. "You know what I told you! I *have* to wear your niece's clothes, to feel her . . . aura!"

"Aura, my foot!" David said.

She stared at him, stunned. Then she fell into the wing chair by the fireplace and sobbed. Aunt Faith quickly repeated her ministrations of that afternoon, and chided David.

"You shouldn't have said that!" she said angrily. "The poor girl is trying to help us, David, and you're spoiling it!"

"Sorry," he said wryly. "I guess I'm just not a believer, Aunt Faith."

"You won't even give her a chance!"

Aunt Faith waited until Iris' sobs quieted, her face thoughtful. Then she leaned close to the girl's ear. "Iris, listen to me. You remember those things you did at the Home? The way you found things for Sister Theresa?"

Iris blinked away the remainder of her tears. "Yes."

"Do you think you could do that again, Iris? Right now, for us?"

"I—I don't know. I could try."

"Will you let her try, David?"

"I don't know what you mean."

"I want you to hide something, or name some object you've lost or misplaced, perhaps somewhere in this house."

"This is silly. It's a parlor game—"

"David!"

He frowned. "All right, have it your own way. How do we play this little game of hide-and-seek?"

Rowena said, "David, what about the cat?"

"The cat?"

"You remember. You once told me about a wool kitten you used to have as a child. You said you lost it somewhere in the house when you were five, and you were so unhappy about it that you wouldn't eat for days."

"That's preposterous. That's thirty years ago—"

"All the better," Aunt Faith said. "All the better, David." She turned to the girl. "Do you think you can find it, Iris? Could you find David's cloth kitten?"

"I'm not sure. I'm never sure, Aunt Faith."

"Just try, Iris. We won't blame you if you fail. It might have been thrown out ages ago, but try anyway."

The girl sat up, and put her face in her hands.

"David," Aunt Faith whispered, "put out the light."

David turned off the one table lamp that lit the room. The flames of the fireplace animated their shadows.

"Try, Iris," Aunt Faith encouraged.

The clock on the mantelpiece revealed its loud tick. Then Iris dropped her hands limply into her lap, and she leaned against the high back of the wing chair with a long, troubled sigh.

"It's a trance," Aunt Faith whispered. "You see it, David, you must see it. The girl is in a genuine trance."

"I wouldn't know," David said.

Iris' eyes were closed, and her lips were moving. There were drops of spittle at the corners of her mouth.

"What's she saying?" Rowena said. "I can't hear her."

"Wait! You must wait!" Aunt Faith cautioned.

Iris' voice became audible. "Hot," she said. "Oh, it's so hot . . . so hot . . ." She squirmed in the chair, and her fingers tugged at the neckline of the evening dress. "So hot back here!" she said loudly. "Oh, please! Oh, please! Kitty is hot! Kitty is hot!"

Then Iris screamed, and David jumped to his feet. Rowena came to his side and clutched his arm.

"It's nothing!" David said. "Can't you see it's an act?"

"Hush, please!" Aunt Faith said. "The girl is in pain!"

Iris moaned and thrashed in the chair. There were beads of perspiration on her forehead now, and her squirming, twisting body had all the aspects of a soul in hellfire.

"Hot! Hot!" she shrieked. "Behind the stove! Oh, please, oh please, oh please . . . so hot . . . kitty so hot . . ." Then she sagged in the chair and groaned.

Aunt Faith rushed to her side and picked up the thin wrists. She rubbed them vigorously, and said, "You heard her, David, you heard it for yourself. Can you doubt the girl now?"

"I didn't hear anything. A lot of screams and moans and gibberish about heat. What's it supposed to mean?"

"You *are* a stubborn fool! Why, the kitten's behind the stove, of course, where you probably stuffed it when you were a little brat of a boy!"

Rowena tugged his arm. "We could find out, couldn't we? Is the same stove still in the kitchen?"

"I suppose so. There's some kind of electronic oven, too, but they've never moved the old iron monster, far as I know."

"Let's look, David, please!" Rowena urged.

Iris was coming awake. She blinked and opened her eyes and looked at their watching faces. "Is it there?" she said. "Is it where I said it was? Behind the stove in the kitchen?"

"We haven't looked yet," David said.

"Then look," Aunt Faith commanded.

They looked, Rowena and David, and it was there, a dust-covered cloth kitten, browned and almost destroyed by three decades of heat and decay; but it was there.

David clutched the old plaything in his fist, and his face went white. Rowena looked at him sadly, and thought he was suffering the pangs of nostalgia, but he wasn't. He was suffering from fear.

In the beginning of May the rains vanished and were replaced by a succession of sunlit days. Iris Lloyd began to spend most of her time outdoors, communing with nature or her own cryptic thoughts.

That was where David found her one midweek afternoon, lying on the grass amid a tangle of daisies. She was dissecting one in an ancient ritual.

"Well," David said, "what's the answer?"

She smiled coyly, and threw the disfigured daisy away. "You tell me, Uncle David."

"Cut out the Uncle David stuff." He bent down to pick up the mutilated flower, and plucked off the remaining petals. "Loves me not," he said.

"Who? Your wife?" She smirked at him boldly. "You can't fool me, Uncle David. I know all about it."

He started to turn away, but she caught his ankle. "Don't go away. I want to talk."

He came back and squatted down to her level. "Look, what's the story with you, Iris? You've been here over a week and you haven't done anything about—well, you know what. This is just a great big picnic for you, isn't it?"

"Sure it is," she said. "You think I want to go back to that sticky Home? It's better here." She lay back on the grass. "No uniforms. No six a.m. prayers. None of that junk they call food." She grinned. "And a lot nicer company."

"I suppose I should say thank you."

"There's nothing you can say I don't know already." She tittered. "Did you forget? I'm psychic."

"Is it really true, Iris," he said casually, "or is it some kind of trick? I mean, these things you do."

"I'll show you if it's a trick." She covered her eyes with both hands. "Your wife hates you," she said. "She thinks you're rotten. You weren't even married a year when you started running around with other women. You never even went to the mill, not more'n once or twice a month, that was how *you* ran the business. All *you* knew how to do was spend the money."

David's face had grown progressively paler during her recitation. Now he grabbed her thin forearm. "You little brat! You're not psychic! You're an eavesdropper!"

"Let go of my arm!"

"Your room is right next door. You've been listening!"

"All right!" she squealed. "You think I could help hearing you two arguing?"

He released her wrist. She rubbed it ruefully, and then laughed, deciding it was funny. Suddenly she flung herself at him and kissed him on the mouth, clutching him with her thin, strong fingers.

He pushed her away, amazed. "What do you think you're doing?" he said roughly. "You dumb kid!"

"I'm not a kid!" she said. "I'm almost seventeen!"

"You were sixteen three months ago!"

"I'm a woman!" Iris shrieked. "But you're not even a man!" She struck him a blow on the chest with a balled fist, and it knocked the breath out of him. Then she turned and ran down the hill toward the house.

He returned home through the back of the estate and entered the kitchen. Aunt Faith was giving Hattie some silverware-cleaning instructions at the kitchen table. She looked up and said, "Did you call for a taxi, David?"

"Taxi? No, why should I?"

"I don't know. But Lucas' cab is in the driveway; he said he was waiting for you."

Lucas climbed out of the cab at David's approach. He peeled off the knitted cap and pressed it against his stomach.

"What do you want, Lucas?"

"To talk, Mr. Wheeler, like I said last week."

David climbed into the rear seat. "All right," he said, "drive someplace. We can talk while you're driving."

"Yes, sir."

Lucas didn't speak again until they were out of sight of the estate; then he said, "I did what you told me, Mr. Wheeler, 'zactly like you said. I hit her clean, she didn't hurt a bit, no blood. Just like an old steer she went down, Mr. Wheeler."

"All right," David said harshly. "I don't want to hear about it anymore, Lucas, I'm satisfied. You should be, too. You got your money, now forget about it."

"I picked her up," Lucas said dreamily. "I took her out in the woods, like you said, and I dug deep, deep as I could. The ground was awful hard then, Mr. Wheeler, it was a lot of work. I smoothed it over real good, ain't nobody could guess what was there. Nobody . . . except—"

"Is it that girl? Is that what's bothering you?"

"I heard awful funny things about her, Mr. Wheeler. About her findin' things, findin' that little kid what fell near Crompton Lake. She's got funny eyes. Maybe she can see right into that woman's grave—"

"Stop the car, Lucas!"

Lucas put his heavy foot on the brake.

"Iris Lloyd won't find her," David said, teeth clenched. "Nobody will. You've got to stop worrying about it. The more you worry, the more you'll give yourself away."

"But she's right behind the house, Mr. Wheeler! She's so close, right in the woods."

"You've got to forget it, Lucas, like it never happened. My sister's disappeared, and she's not coming back. As for the girl, let me worry about her."

He clapped Lucas' shoulder in what was meant to be reassurance, but his touch made Lucas stiffen.

"Now take me home," David said.

He worried about Iris for another five days, but she seemed to have forgotten the purpose of her stay completely. She was a house guest, a replacement for the missing Geraldine, and Aunt Faith's patience seemed inexhaustible as she waited for the psychic miracle to happen.

The next Thursday night, in their bedroom, Rowena caught David's eyes in the vanity mirror and started to say something about the mill.

"Shut up," he said pleasantly. "Don't say another word. I've found out that Iris can hear every nasty little quarrel in this room, so let's declare a truce."

"She doesn't have to eavesdrop, does she? Can't she read minds?" She swiveled around to face him. "Well, she's not the only clairvoyant around here. I can read her mind, too."

"Oh?"

"It's easy," Rowena said bitterly. "I can read every wicked thought in her head, every time she looks at you. I'm surprised you haven't noticed."

"She's a child, for heaven's sake."

"She's in love with you."

He snorted, and went to his bed.

"You're her Sir Galahad," she said mockingly. "You're going to rescue her from that evil castle where they're holding her prisoner. Didn't you know that?"

"Go to sleep, Rowena."

"Of course, there's still one minor obstruction to her plans. A small matter of your wife. But then, I've never been much of a hindrance to your romances, have I?"

"I've asked you for a truce," he said.

She laughed. "You're a pacifist, David, that's part of your famous charm. That's why you came up here in March, wasn't it? To make a truce with Geraldine?"

"I came here on business."

"Yes, I know. To keep Geraldine from sending you to prison, wasn't that the business?"

"You don't know anything about it."

"I have eyes, David. Not like Iris Lloyd, but eyes. I know you were taking money from the mill, too much of it. Geraldine knew it, too. How much time did she give you to make up the loss?"

David thought of himself as a man without a temper, but he found one now, and lost it just as quickly. "Not another word, you hear? I don't want to hear another word!"

He lay awake for the next hour, his eyes staring sightlessly into the dark of the room.

He was still awake when he heard the shuffle of feet in the corridor outside. He sat up, listening, and heard the quiet click of a latching door.

He got out of bed and put on his robe and slippers. There was a patch of moonlight on his wife's pillow; Rowena was asleep. He went noiselessly to the door and opened it.

Iris Lloyd, in a nightdress, was walking slowly down the stairway to the ground floor, her blond head rigid on her shoulders, moving with the mechanical grace of the somnambulist.

At the end of the hall, Aunt Faith opened her door and peered out, wide-eyed. "Is that you, David?"

"It's Iris," David said.

Aunt Faith came into the hallway, tying the housecoat around her middle, her hands shaking. David tried to restrain her from following the girl, but his aunt was stubborn.

They paused at the landing. Iris, her eyes open and unblinking, was moving frenetically around the front hall.

"What did I forget?" the girl mumbled. "What did I forget?"

Aunt Faith reached for David's arm.

"You're late," Iris said, facing the front door. "It's time we were going." She whirled and seemed to be looking straight at her spectators without seeing them.

"We have to be going!" she said, almost tearfully. "Oh, please get my luggage. I'm so nervous. I'm so afraid . . ."

"It's a trance," Aunt Faith whispered, squeezing his hand. "Oh, David, this may be it!"

"What did I forget?" Iris quavered. "Gas, electricity, phone, fireplace . . . Is the fireplace still lit? *Oh!*" She sobbed suddenly, and put her face in her hands.

David took a step toward her, and Aunt Faith said, "Don't! Don't waken her!"

Now Iris was walking, a phantom in the loose gown, toward the back of the house. She went to the kitchen and opened the screen door.

"She's going outside!" David said. "We can't let her—"

"Leave her alone, David! Please, leave her alone!"

Iris stepped outside into the back yard, following a path of moonlight that trailed into the dark woods.

"Iris!" David shouted. *"Iris!"*

"No!" Aunt Faith cried. "Don't waken her! You mustn't!"

"You want that girl to catch pneumonia?" David said furiously. "Are you crazy? Iris!" he shouted again.

She stopped at the sound of her name, turned, and the eyes went from nothingness to bewilderment. Then, as David's arms enclosed her, she screamed and struck at him. He fought to drag her back to the house, pinning her arms to her side. She was sobbing bitterly by the time he had her indoors.

Aunt Faith fluttered about her with tearful cries. "Oh, how could you do that, David?" she groaned. "You know you shouldn't waken a sleepwalker, you know that!"

"I wasn't going to let that child catch her death of cold! That would be a fine thing to tell the Sisters, wouldn't it, Auntie? That we let their little girl die of pneumonia?"

Iris had quieted, her head still cradled in her arms. Now she looked up and studied their strained faces. "Aunt Faith . . ."

"Are you all right, Iris?"

There was still a remnant of the sleepwalker's distant look in her round eyes. "Yes," she said. "Yes, I'm all right. I think I'm ready now, Aunt Faith. I can do it now."

"Do it now? You mean . . . tell us where Geraldine is?"

"I can try, Aunt Faith."

The old woman straightened up, her manner transformed. "We

must call Lieutenant Reese, David. Right now. He'll want to hear anything Iris says."

"Reese? It's after two in the morning!"

"He'll come," Aunt Faith said grimly. "I know he will. I'll telephone him myself; you take Iris to her room."

David helped the girl up the stairs, frowning at the closeness with which she clung to his side. Her manner was meek. She fell on her bed, her eyes closed. Then the eyes opened, and she smiled at him. "You're scared," she said.

He swallowed hard, because it was true. "I'm sending you back," he said hoarsely. "I'm not letting you stay in this house another day. You're more trouble than you're worth, just like Sister Clothilde said."

"Is that the reason, David?"

She began to laugh. Her laughter angered him, and he sat beside her and clamped his hand over her mouth.

"Shut up!" he said. "Shut up, you little fool!"

She stopped laughing. Her eyes, over the fingers of his hand, penetrated his. He put his arm to his side.

Iris leaned toward him. "David," she said sensuously, "I won't give you away. Not if you don't want me to."

"You don't know what you're talking about," he said uncertainly. "You're a fraud."

"Am I? You don't believe that."

She leaned closer still. He grabbed her with brutal suddenness and kissed her mouth. She moved against him, moaning, her thin fingers plucking at the lapel of his robe.

When they parted, he wiped his mouth in disgust and said, "What part of hell did you come from anyway?"

"David," she said dreamily, "you'll take me away from that place, won't you? You won't let me go back there, will you?"

"You're crazy! You know I'm married—"

"That doesn't matter. You can divorce that woman, David. You don't love her anyway, do you?"

The door opened. Rowena, imperious in her nightgown, looked at them with mixed anger and disdain.

"Get out of here!" Iris shrieked. "I don't want you in my room!"

"Rowena—" David turned to her.

His wife said, "I just came in to tell you something, David. You were right about the walls between these rooms."

"I hate you!" Iris shouted. "David hates you, too! Tell her, David. Why don't you tell her?"

"Yes," Rowena said. "Why don't you, David? It's the only thing you haven't done so far."

He looked back and forth between them, the hot-eyed young girl in the heavy flannel nightdress, the cool-eyed woman in silk, waiting to be answered, asking for injury.

"Damn you both!" he muttered. Then he brushed past Rowena and went out.

Lieutenant Reese still seemed half asleep; the stray hairs on his balding scalp were ruffled, and his clothes had the appearance of having been put on hastily. Rowena, still in nightclothes, sat by the window, apparently disinterested. Aunt Faith was at the fireplace, coaxing the embers into flames.

Iris sat in the wing chair, her hands clasped in her lap, her expression enigmatic.

When the fire started, Aunt Faith said, "We can begin any time. David, would you turn out the lamp?"

David made himself a drink before he dimmed the lights, and then went over to the chair opposite Iris.

Aunt Faith said, "Are you ready, my child?"

Iris, white-lipped, nodded.

David caught her eyes before they shut in the beginning of the trance. They seemed to recognize his unspoken, plaintive question, but they gave no hint of a reply.

Then they were silent. The silence lasted for a hundred ticks of the mantelpiece clock.

Gradually Iris Lloyd began to rock from side to side in the chair, and her lips moved.

"It's starting," Aunt Faith whispered. "It's starting."

Iris began to moan. She made sounds of torment and twisted her young body in an ecstasy of anguish. Her mouth fell open, and she gasped; the spittle frothed at the corners and spilled onto her chin.

"You've got to stop this," David said, his voice shaking. "The girl's having a fit."

Lieutenant Reese looked alarmed. "Mrs. Demerest, don't you think—"

"Please!" Aunt Faith said. "It's only the trance. You've seen it before, David, you know—"

Iris cried out.

Reese stood. "Maybe Mr. Wheeler's right. The girl might do herself some harm, Mrs. Demerest—"

"No, no! You must wait!"

Then Iris screamed, in such a mounting cadence of terror that the glass of the room trembled in sympathetic vibration, and Rowena put her hands over her ears.

"Aunt Faith! Aunt Faith!" Iris shrieked. "I'm here! I'm here, Aunt Faith, come and find me! Help me, Aunt Faith, it's dark! So dark! Oh, won't somebody help me?"

"Where are you?" Aunt Faith cried, the tears flooding her cheeks. "Oh, Geraldine, my poor darling, where are you?"

"Oh, help me! Help, please!" Iris writhed and twisted in the chair. "It's so dark, I'm so afraid! Aunt Faith! Do you hear me? Do you hear me?"

"We hear you! We hear you, darling!" Aunt Faith sobbed. "Tell us where you are! Tell us!"

Iris lifted herself from the chair, screamed again, and fell back in a fit of weeping. A few moments later, the heaving of her breast subsided, and her eyes opened slowly.

David tried to go to her, but Lieutenant Reese intervened. "One moment, Mr. Wheeler."

Reese went to his knees, and put his thumb on the girl's pulse. With his other hand, he widened her right eye and stared at the pupil. "Can you hear me, Iris? Are you all right?"

"Yes, sir, I'm all right."

"Do you know what happened just now?"

"Yes, sir, everything."

"Do you know where Geraldine Wheeler is?"

She looked at the circle of faces, and then paused at David's. His eyes pleaded.

"Yes," Iris whispered.

"Where is she, Iris?"

Iris' gaze went distant. "Someplace far away. A place with ships. The sun is shining there. I saw hills, and green trees . . . I heard bells ringing in the streets . . ."

Reese turned to the others, to match his own bewilderment with theirs.

"A place with ships. Does that mean anything to you?"

There was no reply.

"It's a city," Iris said. "It's far away."

"Across the ocean, Iris? Is that where Geraldine is?"

"No! Not across the ocean. Someplace here, in America, where there are ships. I saw a bay and a bridge and blue water—"

"San Francisco!" Rowena said. "I'm sure she means San Francisco, Lieutenant."

"Iris," Reese said sternly. "You've got to be certain of this, we can't chase all over the country. Was it San Francisco? Is that where you saw Geraldine?"

"Yes!" Iris said. "Now I know. There were trolleys in the streets, funny trolleys going uphill . . . It's San Francisco. She's in San Francisco!"

Reese got to his feet, and scratched the back of his neck. "Well, who knows?" he said. "It's as good a guess as I've heard. Has Geraldine ever been in San Francisco before?"

"Never," Aunt Faith said. "Why would she go there? David?"

"I don't know." David grinned. He went over to Iris and patted her shoulder. "But that's where Iris says she is, and I guess the spirits know what they're talking about. Right, Iris?"

She turned her head aside. "I want to go home," she said. "I want Sister Clothilde . . ." Then she began to cry, softly, like a child.

It was spring, but the day felt summery. When David and Aunt Faith returned from the Medvale Home for Girls, the old woman looked out of the car window, but the countryside charm failed to enliven her mood.

"Come on, you old gypsy"—David laughed—"your little clairvoyant was a huge success. Now all the police have to do is find Geraldine in San Francisco—if she hasn't taken a boat to the South Seas by now."

"I don't understand it," Aunt Faith said. "It's not like Geraldine to run away without a word. Why did she do it?"

"I don't know," David replied.

Later that day he drove into town. When he saw Lucas standing at the depot beside his black taxi, he pulled up and climbed out, the smile wide on his face. "Hello, Lucas. How's the taxi business?"

"Could be better." Lucas searched his face. "You got any news for me, Mr. Wheeler?"

"Maybe I do. Suppose we step into your office."

He clapped his hand on Lucas' shoulder, and Lucas preceded him into the depot office. He closed the door carefully, and told the cabman to sit down.

"It's all over," David said. "I've just come from the Medvale Home for Girls. We took Iris Lloyd back."

Lucas released a sigh from deep in his burly chest. "Then she didn't know? She didn't know where the—that woman was?"

"She didn't know, Lucas."

The cabman leaned back, and squeezed the palms of his hands together. "Then I did the right thing. I knew it was the right thing, Mr. Wheeler, but I didn't want to tell you."

"Right thing? What do you mean?"

Lucas looked up with glowing eyes, narrowed by what he might have thought was cunning. "I figured that girl could tell if the body was buried right outside the house. But she'd never find it if it was someplace else. Ain't that right? Someplace far away?"

A spasm took David by the throat. He hurled himself at Lucas and grabbed the collar of his wool jacket.

"What are you talking about? What do you mean, someplace else?" Lucas was too frightened to answer. "What did you do?" David shouted.

"I was afraid you'd be sore," Lucas whimpered. "I didn't want to tell you. I went out in the woods one night last week and dug up that woman's body. I put it in that trunk of hers, Mr. Wheeler, and I sent it by train, far away as I could get it. Farthest place I know, Mr. Wheeler. That's why Iris Lloyd couldn't find it. It's too far away now."

"Where? Where, you moron? San Francisco?"

Lucas mumbled his terror, and then nodded his shaggy head.

The baggagemaster listened intently to the questions of the two plainclothesmen, shrugged when they showed him the photograph of the woman, and then led them to the Unclaimed Baggage room in the rear of the terminal. When he pointed to the trunk that bore the initials G.W., the two men exchanged looks, and then walked slowly toward it. They broke open the lock, and lifted the lid.

Three thousand miles away, Iris Lloyd sat up in the narrow dormitory bed and gasped into the darkness, wondering what strange dream had broken her untroubled sleep.

BORN KILLER

Dorothy Salisbury Davis

Dorothy Salisbury Davis

Complex, often unwholesome, family relationships are hard to convey in the limited space of a short story. As is the revelation of how emotions that have been building over a long period of time can lead to a sudden explosion of violence. In "Born Killer" Dorothy Salisbury Davis has accomplished both feats.

About the story, Mrs. Davis writes from her home in Palisades, New York: "We moved from Chicago to northern Wisconsin when I was five. It was my father's dream and my mother's nightmare, and indeed so our farm life remained throughout my childhood and adolescence, and I grew up with a marvelous and terrible ambivalence.

"The first Christmas I remember my mother and I threshed through the snow and cut down a tree my size which we then trimmed with pictures we cut out of the Sears Roebuck catalogue. It remains the Christmas of my life. I left the farm after my mother's death when I was twenty. "Born Killer" comes out of that background. I suppose there is much of me in George, and now that I think about it, much of my mother as I saw her in Elizabeth. And the father is my father.

"It is my favorite among my own stories, but one with which I have never been satisfied. I have tried to write a screen play and a stage play of it, and perhaps some day, with deeper insight and less fear, I shall attempt it as a novel. I think so far I have only plucked the strings, not yet drawn the bow on the deeper melody I feel. The reader will scarcely see the shadowy threat of incest or the torment of a righteous man who fashions a blind faith in another man out of his own need for that man's decency. Some day perhaps . . . out of the loneliness, the longing, the anger and the flight, George ought to be able to come home."

A.M.

BORN KILLER

There is a sort of legend about Corporal George Orbach. More than one man of his outfit has summed him up as the only person he ever met who didn't know what fear was. They have a good many pat explanations, the way men will when they have nothing to do between patrols but pin labels on one another. "A born killer" is a favorite. A lieutenant called it "a suicidal complex." This particular phrase did not take with the men. A handful of sleeping pills, a loaded .32, they figure, and he could have died in bed without scurvy, without frostbite, and without Migs.

He was up once for rotation and asked to stay. Forced into regulation five-day leaves in Japan, he walks the streets there, striding along them like a farmer behind a plow who sees neither birds nor trees nor sky except to measure the daylight left in them. The one piece of information about himself which he ever volunteered was the remark: "I'll bet I've walked more than any goddam soldier in the infantry."

No one doubted it, which is strange only in the fact that George Orbach is just nineteen years old. He lied about his age when he signed up. At sixteen he said he was twenty-one, and the recruiting officer studied him trying to decide which way he was lying. He was bent like a man with something on his back, and his eyes were old; but his skin was smooth and his dirty nervous hands boy's hands.

"Home?"

"U.S.A."

"Where were you born, wise guy?"

"Masonville, Wisconsin. Ever hear of it?"

"They'll clip your tongue in the army, farm boy. Why don't you take a haircut?"

"I don't have any money."

"Family?"

"Don't have any."

"That's a shame. You ought to have an insurance beneficiary."

"What insurance?"

"What they make you take out before you go overseas."

"Look, mister . . ."

"Sir!"

"Sir. I got a sister. Put her down for it. Elizabeth Orbach, Route Three, Masonville, Wisconsin."

"That's better. How did you get to New York?"

"I walked."

"Fair game for the infantry. Got a police record, Orbach?"

"No, sir."

The recruiting sergeant watched him closely. "They'll extradite you if you have."

George slurred the word wearily. "I don't think they'll extradite me."

"Think it over." The sergeant gave him a card. "If you still want to join up, be at this address at eight o'clock tomorrow morning."

George was born in violence, in a storm that tore great pines out by the roots and so flattened the tall white birches that ten years later George himself, then given to visualizing good and evil, counted the stricken birches pure white souls bowed by the devil, as he scrambled over them on his shortcut home from Sunday school. But on the night he was born, his father killed a horse racing him to Masonville to bring the doctor. Electric wires were down, the phone dead, the truck useless on the washed-out road. George and his mother were attended by Elizabeth, twelve years old. George lived. His mother died.

Elizabeth learned more in going over George's lessons with him than she had in attending school herself. She was more delighted with his first, second, and third readers than he was, and when he was nine or so, he could not quite understand her pleasure in them. By then Elizabeth was over twenty, which to George meant that there was less difference in age between Elizabeth and their father than between his sister and himself.

"Do you believe all that about giants and princes?" he asked her more than once.

"They're nice," she would say. "They're real pretty. I like them."

Mike Orbach, who read only the Masonville weekly, *Hoard's Dairyman,* and the Bible, would shake his head. He should have liked to see her reading the Bible, but all he ever said was, "You just read whatever you like, honey. You got it coming to you."

George was further puzzled when, bringing home a geography and then a history, and books called literature which he could now read himself, he found Elizabeth still smiling over his tattered primers.

The world was at war then, and even to the backwoods of Wisconsin the mobile blood-bank units came. Across the lake, five of the Bergson boys went into service, but four were left and nothing changed very much. At the church basket-suppers there were more women than men, and Elizabeth was not unusual in having her father take her to the dances. Nor did she mind sitting them out. She smiled and nodded as the dancers passed her, and clapped her hands when a couple did an elaborate bow before her.

"She's so good-natured," George overheard Mrs. Bergson say once. "God's been kinder to them than he has to lots of us."

George could not see where the kindness of God had much to do with it. He was fourteen and going by bus to the township high school. Every day when he came home Elizabeth would have his dinner warm on the back of the stove—meat, potatoes, and vegetables, always in the one pot. It didn't have much taste, he discovered, after his lunches in the school cafeteria.

"Can't you put some sugar or salt or something in it, Liz?" he said one day.

The next day there were both sugar and salt, and more of them than his stomach could take. His father had come in from the barn for a cup of tea, for he liked to hear George tell of school as much as Elizabeth did. He scowled when George pushed the plate away.

"For Cripe's sake, Liz, what did you do to this?"

"Eat it," his father said quietly.

Elizabeth went out to the icebox in the back kitchen.

"I can't, Pa," George said.

"God damn you, eat it and keep your mouth shut!"

He had not heard his father swear before. He pulled the plate back and swallowed one mouthful after another, trying to deaden the taste with tea.

Elizabeth returned and watched him. "Sugar and salt," she said.

"It's swell," George murmured.

He went to his room to change his clothes, and changing them, caught sight of himself in the mirror. He moved close to it and examined his face. There was fuzz on his upper lip and on his chin. He twisted his neck that he might see himself from other angles. He was blond like his sister, but there all resemblance that he could find ended. He wondered which one—his sister or himself—did not belong in the family. The possibility that he might be an orphan did not hurt so much as the thought that there might be no bond of family between Elizabeth and him. But there was; he was sure of that. As long as he could remember, Liz had been taking care of him. He could remember her brushing his hair. Then he distinctly remembered his father taking the comb to part it. Liz put his shoes on when he was a child. His father tied the laces.

His face, as he stared at it, seemed to quiver—as though someone were jiggling the glass. He thrust himself into his work clothes and rushed out of the house. His father had already let the cows in and now was in the loft shoveling hay down the chute. The cows nearest it were straining in their stanchions, the metal of their collars jangling.

George measured their grain, and until the last one was fed they snorted and bellowed greedily. It was his practice to start at opposite ends on alternate days, and he was always annoyed that they had no appreciation of his fairness. That day he didn't care.

His father eased himself down the chute, dropping on the hay.

"You'll hurt yourself doing that, Pa. You should walk around."

"I was doing that before you was born."

"Where was I born?"

"Better get the milking pails."

"It's early. Where, Pa?"

"Right in the house there." The old man motioned toward it. The early darkness of winter was coming down fast.

"Was that when my mother died?"

"It was. Your sister took care of you till I got home. It was a terrible storm and I couldn't get Doc Blake to come. He was drunk. That's why I'll whip you if you ever take to liquor. Now get the buckets."

"Pa, what's the matter with Liz?"

His father looked at him. Even in the half-darkness he could see the anger in the old man's eyes.

"Who told you that?"

"Nobody. I can see. Maybe you told me something when you swore at me."

"She's raised you like she was your mother. There ain't ever going to be a woman love you like she's done." The old man drove the pitchfork down on the cement floor, striking sparks. "You've been hanging around that Jennie Bergson . . ."

"No, Pa."

"Don't 'no Pa' me. I seen you cutting out across the lake. Don't you go touching that girl, George. I've been watching her. She's just asking you to get her in trouble. That'd suit Neil Bergson fine. He's got too many girls to home now." He poked his finger into the boy's chest. "You don't touch a girl till you get one you want to marry. If you get feeling queer, you tell me about it, George. Maybe I can help you. I don't know. You can chop down trees." He made a wild gesture toward the woods. "We can read the holy Bible like I did. Now I'm going for the milking pails."

"Pa, what's all this got to do with Liz?"

"She's your sister, ain't she?"

The old man's voice cracked on the words, and George let him go, not wanting to see him cry. Their conversation never did make sense to the boy, although he thought about it many times. He did not try to talk about it to his father again, but he tried to be kinder toward his sister. He did not comment further upon her cooking, and sometimes, making a sort of game of it, he let her wash his hair, and then in turn washed and braided hers.

"Don't you tell," he'd say. "I don't want them calling me sissy."

"It's a secret," Elizabeth agreed. "I like secrets." She would examine herself at the mirror over the kitchen sink, smiling vacantly into it.

Now and then, after staying overnight in town with a schoolmate because of a late basketball game or class play, George would say to his father, "Pa, I need ten dollars for the house."

"Do you?" the old man always said, but it was not a question. He led the way into the parlor, where his rolltop desk stood, and from the window ledge above it took the key and unlocked the desk. Within it he kept a strongbox, also locked, and within that his cash and milk receipts, and over them a pearl-handled revolver.

"That's like giving a burglar a gun, keeping it there, Pa."

"Guns ought to be locked up," the old man said. He carried the revolver in his pocket once a month when he collected on the milk receipts and took the money into Masonville to the bank. Giving the boy the ten dollars, he would say, "Something special?"

"I want to surprise Liz and you."

Thus George brought home now a table lamp, again a cover for the daybed, curtains, and sometimes a dress for his sister. He went alone and picked them out, and watched furtively while he did it that a schoolmate did not come upon him unawares.

His friends began to come to the house, some of them old enough to drive a car, and George had learned to play the mouth organ. In the summertime they swam in the lake below the Orbach farm, and afterwards roasted hot dogs on the beach. George played the tunes he knew, and all of them sang loudly, their voices carrying up to the house so that Elizabeth and her father felt compelled to go down to where they were. They sat quietly, father and daughter, in the shadows, and only when the fire blazed up, were they to be seen and waved at, but not heard.

But one night, above a rollicking song, Elizabeth raised her voice in a high sweet reverie of her own. It was like a bird's song, native to the night and the great high pine trees and the stars. There was no one there who could have said what happened to them, hearing it, but afterwards, the boys always inquired of George about his sister. And they did it reverently, as they might point out the moon's rising or a shooting star. They thought her very shy. Some nights she did not make a sound, as if there was no one song which seemed especially to tempt her. But when she sang, all of them felt happier and somehow wiser, and George thought that it was her way of saying things she never managed to get out in words.

Mike Orbach had never known such prosperous days. He often remarked that things were bound to bust wide open soon. "When a farmer makes a living," he would say, "the rest of the country must be making fortunes." He bought a new car and a good bull, and was at last able to breed his own cattle.

In the late spring the usual migratory strays started dropping off the freight train and applying for work by the day. They would come and go until harvest time. Mostly they were men of George's father's age, lean and grimed with the dust of many roads, and all of them with one habit in common: they were always in search of a place to spit, as though the chaff of a thousand threshings was in their throats. The only qualification on which Orbach ever questioned a man was his sobriety. None of them admitted drinking, and most all of them drank, which he knew, but Orbach calculated his question to have a restraining influence. His only real measurement of a man was his day's work. The summer before George was to enter his third year of high school, Al Jackson came. He was at the breakfast table when George came in from chores one morning.

"This is George, my son," the old man said.

"My name's Jackson, Al Jackson. Glad to meet you, George." He half rose from the chair and extended his hand.

George was pleased at that, the handshake offered him as between men, and in itself a rare custom among the day workers. The handshake was firm but the hand soft, and George made up his mind then to keep his distance when the rookie started to wield a pitchfork.

"Al, here," his father said, "he's been in the army. He's going to take a day or so getting into shape. Man, how your back's going to ache."

There were plenty of men around already in good shape, George thought. There was not even the look of weather about Jackson. His face was newly sunburned, his nose peeling. Still, he was a big man, good-looking, and it might be fun to have someone around whose tongue wasn't wadded in his throat like a plug of tobacco.

"Can you milk?" George asked, for he did love to be relieved of that chore.

"Beg pardon?"

"Cows. Can you milk them?"

Jackson shook his head doubtfully. "I broke my arm a year back. It stiffened up on me. I don't think I'd do 'em justice."

This amused the old man, and Elizabeth, bringing the coffee pot, giggled. Jackson looked up at her and smiled. "That's the best oatmeal I've had since I left home."

Elizabeth blushed and had to set the pot on the table to get a better hold on it.

George, trying to blend his cereal with the milk, said, "It's got lumps in it."

"Maybe it's got lumps," Jackson said, "but the stuff I've been having could've been chipped off a rock pile." He reached across the table for the coffee pot. "Here, let me pour that for you. Sit down, miss."

"Her name's Elizabeth," the old man said.

"Really? That was my mother's name."

The right arm was limber enough with the coffee pot, George noticed.

But that summer George obtained his driver's license, and in the month between haymaking and threshing, and again between threshing and silo-filling, he spent his spare time in Masonville. His father paid him the wage of a hired hand on condition that he outfit himself for school that fall and buy his own books. It left him ample change for the jukebox and the trivia he needed to bolster his attentions to Thelma Sorinson, a classmate of whom he had grown very fond.

Many times, with Thelma sitting beside him in the Ford, he remembered his father's outbreak when he had asked him about Elizabeth, his warning that George was not to touch a girl he didn't intend to marry. George reasoned that he might be willing to mary Thelma some day if she would have him. She was pretty and she could dance like a feather in a whirlwind. Thelma didn't care much what George reasoned, for he had grown tall and he shaved now once a week.

More and more at home he talked about her. His father nodded and asked such questions as what church she attended and what her father did for a living. Al, who had a bedroom in the attic, played a lot of checkers with the old man and a card game called "War" with Elizabeth, so that he was around often enough to take his turn in conversation.

"You ought to invite her out sometime so we can take a look at her, George," Al said one morning.

It was the first time since Al's arrival that George had felt one way or another about him. Now he measured how much a part of the family Al had become. He went to church with them Sundays, having bought a suit with his first pay; he took his bath in the family tub where other hands had always scrubbed down at the dairy pump; his shirts and underwear hung on the line with the household wash every Monday. More than any one thing, it suddenly irked George that Elizabeth should do his underwear.

"What do you mean, 'we'?"

Al shrugged and winked at the old man. "I like to see a pretty girl as much as the next guy."

"I'll say you do."

"That's enough, George," his father interrupted.

"Who's coming?" Elizabeth asked.

"A pretty girl like you," Al said soothingly.

Elizabeth clapped her hands.

The old man was still talking through it. ". . . getting too big for your britches, driving off in a car and your pockets jingling . . ."

"For God's sake, Pa."

"You'll not swear in this house, boy."

George pushed back from the table, the anger choking him.

"He didn't mean no harm," Al said.

"I meant plenty!" George shouted.

Still Elizabeth clapped her hands. "When's she coming, George?"

"She's not coming ever, not here she's not!"

"Out! Outdoors with you." His father pointed, his finger trembling.

"I'll go when I'm ready," George said. "I live here, too."

But he went quickly and strode down the path to the chicken house. He caught up the scraper and basket and flung into the coop with such violence that the birds indoors fled screeching to the entry.

"His arm's not strong enough," George screamed after them, "to clean out a chicken coop, but he can bounce his backside on a tractor seat all day!"

It was milking time before George saw his father, for he did not go into the house at noon, tearing a few ears of corn from the stalks and eating them raw in the field.

"What have you got against him, George?" the old man asked when they met at chores.

"I don't know, Pa. All of a sudden it just seemed to me there was something bad about him. Maybe the way he looks at Liz."

"And maybe the way you're jealous, son?"

George did not look up. He had been afraid all afternoon that that was it. "Maybe," he admitted.

The old man weighed the words before he said them. "I'm hoping he's going to marry Elizabeth."

George could feel a sickness rising in him. "Oh no, Pa!"

"She isn't going to have you and me to look out for her always. Already you got a girl."

"And you?"

The old man squinted at him. "There's a place for me beside your mother. It's just looking at things straight. Nobody lives forever."

George thought about it. "But him, Pa. What's he see in Liz?"

He knew he had put it wrong the moment the words were out, for the anger flickered up in his father's eyes. But he spoke slowly and the anger eased away. "Can you tell me why you think a sunset's pretty and you wouldn't look up at the sun at noon? Can you tell me why?"

George shrugged.

"I couldn't tell you either. I think a shock of corn is beautiful. But there's some folks who'd tell you it reminded them of scarecrows. Now I think Elizabeth is beautiful."

"So do I, Pa."

"Do you, boy? Do you really? You better look down deep inside yourself. I ain't waiting for the answer, but you better look."

George tried to look while he went about the chores, but he knew he was missing the heart of the matter. Still, he searched his memory for moments when he had loved his sister best. He dwelt especially on her singing near the campfire, and since he had not brought about such occasions this summer, he thought he had struck upon his father's meaning. It was true, he had neglected the most beautiful thing about her.

Going into the house at suppertime, he decided that an apology was due Al for the morning's incident. He tried to summon the courage for it. But Al greeted him heartily as though he had been off on a vacation, and because he had decided Al deserved an apology he disliked and distrusted him for not expecting it.

Within the week, George arranged a beach party. It was too late in the season for swimming, but the full moon rose early over the lake, and as they huddled near the fire, boys and girls, their song was like a serenade to its great gold face. They were a long time singing before Elizabeth joined her melody to theirs, and her voice came faint and tentative at first, like a bird's mimicry. George, his arm in Thelma's as they swayed to the music, felt a startled pressure from her, and glanced up to see her smile as she withdrew from him. She was not sharing her discovery with him. It was a quick and private ecstasy, and he realized this must happen to everyone. Catching beauty was a selfish thing. A person had to catch it alone before he could share it. Elizabeth had found the courage of her voice now; she sang out her wordless music as she had never done before. And George had never felt so lonely.

He got up and moved away from the fire. He watched in the shadows while another boy filled in his place. He saw that boy pull Thelma down backwards and kiss her quickly, as one couple and then another were doing.

He turned away and his eyes grew accustomed to far images lighted only by the moon. Elizabeth stopped her song abruptly, and George climbed up from the beach. He trod amid the debris cautiously and searched the shadows. His eyes found her and Al, except that they were almost one person, so close was their embrace. He started toward them. Soundlessly, his father caught him from behind, whirled him around to face his own party and shoved him toward it. George went, but he sat apart and joined no more songs that night, blaming himself for having opened the full measure of his sister's beauty to her lover.

He stayed at home more after that and tried to pretend to a camaraderie with Al, asking him all sorts of questions about the army, his family, his schooling. Al parried the questions like an experienced boxer would an amateur, always keeping him at arm's length. He could tell him he'd served in Afghanistan, George realized, and he could not prove otherwise. On an inquiry about his family, Al said he was an orphan. George remembered the day he came, his saying that his mother's name was Elizabeth. Apparently George showed triumph in his face, because Al drawled, "When you don't have one of your own, you're liable to call any woman who's good to you 'mother.' Ain't that a fact, George?"

He retreated, bested in that as he was in all such encounters, and hated himself for it. He grew sullen, and now when Elizabeth sang often, even about the house as she had never done before, he snapped at her for it. She merely laughed and was still for a few moments. Then, her happiness bubbling up like spittle in a baby's mouth, she would have to let out the sound of it. He fled outdoors.

His father spent almost every evening poring over the Bible. Sometimes, coming on a phrase especially to his liking, he would read it aloud. "Ah," he would say as though he had discovered something for which he had been searching, "ah, listen to this." And he would read a passage, most often describing monumental sins true penitents had been forgiven.

From this, too, George fled.

His father came on him shivering in the pumphouse one night when it was time for him to start back to school. Cornered there, George took a screwdriver to the pump motor.

"There's nothing wrong with that," the old man said, watching him tinker in hurried clumsiness. "Put down your tools for a minute."

George obeyed him.

"A few years back," the old man started, "I was thinking serious of marrying Miss Darling . . ."

Miss Darling had been George's Sunday school teacher.

". . . I figured we'd go away awhile, her and me, and then come back to the farm. That way I thought you and Liz would be so glad to see me, you'd like her here, too. . . ."

George felt something drop down inside him like a plunger.

"But things weren't as good as now, and it just got put off until it was too late. I'm going to send you away to school this year, son. I talked to Reverend Johns about it. He's recommending me a school after service tonight."

"Pa, I don't want to go."

"You always took to books. Now's your chance. No chores, no milking. You can go to the University then."

"No, Pa."

The old man looked at him. "Elizabeth and Al's getting married next week. I don't want you around then, George, the way you're acting."

George could not hold back the tears. "Pa, wait. Make them wait. Ask him where he came from. What does he want with us? Maybe he's got a wife already some place . . . He's thirty, Pa . . ."

"He's being baptized tonight," the old man interrupted. "The Lord is cleansing him whatever sins he's done. I'm satisfied in that. He's seen salvation."

"He's seen a farm and a sucker!" George shouted.

The old man struck him hard across the face, the force of the blow knocking the boy backwards. The fanbelt broke his fall, but before he got to his feet the old man was at the door. He turned and looked back at his son, his eyes streaming. "All we seem to do any more is hurt each other."

When he was gone, the stench of sulphur from the well added to George's nausea. He went outdoors and retched. He was sitting on the stone hedge when he heard the car drive out. He watched for the taillight to appear on the highway, and seeing it, went into the house.

He could hear the clock tick in the stillness, and the water dripping at the sink. There was no other sound and he went up the steps to Al's room. He searched every drawer, finding nothing but clothes; not a letter, not a paper nor a picture, not even an army "dog tag." He almost tore the bed apart, and that search, too, was futile.

"Satisfied, kid?"

The boy whirled around. Al had climbed the stairs without a sound.

"You're supposed to be in church," George blurted out.

"And you're past due for hell," Al said, drawling the words as though there were no threat in them. "What did you find against me, George?"

Everything, George thought, but he could name nothing. He stood, stiff-tongued and awkward in every limb, while Al sauntered to the window and looked out. "I work hard, I go to church regular, and I'm going to marry your sister. I don't know another guy who'd do that."

George clenched his fists and managed but one step forward. Al spun around, holding in his hand the pearl-handled revolver.

"That's Pa's gun," George said.

"Pa's gun and Pa's bullets. You're a fool, kid. We could've got along fine, the four of us."

George was near to tears, fear and hatred torturing him. "Liz," he cried. "You don't love her. I know it. I can't prove it, but I know it."

"So what? Just so what? I never saw the beat of you and your old man for playing God almighty."

Al moved a step toward him, the gun real and steady in his hand.

The fear grew thick in George's throat. "What are you going to do?" he managed.

"You've been on your way to suicide a long time. I'm going to help you."

"Oh no," George moaned.

"Oh yes. Think about it, kid, the way you've been carrying on. Can't you just hear the old man saying, 'I should've put the gun away. I never should've left it where he could get at it.'"

Oh God, George thought, please God, help me. "Pa!" he called out, with the only responding sound the twitter of nesting birds. "Liz!"

"For just once we're going to be real close," Al mocked, coming on.

And at that instant, from the oak tree just outside the window, a bird sounded one last high burst of song.

Al started at the sound and jerked his head. George scarcely knew the impulse, but he leaped at the farmhand, striking the gun from his hand and following it to the floor. Even from there he started firing, the first shots wild, but one finding Al as he plunged toward him. The boy emptied the gun into the fallen body. Then he flung the revolver from him and groped his way through the smoke. Downstairs, he called the county sheriff's office and waited, his mind as empty as the gun.

The sheriff came a few minutes before his father and sister, and he told what he had done while a deputy intercepted the family outdoors. He repeated the circumstances, and took the sheriff to his father's desk to show him where the gun was kept. It had been taken out in haste the moment of his father's departure, George realized, for the rolltop was up and the strongbox gaping. The sheriff shook his head, studying the boy, and George thought vaguely that the truth was not so apparent to the sheriff as it was to him.

Then the sheriff went upstairs, and George heard a car drive out. Presently another, or the same car, drove in again. His father must have taken Elizabeth somewhere. To the Bergsons', he thought. The old man came in. He didn't look at George where he was sitting on the daybed in the parlor. He went to his desk and stared at it without touching anything. He, too, was thinking George had taken the gun and gone upstairs to find Al, the boy reasoned.

The sheriff came down. "Sorry, Orbach," he said to George's father.

The old man looked at him.

The sheriff rubbed his neck. "He was marrying your daughter, was he?"

Orbach nodded, his face a dumb mask of pain.

"You got to believe me," George said then. He knew he was whining, but he couldn't help it. "He'd of killed me. I didn't take the gun, *he* did."

"I believe you, boy," the sheriff said. "Maybe this is all for the best. I just got an alarm on that guy at the office. Murder, while committing robbery. I think he was holing in here."

The old man raised his head and cried out, "It is not all for the best!"

George forced himself to his feet, a terrible realization striking through his sick relief. "Pa! Did you know about him? Did you know that?"

His father lifted his eyes and his voice to the ceiling: "There's things we are not meant to know. God's mercy should not be thwarted by the vengeance of men. Vengeance is Mine, sayeth the Lord."

George stumbled from the room and then outdoors.

"Let him go," he heard the sheriff call. "He'll come back in soon."

But George did not go back. They may not understand him in the army, not knowing all these things. But his buddies are agreed on one thing: he makes a good soldier; and most of them think of George as "a born killer"—that's how little they understand. . . .

PUTTING THE PIECES BACK

Bill Pronzini

Bill Pronzini

According to Bill Pronzini, "Most writers have favorite 'thinking places' whereat—or wherein—they develop ideas for stories and novels. Mine happens to be the bathtub (filled with warm water, naturally), and while I'm tempted to make a pun about all the plots that have ended up going down the drain, I'll refrain from doing so. But the idea for "Putting the Pieces Back" uncharacteristically came in my living room, after I had finished watching a terrible TV suspense movie which featured a character not dissimilar to Fred DeBeque in these pages. The TV character went around doing all sorts of implausible detective-type things, and emerged triumphant in the final scenes mostly as a result of coincidence, illogic, and a rather amazing ability to handle an automobile like a stunt driver. It seemed to me that none of this had anything to do with real life, whereupon I asked myself what might actually happen to such a 'hero' in the real world. My imagination being what it is, the answer I decided on, as you'll see, is somewhat bizarre."

A native of Petaluma, California ("The Egg Basket of the World"), Pronzini sold his first short story in 1966 and has been a full-time writer since 1969. His published words number an impressive two million. He is the author of fourteen suspense novels and approximately a hundred and seventy short stories and articles. He now lives with his wife and two cats in a house in San Francisco, which, he claims, contains the most prolific bathtub west of the Mississippi River.

If, as some maintain, a good short story is harder to write than a novel, a good short short story is even harder. And "Putting the Pieces Back" is a very good short short story.

A.M.

PUTTING THE PIECES BACK

You wouldn't think a man could change completely in four months —but when Kaprelian saw Fred DeBeque come walking into the Drop Back Inn, he had living proof that it could happen. He was so startled, in fact, that he just stood there behind the plank and stared with his mouth hanging open.

It had been a rainy off-Monday exactly like this one the last time he'd seen DeBeque, and that night the guy had been about as low as you could get and carrying a load big enough for two. Now he was dressed in a nice tailored suit, looking sober and normal as though he'd never been through any heavy personal tragedy. Kaprelian felt this funny sense of flashback come over him, like the entire last seven months hadn't even existed.

He didn't much care for feelings like that, and he shook it off. Then he smiled kind of sadly as DeBeque walked over and took his old stool, the one he'd sat on every night for the three months after he had come home from work late one afternoon and found his wife bludgeoned to death.

Actually, Kaprelian was glad to see the change in him. He hadn't known DeBeque or DeBeque's wife very well before the murder; they were just people who lived in the neighborhood and dropped in once in a while for a drink. He'd liked them both, though, and he'd gotten to know Fred pretty well afterward, while he was doing all that boozing. That was why the change surprised him as much as it did.

He'd been sure DeBeque would turn into a Skid Row bum or a corpse, the way he put down the sauce; a man couldn't drink like that more than maybe a year without ending up one or the other.

The thing was, DeBeque and his wife really loved each other. He'd been crazy for her, worshiped the ground she walked on—Kaprelian had never loved anybody that way, so he couldn't really understand it. Anyhow, when she'd been murdered DeBeque had gone all to pieces. Without her, he'd told Kaprelian a few times, he didn't want to go on living himself; but he didn't have the courage to kill himself either. Except with the bottle.

There was another reason why he couldn't kill himself, DeBeque said, and that was because he wanted to see the murderer punished, and the police hadn't yet caught him. They'd sniffed around DeBeque himself at first, but he had an alibi and, anyway, all his and her friends told them how much the two of them were in love. So then, even though nobody had seen any suspicious types in the neighborhood the day it happened, the cops had worked around with the theory that it was either a junkie who'd forced his way into the DeBeque apartment or a sneak thief that she'd surprised. The place had been ransacked and there was some jewelry and mad money missing. Her skull had been crushed with a lamp, and the cops figured she had tried to put up a fight.

So DeBeque kept coming to the Drop Back Inn every night and getting drunk and waiting for the cops to find his wife's killer. After three months went by, they still hadn't found the guy. The way it looked to Kaprelian then—and so far that was the way it had turned out—they never would. The last night he'd seen DeBeque, Fred had admitted that same thing for the first time and then he had walked out into the rain and vanished. Until just now.

Kaprelian said, "Fred, it's good to see you. I been wondering what happened to you, you disappeared so sudden four months ago."

"I guess you never expected I'd show up again, did you, Harry?"

"You want the truth, I sure didn't. But you really look great. Where you been all this time?"

"Putting the pieces back together again," DeBeque said. "Finding new meaning in life."

Kaprelian nodded. "You know, I thought you were headed for Skid

Row or an early grave, you don't mind my saying so."

"No, I don't mind. You're absolutely right, Harry."

"Well—can I get you a drink?"

"Ginger ale," DeBeque said. "I'm off alcohol now."

Kaprelian was even more surprised. There are some guys, some drinkers, you don't ever figure *can* quit, and that was how DeBeque had struck him at the tag end of those three bad months. He said, "Me being a bar owner, I shouldn't say this, but I'm glad to hear that too. If there's one thing I learned after twenty years in this business, you can't drown your troubles or your sorrows in the juice. I seen hundreds try and not one succeed."

"You tried to tell me that a dozen times, as I recall," DeBeque said. "Fortunately, I realized you were right in time to do something about it."

Kaprelian scooped ice into a glass and filled it with ginger ale from the automatic hand dispenser. When he set the glass on the bar, one of the two workers down at the other end—the only other customers in the place—called to him for another beer. He drew it and took it down and then came back to lean on the bar in front of DeBeque.

"So where'd you go after you left four months ago?" he asked. "I mean, did you stay here in the city or what? I know you moved out of the neighborhood."

"No, I didn't stay here." DeBeque sipped his ginger ale. "It's funny the way insights come to a man, Harry—and funny how long it takes sometimes. I spent three months not caring about anything, drinking myself to death, drowning in self-pity; then one morning I just woke up knowing I couldn't go on that way any longer. I wasn't sure why, but I knew I had to straighten myself out. I went upstate and dried out in a rented cabin in the mountains. The rest of the insight came there: I knew why I'd stopped drinking, what it was I had to do."

"What was that, Fred?"

"Find the man who murdered Karen."

Kaprelian had been listening with rapt attention. What DeBeque had turned into wasn't a bum or a corpse but the kind of comeback hero you see in television crime dramas and don't believe for a minute. When you heard it like this, though, in real life and straight from the gut, you knew it had to be the truth—and it made you feel good.

Still, it wasn't the most sensible decision DeBeque could have reached, not in real life, and Kaprelian said, "I don't know, Fred, if the cops couldn't find the guy—"

DeBeque nodded. "I went through all the objections myself," he said, "but I knew I still had to try. So I came back here to the city and I started looking. I spent a lot of time in the Tenderloin bars, and I got to know a few street people, got in with them, was more or less accepted by them. After a while I started asking questions and getting answers."

"You mean," Kaprelian said, astonished, "you actually got a line on the guy who did it—"

Smiling, DeBeque said, "No. All the answers I got were negative. No, Harry, I learned absolutely nothing—except that the police were wrong about the man who killed Karen. He wasn't a junkie or a sneak thief or a street criminal of any kind."

"Then who was he?"

"Someone who knew her, someone she trusted. Someone she would let in the apartment."

"Makes sense, I guess," Kaprelian said. "You have any idea who this someone could be?"

"Not at first. But after I did some discreet investigating, after I visited the neighborhood again a few times, it all came together like the answer to a mathematical equation. There was only one person it could be."

"Who?" Kaprelian asked.

"The mailman."

"The *mailman?*"

"Of course. Think about it, Harry. Who else would have easy access to our apartment? Who else could even be *seen* entering the apartment by neighbors without them thinking anything of it, or even remembering it later? The mailman."

"Well, what did you do?"

"I found out his name and I went to see him one night last week. I confronted him with knowledge of his guilt. He denied it, naturally; he kept right on denying it to the end."

"The end?"

"When I killed him," DeBeque said.

Kaprelian's neck went cold. "Killed him? Fred, you can't be serious! You didn't actually *kill* him."

"Don't sound so shocked," DeBeque said. "What else could I do? I had no evidence, I couldn't take him to the police. But neither could I allow him to get away with what he'd done to Karen. You understand that, don't you? I had no choice. I took out the gun I'd picked up in a pawnshop, and I shot him with it—right through the heart."

"Jeez," Kaprelian said. "Jeez."

DeBeque stopped smiling then and frowned down into his ginger ale; he was silent, kind of moody all of a sudden. Kaprelian became aware of how quiet it was and flipped on the TV. While he was doing that the two workers got up from their stools at the other end of the bar, waved at him and went on out.

DeBeque said suddenly, "Only then I realized he couldn't have been the one."

Kaprelian turned from the TV. "What?"

"It couldn't have been the mailman," DeBeque said. "He was left-handed, and the police established that the killer was probably right-handed. Something about the angle of the blow that killed Karen. So I started thinking who else it could have been, and then I knew: the grocery delivery boy. Except we used two groceries, two delivery boys, and it turned out both of them were right-handed. I talked to the first and I was sure he was the one. I shot him. Then I knew I'd been wrong, it was the other one. I shot him too."

"Hey," Kaprelian said. "Hey, Fred, what're you *saying?*"

THE PHILIPPINE KEY MYSTERY

James Holding

James Holding

The puzzle-type story has probably drawn a larger number of readers and created more fictional immortals than all other types of mysteries combined. Poe's C. Auguste Dupin, Doyle's Sherlock Holmes, Christie's Hercule Poirot, Kemelman's Rabbi Small—the list of famous characters who have come to life for millions by solving seemingly unsolvable cases is a long one. The hidden clue, the unnoticed detail, the incongruous fact picked up by the sleuth but by no one else is the magic of such stories, and powerful magic it is.

"The Philippine Key Mystery" is a fine example of the puzzle story. James Holding, its author, is a native of Pittsburgh, a Yale graduate and a former advertising man. After resigning as vice-president and copy chief of Batten, Barton, Durstine & Osborne, he turned to free-lance writing and has since published nearly two hundred short mystery stories and eighteen children's books, many with foreign backgrounds observed in extensive travels about the world. He lives now on Siesta Key in Sarasota, Florida.

About "The Philippine Key Mystery" he says: "During a visit to Zamboanga in the Philippines, I toured the San Ramon Penal Colony, and in chatting with the prison governor afterward, was told that no prisoner had ever succeeded in breaking out of it. In view of this interesting fact, I was tempted to speculate on how an escape from this high-security prison *might* be effected by a determined prisoner, and the following story was the result."

A.M.

THE PHILIPPINE KEY MYSTERY

Even in the most far-fetched fictional mystery written by the collaborative team of Leroy King, a simple plate of fish soup had never led to the capture of a murderer. Yet in Zamboanga City, on the island of Mindanao in the Philippines, that's exactly what happened. . . .

The cruise ship *Valhalla* anchored in Zamboanga Harbor early in the morning. Immediately most of her passengers debarked by tender for a long, hot, tiring day of sightseeing in the city and its environs. Now, with the cocktail hour upon them, the Danforths and the Leroys decided to have dinner ashore at the Bayot Hotel, attracted to this hostelry by its famous specialty, *sinegang*—a superb fish soup which King Danforth, a fancier of chowders, was eager to sample.

They dined outdoors on a harborside terrace where the sea breeze intermittently afforded them some slight relief from the enervating heat that persisted even after sundown. And the *sinegang,* they unanimously agreed, was all that was claimed for it.

As they ate, a *vinta,* one of those outrigger canoes on which many Moros spend their entire lives, appeared out of the dusk of the harbor and nudged against the sea wall beside which their table was set. A man and woman, dark-skinned, both paddled the craft. A little girl of four or five years crouched amidships among the motley array of tourist goods which those sea gypsies had for sale.

With ingratiating grimaces and pleading singsong words in incomprehensible Tagalog, the child held up one item after another to the

Americans, urging them to buy: shirts of *jusi* and *piña* cloth, made from banana and pineapple fronds; hand-carved statuettes of a lemon-colored wood; bouquets of brilliant tropical blooms; glistening shells gathered from the sea bottom.

Helen Leroy was captivated at once by this small saleslady. "Oh, Mart," she said to her husband, "buy one of her shells for me, please. Isn't she a darling, Carol?"

Carol Danforth nodded. "And the only woman I've seen in Zamboanga who appears comfortably dressed for the climate," she said. The Moro child wore only a sketchy loincloth of a nondescript color —like the lower part of a bikini.

"Just what we need," said Martin Leroy. "A helmet shell from Zamboanga that must weigh five pounds if it weighs an ounce. With the dead animal still in it, too, I'll bet. I think I can smell it from here."

"A bunch of flowers then," urged Helen. "How can you possibly resist that innocent child? Are you completely heartless?"

Leroy stepped to the sea wall. "Flowers it is, then. How much for those flowers?" he asked the child, pointing.

A beatific smile transfigured the thin brown face. "Four pesos," she replied in perfect English. "Or one American dollar."

Danforth laughed. "Some innocent little salesgirl," he said. "I'll bet she speaks Spanish, too."

"*Si. Si,*" the girl piped. "You want flowers? Please?"

"For a buck I'll take a chance," Leroy agreed. He fumbled in his pocket for the money.

"A dollar and a quarter if I dive," the child said quickly. "You got a quarter, Mister?"

The others joined Leroy at the sea wall. "What does she mean?" asked Carol.

"Dive," said the child. "In the water. Here." She handed up the flowers, accepted a dollar bill from Leroy, then passed it to her father. "Now throw quarter in water, sir. Sea very deep here. I dive for quarter and bring it up. You watch, yes?"

"Okay," said Leroy. He tossed a quarter out into the black water about five yards beyond the *vinta*.

Almost before it left his hand, the little girl arched over the canoe's outrigger in a clean pure dive. She stayed under for a few moments, then her head bobbed to the surface. She shook water from her hair. Holding one small hand aloft, she swam rapidly back to the canoe. By the smoky light of the lanterns that were spaced along the sea wall to illuminate the dining terrace and the water's edge, they could see the silver winking of Leroy's quarter in her uplifted palm.

"Wonderful!" Carol Danforth clapped her hands.

The child, all smiles, climbed back into the canoe, with water streaming from her brief bathing costume. Suddenly Danforth smothered an exclamation. "Do you see what I see?" he said to Leroy.

Leroy nodded. "Her—pants?" His eyes were intent.

"Yes." They both stared at the small diver's loincloth, lighted quite well now by the lantern light shining into the *vinta*.

"What are you two muttering about?" Helen Leroy asked, and then she broke off and stared too.

Carol gave an uncertain laugh. "The color?" she said. "Is that what's bothering you?"

Danforth said, "Unless I'm color blind, that's it."

"Masked by some vegetable dyes, maybe," Leroy offered, "but the real color comes through when it's wet."

Helen spoke indignantly. "You can't tell me that little five-year-old is a convicted criminal!"

"Maybe it's her father," Leroy said.

"Nonsense!" Carol joined Helen in protest. "It's a trick of the light, that's all."

Danforth said slowly, "Just the same, I'm going to call Señor Bollo."

Señor Bollo was the governor of San Ramon Penal Colony, situated a few miles outside Zamboanga. They had met him only a few hours before, while sipping tea in the grateful shade of an awning directly across the road from the forbidding stone entrance to the prison farm. Their cruise director had brought the prison governor to their table and introduced him.

"And these people," the director had finished, "are the Danforths and the Leroys, Señor Bollo. You may have heard of the two gentlemen. They write crime fiction under the pen name of Leroy King."

Señor Bollo, short and coffee-colored, inclined politely from the waist. "I have indeed heard of Leroy King," he said. "As who has not? This is a great pleasure, sirs." His English was excellent. "Even here in Zamboanga your fame is known."

"Won't you sit down, Señor Bollo?" asked Helen Leroy, extending a slender hand in invitation. "You might as well, because our husbands will probably want to ask you a million questions about your prison." She nodded toward it. "We've just been given the grand tour, you know."

Bollo took the empty chair at their table. The cruise director excused himself and shot off on another errand. Carol Danforth poured Señor Bollo a cup of tea.

The prison governor waved a hand at the sapphire sea sparkling in the sunlight a hundred yards away, at the strip of white beach that edged it, at the gently swaying palm trees which sheltered the terrace on which they sat. "Have you ever seen a high-security prison in a more beautiful setting?" he asked with pride in his voice.

"Never," said Helen, flashing him her devastating smile. "I'd almost be willing to *be* one of your prisoners, señor, just for the view alone!"

With unmistakable warmth the prison official said, "And I would welcome you as one of my prisoners, Mrs. Leroy!" His glance paid silent homage to her blond beauty.

King Danforth rubbed a palm over his crewcut and burrowed in his chair to get more comfortable. "Judging from our tour of your prison, Señor Bollo, you run a model institution."

Bollo bowed courteously. "Thank you."

"And judging from your handicraft shops and extensive gardens, you place a great deal of emphasis on rehabilitation, don't you?" Martin Leroy asked.

"We do," admitted the governor. "Second only to the emphasis we place on security, of course. One remembers, Mr. Leroy, that most of our prisoners here are murderers."

Momentarily his words caused a slight chill to temper the heat of the afternoon. Carol shivered. Helen said, "Goodness! Then I withdraw my offer to become a prisoner!"

Bollo bared large, square, very white teeth in a delighted grin. "I am desolate, Mrs. Leroy!"

Leroy put down his teacup with a careful impatience which showed how much he would have preferred cold beer to hot tea. "I'm curious about those prison pens inside the compound walls, señor," he said. "The prisoners sleep there? And live there when not working?"

"Yes," said Bollo. "They are quite comfortable."

"But they're very insecure-looking for a high-security prison," Danforth protested. "Walls of vertical bamboo bars four inches apart! That doesn't seem adequate somehow to confine desperate criminals. Why, even a persistent termite—"

Bollo held up a hand in amusement. "Wait. Those bamboo bars are very much stronger than they look, I assure you. They keep our convicts safely confined while allowing them to sleep and live in the open air. Our climate here, you understand, makes enclosed prison cells, such as yours in the States, intolerable. The heat would kill our prisoners. So we use those pens, walled with bars of bamboo"—he smiled—"and periodically we check for termites."

"Oh," said Danforth.

"Yes. The prisoners sleep on floor mats, communally. So only one door is required for each pen, you see? And that one door is fitted with a huge metal lock to which only the particular guard assigned to that pen has the key. He lets the twenty prisoners in his pen out in the morning and he locks them in again at night. During working hours, of course, the prisoners are shackled together. It is a very fine system. Very safe."

"No home-baked cakes with little saw blades in them," Helen asked, "passed through the bars by devoted wives?"

Bollo smiled and shook his head. "No. And furthermore, before he is locked into his pen at night, each prisoner is carefully searched for anything that could possibly serve as a weapon or an escape tool. So you see, escape is impossible."

Leroy said, "Impossible? Do you mean that no prisoner has ever escaped from your San Ramon prison, señor?"

Bollo flushed and looked unhappy. "Never," he said after a brief pause, torn between pride and truth, "except once."

"Ah," said Danforth, "then one criminal did make it?"

"Yes. In shame I confess it. A month ago, for the first time on record. A murderer named Antonio Taal. A man who had callously decapitated a fellow pearl diver in a fit of temper. Your pardon, ladies."

Helen and Carol abruptly pushed back their teacups. Danforth and Leroy sat forward in their chairs, their faces mirroring intense professional interest.

Danforth said eagerly, "Tell us about it, señor."

"There is very little to tell. This Antonio Taal worked in the woodcarvers' shop, which you no doubt visited today. He slept in pen Number Three. One night, after the search of his person which is nightly routine, he was locked into his pen with the other nineteen convicts in his group. The next morning when the guard for pen Number Three went to release the prisoners for breakfast, Taal was gone. Utterly. He had disappeared into thin air. Just like that." Bollo snapped his blunt fingers with a report that made Helen jump.

"Only Taal?" Leroy asked. "No other prisoner was missing from that pen?"

"None. And not a single bamboo bar was broken or damaged. And the pen door was still locked as securely as ever."

"A miracle," said Carol. "More tea, Señor Bollo?"

"Thank you."

Helen said, "I have two ideas about your murderer's escape, Señor Bollo. Associating with Leroy King all these years, you can understand that some of their deductive genius, in quotes, question mark, has rubbed off on Mrs. Danforth and me. Shall I explain Antonio Taal's escape for you?"

Bollo crinkled his eyes and showed his teeth. He was greatly taken with Helen. "Please do so," he begged.

"Well, first of all, I think that Antonio Taal was on a hunger strike over some fancied grievance. Was he?"

"No," said Bollo. "I am sorry. He always ate like a pig."

"Oh. I was going to say that a rigid diet could have made the prisoner so thin that he could have squeezed out of his pen between the bars. If, of course, he happened to have a rather small skull to begin with."

Bollo was convulsed with merriment. "Only four inches between bars," he said through his laughter. "What is your second idea, please?"

"My second idea," said Helen, "would be to interrogate the guard for pen Number Three pretty darn carefully."

Danforth and Leroy grinned at each other. "She has something there," Leroy said.

"We did, Mrs. Leroy," Bollo said, sobering. "At great length. And without result. He was able to prove conclusively that neither he nor his key to pen Number Three had been out of the guard's dormitory all night. Under severe interrogation every one of Taal's penmates denied seeing or hearing anything during the night that could have any bearing on Taal's escape."

"Then," said Leroy quickly, "it becomes simply a matter of a duplicate key, doesn't it?"

"No." Bollo was positive. "For the simple reason that a duplicate key could not conceivably have escaped detection whether it had been hidden on Taal's person or in his prison pen. The keys to our pens are no delicate flat little space-savers, you understand. They are massive. Their stems are three inches long and curved like a half moon; their loops are an inch across; the pins and webs below the collar are made of iron a quarter of an inch thick. Not an easy key to conceal, you must see that. And I assure you that our daily searches of the convicts' quarters and persons"—he cast a sidelong look of faint embarrassment at the ladies—"are thorough in the extreme."

Señor Bollo paused reflectively before continuing. "Even if Taal somehow obtained a duplicate key and somehow succeeded in hiding it until the night of his escape, how, I have asked myself a thousand times, did he manage to get over the prison wall that surrounds the compound? You can see it from here. It is eleven feet high and has that projecting inner catwalk for guard patrol built along its top all the way around the compound. With a ladder or a rope that wall conceivably might be scaled from the inside. But not by a man who had neither. And not by a man who had a seriously injured foot."

"An injured foot?" Leroy pounced.

"Yes. A knife cut between the big toe and second toe of his right foot. Sometime before his escape he had accidentally dropped his woodcarving knife in the shop while working. The knife fell point down, penetrating his bare foot deeply. To complicate matters, the cut became infected, crippling Taal to the point where he needed a walking stick to get around at all—even the short distances between his pen, the workshop, and the dining barracks."

"Do guards patrol the wall all night?" Danforth asked.

"One guard. With a submachine gun. He patrols the catwalk continuously. At any sign of trouble he signals the guards on the main gate to turn on the floodlights, illuminating the whole compound as brightly as day. No such warning occurred the night of Taal's disappearance."

For a few moments no one spoke. A vagrant breath of air from the sea made the fronds of the palm trees rattle. With a conspiratorial twisting of the lips, Leroy looked at Danforth and grinned.

Danforth said, "Señor Bollo, your escaped prisoner—this is the kind of problem that my partner and I concern ourselves with constantly in plotting our mystery stories. We find the discussion and analysis of such puzzles stimulating. They help us to make our living. Will you therefore forgive what may seem like an impertinence to you, and let the two of us speculate on your puzzle? I think we can explain how Antonio Taal escaped."

It was Bollo's turn to sit forward in his chair. "You are joking, surely. You seriously think you can solve a mystery in ten minutes that my staff and I have been working on for four weeks without success?" His square teeth showed a grin that now had a hint of derision.

"Yes," Leroy murmured, his sunburned face assuming the bland expression that his wife called his "Q.E.D." Look. "Yes, I think we can."

"Please don't take offense, Señor Bollo," Helen said hastily, putting a hand on his sleeve. "You are dealing here, don't forget, with a two-headed professional mystery computer into which, or into whom, you merely feed the unknown facts of your puzzle and out of which, or out of whom, the solution is inevitably belched forth!"

Leroy patted her knee under the table. "Isn't that a rather indelicate description of your husband and his partner?"

Carol said, "Yes, Señor Bollo, we apologize for them." She looked around for a waiter. "Don't they serve anything but tea in this place, for heaven's sake?" Her voice was plaintive.

Danforth lit a cigarette and blew smoke into the overheated air. "I can see you're skeptical, Señor Bollo. And I don't blame you. Will you let us try, however? And answer just one more question first?"

"It will be my pleasure." Bollo had the air of a man trying to go along with a gag thought up by idiot children.

"This walking stick used by Taal to hobble about on," said Danforth. "Was he allowed to take it into his pen with him at night?"

"He was. He could not walk without it. And it is sometimes necessary, you understand, for a prisoner to get up at night . . ." Bollo let his words trail off, again glancing self-consciously at the ladies.

"A fact of nature," Leroy said sententiously, "and not to be denied, even in a prison pen. Exactly what kind of walking stick did Taal use?"

Bollo pointed at the souvenir walking stick that Helen Leroy had purchased an hour before from a shackled woodcarver in the prison shop. "One of those," Bollo said. "The kind Taal himself carved for sale to tourists."

Danforth, in high spirits, struck the table a light blow. "I thought so," he said. "You begin, Mart."

Leroy nodded. "Señor Bollo. Taal was a woodcarver in your prison shop. So he must have been skilled with a knife."

"Skilled enough to cut off a pal's head over a pearl," Carol offered.

"Quiet," Leroy admonished her. "I was saying. Antonio Taal undoubtedly made the duplicate key to pen Number Three himself. Carved it out of wood, at odd moments when he was unobserved in the shop."

Bollo started to protest. Danforth interrupted him. "Wait, now, give us a chance. Taal saw the guard's key to pen Number Three hundreds of times, eh? A keen observer could have registered its size, shape, and general configuration quite accurately after a few years of looking at it every day, couldn't he? And kept the details in his memory? Besides, Taal also had the lock itself, into which the key fitted, before his eyes every day. So he decided to try his hand at *carving* a key that would lead him to freedom. Isn't that a reasonable assumption."

"Impossible."

"Not at all." Leroy took up the argument. "You are going to say, where could Taal keep his wooden key while he was laboriously carving it over a period of many weeks so that no guard or other prisoner would suspect its existence?"

"Where?" said Bollo. "Exactly."

"In the handle of one of the walking sticks he was carving in the shop," Danforth supplied the answer promptly. He reached out and took Helen's walking stick, which was hanging by its handle over the back of her chair.

It was a handsome cane. A thick curved hand-grip, shaped like the grip of a revolver, topped a stout stick of beautifully carved mahogany. The stick tapered in a graceful series of octagonal, round, and spiral sections to a slender ferrule. Its entire length was embellished with bands, studs, and floral designs of mother-of-pearl, delicately inlaid in the wood. The butt end of the stick's grip was faced with a large oval lozenge of mother-of-pearl, two inches in length and one inch in width.

"He hollowed out the handle of one of these sticks," Danforth went on. "Made a cavity big enough to hold the duplicate key. Then he covered the cavity with a big wafer of mother-of-pearl like this one, easily removable, easily replaced. And he merely refrained from finishing the carving and decoration of that particular stick so it would not be sold to a tourist before he was ready to use the key inside its handle."

"But," said Señor Bollo, still humoring these odd Americans, "he could not have known that his wooden key would actually turn the pen lock. Not possibly. The chances of carving from memory a key that would fit the lock are a million to one!"

"True," Leroy admitted. "So Taal made sure that the key he was carving *would* fit."

"How?"

"By deliberately cutting his foot with his carving knife," Leroy said. "How else?"

"Oh, come now," Bollo said indulgently. "It was an accident. There was nothing deliberate about it. The other woodcarvers in the shop testified to that."

"Naturally," Danforth said. "Taal meant it to look like an accident. But we would be naive to believe it, wouldn't we? A man so skilled in handling a knife as Taal? No. He cut his foot on purpose. And infected it deliberately, too, I'll bet, so that your prison doctor would recommend that he be allowed to use a cane. In any event, he *was* permitted to use the cane, wasn't he?"

"He was."

"So what have we?" Danforth spoke with relish. "A convicted murderer, a crippled murderer, with a wooden key to his pen door concealed in his cane's handle. And a natural need, like all of us, to get up at night occasionally. Surreptitiously on these occasions he tries his key, removed from the cane handle, in the lock of the pen door. And guided by these clandestine nocturnal tests, he adds refinements, the finishing touches, to the web of his carved key next day in the shop. Finally one night the key *works* when he tries it in the pen lock. He thereupon seizes the first opportunity, when all his penmates are sound asleep, to unlock the door of the pen, hobble out cane in hand, relock the door from the outside, and make himself scarce. It could be, couldn't it, Señor Bollo?"

Bollo shook his head. "What of the compound wall?" He pointed dramatically across the road. "What of the patrolling guard on top of the wall? And how could a crippled man, whose foot was agony to touch to the ground, possibly run far enough to escape?—even if he *did* miraculously manage to get over the wall."

"That's not too difficult to explain," Leroy said placidly. He and Danforth were enjoying themselves. "One guard patrolling the catwalk on top of the wall means there would be intervals of several minutes between his successive visits to any specific point on the perimeter. Especially if he walks clear around the compound on each pass, as you say he does. Antonio Taal, it seems to me, would merely time the guard's patrol and go over the wall while the guard was on the other side of the compound. Simple."

"How?" asked Bollo, beginning to perspire. "How did he scale the wall?"

"How tall was Taal?" Danforth asked.

"Perhaps five and a half feet."

"Figure it out then," Danforth said. "If he's five and a half feet tall, he probably has a reach of about seven feet, give or take a couple of inches, when he stands on tiptoe and reaches upward. Add to this the three-foot length of the walking stick in his hand. And the few desperate inches he could force himself to jump off his uninjured foot. Holding his cane by its ferrule end, and using the handle of the stick as a hook to catch over the inner rail of the catwalk on the wall's top, an agile man could climb up his cane, hand over hand, and reach the top of an eleven-foot wall quite easily. And descend the same way on the other side." Danforth winked at Leroy. "*Was* Taal an agile man, Señor Bollo?"

Bollo coughed. "Yes," he said slowly. "He was as muscular as a monkey."

"Which, incidentally, have no tails in Zamboanga, I understand," Carol murmured.

Bollo exclaimed, almost to himself, "By our Lady of Pilar! Yes. Yes. It is barely possible." He half stood, then sat again, looking crestfallen. "But no," he said, his coffee-colored face solemn, "not with a foot like Taal's. He could not have traveled a quarter of a mile from here by morning—even if he had crawled on his belly. Yet the greatest manhunt Zamboanga ever saw combed every rock, beach, blade of grass, and patch of jungle within a ten-mile radius of this prison within six hours after Taal was discovered missing, and no trace of him was found. Nor was any cart, car, boat, or outrigger in which he might have escaped reported missing."

He broke off abruptly as a file of men in shapeless garments of an odd orange-russet color trudged slowly down the road toward the prison gate, trying to walk in step through their own dust. The chains connecting them leg to leg made a metallic clinking, plainly audible to the tea drinkers under the awning opposite the gate. A guard carrying a shotgun walked beside the file of prisoners.

"A road gang coming in for dinner," Bollo said, gesturing. Then, "And that is another thing. Those prison clothes—"

Helen interrupted him. "They're a darling color, Señor Bollo. Such a chic orangy-red! I wish I could buy some of that cloth to take home with me. It would make awfully cute slacks, Carol."

Bollo showed his big white teeth. "I'm afraid that is out of the question, Mrs. Leroy. The cloth is not available to the public. Only my prisoners wear it. Its color is unique, as you say. That special orange dye is used only for prison material. Very high visibility color, do you see? Anyone wearing clothes of that color is instantly recognized as a convicted criminal. That is what I meant, gentlemen—another puzzling factor about Taal's escape. Dressed in prison clothes of that color, he would have stood out like a shark among pilot fish. Yet no one in Zamboanga saw him."

He shrugged and smiled at Helen. "I think you are right, after all, Mrs. Leroy. More right than your husband. Antonio Taal starved himself to nothing and was spirited out of my prison camp to heaven, a disembodied ghost."

Leroy laughed. "There's a simpler explanation than that. I think you may have inadvertently overlooked one important fact in connection with your murderer."

"What fact is that?"

"He was a pearl diver," Leroy said. "Therefore an excellent swimmer. A man used to the water, at home in the sea. I think he *swam* away from your prison by night, when his orange clothing could not be seen, and laid up for rest at daylight in some lonely cove along the shore between here and Zamboanga City." Leroy thumbed at the murmuring surf a few yards away. "We saw plenty of likely spots as we drove out here today along the coast road. And a very good swimmer could easily swim ten miles before daybreak in a calm sea if he escaped from the pen in the middle of the night."

Explosively Señor Bollo called once again on Pilar, patron saint of Zamboanga. The expression on his face was a comic mixture of sudden enlightenment and chagrin, mixed with anger, astonishment, and at last, healthy amusement. When Danforth added innocently, "And as for Taal's infected foot, its long immersion in salt water might have proved most beneficial," the amusement won out over his other emotions, and Bollo laughed heartily.

"A remarkable reconstruction," he said, "thoroughly worthy of Leroy King. *If* it happened that way, of course."

Danforth grinned. "It *may* be a little far-fetched," he conceded, "but it is not at all incredible."

"In any event," Bollo said, "Taal escaped and is still at large. He is a brutal short-tempered murderer who will almost certainly kill again. If I could get him back in San Ramon prison before he does so, I would be a very happy man."

"So here's to a very happy man," said Danforth, taking a sip of his nightcap. It was shortly after midnight. They sat in the Horseshoe Bar of the *Valhalla,* now breasting the long swells of the Celebes Sea, Borneo-bound. "To Señor Bollo, who has his wandering murderer safely behind bamboo bars once more."

"Thanks to our sharp eyes and sharper minds," said Leroy self-satisfiedly.

Helen bristled. "Thanks to a four-year-old child, you mean!"

"What?" Danforth was bland. "Just because the kid happened to be diving and found Taal's orange convict suit on the sea bottom, weighted down with rocks under some widow's house in the Mohammedan settlement? And told Bollo where it was so he could raid the place earlier tonight?"

"Isn't that enough?" Helen said. "They caught the escaped murderer there, didn't they? Terrorizing the widow into feeding and hiding him!"

"True. But what about the child's mother, if it comes to a question of who's responsible for catching Taal? *She's* the one who made bathing trunks for her youngster out of the orange material the kid found." Danforth winked at his partner. "And if we hadn't noticed the color of the child's bikini—"

"Which brings us back to those sharp eyes I mentioned," said Leroy. "Ours."

"Then your sharp eyes are also responsible, I take it," said Carol with some spirit, "for the poor constable's arm that Antonio Taal broke with *that* while resisting arrest." She pointed to a walking stick Leroy held between his knees—a parting gift from Señor Bollo. Behind a large disk of mother-of-pearl in the hollow handle of the cane the prison governor had found the duplicate key—a massive key crudely carved out of hardwood.

"It seems to me," murmured Leroy soothingly, "that perhaps the best case of all could be made for the fish soup."

"I know it is undignified to bicker with one's wives," remarked Danforth with the air of a man much put upon, "but simple justice requires me to point out, all the same, that Leroy King's reconstruction of the escape was flawless."

Helen laughed. "Yes, but it was a very simple puzzle," she said.

"Why, even stupid little me had several perfectly good explanations."

"Yeah," her husband jeered affectionately. "Between you and Bollo you had Taal starving himself to death and rising up to heaven as a disembodied spirit! Is that what you call a perfectly good explanation?"

Danforth chuckled. "You know something? *I* would have favored that theory too, except for one thing."

"What?"

"I just couldn't seem to picture a disembodied spirit wearing orange pants!"

THE LOST HEIR

Lillian de la Torre

Lillian de la Torre

In *The Seven-Per-Cent Solution* Nicholas Meyer re-created a fictional personage: Sherlock Holmes. In "The Lost Heir" Lillian de la Torre re-created an actual personage: Samuel Johnson. And made him a detective.

Her task involved not only the usual problems of narrative fiction; it also involved a vast amount of scholarship. At both of which she excels.

"I was born in New York, and brought up in a house full of detective stories," she explains. "It marked me for life.

"I didn't know that yet, however, when, resisting the temptations of the stage and journalism, I determined to become a scholar. (I have been treading the boards and writing for the papers intermittently ever since, but that's on the side.)

"As a scholar I discovered the raffish charms of the Age of Johnson. I married a Johnsonian, moved West, and lived happily ever after. We never argue. Well, almost never. Our most memorable argument was about detective stories. He was crying them down:

" 'Detectives, bosh!' he snorted. 'Drawling dilettantes, cute brides, sententious Chinamen, dear old ladies—next thing, I suppose, a police dog!'

" 'There's been a police dog,' I admitted. 'Granted, if the detective's flimsy, the story's flimsy. But take a character as solid and many-sided as, for instance, Dr. Sam Johnson in Boswell's great biography—'

"No sooner said than done! Dr. Johnson, the Great Cham of the 18th Century, forthwith became by my pen a 'detector' of crime and chicane, and Boswell narrated his exploits.

"For plots I ransacked the criminal annals of the 18th century, and pursued old-time mysteries from Paris to Dublin, from London to Edinburgh. My most formidable find turned up at Foyle's: *The Tichborne Trial* in nine volumes folio (1876), a wild account of the 'lost heir' of Tichborne by the egregious Lawyer Kenealy, who was disbarred for his pains.

"The 18th century fancied long-lost heirs, and so do I. Naturally my 'Lost Heir' smacks slightly of Tichborne, and here he is."

A.M.

THE LOST HEIR

"I implore you, Dr. Johnson, help a grieving mother to find her lost son!"

Thus impulsively spoke Paulette, Lady Claybourne, as she crossed the threshold at Johnson's Court. We saw a delicate small personage, past youth indeed, but slim and erect in the most elegant of costly widow's weeds. Her face was a clear oval, cream tinged with pink, and her large dark eyes looked upon us imploringly under smooth translucent lids. In Dr. Johnson's plain old-fashioned sitting room, she looked like a white butterfly momentarily hovering over the gnarled bole of an oak tree.

Dr. Sam Johnson, *detector* of crime and chicane, and friend to the distrest, bowed over the small white hand. Then in his sixty-third year, tall and burly, aukward and uncouth, he yet valued himself upon his complaisance to the ladies. His large but shapely fingers engulfed the dainty digits of our guest as he led her to an armed chair, the while replying:

" 'Twere duty, no less. But first, ma'am (seating her), you must tell me how you came to lose the child. Pray attend, Mr. Boswell, I shall value your opinion. Ma'am, I present Mr. Boswell, advocate, of Edinburgh in Scotland, my young friend and favourite companion."

Smiling with pleasure to hear myself thus described, I bowed low. The lady inclined slightly, and began her story:

"My son, Sir Richard Claybourne, is no child. He is in his twenty-seventh year, if—if he is in life. His father, Sir Hubert Claybourne, of Claybourne Hall in Kent, left me inconsolable ten years ago, and our only son, Richard, then sixteen, acceded to the title and estate.

"Well, sir, 'tis a common story. Tho' we had been close before, once he came into his estate, I could not controul him. Claybourne Hall saw him but seldom, for he preferred raking in London, running from the gaming tables to—to places more infamous yet.

"Then, as he approached his majority," the soft voice went on, "Richard fell deeply in love, and proposed to marry. 'Twas against my wishes, for tho' the young lady's fortune was ample, she was brought up in a household where I, alas, have no friends. But being neighbours, Cynthia Wentworth drew Richard home to Kent, and at Claybourne, on a day in spring, they were wedded and bedded.

"Alas the day! That very night, Richard burst into my chamber, where I lay alone waking and fretting. He was dishevelled and wild, and, Damn the bitch, says he (pardon me, gentlemen), she has broken my heart, I shall leave England this night. I'll go for a soldier, and never return while she lives. Nothing I said could disswade him. Take care of Claybourne estate, cried he to me, and was gone."

The low voice faltered, and went on:

"With the help of Mr. Matthew Rollis, my trusted solicitor, I kept up the estate. Cynthia Wentworth, mute and grim, went back to her foster folk at Rendle. No word came from Richard; but enquiring of returning soldiers, once or twice I heard a rumor of him in the New World, at New-York, at Jamaica. Since then, nothing. Six years have now passed. I can bear it no longer. I must find my boy."

Dr. Johnson looked grave.

"'Tis long for a voluntary absence. Who is the next heir? Who had an interest to prevent Sir Richard's return?"

"Good lack, Dr. Johnson, you do not think—?"

"I do not think. I ask meerly."

"You alarm me, sir. The next heir is Jeremy Claybourne, a lad now rising twenty. He springs from the Claybournes of Rendle, a family I have long lived at enmity with. His father, my husband's late brother Hector—well, I say nothing of him; he was kind to me while he lived. But his wife was a venomous vixen, and never spared to vilify me. In that house Cynthia was brought up and her mind poisoned against me. On them I blame the whole affair.

"Indeed it is pressure from that quarter that drives me to action. The lawyers will have Richard declared dead, and his cousin Jeremy put in possession. On that day they will turn me out into the world without a friend. He must come home and protect me."

"Then we must find him. You say your son departed on his wedding night. How did he depart?"

"I know not how, sir, but Claybourne estate is on the coast; I have thought he went by sea, perhaps in some smuggler's vessel."

"A course full of peril," commented my friend, who considered that being in a ship was like being in gaol, with the likelihood of being drowned. "Alas, madam, what assures you that he is still in life?"

"A mother's heart! I *know* that, somewhere, he is alive!"

"Then we must appeal to him to shew himself, wherever he may be. Bozzy, your tablets. By your leave, ma'am, we'll address him thus in all the papers (dictating):

> "Sir Richard Claybourne went from his Friends in the year '66, & left his Mother bereft & his Affairs in disorder. Whosoever makes known his whereabouts shall be amply rewarded, & he himself is implored to return to the Bosom of
>
>   his grieving Mother.
>
> Claybourne Hall in Kent
> April ye 10th, 1772

"There, madam, let this simple screed be disseminated, especially in the seaports of the New World, where he was last heard of; and my life upon it, if he be alive, Sir Richard will give over his sulks and return to his duties."

"I pray it may be so," murmured my Lady.

Dr. Johnson looked after the crested coach as it left the court, and shook his head.

"Let us all pray, for her sake, it may be so."

Time passed. I returned to Edinburgh, and quite forgot the problem of the missing Sir Richard Claybourne and his whereabouts; until once more, in the spring of 1773, I visited London.

I was sitting comfortably with my learned friend in his house in Johnson's Court, when a billet was handed in. Dr. Johnson put up his well-shaped brows as he read it, and passed it to me.

> By the grace of Heaven, Sir Richard Claybourne is found! Come at once to the Cross Keys.
>
> P. Claybourne
>
> at the Cross Keys,
> Wednesday, 10 of ye clock

"I suppose we must go," said Dr. Johnson.

Wild horses would not have kept me away. We found Lady Claybourne in the wainscotted room abovestairs at the Cross Keys, sitting by the fire in a state of agitation. By her side, in silent concern, stood a grave, smooth-faced person in a decent grey coat. He proved to be Mr. Rollis, the manager of the Claybourne estate. My Lady started up at our advent.

"O bless you, Dr. Johnson, your screed has brought my Richard home to me!"

"Is he here?"

"Not yet. He is but now come into port, and gives me the rendezvous here."

"That is so," murmured Mr. Rollis in a low caressing voice, seating her gently.

"Then, my Lady, how are you sure it is he?" asked Dr. Johnson gravely.

"Old Bogie says so."

"And who is old Bogie?"

"My son's bodyservant from his childhood. To this trusted retainer I gave the task of disseminating your screed in the New World. You understand, Dr. Johnson, I am of French extraction, and come from the island of Haiti, where I still possess estates. There Bogie was born and bred, and there, his task done, he was instructed to await developments."

"And there he found Richard?"

"Sir, strolling in the gardens at Port au Prince, by chance he comes face to face with Richard. What, 'tis Bogie! cries Richard. Master Dickie! cries Bogie, and they embrace. In letters sent before, they describe this affecting scene."

"Indeed, my Lady, so they do," asseverated Rollis.

What more these letters imported was not revealed, for just then there was a knock at the door, and two men appeared on the threshold. One of them, a little old Negro with such a face as might have been carven on a walnut shell, was but a shadow behind the shoulder of the other. On this one all eyes fixed.

We saw a tall young man, dark tanned and very thin. His swarthy face, tho' gaunt and worn, yet strikingly resembled my Lady's about the eyes, which were brilliant and dark, with smooth deep lids under arching brows. He smiled her very smile, his delicately cut mouth, so like hers, flashing white teeth. His own dark hair was gathered back with a thong. His right sleeve hung empty.

The length of a heartbeat the room was poised in silence. Then my Lady rose slowly to her feet.

" 'Tis Richard," she whispered.

"Aye, 'tis Richard," murmured Rollis.

" 'Tis Richard: but O Heaven, how changed!"

In an instant the tall young man went to her, and she gathered him to her bosom. Let us draw the veil over a mother's transports.

After these sacred moments, Richard made known to us his story.

"I went from England," he said, "resolved never to return. But I soon tired of the soldier's restless life, and I resolved to seek some idyllic shade, far from the haunts of man, and there forget the past. From Jamaica I made my way to Haiti. With forged letters and a false name I obtained employment from our own factor on our own plantation. There all went on to a wish, marred only when in the late earthquake I was pinned by a fallen lintel, which paralyzed my right arm (touching the empty sleeve). Alas, Mother, I have brought you back the half of a man."

"Not so!" cried my Lady stoutly. "The arm is there. (So it was, close-clipped to his side within his fustian coat.) We'll have the best surgeons to it, and it shall mend!"

"Meanwhile," he smiled, "you shall see how my left hand serves."

To proof, he took her white fingers in his brown ones, and kissed them the while my Lady melted in smiles.

"Tho' 'twas my intent never to return," he went on, "your eloquent appeal, making its way to me, moved my heart towards England."

"The thanks be yours, Dr. Johnson," uttered my Lady.

"Aye, our thanks to you," seconded Rollis.

"And so I came down to Port au Prince, with intent to take ship, and there at the dock I met with dear Bogie—"

The black man bowed, and wiped a tear with the heel of a dusky pink palm.

"—and here I am!"

"There will be rejoicing at Claybourne," smiled my Lady. "You must be present, Dr. Johnson, Mr. Boswell."

Assenting, we parted with a promise to visit the Hall for the coming festivities of the Claybourne Dole on St. George's Day.

'Twas April, with spring in the air. We proceeded forthwith into Kent, tho' not to Claybourne Hall. Dr. Johnson had a mind first to visit friends at Kentish Old Priory, hard by.

Our welcome at the Priory, and our diversions thereat, form no part of this tale, except insofar as diversion was afforded at every social gathering by speculation upon the romantic recrudescence of Sir Richard Claybourne. Those who had caught a glimpse of him importantly expatiated on his resemblance to his lady mother. Some even saw in him a look of his late father, Sir Hubert. Others again thought he resembled nobody, and suspected my Lady had been bamboozled by an impostor. She was just asking to be bamboozled, added certain cynics; while the sentimental joyed to share the bliss of a mother's heart.

As to myself, being a lawyer I took it upon me to expatiate in all companies on the great principle of filiation, by which the romantick Douglas Cause had been newly won: that, in brief, if a mother declares *This is my son,* it is so.

Heedless, the young ladies would twitter the while over the folk at Rendle. How were they taking it? How would Cynthia receive the return of her long-lost bridegroom? What would Jeremy say, now that his cousin had returned to cut him out?

As the group around the tea table was enjoyably speculating thus, one afternoon, a servant announced:

"Lady Claybourne. Mr. Claybourne."

At the names silence fell, and every head turned. Into the silence stepped a blonde girl in sea-green tissue, snug at her slender waist, and draping softly over a swaying hoop. Her sunny hair was lightly piled up à la Pompadour. There was pride in her carriage, and reserve in her level blue gaze and faint smile.

Attending her, nay, hovering over her, came a broad-shouldered youth in mulberry, whose carelessly ribbanded tawny hair, square jaw, and challenging hazel eye delineated a very John Bull in the making.

Thus I encountered at last Cynthia, Lady Claybourne, whom Richard had loved and left, and Jeremy Claybourne, his cousin and heir.

Constraint fell on the tea table. After a few observes on the weather (very fair for April), the company dispersed. The Claybournes lingered, having come of purpose to bespeak Dr. Johnson's advice in the matter of the claimant at Claybourne Hall.

"They say you have met this person," said Cynthia. "I have not. Tell me, is he Richard indeed?"

"Of course he is not!" uttered Jeremy angrily.

"The great principle of filiation—" I began.

"As you say, Mr. Boswell: the mother avers it is her son. Moreover," added Dr. Johnson, "the man of business says it is Richard; and the oldtime servant asserts it is Richard."

"My Lady's too tender heart is set on the fellow," growled Jeremy, "and everybody knows Rollis and Bogie will never gainsay her. She has them under her spell with her coaxing ways: as she has everybody. Only my mother saw thro' her. Cupidity, wilfulness, adultery, bastardy—in such terms my mother spoke of her."

"Enough, Jeremy," said Cynthia quickly, "your mother ever spoke more than she knew about her sister Claybourne."

"Never defend Lady Claybourne," muttered Jeremy, "for she is no friend to you."

"Yet Richard loved me," said the girl. "Can he be Richard, and never come near me?"

"Yet, my dear—if he left you in anger?" murmured Dr. Johnson.

"That is between me and Richard," said Cynthia stiffly.

"Then there's no more to be said."

"Oh, but there is," countered Cynthia quickly. "I'll not see Jeremy dispossessed by a pretender. Pray, Dr. Johnson, will you not scrutinize this fellow, and detect whether he be Richard indeed, or an impostor?"

"Why, if he be an impostor, 'tis my hand in the business has raised him up," observed Dr. Johnson. "I'll scan him narrowly, you may be sure. But why do you not confront him yourself?"

"The door is closed against me."

"We'll confront him at the Dole," said Jeremy grimly.

"What is this Claybourne Dole we hear so much about?" I enquired curiously.

"Sir," replied Cynthia, " 'tis a whimsy from the Dark Ages, of a death-bed vow to relieve the poor forever, and a death-bed curse, that if 'tis neglected, the Claybourne line shall fail. For six years past Jeremy, as the heir, has upheld the custom; and all Claybournes, even I, must play their part on St. George's Day."

"Which is this day week," remarked Dr. Johnson. "Well, well, I'll note Sir Richard's proceedings in the meantime."

Next day, according to our invitation at the Cross Keys, we became guests at Claybourne Hall. We found the Hall to be a stately Palladian mansion, with classical pilasters and myriad sashwindows taking the light. Here the dowager Lady Claybourne reigned in splendour, and now that her Richard was beside her, all was love and abundance.

Richard indeed moved as one waking out of a dream, from the formal garden to the bluffs above the sea, from the great hall to the portrait gallery. As he stared at the likenesses of his ancestors in the latter, we were enabled to stare at him, as a youth on canvas, as a man in the flesh. As my Lady had said, how changed!

The youthful face in the portrait was smooth and high-coloured. The face of flesh was now thin and sallow. But in both countenances, the fresh and the worn, the look of my Lady was apparent in the large thin-lidded eyes and the curve of lip. In the portrait, young Richard rested his left hand on the hilt of his sword, and held in his right the bridle of his favourite horse.

"Gallant Soldier, remember, mother?" murmured Richard. "He bade fair to be the fastest horse in the county."

"He is so still. You shall ride him yet, my son, when the arm mends."

Following her glance, I perceived that the useless arm had been coaxed into its sleeve, and saw in the hand the ball of crimson wool whereby, with continual kneading and playing, the atrophied muscles were to be, by little and little, restored to use. The slack fingers with an effort tightened about the crimson wool and loosed it again, tightened and loosed.

"I'll ride Gallant Soldier yet," vowed Sir Richard.

Meanwhile, the swift steed was Richard's delight and wherever he went, out of doors in the fresh April weather, horse and groom were sure to be near him.

The out of doors was Richard's element. The old gamekeeper rejoiced to have him back, and marvelled at his undiminished skill, tho' with the left hand, at angling and fencing and shooting with the pistol; tho' the sporting gun was no longer within his power.

Indoors, other times, the restored Sir Richard would be busied with Mr. Rollis, turning over old deeds or signing new ones, as to the manner born. Mr. Rollis exclaimed in wonder, that the new signature, tho' left-handed, so closely resembled the old.

In certain respects, methought, the long sojourn in the wilds shewed its effects. The skin was leather-tanned by the furnace of the West Indies. The voice was harsh, and so far from smacking of his upbringing in Kent, the manner of speech had a twang that spoke of the years in Haiti.

At table, also, the heir's manners, to my way of thinking, left something to be desired. But what can a man do who must feed himself with one hand? Old Bogie hovered ever at his shoulder, ready to cut his meat; while at his knee, rolling adoring eyes, sat Richard's old dog, a cross fat rug of a thing named Gypsy. I noticed she got more than her share of titbits.

Only once during that week was the name of Cynthia mentioned, when Dr. Johnson took opportunity to say:

"Sir, will you not see your wife?"

Richard shook his head.

"Not yet. Do not ask it. Let me mend first."

"Cynthia's suspense must be painful," observed Dr. Johnson.

Wherever Richard was, my Lady was sure to be close at hand. Now she came between to say coldly:

"Cynthia has Jeremy to console her. Let her alone."

Richard turned away in silence.

St. George's Day, April 23, 1773, dawned fair. Claybourne Hall hummed and was redolent with final preparations. At the farther edge of the south meadow they were roasting whole oxen, and putting up long tables on trestles to set forth the viands to come. At the near end a platform under a red and white striped canopy offered shelter against sun or shower, whatever April weather might ensue.

At the Hall as morning advanced, Lady Claybourne bustled about; but Richard did not appear. Soon he would face his first meeting with the world. How would he be received?

At mid-morning, we all attended Sir Richard's levee in the old-fashioned way. A rainbow of splendid garments had been kept furbished for him from his raking days. For this great occasion, he chose a suit of cream brocaded and laced with gold, in which he looked like a bridegroom. A modish new wig with high powdered fore-top well became his flashing dark eyes and haggard face. In this he shewed his only trace of foppery, the outmoded hats and wigs of past days having been condemned *en masse,* and new ones bespoke from London.

My Lady, too, was adorned most like a bride, for she had given over her mourning weeds upon Richard's return, and now wore silver tissue edged with bullion lace. As to me, I had donned my bloom-coloured coat, while Dr. Johnson was satisfied to be decent in chestnut broadcloth.

On the stroke of noon we issued forth to greet the quality and commonalty already gathering to honour the day. Richard vibrated like a wire; my Lady, glowing with joy, never left his side. Thus, strolling in the meadow, we exchanged bows with the neighbouring squires, and nodded condescendingly to the assembling tenantry. Sometimes Richard uttered a name; sometimes he only made a leg, bowed and smiled. His eyes shewed the strain he was under.

As we strolled, suddenly my Lady took in a sibilant breath, and gripped her son's fingers. Two persons stood in our way. Richard uttered one word: "Cynthia!"

Her hand on Jeremy's, the girl stood and eyed the speaker, utterly still. At last she spoke:

"Who are you?"

"I am Sir Richard Claybourne, your humble servant, and your husband that was."

She searched him deep, the sallow face, the dark eyes, the useless arm.

"Make me believe it," she said. "Answer me but three questions."

"Not now," snapped Lady Claybourne. "The Dole begins."

"I think you must, Sir Richard," said Dr. Johnson gently.

"Very well, sir. But think well, Cynthia, you may not like the answers."

"If true, I shall like them very well. One: when we began our loves (the clear skin rosied), what was my name for you?"

"Dickon," said the claimant instantly.

"No, 'Rich,' you are wrong. Now say: where was our secret post office?"

"In a hollow tree."

"That is true. Which one?"

"Ah, that I have forgotten."

"Never mind. Why did you leave me as you did?"

"You know why."

"I know why. Do you?"

"I beg you, Cynthia, spare me saying it."

"I do not fear to hear it."

Eyes downcast, Richard uttered low: "You force me to say it. Because I found you to be used goods."

Jeremy doubled his fists and aimed a blow, which Richard swiftly fended with his own.

"Stand back, Jeremy," said Cynthia coolly: "he knows he lies."

Jeremy, muttering, dropped his arms, and the claimant followed suit, as the dowager cried:

"Of course the little trollop must deny it. Enough of this farce!"

"Answer me but this, if you be Richard," pursued Cynthia steadily, "what did you say in your farewell note?"

"An unworthy trick, Cynthia, I left you no farewell note."

"Shall I shew it you?"

"I forbid it!" cried the dowager angrily. " 'Tis clear Cynthia will tell any lie, pass any forgery, to do away with you and get the estate for Jeremy. Come, begin the Dole!"

She swept Richard away. At her gesture, he mounted the platform and spoke:

"My people—my dear friends, companions of my youth! Richard is returned, and we shall have better days at Claybourne Hall. I am too moved to say more."

A silence. Would they reject him? Then the cheer burst forth: *Huzza!* It was Mr. Rollis who gave the triple "Hip hip!"

Bowing, the master of Claybourne reached his hand to his lady mother, and descended to the level. Old Bogie with a basket of loaves and Mr. Rollis with a purse of crown pieces fell in on either side. Jeremy and Cynthia, stiff-backed, followed; and we, Sir Richard's guests, brought up the rear.

Drawn up before the dais, shepherded by friends and relations in gala array, stood two dozen hand-picked and hand-scrubbed antients of days. Clean smocks cloathed the toothless gaffers, and snowy aprons adorned the silver-haired gammers. The Dole began: to each, a gracious word from Sir Richard, a crown piece from Rollis's purse, and a fat brown loaf from Bogie's basket.

The entourage had gone part way down the line, when a boy with a billet pushed through the crowd and handed the folded paper to Sir Richard. The latter snapped it open, read, and scowled. Then he shrugged, threw down the crumpled paper (which in the interest of neatness I retrieved and pocketed for future destruction) and stepped forward to the next curtseying old crone.

There was still bread in the basket and silver in the purse when again a newcomer pushed his way importantly through the crowd. I recognized the burly fellow with his staff and his writ. 'Twas the parish constable, come as I supposed to bear his part in the drama of the Claybourne Dole. At sight of him, Richard stopped stock-still. Then he bowed abruptly, and strode swiftly away. We saw him reach the edge of the meadow, where as usual the favourite steed, Gallant Soldier, saddled and bridled, stood with his groom. The Dole party stood and gaped as Richard leaped to the saddle, slapped the reins two-handed, and tore off at a gallop.

As we stood staring, the dowager rounded on Cynthia.

"You wicked, wicked girl!" she cried. "Now what have you done! You have driven Richard from home a second time!"

"Be that as it may," said Dr. Johnson, "continue the Dole, Sir Jeremy, lest the Curse fall upon you."

Under his commanding eye, the Dole party re-formed about Jeremy. I noticed that the constable, stately with writ and staff, belatedly brought up the rear; and so the Dole was completed.

Cheering, the tenantry broke ranks and attacked the tables; but there was no feasting for us. Marshalled by Dr. Johnson, we found ourselves indoors in the withdrawing room, sitting about on the stiff brocaded chairs as the late sunlight slanted in along the polished floor. We seemed to sit most like a select committee, myself and Cynthia and Jeremy, Lady Claybourne and Rollis and Bogie, with Dr. Johnson as it were in the chair, and the constable like a sergeant-at-arms, solidly established just outside the door.

"Where is Sir Richard?" demanded Mr. Rollis.

"Vanisht," replied Dr. Johnson with a broad smile. "We have put the genie back in the bottle."

"How do you know he is vanisht?"

"Because 'twas I conjured him away."

"Alas for my Lady!" cried generous-hearted Cynthia, "to lose her son a second time."

With a heart-broken gesture, Lady Claybourne put her kerchief to her eyes.

"Save your sympathy, she has not lost him," said Dr. Johnson calmly.

"Unravel this mystery, sir," exclaimed Cynthia.

"I have not all the strands in my fingers, but the master string I have pulled, and the unravelling begins. You have heard the cynical saying, if you should send word to every member of Parliament, *Fly, all is discovered,* the floor would be half empty next day."

In a trice I had out of my pocket the note the claimant had thrown down. *Fly, all is discovered,* it read.

"But he did not fly," I objected.

"Not then," conceded my friend. "But upon the heels of the warning came the constable with his staff and a great writ in his hand—instructed by me, I confess—and that did the business. The false Richard is off, and I venture to suppose he'll not return."

"How could you be so sure he was not the true Richard?" I asked curiously.

"Sir, the affair of Susanna and the elders was my first hint. As the lying elders could not say with one voice under which tree she sinned, so there was no agreement on the scene of that romantick meeting with old Bogie, whether the gardens or the docks. Was there such a meeting? It occurred to me to doubt it. Yet the positive voices of all three, mother, man of business, and old servant, overbore me for the nonce."

"Not to mention," said I, "the devotion of the dog Gypsy at Claybourne."

"Cupboard love," smiled Johnson. "Had you fed her, she would have drooled in *your* lap. No, the dog did not move me. For at Claybourne, I was again observing matter for doubt. There was, for instance, the affair of the wigs and hats. The false Richard wore his predecessor's garments very well. But the headgear would not fit; he was obliged to obtain a new supply.

"Moreover," my friend continued, "the real Sir Richard was right-handed. The sword in his portrait was scabbarded to the left, as it must be for a right-handed man to draw. But I soon perceived this fellow was always left-handed. He wrote, he shot, he fished left-handed with the perfect ease of a lifetime. Therefore must his right arm seem to be stricken. Then if he had learned from someone to write like Sir Richard, yet perforce not perfectly, the shift of hand explains all. Thus too, the arm must seem to mend. Who would willingly go one-armed forever?"

"And it mended miraculously," added Jeremy drily, "when I struck at him and he struck back two-fisted."

"So I saw," remarked Dr. Johnson, "tho' 'twas over in the blink of an eye. Yet it shook him, and Cynthia's tests still worse, making him all the more ready to believe *All is discovered,* and fly at once, by that mount he had always ready."

"Then where is the real Sir Richard?" I put the question that was hanging in the air.

"Ah, there's the question," said Dr. Johnson. "Let us ask Cynthia. Forgive me, my dear, do not answer unless you will; but had you really a note of farewell?"

"I will answer," said Cynthia in a low voice, "for Jeremy has the right to know. There was a note of farewell left for me in our hollow tree." Reaching into her bodice, she brought it forth. "Here it is."

With compressed lips, Lady Claybourne turned away. Three heads bent over the yellowing scrap. The message we read was brief and bitter:

> Now you know me, I am unworthy to touch you. But be comforted, you shall be rid of your incubus when the tide goes out. Farewell, for you'll never see me more.
>
> Rich

"I made sure he had thrown himself into the sea," whispered Cynthia.

"Dear heart," cried Jeremy, "on his wedding night, why would he so?"

"Because," said Cynthia, low, "he came to me with the French disease, and left me rather than infect me. He was half mad with remorse and drink taken, and I feared what he might do. 'Twas pure relief when I heard his mother had seen him and set him on his way."

"But had she?" asked Johnson gravely. "—Sit down, Lady Claybourne. You need not answer. I will answer for you. You never saw Richard that night. He was drowned. But you were determined still to rule Claybourne estate, and you had the wit and the will to invent a story to keep you there tho' Richard was gone. How long, think you,

Cynthia, could she have remained, had you displayed this everlasting farewell?"

"I was but fourteen, and I wanted so to believe," murmured Cynthia. "But now—I know not."

"Perhaps," said Dr. Johnson, turning a stern face on the old Negro, "perhaps Bogie knows."

The dark eyes darted left and right. No sign came from my Lady, but Jeremy spoke with gruff gentleness:

"Speak up, Bogie. Tell us the truth; it shall not be held against you."

"I know," whispered the black painfully. "When Sir Richard was gone, none knew whither, I was set to search, and so 'twas I found at the cliff top his wedding coat folded, and a note held down by a stone."

"What said the note? Or can you not read?"

"I can read. It began: Honoured Mother, When you read this I shall be dead—"

Cynthia hid her face in her hands.

"I read no more," went on Bogie, "but took coat and note to my Lady in her chamber. She read it dry-eyed, and mused long. At last, Bogie, says she, I learn by this billet that your young master has left England, and we are to keep all things in readiness for his return. Was I to gainsay her?"

Lady Claybourne sat like a figure carved in ice.

"Yet Sir Richard would never return," went on Dr. Johnson, "and Jeremy's guardians became more and more pressing. I suggest that as Jeremy approached his majority, a scheam was conceived to hold the estate, a scheam in which you three—you, my Lady, and Rollis and Bogie—had your parts to play."

"And you too, Dr. Johnson," smiled Rollis, unabashed.

"And I too," said the philosopher wryly. "My part was to be the dupe, and lend my authority to the comedy of 'The Return of the Long Lost Heir.' 'Twas all too pat. He will be found, predicts my Lady like a sybil, and found he is, on her own ground, in Haiti. How? Because—as I now perceive—she arranged it—through a trusted messenger, her old slave from Haiti, our friend Mr. Bogie. Well, Bogie?"

The old man almost smiled as he inclined his head.

"But who was he, then, whom Bogie found in Haiti," I demanded, "so miraculously suited to the part?"

"I know not," replied Dr. Johnson; "but I can guess. I think we shall find that there was someone in Haiti whom my Lady sent there out of the way long ago; someone whom she would gladly establish for life at Claybourne Hall; someone who so closely resembled her that he could win wide acceptance as the lost heir. To speak plainly: her son."

"Her *son?*"

"Her bastard son, Sir Jeremy, whose existence your mother railed at in years past. Is that not so, Lady Claybourne?"

My Lady disdained to answer.

"Is that not so, Mr. Rollis?"

"That is so, Dr. Johnson." Mr. Rollis smiled thinly. "The lad was troublesome, and 'twas I who secretly shipped him off for her to the Haiti plantation. Thither my Lady sent Bogie, to instruct him and bring him back. Bogie is not as simple as he seems. Come, my Lady, say this is so, for our best course now is to compound the matter with Sir Jeremy."

"Compound, will you?" said Jeremy darkly. "I'll look to the strong-box first."

"As to the strong-box," said Rollis calmly, "you may set your mind at rest, for I have kept the keys. Tho' in indifferent matters I was ruled by my Lady—"

"D'you call it an indifferent matter, raising me up a false husband!" cried Cynthia indignantly.

"As to that," returned the solicitor coolly, "I never expected my Lady's mad scheam to prevail; and as to the estate, I have kept it faithfully for whoever comes after."

"What impudence!" cried Jeremy. "Dr. Johnson, say, shall we not give these conspirators into custody, and send after the fleeing impostor?"

Lady Claybourne spoke for the first time:

"He'll hang for it. Would you hang your brother, Jeremy?"

"My *brother?*"

"Your father's son."

"Of the blood on both sides!" exclaimed Dr. Johnson. "Small wonder he passed for the heir!"

"And small wonder my mother railed," added Jeremy.

"Sir Jeremy will not desire a scandal at Claybourne," said my Lady with perfect calm. "He will prefer that I should take my dower right and withdraw to Haiti. My son Paul—whom, as you say, I have not lost—shall join me. Now I will bid you good night. Come, Rollis. Come, Bogie."

" 'Tis for the best. Let it be so, Sir Jeremy," said my wise friend.

My Lady, head held high, sailed out at the door, and Rollis and Bogie followed.

"Be it so," assented Jeremy gravely, and the constable let them pass. "Now," he went on, his face softening, "there is but one more word to say. Cynthia (taking her hand)—Lady Claybourne, will you wed with me, and be Lady Claybourne still?"

"Yes, Jeremy," said Cynthia.

NADIGO

Stanley Cohen

Stanley Cohen

Is this really happening, we sometimes ask ourselves, or am I only imagining it? The seemingly impossible does occur, often to our disbelief—and horror.

In "Nadigo" Stanley Cohen has dealt with the shadowy area where the seemingly impossible and the actual meet, and has come up with a story that is disturbing, alarming and in its quiet way haunting. He has dealt with the world of the inexplicable.

"Although a chemical engineer by education," Cohen says, "I became interested in writing some fifteen years ago as an outlet for my excess creative energy. I turned to mystery writing when my agent sold my first novel, *Taking Gary Feldman,* as a mystery. I've completed four books and three have been mysteries as have most of my published short stories."

As for this particular story, he goes on, "We all agree there's something corn-ball about a writer who states that the idea for a story occurred in a dream. Nevertheless, the essence of the story "Nadigo" did emerge during a restless and unsettling night a few years back. Perhaps it was something I ate. At any rate, I did have a friend in college named Bert who did have a brother in Hollywood."

A. M.

NADIGO

David Klemmer stood at the corner of two streets, shaken with disbelief at how he had come to be there alone. The town was small and flat. He could see the edges of town in all four directions, the faded little houses thinning out into desert. The horizons rippled with heat, exceptional heat for late afternoon in late December. Beyond miles of desert loomed tall bluffs. He was somewhere in Arizona.

The town was old and ugly. Two filling stations, a few parked or slowly moving cars, electric wires, and the black highway with the white line kept the town from being a perfect setting for a western. The buildings and even the sidewalks were mostly wooden, except for aprons to the service stations.

The idea had been preposterous from the beginning. He should never have left New York. Three days before, in the rooms they shared on West 123rd Street, he should have shrugged off Bert's invitation. But Bert's glowing word pictures were more than he had been able to resist.

"The glitter and green of California call," Bert had said. "We leave Wednesday for the Coast."

"Sure, Bert, what I need is a trip to California for the holidays."

But Bert had been serious. And he had the railroad credit card his very rich brother in California had sent. The winter of 1950 was tightening its grip on New York; and California, some far-off land he had never seen, was a tempting contrast to the nearby rumble of trains and the freezing rain outside. Work or no work, Dave had gone past the point of simply weakening. He continued to voice negative noises but in his own mind he had accepted the invitation and was planning to go.

The train ride had been all Bert had promised—a kaleidoscope of panoramic landscapes. Yet Dave struggled to keep himself tuned in, absorbed in thoughts of his work, suffering guilt for being away from it. Something in his thesis lab work just wasn't right. "Dave's a chemist," he heard Bert say to a quietly dignified elderly couple across the breakfast table on the third day. "He hates his work so much, that's all he ever thinks about. Me, I'm an English major," Bert continued. "We're going to California for the Christmas break. My brother's got an eleven-sided swimming pool." The couple opposite them studied them quietly, listening but seldom speaking. Outside the window, a brilliant diamond-clear western day was opening up and sweeping by.

Around midafternoon, Bert became sick and began complaining of excruciating stomach cramps. "We've got to get off this train," he said.

"This train's non-stop the rest of the way, Bert. You'll feel better in a little while. We'll be getting into L.A. soon."

"I've got to get off this train."

"This train doesn't stop around here. We're in the middle of nowhere."

"All trains stop." Still holding his stomach, Bert got up and lurched forward.

"Bert, where're you going? Wait. Maybe there's a doctor on the train." Other passengers began to look up at them.

"I'm going to stop the train," Bert answered.

"You can't stop this train," Dave said, starting after him.

"I can stop any train!" He reached the front of the car and reached up for the emergency brake pull with the DO NOT TOUCH sign.

"No, Bert, No!" Everyone in the car was standing.

Bert grabbed and yanked. Then he dropped into an empty seat and doubled over, holding his stomach.

A conductor burst into the rear of the car and came running up the aisle. "Who the hell pulled the rope?" Passengers began gathering.

"I did," Bert shouted. "Stop the train. I've got to get off." He was rolling from side to side.

"We're in the middle of the desert," the conductor said.

"He's sick. He needs a doctor," Dave said. "Maybe there's a doctor on the train."

The conductor disappeared, and the train continued at a slightly slowed pace. Bert began to moan and continued rolling back and forth on the seat. Passengers gathered around them offering suggestions and sympathy. Bert practically cursed them back to their seats.

The conductor returned. "There's a small town in about five miles. You sure you want off?"

"Tell 'em to stop," Bert shouted. "We want off."

"What town is it?" Dave asked.

"We're still in Arizona, I think. That's the best I can tell you." The conductor started down the aisle again.

"Just get us off this goddamn train! You hear?" Bert shouted. Dave looked around quickly at Bert.

In a few minutes the train began slowing down to stop, the clean, rhythmic click of wheels starting to grind and grate.

They stepped from the train into choking heat on a side street in a tiny desert town. There was no railroad station. They were wearing winter clothes. Bert was still doubled over, holding his stomach, moaning. Dave carried their two suitcases. He glanced around and led Bert toward a slightly built-up area alongside a black highway with white lines. "C'mon, Bert, that looks like a main drag. We'll find a doctor."

They walked along the side street, in front of an auto repair shop and several small grubby houses and buildings, until they came to the highway, obviously the main street of the town. Dave looked around for some indication of the name of the town, some business named after it, a lumberyard, a post office, anything. The buildings were one and two story, mostly wood frame. Fred's Cafe. Sidewalks were wooden all along one side of the road and covered, like in a western. Davis' Feed Store. General supplies. Across the street a dress shop, Mae's, with a garish, black-glass storefront. A drugstore, Hickman's.

About two blocks down, two filling stations on opposite corners of an intersection. Standing alone, surrounded by cars, a small brick A&P.

They walked up on the covered sidewalk and approached a young man, perhaps their age, a handsome boy with steel-blue eyes, wavy hair, and neat shirt and slacks. "Could you tell us where we can find a doctor?" Dave asked.

The boy was leaning against a post with a match in his mouth. He straightened up and removed the match. "You two just get off the train? First time I ever saw it stop."

"My friend got sick on the train. Could you tell us where there's a doctor?"

"Sure, we got one. Old Doc Finger. He's a good doctor. He'll take care of him."

"Where's he at?"

He pointed down the covered walk. "About six doors down. There's his shingle hanging. Go up the steps."

"Thanks. Incidentally, what town is this?"

"You'd better get your friend on over to Doc Finger's. He looks like he's feeling pretty bad." The handsome boy turned and walked away.

Dave and Bert walked up the steps to a little foyer. A door to the left of the foyer led into a dingy, crowded waiting room. They went in, found two empty chairs, and sat down. Bert was pitched forward in too much pain to remain quiet. Dave did what he could to calm him, finally slumping back to match stares with the other patients, all older men. There was no receptionist, no nurse, no sign of the doctor or of any activity. As Dave stared at the other men sitting quietly, his mind blurred for a moment and he imagined the other men derelicts, rather like sunken boats in low water, one missing an arm, another a leg, an eye or an ear or a nose, even an entire face. One man had a four-inch hole in his chest through which the chair-back was visible. For an instant he thought he heard a train. He shook his head to clear it, and his thoughts wandered back to his thesis work. He cringed.

"If you hate chemistry so much, why don't you get out of it?" Bert often said.

"I've gone too far to turn back. Besides, what else could I do?"

He felt a need and nudged Bert. "Looks like it's going to be a few minutes. I'm gonna go look for a head. Be back." He turned to the man sitting to the other side of him. "Excuse me. Can you tell me where the nearest men's room is?"

The man thought a minute. "Don't know. Probably the back of the bar and grill across the street."

Dave reached the street and looked for a bar and grill. Probably Fred's Cafe. He crossed and went in. The empty cafe was hot and the air heavy with beer and fried food. The heat was beginning to reach him. The waiting room had been hot. He walked straight to the back of the room and found a door marked MEN. The air in the tiny cubicle was almost unbearable. There was no basin in which to wash his hands.

He headed out, saying thanks to a man in a white paper cap and filthy white apron behind the cash register.

"Come back," the man answered.

As he reached the street, he thought about the crowd in the waiting room and wandered into the drugstore, over to the magazine rack. He stood for a few minutes thumbing through magazines, became absorbed in an article, and squatted to read it. He read another and, realizing some time had passed, dropped the magazine and walked back to the doctor's office. As he headed up the narrow wooden staircase, he found a padlocked steel folding lattice across the foyer. It was like the steel grillwork in front of New York pawnshops. Beyond it, the door to the doctor's office was closed, the glass window dark. He went up to the lattice and shook it.

Back on the street, wondering where Bert could possibly be, he spotted the boy who had directed them to the doctor. Dave hailed him and trotted over to him. "You haven't seen my friend, have you? You know, the one I got off the train with."

The handsome boy grinned at him. "Why? Should I have?" The boy's eyes were so clear blue it was like staring through two holes in his head at the sky beyond.

"I left him in the doctor's office and went out for a few minutes. The place was full of patients. When I got back, the place was locked up with that steel fence."

"Doc Finger's quick. Good hands."

"But where could they have gone? My friend was sick. Is there a hospital?"

"Nearest thing like a hospital is ninety miles. Your friend's probably well now and around someplace looking for you. Doc Finger's pretty good."

"Incidentally, why does he have that steel fence?"

"He keeps a little strong medicine up there. Kids broke in a couple of times."

"Where could I find Doc Finger now?"

"Maybe home if he didn't go hunting."

"Thanks. Incidentally, what's the name of this town?"

"You'd better quit worrying about a little thing like that and find your buddy, seems to me," he said with his persistent unwarm grin. Then he walked off.

Dave looked up and down the highway. There wasn't much activity, and he didn't see Bert anywhere. He could see to the horizon and would spot Bert if he were standing in a crowd five miles away. He went back into the drugstore and asked the old pharmacist if he could use the phone to call Dr. Finger.

"His office is just across the street."

"I just came from there. Place is all locked up." Dave reviewed his story for the old man.

"Sure, help yourself to the phone. Just pick it up and ask Annamarie, that's the operator, for Doc's house."

After several rings, a sullen woman's voice answered.

"I'm looking for Dr. Finger. Are you Mrs. Finger?"

"Yeah, I'm his wife, 'n' he ain't here. Call him at his office." She answered as if she couldn't possibly imagine any other approach, as if no one had ever called for him at home before.

Dave repeated his story for her. "Has he called you or said anything about my friend or about taking him to the hospital or anything like that?"

"I ain't heard from him since this morning. Said he might go huntin' when he got through this afternoon."

"Thanks just the same." Dave hung up, looked helplessly at the old druggist, and went back out into the street. Sunset was approaching and the town was getting uglier as the light changed. The realization began to slowly descend on him that he was dependent on Bert and the card, that he was in the middle of a nowhere of strangers with remarkably little money. He clutched at his pants pocket to make sure at least his wallet was still there. He walked back to the intersection of the highway and the street where they had gotten off the train. Surveying the town, he realized he could walk in and out of every public place in the town in thirty minutes. He had to find Bert.

He stepped into Davis' Feed Store and the sweet heavy smell of sacks of grain hit him. There were farm tools, a rack of rifles, counters stacked with men's work clothing, and two small-screen televisions. He smiled at the proprietor and left.

Black's Men's Shop, one of the few non-wooden buildings. He asked the proprietor if a . . . a stranger—and he described Bert—had been in.

The man laughed sarcastically. No. Nobody fitting that description. Dave flushed with intense dislike for the man and walked out. He surveyed a brightly lit well-stocked appliance store through the large glass window. There was only one person in the store. He stepped inside the dress shop, Mae's, and looked around. A fat proprietress with wild artificially blue-white hair and heavy make-up approached him. He quickly walked out.

He spotted the red white and blue of a revolving barber pole. An arrow pointed up a flight of stairs: *Sweets Brothers Tonsorial Parlor.* He walked up the steps and through swinging doors into the sweetish stench of barbers' tonics and preparations. Five barber chairs were full and some ten or twelve young men sat in chairs ringing the room. They talked, waiting. This room, with the thick layer of matted hair covering the floor, was clearly one of the town's popular gathering spots. Dave noticed a striking similarity between three of the barbers. The Sweets Brothers. As he looked at them, their similarity, except for height, became more and more remarkable. They were one short, one medium and one tall; but their identical heads were covered with thin blond, almost nonexistent hair, and their faces were pinkish and boyish and bright-lipped, and they had matching incredibly sweet smiling countenances as they chatted with their particular customers of the moment and with each other. Dave turned and walked quickly out of the shop. As he ran down the steps toward fresh air, he thought he heard the fading sound of a distant train.

When he reached the street, he ran into the handsome blue-eyed boy. "I just thought I heard a train."

The boy shook his head no. "Only passes through once a day and you were on it. You must be hearing things. You look like you just saw a ghost."

"That barber shop up there."

"The Sweets boys?" The boy grinned. "Yeah, they're some matched set. Find your friend yet?"

"Does it look like it?"

"Try the A&P. Maybe he wanted to pick up a few things."

Dave studied the boy for a moment. "Tell me something. What do you do for a living? You work at something? Go to school? Or do you just stand around and help tourists?"

The boy continued grinning. "I ride the range on my trusty steed." He pointed at a '49 Ford parked on the street.

"Is that all?"

"Why? Isn't that enough? You like what you do any better?"

"You don't hang your whole life on doing something you don't want any part of," Bert had once said.

Dave walked away from him and crossed back to the drugstore. "Like to use your phone again," he mumbled at the old pharmacist. He picked up the phone. "Annamarie?" he said, like a native.

"She went home."

"Well, could I have Dr. Finger's house?"

The sullen woman's voice answered after several rings.

"Uh, hello, is Dr. Finger there yet? Or has he called you in the last little while? You may recall I called a little earlier about—"

"I remember ya', and I ain't heard from him."

"Do you know when to expect him?"

"Not if he went huntin'."

"Okay, thanks. Maybe I could call back later."

"I go to bed about nine-thirty."

"Does he have office hours tomorrow morning?"

"Course he does. Tomorrow ain't Sunday."

"Okay, thanks." Dave hung up. "I'd like to call the hospital," he said to the old pharmacist.

"Have to charge you fifty cents. That's long distance. Just ask the girl for the hospital."

A voice mouthed, "Something-Hospital," after one ring.

"I'd like to know if you have checked in a new patient there in the last couple of hours. A patient of Dr. Finger's."

"What's the patient's name?"

Dave told her, and spelled Bert's last name.

"I'm sorry. Dr. Finger has no patients here at this time."

"Would you just check the name to be sure?" Dave spelled it again.

"There's no one here by that name. Sorry."

Dave paid the pharmacist and walked out into the street. Bert had to be somewhere. He decided to continue his search of every public place in the town. He walked into the beer-and-grease air of Fred's Cafe and looked around. He even walked to the rear of the room and glanced through the open door to the men's room. Again he thought he heard a distant train. He walked back out into the air. It was dusk. Mae's and Black's and Davis' were all closed. Ritter's Grocery, The People's Savings Bank, and Early Brothers Real Estate and General Insurance were closed. The Sweets Brothers' barber pole was still and dark. Red's Whiskey Store was open, but Red sat alone behind the counter, picking his teeth. Dave came to the sheriff's office—the police, of course—but it, too, was closed.

Dave crossed an intersection to the red-brick A&P. He stepped inside and for a moment felt surrounded by normalcy. It was like all A&P's, bustling with housewives, boys in white aprons, aisle after aisle of brightly displayed groceries. For a moment in the more familiar surroundings he felt more secure and a little hungry. He paced the area just behind the check-out, looking up and down each aisle. He went down the last aisle and into the open area in front of the meat display. Bert wasn't in there, but then, why should he be? Why possibly? But where was he? His momentary sense of security faded. Dr. Finger was apparently his only lead and where was Dr. Finger?

He went back out into the street. The town's two filling stations were at the next corner, one closed. He went into the other, which wasn't busy.

"You haven't by any chance seen a stranger in a gray jacket and gray pants, maybe with two suitcases."

"Friend of yours?" the attendant asked.

"Yeah. Can't see why he would have come out this way, but I'm looking everywhere. We got off the train when he got sick and—"

The attendant jumped up and dashed out to pump gas for a car that had just pulled in. Then another rolled in. "Haven't seen him," the attendant shouted, looking back at Dave.

Dave walked out to the street and looked toward the edge of town. The highway was flanked on each side by houses. Several hundred yards out stood a small horizontal white sign on a white post. A town name sign, maybe. Dave started walking toward it and then broke into a trot. The sign was farther away than it had appeared. He finally reached it. In the rapidly dimming light, he read, NADIGO, ARIZONA, POP. 1230.

He turned and walked back toward town. The filling station attendant had two cars. The A&P was closed. He suddenly felt very frightened. It was nearly dark. He had less than seven dollars. He went into Fred's Cafe and found the handsome boy sitting alone in a booth, a bottle of beer and a glass in front of him. "Nadigo," Dave said, walking over to him.

"Sure. Why not?" the boy answered.

"Where's the town's sheriff? I notice you have an office for one."

"He went to Phoenix today." The boy grinned.

"Well, isn't there any other police protection in the town? A . . . a deputy or something?"

"Springer went with him. He wouldn't think of missing a trip to Phoenix."

"Suppose something happened around here."

"Nothing much ever happens here. The sheriff'd take care of it when he got back."

"Nothing happens? My friend sure as hell disappeared."

"He probably just left. Got well and left." The boy grinned.

"He wouldn't leave without me."

"Might have. Certainly could have if he'd wanted to."

"How? You said there's no train stop."

"Could've taken a bus. Bus comes through twice a day, once around suppertime. Could've also hitched a ride."

"I haven't seen any buses."

"They come through. They don't usually stop unless you call Mason City. I guess you could flag them down, though."

"Is there a Western Union in this town?"

"Doc Hickman's."

"What about a post office?"

"Doc Hickman's, too."

Dave remembered seeing a barred window in the back of the drugstore which, as he thought about it, was marked for mail. He was hungry, but as he stood in the restaurant the foul smell discouraged any thought of buying food there. Then, too, he had very little money and wondered how long it would have to last. He glanced at the cash register and the candy display. He decided to have a candy bar, a big double coconut Mounds, and he began salivating at the prospect. He walked over, bought one, went out into the air, and opened it. It was stale, very stale, thick, dry, chewy. But he ate it.

He went back to the drugstore. "I don't suppose my friend's been in here," he said. The old druggist shook his head. "Just thought I'd ask. Gimme a Hershey bar," he said, taking one, "and let me use your phone again." The candy was fresher than the first one had been. He called Dr. Finger's house.

"No, I ain't heard from him yet."

"Well, when he gets in, would you ask him to call Hickman's."

"I close at ten," the old man said.

"I suppose," the woman said, "if I'm still up."

Dave called the hospital again and had another fruitless fifty-cent exchange with the woman on the desk there. He put the phone down. It was a few minutes after eight. He tried to reconstruct the day's events, to make some sense out of the situation. It was inconceivable that Bert could have left without him. But where was he? Perhaps he was seriously ill, too sick for the hospital ninety miles away. Perhaps Doc Finger had to take him somewhere better, farther away. He was sorry he hadn't stayed in New York. But what would Bert have done without him on the train? It was good he had come along. But then, why had he left Bert alone for so long while he read a couple of crummy magazine articles? Bert had needed him and he hadn't been around. Or *could* Bert have left?

But the fact remained he was in Nadigo, Arizona, wherever the hell that was, and he didn't know where Bert was, and he might have to get out of there on his own. He needed help, or at least money. He picked up the phone again. "Operator, I want to place a collect call to Mr. or Mrs. Herman Klemmer in Macon, Georgia. My name is David Klemmer."

He listened to his sleeping mother being aroused by the phone call. She wasn't used to getting calls that late. There was a three-hour time difference. She seldom had long distance calls of any kind. Dave never called home. There were too many other more essential expenses in life. A long distance collect call from Arizona? From David? "David? Is that you, son?"

"Hello, Ma."

"Will you accept the charges?" asked an operator somewhere along the line.

"David? Is that you?" she shouted. Long distances are always shouted. "Are you all right? Where are you?"

The line went dead. The operator must have been getting Mrs. Klemmer's assurance that she would accept the charges. She had so little experience handling these matters, especially on being roused out of sleep.

The line opened again. "Hello? Hello? David, is that you? Are you all right?" she shouted.

"Hello, Ma, now listen, I'm fine but I need your help."

"David, where are you? The operator said Arizona?"

"Ma, please listen a minute and I'll try and explain. I'm fine. If you'll let me talk a minute, I know it sounds crazy, but I can explain. You know my roommate? You know, that I've written you about? Bert? Well, he's got a rich brother in Hollywood and we were going out to visit him during vacation and—"

"Hollywood? David, you don't have money to go to Hollywood."

"Ma, let me finish. It wouldn't have cost much of anything. Bert's brother has all kinds of connections. The problem is that Bert has both railroad passes and he got sick on the train, so we got off in this little town so Bert could see a doctor and now Bert's disappeared and I may need money—"

"Disappeared? What do you mean disappeared? Where is he? David, is everything . . . Are you all right?"

"Ma, if I knew where he was, I'd go to him. I left him with the doctor for a minute and when I got back he was gone."

"Where? Ask the doctor."

"Ma, the doctor's gone, too. He went hunting, or something. I didn't want to call and alarm you, but I need your help. You've got to wire me some money, right now, just in case I'm lost from Bert."

"David, are you sure . . . Is someone there with you . . . forcing you?"

"Ma, I promise you, everything is O.K. I know this whole thing sounds crazy, but it's just like I told you. I'm going to keep looking for Bert. But just in case I can't find him, go down to Western Union and wire me some money. Just send it to me, care of Western Union, Nadigo, Arizona. I'm in the Western Union office."

"David, it's late. Your father and I are in bed. We were asleep."

"Ma, I need your help. I'm all alone in this little town. I'm stranded. You've got to send me some money."

"How much money do you need?"

He thought a minute. "You'd better send me two hundred dollars. I may need enough to get back to New York and I don't know what the fare is. And I have to look for Bert."

"We don't have that much at home. We'll go to the bank tomorrow—"

"Get it from Uncle Max. He's always got that much. The son of a bitch is loaded. Wake him up if you have to and get it from him. Just send it to me care of Western Union in Nadigo, Arizona. That's N-A-D-I-G-O. I'll be waiting right here in the Western Union office. Now, Ma. They close this office at ten, and it's eight-thirty here. Did you get the town? N-A-D-I-G-O."

She sighed. "I've got it all. We'll manage. David? David? . . ."

He put the phone down gently, as if the least disruption might make something go wrong. He looked at Doc Hickman, who had been watching him from behind the cash register. The old man smiled with quiet concern but said nothing. He only smiled and observed. He was the image of all the old Docs in all the drugstores Dave had ever seen.

"Nothing to do now but wait," Dave said.

The old man continued smiling.

Dave walked back over to the magazine display and squatted down on a low shelf of magazines to occupy himself while waiting. He watched the old pharmacist move into the back of the store and busy himself. He glanced at the clock. He thought about his mother calling her brother, Max, waking him with a story about her son, David. The college boy, Max would say, the scientist, like some kind of crazy person, stranded in some little town without money. Where? In Arizona? He could see his parents getting dressed, driving out into the night to Max's, pleading to make the story sound plausible for Max and the money, and then driving to Western Union. He tried to submerge himself in a magazine but the words ran together and he turned page after page, staring blankly at pictures, frequently glancing up at the clock and in the direction of the old pharmacist, expecting him every minute to come walking forward with his perpetual smile and a handful of money.

As the clock edged past nine-thirty, Dave took the phone and placed the long distance collect call home. There was no answer. Perhaps the weather was bad there. Perhaps they had had car trouble, maybe even an accident. Ordinarily, Dave always went to great lengths to avoid being a burden. He thought for a moment about Bert's whereabouts and his face grew hot with fear of something so incredibly unknown. He thought about his thesis work and another flush of heat swept through him. He wandered back to the magazines and squatted back down.

He watched the clock and waited for some sign of activity from Doc Hickman. There had been no customers in the store for some time. His parents had had time, plenty of time. He had stressed time. Don't telegrams travel with the speed of electricity in a wire? As the clock approached ten of ten, he went back to the phone and placed the collect call again. His mother answered and quickly accepted charges. She was more experienced now. "David? Where are you?"

"Ma, you know where I am. Where's the money?"

"The man at Western Union says there's no such place. He had a book and he said it had every Western Union office everywhere and he said there's no such place as Nadigo, Arizona."

"But Ma, that's crazy. I'm standing here. He must have made a mistake. Did you spell it right?"

"I wrote it down. N–A–D–I–G–O, Arizona. I even tried calling you there at Western Union but the telephone operator said the same thing. She said there's no such place. David, are you sure you're all right?"

"Look Ma, I'm talking to you from here . . . What did the operator say when she asked you to accept my call?"

She paused a moment. "She asked if I would accept a call from you from Nadigo, Arizona."

"Ma, now listen. It's too late to do anything tonight, but first thing in the morning . . ." Dave glanced toward the back of the store. The old man was turning off lights. ". . . first thing tomorrow, go back to Western Union and don't take no for an answer. It's N as in nowhere, N–A–D–I–G–O, Nadigo, Arizona. You've got to do it, Ma."

"Where are you going to sleep tonight? Will you be all right?"

"I'll be fine. Just send me the money in the morning. O.K.? I've got to go now, Ma."

Dave hung up and walked out onto the planked walk with the pharmacist. The old man locked the door. "Guess I'll see you in the morning," Dave said. The old man nodded, smiled, and disappeared around the corner, leaving Dave very much alone. Dave looked up and down the totally deserted street. There was no automobile traffic. The buildings were all dark. A few widely spaced street lights produced splotches of dirty illumination. Where would he wait till morning? He was suddenly overcome by a wave of extreme terror. He wanted to cry out for Bert, for any friendly face. He turned around and around, staring helplessly in all directions at the desolation that contained him. The blue-eyed boy with the cold smile who always appeared when he had a question—where was he now? The little black Ford was gone. Fred's Cafe was dark. "Oh, my God," he muttered to himself, beginning to feel the nausea of overpowering fear.

He glanced at Doc Finger's dangling shingle. He could barely make out the stairwell leading up to his office. Doc Finger had seen Bert. He was the last link with Bert. Dave crossed the road and walked toward Doc Finger's. He would wait there for him, at his door, taking no chances on missing him the next morning. He climbed the stairs in the dim light that leaked in from the street. The landing was hot and dark, almost pitch black.

Dave took off his jacket and slumped down into the corner where the steel fence met the wall. Below him the doorway onto the wooden sidewalk glowed in the darkness like the square mouth of a cave or a mine.

He began to think about his work, about what he'd done last and what he'd do next. He could almost smell the sweet chemical air of his lab. This was a sensation he liked, wasn't it? He did look forward to a lifetime of solvents searing the inside of his nose and cracking the skin on his fingers, didn't he? What choice did he have? The face of the blue-eyed boy with the cold grin suddenly appeared in his thoughts. "I ride the range on my trusty steed. Do you like what you do any better?"

Bert drifted back into his mind as he sat in the darkness staring at the door below. A wave of guilt swept over him and he tried to retreat further into his little corner of floor, wall, and steel fence. He closed his eyes, and Gorman moved into his mind. Professor Gorman and the undecipherable molecular models on the lecture bench. "Do something else, Dave. Chemistry's obviously not for you." "But Bert, I'm already in graduate school. It's too late." "It's not too late, Dave. Don't you understand? It's *not* too late."

The boy with the blue eyes crossed his mind. Then Nadigo's main street. Yes, Nadigo. It was warm in Nadigo. It was cold in New York. Cold and damp. Nadigo was warm and dry. He thought about his parents going to Uncle Max—No! Not back to Uncle Max for more money! Let Max keep his lousy money. . . .

The doorway below was the slate gray of dawn. He had been asleep. He raised his cramped body and stretched and walked slowly down the steps. The street was still deserted. He sat down on the wooden steps at the edge of the street to watch the town wake up. The early morning air was crystalline. The monumental bluffs seemed a short drive away.

He waited and watched. The day gradually warmed and brightened. A man in work clothes, the first person of the new day, walked by and nodded. A car moved slowly by. Mr. Davis opened his feed store. More cars passed. The lights were on in Fred's Cafe across the street and the tiny thread of bacon scent that reached Dave was sweet, as sweet as he had ever smelled. Old Doc Hickman smiled and waved as though he had seen Dave there every day. The town was fully alive and the sun warm. The A&P and the filling stations had traffic.

The little black Ford pulled up in front of Dave and the boy with sky blue eyes smiled at him. "Find your friend?" His smile was suddenly warmer, more sincere.

"I don't need to find him any more."

"What about you? You planning to go back?"

"What for? I like it here."

"A little later, why don't we go out for a ride? Ride the range. Pretty country around here. I'll show you sights you can't see back East."

"I'd like that. I'd really like that."

"Meet you in half an hour up at Sweets," the blue-eyed boy said. "I need a haircut. Wait for me up there." The boy pulled the Ford away from the wooden sidewalk and moved down the street.

Dave glanced toward the stairway to Sweets. The barber pole was turning. He sat in the sun for a few more minutes and then walked up to the barber shop. All five barber chairs were occupied and most of the ring of waiting chairs were full. Dave went over to an empty one and sat down.

While he was waiting, a young man came in, somewhat in a hurry, an intense dark-haired young man wearing winter clothes. His facial expression was harried, unnerved. He looked around as though looking for someone. He walked over to the closest of the Sweets brothers. "Did a friend of mine come in here? Guy named Dave Klemmer? He was about so tall and was—"

"Look around," Sweets interrupted. "See if he's here."

The young man slowly scanned the faces of everyone in the shop. Dave smiled as the stranger's scanning eyes touched him and moved on. Dave continued to smile for a moment or two as he watched the young man complete his scan and hurry back down the steps to continue his search.

THE DOG INCIDENT

Patrick O'Keeffe

Patrick O'Keeffe

Patrick O'Keeffe has spent most of his life on ships. At sixteen he joined the British Navy during World War I and served three years as a wireless telegraphist aboard a destroyer in the North Sea. After that, he writes, "I went into the British merchant marine as a wireless officer. Later, I transferred to American-owned, British-flag freighters operating out of U.S. ports, and eventually to American passenger vessels as chief radio officer.

"The passenger ship I was in at the time of the Pearl Harbor attack was commandeered by the Navy, and I had to make way for Navy personnel. I sailed throughout the rest of the war as sole radio officer in war-materiel ships, ammunition ships, meat ships, plying the Caribbean, the North Atlantic, the Mediterranean, convoyed or running independently without escort. When the war ended, I returned to normal passenger-ship service."

Now retired and living in Brooklyn, O'Keeffe has turned from the sea adventures he wrote during his years in the merchant marine to mysteries. In "The Dog Incident" he presents a setting that is found all too seldom in fiction these days, and a story that has the sort of wry ending that O. Henry would have appreciated. He also presents a missing person.

About the story's origin, O'Keeffe says: "During one of my cruise-ship voyages, a valuable pedigreed dog believed to be owned by the president of a Central American republic accidentally leaped overboard in a calm sea. The dog could be seen swimming in the wake. The captain refused to turn back, peeved by a recent dispute over which department was responsible for animals. Talk around the ship after the voyage had it that he defended his action to company officials by saying that he didn't wish to endanger human life by ordering a boat away. Out of this came 'The Dog Incident.'"

A.M.

THE DOG INCIDENT

The disappearance of Captain Delf still remains one of the most baffling mysteries of the sea. Three years ago, on the evening before the freighter *Juron* was due to arrive in Los Angeles, Captain Delf left the supper table and presumably went straight up to his cabin. When the second mate went there with a query ten minutes later, the captain was not inside. During those ten minutes he had vanished as completely and silently as if he had been spirited up into outer space by an invisible flying saucer, with not even the Devil's Triangle to be adduced as a solution.

To the two FBI agents who came aboard to investigate, Mr. Kruper, the chief mate, said, "Captain Delf wasn't really missed until around seven o'clock, when the chief steward went to his cabin to get the captain's signature on his arrival papers. I turned the ship about at once, even before making absolutely sure he wasn't aboard. I steamed back along our course for a full two hours. There was no trace of him. That delayed our arrival until early this morning."

The two agents then went out to pursue their inquiries among the rest of the officers and the crew. After a while, one of them returned alone. He was a clean-shaven young man with perhaps slight knowledge of merchant ships and their personnel. "About the dog incident, Mr. Kruper, it seems to have caused a great deal of anger and resentment on board. Would you consider it feasible that a psycho of a dog lover could have been responsible for the captain's disappearance?"

The chief mate shook his head. "I don't know of a single man on board who'd match up to that description. Nor could such a man have attacked the captain in his cabin and disposed of his body overboard unseen. Also, as I wrote in the official log, the captain's cabin was in perfect order, no sign of a struggle."

"Captain Delf may have suddenly become deranged and rushed out on deck and jumped overboard."

"He appeared to be in the best of health and good spirits at the time, and had been so since he took command of the ship two weeks ago. He was a bachelor, without a hint of family troubles of any kind, apparently of sound mind. Let me point out something else to you."

The chief mate stepped from his cabin into the passageway, followed by the agent. The passageway ran across the entire length of the deck-officers' quarters. The chief mate's cabin was next to the captain's. At one end of the passageway was the stairway down to the dining saloon and the engineers' quarters, close to a door opening onto the boat deck; at the other end was a similar door to the boat deck on that side.

"Above each door," Mr. Kruper said, "a crew member was at work during those ten minutes. A young seaman was painting the bridge rails on one side, Old Ben stitching canvas on the other. One or the other would have seen the captain either being carried out and dropped overboard, or rushing out and jumping over."

"Captain Delf may have gone back down the stairway to the engineers' quarters."

"He'd only have gone down to see the chief engineer about something. The last time the chief saw him was when the captain got up from supper, cracking a joke with the chief engineer about his fuel report."

The agent assumed a perplexed frown. "Captain Delf simply didn't evaporate from his cabin. He was either carried out to the ship's side and dropped overboard, or he went out of his own free will and jumped over. There can be no other explanation."

There was another explanation, but the two agents went ashore to make their official report without having uncovered it.

THE DOG INCIDENT

When old Captain Bridges died of a heart attack aboard the *Juron* while she was en route from Guayaquil to Balboa, Captain Delf, then chief mate of another of the Line's vessels, had just reported back to the main office in San Francisco from his summer vacation. As the next in line for promotion to captain, he was flown down to Panama to take permanent command of the *Juron*.

During the forenoon of the first day out from Balboa, bound for Los Angeles and San Francisco, Captain Delf made a preliminary inspection of the ship by himself. At the end, he appeared in the chief mate's doorway. Captain Delf was a short, stubby man with a dour expression, about forty or so, with cropped black hair and mouse-size eyebrows. For this inspection he had worn fresh khakis, with black tie and brass hat, to show himself off to the crew.

Slowly removing the brier pipe from between his yellowed teeth, he said, "Mr. Kruper, there's a dog on board."

Mr. Kruper, taking a respite with a cigarette and still in the boiler suit he had worn for an inspection of the forepeak with the bosun, looked up at the captain serenely. "It belongs to old Ben, the four-to-eight helmsman. Captain Bridges gave him permission to keep it on board."

"See that it's put ashore in L.A."

"That will hit old Ben pretty hard," Mr. Kruper demurred. "That dog's about all there is in life for him."

"I don't want any animals aboard my ship." The captain put his pipe back between his teeth and walked away.

Mr. Kruper sat in gloomy dejection long after the captain had departed. He was a year or two younger than Captain Delf, taller and with a more agreeable expression. He had sailed as second mate under Delf as chief mate, and their relations had been anything but cordial, and more than once Mr. Kruper had spoken his mind. Chief Mate Delf had been the most disliked officer in the line among both crew and officers. Now that Mr. Kruper was under him as captain, he was only too well aware that he'd have to guard his tongue if he wished his own prospects for promotion to remain bright.

Mr. Kruper didn't break the news to old Ben until his bridge watch that same evening. The steering was on gyro, and old Ben was wiping off the binnacle cover. "Ben, I'm afraid you're going to have, to put Stumpy ashore in L.A. Captain's orders."

The old sailor stared at him in dismay. "What's Cap'n Delf got against Stumpy?"

"He doesn't want any animals on board."

"Stumpy ain't no animal. He's my dog."

"I tried to tell him that, Ben."

Ben turned and gazed bleakly through the wheelhouse windows across the smooth blue Pacific. He was tall and lean, the lines of sixty years running deep in leathery skin. Ben was believed to be without a relative of any sort, his shore address and next of kin the Seamen's Mission. The dog had hopped hesitantly up the accommodation ladder one afternoon in San Diego about a year before, wagging its stump of a tail hopefully at old Ben, who was on gangway watch. It was a small brown terrier of dubious ancestry; the end of its tail had been bitten or chopped off. Ben carried it down to the crew mess and fed it. No one came aboard looking for a lost dog, and so old Ben asked the captain's permission to keep it on board. The bosun named it Stumpy, and while Stumpy became the ship's pet, it was regarded as Ben's dog.

"If Stumpy goes ashore," Ben said bitterly, "I goes with him."

"Think it over, Ben. Shipping's not too good on the Coast right now. You might pound the bricks a long time before finding another ship."

"It's like the bosun said when he heard Delf was comin' here—she ain't goin' to be a happy ship no more."

During the next two or three days, Captain Delf made further rounds of the ship alone, but in coveralls. He first went into the four lifeboats to check the equipment. He went over the entire part above deck, from the anchor cables on the foc's'le head to the emergency steering gear aft. He climbed the radar mast to look at the scanner platform, and up to the crosstrees to inspect the topping-lift shackles.

"One of these days," the bosun growled to old Ben, perhaps hopefully, "he's gonna fall and break his neck through lookin' for somethin' to pick on to Mr. Kruper."

Mr. Kruper was indeed duly informed caustically of any adverse findings, and not always beyond the hearing of crew members. He was

THE DOG INCIDENT

in no doubt regarding the meaning of the inspections: Captain Bridges had always left the upkeep of his ship to the chief mate; Captain Delf was making it quite clear that henceforth Mr. Kruper would come under strict supervision, and no slackness would be tolerated.

When the ship was off the coast of Mexico, the dog went overboard. The weather was still balmy, and a young sailor was playing with Stumpy on the poop, teasing it with a piece of rag, darting aside whenever the dog leaped at it. Without realizing the danger, the young sailor had worked close to the ship's side, with his back to the rails. He stepped away again as the dog sprang, and Stumpy shot clean between the two lower rails and overboard.

Captain Delf was on the bridge at the time, leaning over the fore rail beside the chief mate. The rudder being on gyro, old Ben wasn't needed at the wheel, and was seated on an old wooden bench behind the wheelhouse, stitching a torn awning. As an old-timer, Ben was as proficient as a sailmaker with the leather palm and needle, and at such intervals, Mr. Kruper gave him odd jobs sewing canvas. The after area of the bridge stretched back to form the roof of the deck-officers' quarters, above the boat deck.

From his seat beside the bridge rails, Ben saw the young sailor run past beneath him and up the bridge ladder, coming to a halt behind the captain. He heard the sailor gasp, "Cap'n, Stumpy's overboard. I threw a life ring after him."

Mr. Kruper ran out to the wing and then back to the captain's side. "Stumpy's okay, didn't get foul of the propeller. He's bobbing in the wake."

The captain ignored him. He had turned in slow deliberation and, having removed his pipe, he was regarding the young sailor as if he had confessed to throwing the chartroom chronometer overboard. "You threw a life ring overboard?"

"That's right, sir. So you'd have a marker for finding Stumpy," the young sailor said eagerly, pleased with his quick thinking.

"You'll be logged one day's pay for destroying ship's property. Now get off the bridge."

The young sailor stared at the captain in disbelief. He looked around as old Ben came up beside him. Ben had dropped the canvas and run after the chief mate for a quick glimpse astern. He eyed the captain in alarm.

"Cap'n, ain't you goin' to turn back an' pick up Stumpy?"

"I don't risk human life for a little mongrel," the captain snapped.

Ben turned to the chief mate blankly. It was obvious what the old sailor was thinking. Wispy white clouds floated lazily in the red of approaching sunset; the sea looked as if it had just been ironed to a smooth sheen; a small fishing vessel lay becalmed with sail hanging slack. Lifeboats were often lowered during drills in port in weather that was a howling gale in comparison.

"But, Cap'n," Ben went on, "every man aboard 'ud be willin' to go away in a boat. I'll—"

The captain cut him short. "Get back to your stitching." Glaring at the young sailor, he snapped, "I ordered you off the bridge."

The captain stuck his pipe between his teeth and turned to lean over the rail again. The young sailor hurried down the ladder. Ben hastened out to the wing again and gazed astern. As though unable to bear the sight, he came back and looked at Mr. Kruper. The chief mate stared back at him helplessly.

"Cap'n," old Ben pleaded, "I ain't askin' you to lower a boat. Only to turn back an' drift up alongside old Stumpy. I'll shin down the ship's side on a rope an' grab him, take all the risk."

Captain Delf continued to gaze ahead as if he were a deaf mute. Ben stared at the captain's back for a few more seconds; then, with an expression of bitter hatred, he went back to his stitching.

As the chief mate feared, the incident inflamed the crew. When the bosun reported to him on the bridge next morning for his day's work orders, he told Mr. Kruper that all hands were boiling mad. "Some of 'em are talkin' about refusing to sign on for the next voyage if Cap'n Delf stays as master."

"Bosun," Mr. Kruper said sympathetically, "it won't get them anywhere. There's nothing in the Navigation Laws requiring a captain to order a lifeboat away to pick up a dog."

"Then there oughta be. We're all gonna take it up with the union if he holds to logging a man a day's pay over the life ring. We're gonna bring up all the beefs we've got a right to bring up. Show the Line this ain't the ship she was under Cap'n Bridges. We're gonna make a big stink about old Stumpy."

It was on arrival day that Captain Delf disappeared. The *Juron* was due in Wilmington late in the evening and, the weather being ideal and the forecast favorable, the chief mate told the bosun in the afternoon to rig the accommodation ladder, the type of gangway that hugs the ship's side down to a pier instead of out at an angle. At sea it was kept dismantled and lashed to the outside of the boat-deck rails, to prevent it from being washed overboard in rough seas.

Old Ben watched the men from above, seated on the old wooden bench, making a canvas cover for a boat reel. The bosun and his deck gang finished the job toward five o'clock, and after testing the electric winch used for lowering the free end of the gangway, the bosun and his men went below for supper.

The third mate came to the bridge to relieve the chief mate for supper. Also relieved on the bridge were old Ben and the young sailor who had been the cause of losing the dog overboard. All returned to the bridge about five-thirty. Ben resumed work on the canvas cover.

Presently he saw Captain Delf step from the doorway of the officers' quarters below him, chewing a toothpick. What apparently had attracted him out to the deck was the newly rigged gangway. It hung outside the rails like a painter's stage or scaffolding on the side of a building, ready for lowering.

Captain Delf gazed at the gangway for several moments, and then apparently decided to make an immediate inspection, now that it had been assembled. He climbed over the rails and onto it and worked toward the open end, one hand on the gangway rail. Near the end he went down on one knee for a closer look at something, perhaps a rusting shackle attaching the bridle chains to the gangway.

"Maybe something else to pick on the chief mate about," old Ben muttered to himself. "Serve him right if he fell off."

And then, though not quite as the bosun had predicted, the accident came about. Old Ben had glanced away at the moment and wasn't sure whether the captain slipped, or lost his balance, or a kink in the bridle chains suddenly cleared under the captain's weight and jerked the gangway. Ben heard a frightened gasp and was in time to see the captain tumbling backward into the sea.

Ben came to his feet. The chief mate had just gone into the chartroom, and the young sailor was painting the rails on the other side. For a long moment old Ben stood gazing astern at the black object bobbing about in the frothing wake. Then sat down again and went back to his stiching.

THE BLUE DOOR

Vincent Starrett

Vincent Starrett

The history of the detective story in the United States can be said to fall into two periods: before Dashiell Hammett, and after. He invented the hard-bitten private eye and brought to mystery fiction an air of realism that had been lacking in it before. So great is his influence that readers sometimes forget how mystery stories were told during the 1920's, before tough guys and cops with cynical viewpoints took them over.

Vincent Starrett's "The Blue Door" is a story of the 1920's. Specifically, the 1920's in Chicago. Speakeasies, gentlemen's clubs and a code of behavior that still bore traces, if not of Victorianism, at least of Edwardianism. The world of Conan Doyle, updated a few years and transported to the shores of Lake Michigan.

The late Vincent Starrett was a past president of Mystery Writers of America and the recipient of its first Grand Master of Mystery Award. According to his friend Robert Hahn, Starrett is "almost invariably referred to as a bookman. And that he was. But for a 'bookman' he had a most active and adventurous background. His work as a crime reporter, feature writer, and foreign correspondent made him as much at home in China or Mexico as in his book-filled apartment near Chicago's Wrigley Field; and as conversant with political personalities and literary luminaries as he was with cab drivers, conmen and Baker Street Irregulars.

"He is best remembered for his literary essays and *The Private Life of Sherlock Holmes,* but he left a significant body of work in the mystery genre." He was both a novelist and short story writer, his principal character being Jimmy Lavender.

"The Blue Door" is a piece of "classic" mystery writing. The war to end all wars had been fought, the Great Depression hadn't struck, it took four days to go from the East coast of the United States to the West Coast. But then, as now, mystery stories were being written. Then, as now, very good ones.

A.M.

THE BLUE DOOR

1

Obliquely returning, at a late hour (or early, as you prefer), from the Sea Lions' Saturday Nite Frolic, two shirt-fronted gentlemen, who addressed each other as Norway and Pemberton, affectionately linked arms and paraded, somewhat crazily, down the center of the street.

There was no mistaking their condition, and night-roaming taxi drivers, realizing the situation, hailed them hopefully. But the survivors of the recent hilarious celebration shook jovial heads and plodded onward in the Sunday morning silence. At intervals, however, the older of the two men tugged at his companion's arm, endeavoring to draw him over to the sidewalk.

"Come 'long, Norway," he urged, a little thickly. "Don't be a damn' fool. Let's get home."

"Let's not," suggested young Mr. Norway, with surprising clarity. He brandished his stick at a leering street lamp and tightened his grasp on the other's sleeve. " 'S the use of going home? There's nobody there."

The older man failed to appreciate this flight of logic. "We'll be pinched, first thing we know," he complained. "You don't want to be pinched, do you?"

"Let 'em," responded Norway, with some irrelevance, and continued his calisthenics with his stick. After a moment he added: "Tell you what let's do. Let's get some more Scotch and go to my place. No use going to bed now. Time to get up, Pemberton, ol' man. Time for breakfas' pretty soon. Whatcha say? Couple more little drinks, then we'll call it a night. Gotta get some more Scotch, though. Well, whatcha say?"

The man called Pemberton made a gesture of resignation. "All right," he agreed, "let's go to your place, wherever it is. But what's the sense of drinking all night? Besides, you can't get anything now. Everything's closed up—tight."

"H'm!" said young Mr. Norway scornfully. "I can get it any time I want it. *Any time,*" he repeated firmly. "Day or night," he added with conviction. "Know how to get a drink after midnight, Pemberton?"

"How?"

"Ask a cop!"

"You're drunk as a fool," said Pemberton.

His companion stood upon his dignity. "Not drunk at all," he retorted. "But I'm going to be. Know what'm talking about, ol' man. There's a cop at the next corner. You'll see."

Mr. Pemberton became uneasy. "Good God, Norway," he protested, "you can't ask a policeman for liquor! Do you know this man?" His own wits were clearing under the effect of apprehension.

"Don't know him at all," said the younger man, "but he's a cop, ain't he? An' all cops know where the liquor is, don't they? Can't fool me."

Mr. Pemberton became more and more perturbed. His perturbation increased as relentlessly they bore down upon the policeman at the corner. He made an effort to stop the headlong progress of his companion, but Norway had already engaged the attention of the patrolman. Mr. Pemberton sighed, and assumed a subservient position in the rear.

"Morning!" observed Norway cheerfully, bracing his feet and slightly rocking.

The bluecoat stared suspiciously.

"Awful sorry to bother you, ol' man, but we gotta get some liquor. Couple o' thirsty Sea Lions in need o' liquor." He stepped back and cupped his hands to his mouth. *"Whoo-o-o Whoo-o-o!"* he rumbled, with a sound like a contralto fog siren, and immediately explained, "Sea Lions—see? Y'ain't a Sea Lion yourself, officer?"

The officer was not. He was deeply interested, however.

"Thirsty, eh?" he countered.

"You bet," said Norway earnestly. "Wanta get some Scotch. *Good* Scotch," he added with great solemnity, "solid wool, eighteen karat. You know? Don't happen to know a good place, do you?"

Suppressing a smile, the policeman appeared to think deeply. After a moment he replied: "Well, yes, I do know a place not far from here." His glance took them both in, swiftly and shrewdly; but there seemed no doubt that they were quite innocent of guile. They appeared sincerely to want a drink. Furthermore, they were both already sufficiently liquored not to be likely to remember the incident.

"I'll tell you what you've got to do, boys," said the policeman. "This is Dearborn Street; I suppose you know that. Well, you go along here, the way you were going, for two blocks, then turn over west one block, then south again. There's a little street cuts in there, only a couple of blocks long, and in front of one of the houses you'll find an old cab—the only one left in the world, I guess. An old cab with a tired old horse attached to it. He stands with his head down, all the time, as if he was asleep, which maybe he is, and up on the box there'll be an old cabby, with his head down, and for all I know maybe he's asleep, too. Well there you are! All you got to do is get into the cab, then wake up the old cabby and tell him what you want. He'll take you where you can get it."

Pemberton stared, amazed at such directions from a policeman. Norway, however, received the nightmarish direction with gratitude and assurance. It was as if he had been given merely a street number and a name. He turned at once.

"Many thanks, ol' man," he nodded. "Knew you could fix us up. Well, many thanks!" And the hand that had been fumbling the change in his pocket came out with a reckless handful. It was the policeman's turn to thank his interrogators.

"There!" said Norway triumphantly, as they moved away. "What'd I tell you? Any time you want a drink in this town—just ask a cop!"

Pemberton breathed a long sigh of relief. "By Golly, I *need* one," he remarked plaintively.

"Now," continued the younger man, as briskly as ever, "what'd that cop tell us to do?"

"I know the street," answered his companion. "It must be Baker Street. Let's get there in a hurry. I'm sober as a judge."

He led the other to the sidewalk, this time without demur, and they continued their advance for two blocks, as directed, before turning to the west. At Baker Street they halted and looked quickly at each other. Suddenly both were smiling.

For two squares to the southward the little thoroughfare extended, lined on either side with tall residence buildings; and before the second house from the corner stood a tired horse attached to a decrepit cab of World's Fair vintage—Chicago, 1893. Asleep upon the box sat an ancient cabman.

"Well," observed Pemberton, "he's there."

"Sure he's there," said young Mr. Norway in a matter-of-fact tone. "Did you think he wouldn't be? Any time you want anything in Chicago, ol' man, just call a cop. Wanta taxi? Call a cop! Wanta cab? Call a cop! Wanta drink? Call a cop! Wanta policeman? Call a cop!"

He bore down upon the antique vehicle and, opening the door, climbed in and sat down. More slowly, Pemberton followed him. Neither horse nor driver stirred. The older man reopened and again closed the door, with some violence. Mr. Norway, a wizard of resource, thrust his stick through the open front window and sharply prodded the cabman with the ferule. "Probably dead," he observed casually; and then the sleeper stirred and turned upon them.

The wrinkled face of the old driver was thrust toward them beyond the open window; his eyes were blinking.

"*Whoo-o-o!*" roared young Mr. Norway, in imitation of a sea lion. "Attaboy, Methuselah. All together now, gentlemen! *We want liquor! We—want—liquor!*"

"Shut up, you damned fool!" said Pemberton tensely. "Do you want to wake up the neighborhood?" Leaning forward toward the peering countenance, he asked in a low voice, "Can we get a drink, brother?"

"Right!" said the driver, and turned to rouse his slumbering animal with a long whip.

"Right away," said young Mr. Norway, and fell asleep in his corner of the cab.

Pemberton looked at his companion with disgust in his glance. The opportunity to escape from the turbulent Norway seemed to have arrived. Still, he decided, after a moment, he might as well see it through. Norway might wake if he stopped the cab to get out, and then there would be another scene. Besides, he had no idea where Norway lived when he was at home, and it was probably necessary —decent, anyway—to get the idiot home, somehow. Let him have his drink, and possibly he would go along by himself.

He leaned back in his own corner and noted the curious career of the cab. Ingenious, he told himself; very ingenious indeed. The course, while erratic, was very methodical, and he was not surprised when, twenty minutes after they had departed, they drove up to the same house in Baker Street from which they had embarked.

He wakened Norway without ceremony and bundled that sleepy inebriate out onto the sidewalk. A door, slightly below the level of the sidewalk, stood open, and at the top of a flight of steps inside an unseen light was burning. The morning air was raw and chilly, and Norway shivered.

"The blue door at the top of the first flight," said the driver, accepting a gratuity. "Tell 'em that the sleeping cabman sent you."

Pemberton nodded curtly and led his companion inside. By degrees Norway was coming back to consciousness.

"Funny steps," he muttered, looking vaguely up the stairway, and pronouncing the word *shteps*. "Got brass trimmings, ain't they?" At the edge of each step the runner was bound with a strip of metal.

He stumbled after his companion until they stood upon a landing confronting a door that had been painted blue. Pemberton knocked softly with his knuckles against the panel, and the blue door was slightly opened. In the aperture was framed a hideously ugly woman, who looked back at them with unfriendly eyes.

"Well?" asked the woman sharply.

"We were told," explained Pemberton, "that we could get—ah— something to drink here."

"Were yese now?" sneered the woman, and her ugly face seemed to contract with malevolence. "Who told yese that maybe?"

"The sleeping cabman," replied Pemberton politely, and gave her a smile.

For an instant she continued to stare at them, as though upon the instant she had conceived for them a dislike and an antipathy that would never end. Then, "Come in," she said abruptly, and they passed into a sudden blaze of light.

2

Arthur Norway came slowly out of a deep slumber and looked about him at the familiar furnishings of his own room. Everything was as it should be, and for some moments he lay quietly on his pillow without memory of the events of the preceding hours of darkness.

After a time it occurred to him that his head was aching with quiet persistence and his tongue was thick and coated. An instant later, as he started to sit up, his dark sleeve attracted his attention, and he noted with a sense of bewilderment that he was fully dressed. At that point memory began to function, and with a bound he was out of bed and standing stupidly in the center of his chamber.

The declining sunlight of afternoon was coming in through his window, and a glance at his watch confirmed his suspicion that he had been asleep for a number of hours. It was, in point of fact, three o'clock Sunday afternoon.

Suddenly he became conscious that the telephone bell was ringing; that it had been ringing for some time. Probably it was that which had awakened him. There was an exasperated note in the outcry of the alarm bell. Pemberton probably, ringing him up to ask how he felt. The answer to that one was easy. He felt like hell.

Slowly he moved to the instrument and placed the receiver against his ear. After a moment it occurred to him to say "Hello," and he said it.

It was not Pemberton; it was Taylor, reminding him of an engagement for that evening. Well, to the devil with Taylor! Without troubling to speak, he hung up the receiver and was called back a few minutes later. Taylor was under the impression that he had been cut off by the operator. Norway disillusioned him and again hung up the receiver.

Wow, what a head! And his tongue tasted like a brown plush vest. He had a policeman to thank for that. A policeman and a sleeping cabman. Poor old Pemberton! He was probably a wreck, too. He remembered everything very clearly now. At the top of the steps there had been a blue door, and then—in the doorway—an ugly woman with red hair. She had passed them in, and then there had been a barroom and a lot of people drinking. Lots of light, lots of glasses tinkling, lots of men, but not so many women. A flashy place with a long mirror and a lot of tables. A regular old-fashioned bar, though, with a brass rail and everything. The bartender's hair, he recalled, was parted in the middle and plastered down on the temples just the way a bartender's hair should be.

He supposed he had done a lot more drinking himself; in fact, he remembered some of it. He remembered it all, up to a point. Then everything had sort of faded out, like a picture on the screen. He and Pemberton had got separated somehow, he supposed. But no! Pemberton must have seen him home. Who else would have bothered?

"Wotta head!" observed young Mr. Norway idiomatically, and returned to the telephone.

He gave the number of the club where he had met Pemberton and asked for that member. Mr. Pemberton, the operator told him, was not in.

"When did he go out?" asked Norway.

The operator consulted someone else. "He didn't come here last night," she reported.

Good night!

What had happened, Norway wondered, to old Pemberton?

The operator was asking, "Who *is* this?" as he started to hang up. "Norway," he said. "Tell him Norway called, when he comes in."

"Oh, *yes!*" said the girl, with heavy sarcasm. "Why not Portugal?" She terminated the connection with a spiteful *click*.

Mr. Norway sat down in a chair to think it over. After all, he had got Pemberton into this mess, by insisting on approaching the policeman. What ought to be done about it?

But—pshaw! Pemberton was a grown man, capable of looking after himself. Probably a good drinker, too. He had gone to a hotel, no doubt, or to a Turkish bath. Probably he hadn't gone to bed at all.

"You're a better man than I am, Gordon gin," said Norway aloud, and decided that he was an ass to worry about Pemberton. Pemberton had been drinking prewar cocktails when Arthur Norway had been drinking root beer at school.

A little later in the day, however, when he had bathed and dined and was feeling somewhat more human, Norway again called his companion's club. Pemberton had not yet returned, and there had been no word from him.

"Is this Sweden again?" asked the operator, recognizing his voice. "No, Mr. Pemberton hasn't come in yet."

With a mild oath, Norway replaced the receiver.

Well, that was that. Then, his conscience reproaching him, he called up Taylor, apologized for his rudeness, and the two friends foregathered for the evening. Norway said little about his exploits of the preceding night, beyond explaining that he had done some important drinking.

In the morning he called Pemberton again, and learned with genuine alarm that still there had been no word of him. The operator was brusque and indisposed to answer questions.

Norway's elastic conscience again smote him. If anything had happened to Pemberton, he was to blame. He didn't know where Pemberton worked, or he would have called his office. Maybe Pemberton didn't work at all; he looked like a bit of a capitalist.

"Ought I to call the police?" asked Norway, addressing the scratch pad on his telephone. There was no reply to his question, which, in consequence, remained unanswered. He fell into a panic of thinking.

If he called the police and nothing had happened to Pemberton, his friend might be angry. A lot of undesirable publicity might result about nothing. After all, Pemberton didn't owe him any explanations. Pemberton wasn't bothering *him* with telephone calls about his health.

Monday evening Mr. Norway was seized of a brilliant idea. He had them at times. Before leaving the office he telephoned one Honeywell, an old friend whom he had neglected in recent weeks, and asked him to dinner at the Belle Isle. Mr. Honeywell was charmed to accept.

They met in the lobby and went into conference over the oysters.

Bartlett Honeywell was a name well known to a vast section of the American public. It was a name that appeared over exciting mystery tales in popular magazines for sale at all newsstands. But Bart Honeywell was known to Arthur Norway chiefly because they had attended high school together. In those days Norway had worked out Honeywell's mathematics for him, and in return Honeywell had written Norway's "compositions." Although their ways lay widely apart, they were still friends, and each admired the other as much as he deserved to be admired. Honeywell admired Norway because he made a great deal of money in an office, and Norway admired Honeywell because he wrote stories that editors bought and printed and that other people read.

The amateur detective nodded sagaciously throughout his friend's recital, and seemed to understand perfectly.

"So there you are," concluded Norway. "Pemberton's probably missing—God knows where!—and it's my fault. Now the question is, ought I to go to the police—I've told you why I don't like to—or just go on making inquiries myself? Or ought I to forget the whole business?"

"Forget nothing," answered Honeywell promptly. "The man may be murdered!"

Norway hadn't admitted that possibility even to himself. He jumped nervously. "By Jove!" he observed, weakly inadequate.

"What we've got to do," continued Honeywell, "is find him ourselves. I'll help you. You can't do it yourself; you've got to be at the office during the day."

"Oh, I could get away," said Norway easily.

"Well, if I need you," conceded Honeywell, "we'll think about it." He frowned thoughtfully. "Not much to go on, I'm afraid. I wish you hadn't been so drunk, Norway. You forget the most important details."

"We can find the house again," protested Norway. "I'd recognize it in a minute."

"You don't even remember the name of the street," commented the writer, "yet you remember Pemberton mentioning it. And you can be sure of one thing: that old scoundrel with the cab won't be there during the day. He's the *night* lookout. The policeman, too, is a night man, and probably he won't admit anything. It's one thing to ask a policeman what you did when you're drunk, and another thing to ask him when you're sober."

"I wish I'd never seen him," declared Norway earnestly. "Well, we've got to do it at night then, Honeywell."

"Yes," agreed the other, "I guess we've got to do it at night. *This* night, as a matter of fact. Already too much time has been allowed to elapse. You're sure you never heard anything about Pemberton's place of business?"

"I know I never did. He's a new acquaintance, as I told you; and that's the worst of it. A nice fellow that I meet, whom I like and who likes me; and first shot out of the box I run him into this!"

"Well, he must have a business some place, where they may know what's become of him. Some place where people are agitated about him. Anyway, there's the club. You'd better try it again, before we start out. He may have come back."

However, Pemberton had not been heard from by anyone at the club; but in the telephone booth of the restaurant Norway had a shock. In the side pocket of his light overcoat he found a strange card.

"Now, how the devil did that get there?" he asked his friend, as they stood together in the lobby, preparing to go out.

The author-detective took the card and read: "Mademoiselle Marie Stravinsky, Russian Dancer." He turned his peering, thick-lensed eyes upon his friend.

"You never heard of her?" he asked.

"Never in my life."

"Of course," said Honeywell, "a man gets a great many cards thrust at him. Some of them he accepts and absently drops into his pocket."

"No," asserted Norway, "nobody handed it to me. I'd be sure to remember."

"I'm inclined to doubt it; but maybe! What you are thinking, of course, is that this card was put in your pocket, by someone in the speakeasy while you were intoxicated."

"Something like that," admitted Norway.

"Did you take your overcoat off?"

"I don't know. I think it was off when I went in. Oh, hang it, I don't remember!"

He knotted his brows for an instant. "Wait a minute! Honeywell, I'll bet I found that card in the cab. It just popped into my head. I can't swear to it, but I have a hazy sort of recollection about it. I seem to remember finding something on the seat when I climbed in."

"Why should you stuff it in your pocket?"

"Good God, why should I do *any* of the things I did? Why should I want more liquor? Why should I ask a policeman for directions to a gin palace?"

The amateur detective was thoughtful. "You may be right," he said, after a moment. "If you *did* find it in the cab it's important—or it may be. Of course, someone else may have dropped it there. In fact, someone else *did* drop it there. Of course! It's an admission card, see? It's one way of getting into the place with the blue door."

Again he was thoughtful.

"Or possibly it was dropped there by Pemberton, and you picked it up *after* he had climbed in. In which case it's a clue also, for she will be a friend of Pemberton's and may have heard from him."

Mr. Norway again felt inclined to say "By Jove!" and said it before he could stop himself. "Bart," he added with enthusiasm, "you're a marvel!"

"No, I'm not," said Honeywell, who knew very well his limitations; "but the card is something to work on, anyway, and I'm glad you found it. Look here, Norway, this is only Monday night, after all. Pemberton may be all right. Let's give him until morning to show up at the club. Meanwhile, I'll take this card and try to get a line on Mademoiselle Stravinsky. If she's at all well known somebody will know where she lives; and I'd like to be able to call on her tomorrow."

"All right," agreed Norway, "whatever you think best."

Vastly relieved by the knowledge that his clever friend was at work on the mystery, he went about his own business, while Honeywell, proud of his first real detective case, immediately set to work to discover the whereabouts of the Russian dancer.

"She's probably not a Russian," muttered the amateur detective, "and probably not much of a dancer, or it wouldn't be necessary to have that kind of a card to advertise her. On the whole, I fancy it's an admission card to the place with the blue door. Now, if I only knew how to find that place!"

The ease with which he discovered the address of Mademoiselle Stravinsky shocked him. The first man he asked seemed to know all about her. His informant was the leader of the restaurant orchestra, to whom the investigator had gone as soon as his friend's back was turned.

"Sure," said the orchestra leader, "I know her. Not personally, y' understand; but I know who she is. She's a cabaret dancer; everybody knows her. Used to be at the Whip-poor-Will, over in State Street, but I don't know just where she works now. Anyway, she lives at the Sandblast. You know the big apartment building over near the lake? She's got an apartment there."

Honeywell, deeply grateful, wasted no further time. If she lived at the Sandblast, she wasn't so far away at that minute; and there was no time like the present. He commandeered a taxicab and drove rapidly to the lake-front apartments.

What luck, he thought, if he should find Pemberton that very night! But that would be almost too easy. Furthermore, it would probably mean that nothing had happened to Pemberton. It didn't take much of a detective, he reflected, to find a man who wasn't lost. As reflecting credit upon Bartlett Honeywell, the case would be somewhat of a flop.

"Great Scott, what a bloodthirsty fellow I'm getting to be!" murmured the young man. "Here I'm almost hoping something *has* happened to him!"

At the Sandblast he ran his eye down the roster of names that appeared over the doorbells, and found a duplicate of the line of type on Norway's card: *Mademoiselle Marie Stravinsky.* The additional words, *Russian Dancer,* had been scissored off to make the strip fit into its frame. He plunged his thumb into the minute button underneath. After a moment the release clicked like a telegraph instrument, and he adjusted his cravat and mounted the stairs.

Honeywell was not disappointed. Russian dancers, in anticipation, are lithe and beautiful. This one was both. She was not notably Russian, he reflected; she was, in point of fact, dark and Hebraic.

However, she was radiantly young. How jolly it was to be an amateur detective, thought Honeywell, jiggling his cuffs into view.

Mademoiselle Stravinsky, however, was taken aback.

"Oh!" she exclaimed, then hesitated. "I thought you were someone else," she said, after a moment.

"No, mademoiselle," said Honeywell pleasantly. "May I introduce myself?" He did so. "The gentleman you were expecting is not Mr. Pemberton, by any chance?"

The dancer stared and frowned. "I do not understand you, sir," she answered, clipping her words in foreign fashion. "Perhaps it is the wrong bell that you have rung?"

"That may be," admitted the amateur. "You don't know anyone named Pemberton, you mean?"

"I am sorry, but I do not know the gentleman you mention. You will pardon me if I close the door?"

She had begun to do so when Honeywell recovered his wits. "I beg your pardon," he continued hurriedly. "The fact is, I was led to believe that he was a friend of yours. I'm sorry if I have made a mistake. You see, I found your card in his room."

He made the last assertion boldly and untruthfully, and waited to see its effect.

"My card?" The pretty young woman was perplexed. "In the room of a Mr. Pemberton?"

The investigator conceded a point. "Well, in *one* of his rooms."

"I must ask you to explain."

"I should like to, mademoiselle. May I come in for a moment? I am quite respectable, I assure you."

She flung open the door, and with a gesture invited him to enter. The apartment, he noted, was small and all but incapable of secreting anybody for long. After all, he decided, the truth was best. Certainly this charming creature was no criminal. He dropped into a big chair and told the story, suppressing only the fact that the card had been found in the ancient vehicle of the sleeping cabman.

"Why, it is wonderful!" she breathed when he had finished. "It is like a novel, is it not? And you—you are one of those clever detectives, Mr. Honeywell?"

"No," asserted the clever detective, "that would be a bit thick, you know. I'm just a friend of Mr. Norway's, trying to help him out."

The dancer drew another breath of enchantment. "How sorry I am not to be able also to help," she cried. "But you can see how impossible that is. I do not even know this Mr. Pemberton. As for my card, I can only suppose that it was given to him by someone else."

"I understand," said Honeywell. By George! She was stunning! "Well, thank you, anyway. And now I'll run along." He stood up and reached for his hat.

"Thank *you,*" said Mademoiselle Stravinsky. "Why, it is as good as a play, is it not? Except for your poor Mr. Pemberton. He, of course, is probably most unhappy. But may I not make a suggestion? Possibly he is ill. Possibly he was taken to a hospital. Have you called at the hospitals, Mr. Honeywell?"

Mr. Honeywell, feeling abysmally juvenile, admitted that he had not. "I never thought of it," he confessed. "It was a good idea, my coming to you, if only to get a common-sense view of the case."

On the steps, the amateur detective decided that he had been an ass. As for Mademoiselle Stravinsky, she was a beauty, and she had treated him very well indeed. Not many women would have bothered to listen to him.

He caught another taxi and headed for the apartment of Arthur Norway. There was a telephone there, anyway, and between them they could call up the different hospitals.

A disturbing thought began to gnaw at his mind. Surely that card meant something. Maybe the girl was telling the truth. Maybe she *didn't* know Pemberton. But that didn't prove that she had no connection with the place of the blue door. Had he been fooled? She had been very smooth, that good-looking girl. Had she been playing with him? But no, she had been very open and aboveboard; and he had mentioned the blue door. And yet . . . He leaned back in the taxicab.

Ho hum, thought Bartlett Honeywell, a bit wearily, this playing at detective wasn't as easy as he had thought. In fiction, now, he would have had a confession in five minutes. It was odd how clever his creations were, when he himself was so bungling.

Norway greeted him with eagerness. "What luck?" asked that young man, even before the writer could remove his hat.

The amateur shrugged. "I've seen the Russian dancer," he replied.

"In fact, I've talked with her. She's a knockout!"

"A knockout?"

"You know what I mean. She's very good-looking. Anyway, she knows nothing. But she made a whacking good suggestion. She suggested that we call up the hospitals."

"By Jove!" cried Norway. "Well, I suppose we *could* do that. You must have made quite a hit with the lady, Bart, to have her making suggestions. She didn't pull the wool over your eyes, I suppose?" He chuckled.

Honeywell grinned provokingly. "She isn't the woman who let you in at the blue door, anyway," he retorted. "This one is a real beauty. Just the same," he admitted, "I've been wondering, since I left her, whether she wasn't almost *too* nice to me."

"The woman at the speakeasy had red hair and a face like the wrath of God," said Norway.

"This one has black hair and a face like a—like a—"

"I know," nodded Norway. "Let it go at that, old man."

He picked up a telephone directory with a red back and turned to the list of hospitals. After a moment he groaned. "Lord, what a lot of them!"

"This one wore a seal ring," continued Honeywell casually. "You don't remember a seal ring anywhere around that blue door, I suppose?"

Norway was suddenly interested. He hung up the receiver, which he had just plucked from its hook. "A *seal* ring?" he echoed.

"A regular man's ring; I noticed it particularly. The design on the stone intrigued me; it was the head of a sphinx."

"The head of a *sphinx!*" shrieked Norway.

"Something like that. You don't mean to say you *do* recognize it?"

Norway collapsed into a chair. "Good God, Bart," he cried, "it's Pemberton's! I remember every line of it. I saw it on his finger that night!"

Bartlett Honeywell got quickly to his feet. For a moment he stood silent, his eyes on those of his friend. Then he spoke slowly.

"I guess I've been a fool, Norway," he observed. "But she won't fool me again. Will you come along?"

Their progress to the Sandblast was marked by an array of speeding street lamps that fell behind them like a comet's tail; but even so they were too late.

"Miss Stravinsky has gone away," said the resident manager of the apartment building, when they had routed him from his chambers. "She left about half an hour ago. . . . No, sir, I don't know where she went. She was called away suddenly, she said, and might be gone for some time. She's given up the apartment. . . . Yes, sir, she only had it by the month; the furniture is ours. . . . No, sir. . . . Yes, sir. . . . Yes, sir. . . . No, sir. . . . I'm afraid not, sir. . . . Very well, sir. . . . Good night, sir!"

3

There are parts of Chicago that are as satisfyingly picturesque as anything Europe can show. At night, when the shadows have painted out the ugliness that the sunlight loves to reveal, there are old-world glimpses that are worth going a distance to see. This is particularly true of what is locally known as the Near North Side, a district not too far from the roaring heart of the Loop, in which a motley of peoples and of passions have taken up their abode.

The neighborhood is known by its show spots, which is too bad, for they are quite the least attractive of the scenes it has to offer. There is that place, up a flight of stairs, where the waiters dance as they carry in one's midnight supper, while the cook howls doleful ballads in the kitchen. And there is that blowsy club, up a miserable alley, that is a rendezvous for near-thinkers of a radical turn of thought. Free-thinkers, sex adepts, and notoriety seekers generally, speak their mind there, receiving for their performances half the contents of an impromptu tambourine. And there are little obscure back parlors, yet, where obscure poets and their lights-o'-love sit at sloppy tables and in the swash of dubious Budweiser catch a remote echo of the waves that beat on seacoast Bohemia.

But these are not the places to see. It is the accidental vignettes, the little washed-in sketches that are worth the journey. There is Elm Street, for instance, with its quaint old houses with white porcelain doorknobs and brass knockers. It progresses soberly westward from the Drive and almost ends in the broad front of a church then queerly changes its mind and winds up in a narrow byway west of LaSalle. It is like a bit of old London. The great gray mass of the Newberry Library bulks through the trees at Walton Square, and among its treasures are Latin breviaries, Sanskrit volumes with copper leaves, and an illuminated manuscript roll of the Bhagavad Ghita. To those who rest on the benches in the square there comes at times a silver chiming of bells from a neighboring temple, lost at intervals in the whir of motors in the avenue beyond and the strident voice of the fanatic who harangues an audience from a soapbox on the corner.

To the east, in Dearborn Street, the houses are elderly and tall, and once they were fashionable; but to-day placards stand in the windows or creak at the end of metal arms thrust outward from the stairheads. "Furnished Apartments," the placards say, or, more simply, "Rooms." Crossing the long thoroughfare at intervals, from east to west, are other streets of similar appearance, lined with gaunt, solemn houses, which at night, by the curious suggestion of darkness, sometimes seem fraught with sinister significance.

In one of the tall houses of this district was a large apartment on the second floor, to which access was gained by means of a blue door. And it was to seek this door, and that which lay beyond, that Messrs. Bartlett Honeywell and Arthur Norway went forth on the evening of the day that followed their fiasco at the apartment of Mademoiselle Stravinsky.

The hour was sufficiently late, and near an important intersection in Dearborn Street they halted their steps.

"Well," observed Norway, "there's the policeman, anyway." He indicated the tall figure of a man in uniform some distance beyond them.

"There's *a* policeman," corrected Honeywell. "Whether or not he's *your* policeman remains to be seen."

"I'm almost certain this is the corner," insisted the other, a bit nervously. "Besides, I ought to be able to recognize the fellow."

The amateur detective shrugged dubiously. "We can only try," he said. "Will you do the talking, or shall I?"

"If he recognizes me I'll do it," replied Norway. "If not, *you'd* better take him in hand."

They approached slowly and halted before the policeman, who turned brusquely to confront them. There was no gleam of recognition in his glance. Norway, lacking the liquid courage that had fortified him on the preceding Saturday, made apologetic noises in his throat. His companion spoke.

"Beg pardon, officer," he began, "but do you recognize this gentleman?"

The policeman's gaze became more intent, and the unfortunate Norway squirmed.

"I can't say that I do," answered the policeman, and asked a question of his own: "What's the idea? Am I supposed to know him?"

"The fact is," continued Honeywell, "he was drunk last Saturday night and you gave him certain directions, he believes. He was with another gentleman, somewhat older and, I believe, somewhat less intoxicated. As the other gentleman has disappeared, we are naturally anxious to locate him."

The policeman was interested. "*I* gave him directions?" he echoed. "I don't remember them. What were the directions?"

"He and his friend were looking for some liquor, and they asked a policeman where they could get some. The policeman told them. I don't know that you were the policeman."

"Oh, you *don't!*" cried the bluecoat with solemn irony. He added: "Say, what are you fellows trying to do? Kid me?"

"On my honor," replied Honeywell, "I'm telling what I believe to be the truth. A policeman told my friend here of a place where he could get some liquor; where, in fact, he *did* get some liquor. Later, the gentleman who was with my friend disappeared, and we are afraid that something has happened to him."

"Oh, you are afraid that something has happened to him?" The policeman's sarcasm became more profound, a thing of weight and substance. After a moment he spoke again, gently and with an almost friendly smile. "Look here, buddy, I don't know whether you're coo-coo or *I* am, but just you move quietly along and forget that stuff, or something *might* happen to *you*. See? Take a tip from a friend, and get started."

"If you're not the man," said the amateur detective in friendly tones, "of course you think I'm crazy. I don't blame you. But let me ask you just one more question: Do you know anything about the sleeping cabman?"

The burly policeman retreated a step. "The *what?*" he demanded.

"The sleeping cabman. An old fellow asleep on a cab, you know, who takes people where they want to go. He only lets on he's asleep until you climb into his cab; then he whips up his horse and—"

The policeman's hand fell lightly on the speaker's shoulder. There was a smile on his lips. "Never heard of him, buddy," he interrupted. "So he lets on he's asleep, does he? Cunning old rascal! Sorry I can't help you. You might ask the copper on the next corner, though; he's pretty keen after sleepers. But if you'll take a tip from me, you won't ask anybody, but just run along home and get into bed. Wonderful place—bed—when you ain't feeling well," he added sententiously.

Honeywell burst into a fit of laughter. "You still think we're a couple of lunatics," he cried. "I'm beginning to think so myself. It's pretty wild, isn't it? And yet, it's all true. Well, thanks anyway. I imagine we're lucky we're not taking a ride with *you.*"

The two friends tramped off in the darkness and no word was spoken between them until they had reached the next corner. Then Honeywell said dryly: "I think we've had enough of policemen, Norway, until we go to them in the regular way. We're going to find this damned blue door by ourselves."

"You didn't ask him about that," said Norway.

"No, I knew just when to quit."

Norway nodded. "All right," he replied; "but listen, Bart—*that* was the policeman! Don't contradict me. I *know!* I was too scared to tell him so—but he's the man, and don't you forget it. Now, come on."

He cast about him for a moment, and then turned briskly up the side street. "It's either this street or the next one," he said. "I've forgotten the exact directions, but I know the way we walked."

They stopped at the first north-and-south intersection and looked blankly at each other. There was no ancient cab at the curbstone of any house in view; no tired horse, no sleeping cabman; no cabman living or dead, awake or slumbering.

"And yet," muttered Norway, "those look like the houses."

They crossed the street and entered the narrow residence block that paralleled Dearborn Street. In one doorway, level with the sidewalk, from which it was only a few steps removed, a dim light was burning. Beyond its feeble illumination a flight of steps ascended. The door was open. Pushing closer in, Norway observed that the steps were bound at every edge by a metal strip. The fact woke a slumbering memory in his brain. He turned to his companion.

"Bart," he said, "either this is the very place or its twin brother. Shall we risk it?"

For answer, Honeywell stepped forward and passed through the open door. Then in silence they ascended the poorly lighted stairway until they stood upon a landing before a door that certainly once had been painted blue.

"The blue door!" whispered Norway, and Honeywell raised his hand and rapped with his knuckles against the panel. Within were the familiar sounds of subdued revelry.

The story writer knocked more loudly, and suddenly all sound ceased. In a moment steps were heard beyond the barrier, and the door creaked open on ancient hinges. A formidable-looking man stood in the opening; he glared out at them with baleful eyes.

But Norway, timorous in the presence of uniformed law and order, in the presence of this stranger was undismayed. To the snarling "Whadda yuh want?" of the man in the doorway, he replied smilingly, "Liquor."

The mountainous bouncer sneered. "Who sent yuh *here?*" he demanded, truculently. "This is a private home."

"The sleeping cabman," said Norway, and stepped six inches nearer. The door was beginning to close in his face.

"Mademoiselle Marie Stravinsky," said Honeywell suavely, and shoved the card he carried under the man's red nose.

The fellow shrugged. He pulled the door open half a foot. "You're new ones to *me,*" he observed ungraciously, "but I s'pose you're all right. Don't make so much noise next time you come, boys," he added in better humor. "We thought the place was pinched."

They slid through and looked about them with eager eyes.

Norway's first impulse was to say quickly, "This is not the place," and go out; but his friend's fingers were on his arm, as if he sensed the danger, and together they strode forward to the long bar that flanked one side of the room.

"All right, Jim," said the man at the door, and an oily barkeep glided forward to receive their order.

In the wide mirror that hung behind the bar Honeywell studied his friend's face and read the doubt written there. "We're in wrong," he said inwardly, and gave his order with great nonchalance to the oily barkeep.

"Let's sit down, Artie," he remarked to Norway, avoiding a reference to his friend's surname, and when their drinks had been set before them they carried them to a table, which fortunately was unoccupied.

"Wrong place?" asked the writer casually, as if passing the time of day; and Norway nodded.

"The glass is on the wrong side, and so's the bar," replied his friend. "Less swanky, too. All men here. The other place was—ah—co-educational."

Honeywell laughed. "We'll leave after a drink or two," he said. "Take it easy, old chap. Lots of time."

Over the rim of his glass he began a careful scrutiny of the long room. There were perhaps thirty men present, all drinking, and three youngish citizens were doing duty behind the bar. There appeared to be everything on hand that anyone might care to drink, and a great deal that Bartlett Honeywell had no notion of trying. On the whole, the appearance of the place was much similar to that of an old-fashioned barroom of the better sort. The men, for the most part, seemed harmless enough Republicans and Democrats.

Mr. Honeywell sipped leisurely at his Scotch-and-soda and decided that he was beginning to enjoy the chase. At the bar he had asked for a Scotch highball, but in private he preferred to think of the compound as Scotch-and-soda; the phrase had greater literary connotations. It pleased him now to fancy himself a private detective of wide clandestine celebrity, sipping the drink that such detectives like best.

In a little while a small man came out of a back room and, glancing quickly about the place, came over to their table and sat down. A waiter from behind the bar came to his side and received his order. Messrs. Norway and Honeywell accepted his company without outward demonstration. When he had inhaled a draught from his tumbler the newcomer became friendly.

"Don't think I've seen you here before, boys," he said affably. "Glad to see you. Any friend of the house is a friend of mine." He made the remark with proper modesty, yet with a proper appreciation of the honor he was conferring upon the newcomers by his interest. He added: "Name's Silvernail—Julian Silvernail."

Withholding his own name and that of his friend, Honeywell hastened to indicate that they were delighted to make Mr. Silvernail's acquaintance. They hadn't been in before, he added, but they hoped to be in again often, now that they had found the place.

Julian Silvernail understood perfectly. "Nice little place," he observed with some condescension. "Gawd knows who gets the graft, but it's a nice little place. Maybe you know my name. I do a little turn over at the Pollymabel. Song and dance."

"An actor!" cried Honeywell in ecstasy.

"Well, something like that, you know." Mr. Silvernail was deprecatory. "Everybody seems to know me, anyway." He smiled and inhaled another draught of liquid, setting down his glass to wave a friendly hand at the huge man at the door. "Everybody knows *me*," he repeated. "I'm wise to all these places. Lead you to 'em with my eyes shut."

Honeywell's suspicions began to diminish. The man was patently an egotist, and probably just what he claimed to be, a cheap artist in neighborhood vaudeville. It was just conceivable that he might be made useful.

"We thought we might run into a friend of ours here," said the writer after a moment. "He comes here sometimes. Haven't seen him for a day or two. Maybe he's sick." There was considerable noise at the moment; he resolved to risk the name. "His name's Pemberton," he continued. "You don't happen to know him?"

"Pemberton?" repeated Silvernail. " 'S funny. I seem to know that name. Knew a fellow named Pemberton out in 'Frisco, once; probably not the same fellow, though."

"The fact is," Honeywell went on, "we're a bit worried about Pemberton. He drinks too much. Goes on a bat, sometimes, and disappears. May be dead, for all anyone knows, once he lets himself go. I'd certainly like to run across him."

"Comes here, does he?" asked the vaudevillian. "Some of the

boys'll know him, maybe. Big Ed, over there at the door, ought to know him. I'll ask him."

"No, don't bother," cried Honeywell quickly. "He'll turn up." And Norway hurriedly added, "I saw him a couple of nights ago, over at another place. Place just like this, about a block over. You know it? Don't know it very well myself; but I know it's got a blue door, like this one."

Silvernail chuckled. "Second floor?" he asked. "Old boy outside, asleep on his box? Redhead Annie at the door? I'll say I know it! But, say, it's hard to get in there. Sort of fancy club, that."

"We thought we'd drop in, later on," added Honeywell, pleased at the way the conversation had turned.

"Drop in now," cried Silvernail. "Why not? I'll go with you. Say, I know that whole crowd. Wait'll I come back, boys. Won't be a minute."

He hastily swallowed what was left of the liquor in his glass and got to his feet. In a moment he had disappeared into the back room from which he had emerged.

Honeywell looked at Norway. "Have we been damned fools?" he asked in a low voice. "I was suspicious of that fellow at first, and I think I'm more suspicious of him now."

"Oh, he's all right," answered his companion, excited at the prospect of finding the trail of the missing Pemberton. "He certainly looks the part he calls himself. I know the type, Bart. Take a chance; it may be the only one we'll have."

"No hope for it, I guess," muttered Honeywell. "Here he is. What's he talking to that fellow behind the bar for?" he asked complainingly. "They're both looking over here at us."

"Telling him about Pemberton, I imagine," replied Norway. "It can't be helped. And we *are* looking for him, you know! I don't know why we shouldn't ask questions, wherever we go."

The dapper Silvernail rejoined them, smiling. "All set?" he asked. "Here we go!"

The man-mountain who had been called Big Ed opened the door for them, smiling evilly, and they descended to the street in silence. A light drizzle of rain was falling and a touch of fog was in the air. The street lamps gleamed somewhat ghostily in the silver darkness.

A purple taxicab was coming along the slippery street, feeling its way toward the curb. Silvernail flung up an arresting hand.

"Hey, Purple!" he called.

The driver brought his machine to a standstill. "Sorry," he said courteously, "but I've got a call."

"To hell with it," said Silvernail cheerily. "I've got a new suit, and it's raining. We're only going a block or two, anyway. You can be back in ten minutes."

He yanked open the door as he spoke. "In you go, boys." The driver laughed and surrendered. Norway and Honeywell climbed in, and the song-and-dance artist followed.

"Do you know a place called the Blue Door?" asked Silvernail of the chauffeur.

"I've heard of it," admitted the driver cautiously.

"Take us *there*," said Julian Silvernail. "It's in the next block, in the same position as this place we're leaving."

The driver nodded and the taxi moved away from the curb. At the corner they turned and began to circle the square.

"You know," cried the irrepressible Silvernail, "I wouldn't be surprised if I knew your friend Pemberton, once I see him."

"I hope so," said Honeywell politely, "but I'm afraid there's not much chance of your seeing him. As we told you, Mr. Pemberton has been missing for some days. We don't exactly want to advertise it, but we *would* like to get some sort of a line on him. The fact is, we're afraid something may have happened to him."

"Things *do* happen," admitted Mr. Silvernail with great originality. He brought forth a package of cheap cigarettes and proceeded with difficulty to light one. The street lamps were eerie in the wet darkness. The rain was increasing.

"Hello," cried Norway suddenly, "this fellow's going all wrong! He's turning north."

"That's funny," said the actor. "He ought know better than that. Hey, buddy!" he called through the glass pane before him. "Not north —*south!*"

Instead of replying, the driver stepped on his accelerator and the car leaped forward as if it were an animal. Reaching an east-and-west crossing, it turned westward with undiminished speed and rushed blindly along the strange thoroughfare, while Julian Silvernail swore and tugged frantically at the window.

Honeywell started to rise to his feet, but a lurch of the car threw him into a corner with a shock that bruised his elbow. He subsided in his seat with a curious smile on his lips. Norway was rapping with his cane against the driver's window, threatening to break the glass. A moment later he, too, subsided, and all three looked at one another in the darkness.

"Well, I'm damned!" said Julian Silvernail. "What does this mean, boys? Are you running away with me?"

"No more than you are running away with us," replied Honeywell. "The driver would appear to be running away with us all. If I am not mistaken, we are being kidnaped." The words were jerked out of him by the headlong speed of the taxicab, which now seemed to be running wild toward the western frontier.

"But this is infamous," cried Norway. "Isn't there something we can do?"

"We can break the glass and yell for help," answered Honeywell, "but I doubt if it would do us any good. Anyone who heard us would only think we were all drunk. Or we can try to force the door open and jump for it; but it would be unsafe to try it. One of us would be sure to be killed. For my part, I'm going to sit tight and see what it all means. At any rate, we are three to one, if this fellow tries any funny business."

Silvernail grunted. "We can knock his block off at the end of the line," he suggested; "but where is the end of the line?"

Then suddenly, the taxicab swung north again, and plunged into a maze of small, dark streets and shadowy houses, to emerge at length in a barren district backgrounded by railroad tracks and the distant hoot of locomotives. In a narrow street that was little more than a blind alley it slackened speed and soon came to a stop. The driver sprang down from his seat and wrenched open the door at Honeywell's side. In his hand there had appeared a menacing pistol of sinister reputation.

"Well, here we are," he observed with acrid sarcasm. "Keep your faces shut, and get out quick."

In silence, the trio descended to the sodden earth, and suddenly

Norway and Honeywell were aware that two pistols were covering them. The second was in the hand of Julian Silvernail.

"End of the line, boys," said their companion of the wild ride, "and a long walk back. You're lucky to be getting back at all. You look like a couple of sensible young fellows to me. Take a tip from a friend, and keep out of this business. It ain't healthy."

The voice was detached and cool, but not unfriendly. Honeywell, when he had recovered his own, answered.

"Who do you think we are?" he asked.

The two strangers laughed.

"Forget it now, boys," continued their acquaintance of the barroom. "We weren't either of us born yesterday. Big Ed was wise to you as soon as you opened your traps. If he'd had *his* way, you wouldn't be going home to-night. You're only doing your duty; I know that, and I ain't unfriendly; but we're making *our* living in *our* way, too, and all we want is to be let alone, see? There's no harm in selling good liquor to good fellows, now, is there?"

"I see," said Honeywell; "you think we are government detectives, do you?"

"Government, or state, or anti-saloon league, or whatever you are, you've had your warning," said the taxi driver. "Next time there'll be less talking."

He climbed back into his seat and Silvernail jumped quickly into the body of the cab. The engine was still running. In a moment the car was in motion. It turned slowly, and Honeywell, straining his eyes in the darkness, saw that the license plate had been painted over. There was a dark line about the body of the cab, too, that was unfamiliar. It was, in point of fact, he realized quickly, not a Purple taxi at all, but a private cab of similar hue and build; an owl taxi, probably, trading on the color of the popular company whose name was in everybody's mouth.

With a final shifting of gears, it moved off in the darkness, leaving the two friends to silence and their thoughts.

Their thoughts were neither pleasant nor printable.

4

The sun, rising early next morning after the rain, found the two adventurers soundly sleeping, and had been up a number of hours before either opened his eyes upon a lunatic world. The long, wet tramp through the night before a respectable taxicab could be encountered had had its inevitable effect upon the two friends; it had tired them so completely that sleep had overwhelmed them almost before they could undress.

About ten o'clock, however, Norway stirred, troubled by vague thoughts of the office, and, rolling over in bed, beheld the tousled head of Bartlett Honeywell outlined upon a sofa pillow. The story writer had spent the night upon a couch. Instantly Norway was wide awake, the details of the preceding evening vivid in his mind. His vocal shudderings in the cold shower awoke Honeywell, who hastened to join his friend in the workaday world, however lunatic.

Some minutes later they descended to breakfast. Their plans had been perfected the night before, during that long, damp walk. They were through with private detecting: it was a delusion and a snare. The police should hear of these outrages, and that shortly.

Without difficulty, they gained the ear of a police captain and told their story. The officer smiled understandingly.

"Don't those fellows do the damnedest things?" he asked. "I hear they have airships now, and fly the stuff over from Canada to some place in Michigan. Then they bring it down the lake and land it some place right under the noses of the government fellows. They're sure getting cute. Well, gentlemen, I'll do what I can to help you. I suppose you can find the place again where you met this fellow—what's his name?—Goldstein?"

"Silvernail," said Honeywell.

"Of course he lied about being a vaudeville actor," continued the captain, "but he's a *bad actor,* I'll make a little bet on that. We'll raid the place before they can get time to turn around, and maybe we'll find a clew to your friend—what's his name?—Emerson?"

"Pemberton," said Honeywell.

"Whatever it is," agreed the captain. "You fellows'll have to go along, see?"

He bustled about for some moments and came back with a square-shouldered, powerful fellow in plain clothes, who was introduced as Detective Sergeant Brady.

"Take a couple of men with you, Brady," ordered the captain, "and get the whole gang."

"Oughtn't we to go at night, Captain?" asked Norway. "There'll be a bigger crowd there at night."

"Oh, we don't want the customers," grinned the officer. "They're decent enough citizens, like yourselves. All they go there for is a drink. We want the fellows who run the place; the fellows behind the bar, and this Big Ed you were talking about."

"How about the policeman who directed Mr. Norway?" queried Honeywell.

"Don't you worry about *him*. That's our job. He'll get all that's coming to him and then some. Leave that to *me*."

A police car was waiting at the curb, and they all piled in, while a small crowd collected before the station to see them off. Honeywell dimly wondered how many bootleggers were in the throng.

Under the guidance of Norway, who sat beside the driver, the police car rapidly covered the distance to the scene of their adventure, and in an instant the whole posse was in motion. Two of the detectives scurried around to the back of the house, to interrupt any possible egress at that point, while Brady and the two adventurers proceeded up the stairway at the front.

At the door leading to the apartment, which seemed somewhat less blue than the night before, Brady hammered briskly and received no reply. He pounded again with the same result.

"Well," said Detective Sergeant Brady, "down she comes!"

He flung himself sharply against the door frame and rebounded, rubbing his shoulder. "All together, boys," he said; and the trio hurled itself in a knot at the withholding door.

Twice they repeated the performance, and then there were running steps inside and the bolts were withdrawn. The men who opened the door were Brady's companions, who had effected an entrance at the rear. They grinned sheepishly and flung out empty hands to indicate the condition of the barroom.

Brady and the two adventurers pushed in and looked about them; but the place was vacant. Everything had been removed overnight. There was not even a clue to the illegal business that had been conducted there only a few hours before.

They returned, crestfallen, to the station, where they listened to a brief lecture from the captain.

"That's the way it often happens, gentlemen," said the officer sympathetically. "Maybe you got the wrong house, and maybe you didn't. Maybe they got a tip-off and scuttled the ship; maybe they just suspected there'd be trouble after they kidnaped two American citizens. I don't know. We're up against that sort of thing all the time, you know, and there's nothing we can do about it but try again. 'Better luck next time' is our motto, these days. Well, gentlemen, any time you get another hunch, look us up. We're always glad to help."

He relighted the stub of a frayed cigar and ushered the friends to the station door.

"Well?" asked Honeywell, cocking an eye at Norway as they stood on a corner a block removed from the police station.

"I think that captain tipped them off himself," asserted Norway promptly. "The police are in this bootlegging business themselves, up to their necks."

"No," demurred the amateur detective. "They wouldn't have had time to clean out that place between the time we left the station and the time we reached the apartment. I'm not defending the police; they may be as bad as you think they are. One of 'em certainly sent you and Pemberton to that first place with the blue door. But there's something else behind all this, something big that's blocking us. I'm beginning to think that something pretty serious has happened to Pemberton, and somebody's afraid we are going to uncover it." His lips set in a thin line. "Well, we *are!* I'm not through with this case yet, Norway. If they've killed Pemberton we'll get the men who killed him. If they're just keeping him locked up some place, we'll find him, and he'll have the evidence we need to put the others where they belong. That's why Pemberton is missing. Somehow, somewhere, he got the goods on this gang—so the gang got Pemberton."

"The place with the blue door is the place we've got to find, Bart," declared Norway with emphasis.

"I know—and thanks to Silvernail, we can find it. He said it was in the next block, and I don't think he lied about that. You thought yourself that we might be a block off in our calculations. Well, I'm going there, myself, to-night."

"Alone?" Norway's question was a protest.

"Yes, alone. We're probably being watched and followed, Norway, and you're more dangerous than I am, because you know Pemberton. I've got a plan turning in my mind, and I'll tell you about it when it's ready."

In Norway's mailbox, when they returned to his apartment, there was a letter in a strange hand, and its recipient quickly tore open the envelope. After a moment he whistled in surprise, and then he laughed.

"By heaven, Bart," he cried, "we've been on a wild goose chase all along. Nothing has happened to Pemberton at all! This is from *him*. He's simply out of town."

"*What?*" cried the writer, snatching the paper from his friend's hand.

But the letter, which was only a friendly note, said quite plainly that Pemberton, who had been out of town for a few days, would be back shortly and hoped to see Norway upon his return.

"Let's get upstairs," said Honeywell; and in the apartment he slumped down in a chair and reread the surprising letter a number of times.

"It certainly takes the wind out of our sails, doesn't it?" asked Norway.

"It does," admitted the story writer, "and I'm wondering if it wasn't intended to do *just* that."

"Now what the devil do you mean?"

"I'm wondering whether the writer of that note isn't trying to call us off the chase."

"But the writer of the note is Pemberton," protested Norway. "There hasn't been any chase except the one we cooked up for ourselves."

Honeywell was again deep in thought. After a few minutes he asked: "How do you know the note is from Pemberton? Because it's signed with his name?"

"Why—yes—I suppose so."

"Did you ever have a letter from him before? Do you know his handwriting? As I understand it, you met Pemberton at the Jack o' Lantern Club the night of the Sea Lions' Frolic. If nothing has happened to Pemberton, there was no occasion for this note. He could have waited until his return and then called you up. No, this note is too damned *timely,* Norway; and I don't believe your friend ever wrote it. It was written by someone who knows you are searching for Pemberton, and who is desperately afraid you are going to find him —or what's left of him, maybe! It was written to call off the hunt, to allay suspicion, to help you to forget your fears for Pemberton's safety."

"Good Lord!" ejaculated Norway. "Who could *that* be?"

"Who? Well, it might have been written by Silvernail, just for instance, or by somebody else at Silvernail's dictation. He knows about Pemberton. We babbled about him enough to that little thug, and he probably knew all about him before."

Again for a time the writer became thoughtful. Then, "I'm going to find that other place to-night," he said grimly. "I've *got* to. It holds the secret of Pemberton's fate. And I'm more than ever certain, now, that Pemberton has either been murdered or is being held captive by those who are afraid of what he has seen."

Thus it fell out that Arthur Norway sat at home that evening, close to a telephone, while Bartlett Honeywell, creator of mysteries, fared forth alone on the trail of the blue door.

It was close to eight o'clock when the amateur detective turned briskly out of Dearborn Street into the little thoroughfare of tall houses that held the bootlegger's palace which he sought. He was exactly a block removed from the scene of their earlier exploit, and no sleeping cabman nodded on his box to mark the entrance. But Honeywell was not disturbed. He realized that the cabby had been removed for good and proper reasons. So long as the search for Pemberton continued, no helpful clue would be furnished by the opposing forces.

It was a night of stars and soft breezes, and the writer's mind reacted happily to the background of vibrant darkness. He strolled casually past the suspected doorway and glanced casually in at the open door. He noted the metal-bound edges of the steps and the soft pile of the scarlet stair runner; but he made no attempt to enter. He was merely an honest citizen out for a stroll on a balmy evening of spring. His light cap was pulled a little sidewise on his head, a pipe was in the corner of his mouth, his hands were in his trouser pockets. On the second floor the blinds were drawn, but a thin line of light escaped beneath the edges.

He circled the block at easy gait and, returning, noted that the nearest intersecting highway was Baker Street. The house he watched was the second from the corner.

In Baker Street, too, the houses were tall and solemn, the very twins of those in the little street that held the apartment with the blue door. The entire square was small, and in a moment he knew why. There was no intervening alley. If an alley existed, it was a private one, somewhere in the center of the buildings, reached probably from the courts. In that case, he reflected, the rear entrances of the several buildings that clustered at the corner would be rather near together. Perhaps they even adjoined.

An odd idea occurred to him. Was it not even possible that the entire square was given over to the lucrative business of selling illegal liquor? A speakeasy in every flat! Dumbwaiters that lifted the "stuff" from huge storerooms in the basements! An entire city block that was a stronghold of criminal enterprise! A great fortress made up of adjoining buildings, connecting from the inside! The headquarters of a vast bootleg industry whose ramifications extended to all quarters of the city!

It was *not* possible, of course; but the idea pleased him. It was the sort of fancy that made his stories popular in the magazines, an extravagance of imagination that made him the one and only Bartlett Honeywell, purveyor of mystery fiction to innumerable thousands.

With this notion running pleasantly through his head, he continued his stroll, and out of the wild idea was born another and less spectacular one. It was at least probable that there were *two* entrances to the house with the blue door and the scarlet stair runner. Since there was no visible access to the rear, where could the second entrance be?

Approaching the Baker Street intersection from another direction, he looked with close attention at all the houses within eye sweep and reached a tentative decision. If there were any connections between the houses at the corner, they would be between the three that made the triangle, that is, the corner house itself and those that stood on either side of it, one in Baker Street, one in the little street of the sleeping cabman.

Here, at any rate, was a valid idea. The commercial entrance to the gin palace was obviously the stairway that led to the blue door. Ergo, the private entrance would be in Baker Street. There might be a flaw in his reasoning, he realized; it was quite possible that no connection existed whatever; but it might pay him to give a trifle of attention to the corner house and to the second house in Baker Street.

He crossed the street and resumed his stroll upon the sidewalk directly across from the two houses that had interested him. Low lights burned in several of the windows, but the shades of all were drawn.

Then, with startling suddenness, his dream castle was given a foundation. A door opened in the second house, and a woman came out and stood upon the steps. She was clad in a light coat over a dark suit, and something in her height and manner made the writer's heart beat rapidly. He shrank back in the shadow of a bush upon a neighboring lawn and watched her.

The young woman—she was obviously young—seemed impatient; but in a moment a taxicab swung into view from Dearborn Street and glided to the curb before the house upon whose steps she stood. She ran quickly down and pulled open the door before the driver could leave his seat. A dim light burned in the interior of the cab, and Honeywell, reckless and excited, ran halfway out into the street for a view of the passenger's face.

Then quickly he turned his back and walked away. He had been right. The second house harbored at least one member of the criminal crew. The young woman who was rolling away in the taxi was Mademoiselle Marie Stravinsky.

Honeywell paused under a lamp post to look at his watch. It was now nine o'clock and the night was yet young. But what should his next step be? To try to force an entrance by either door would be madness, singlehanded; and, anyway, what could he hope to find? Would he not do well to return to Norway for a consultation, or perhaps hurry at once to the police with this new clue to the whereabouts of the man he sought? For that Mademoiselle Stravinsky knew all about the missing Pemberton he had no doubt at all.

Fortune, as he debated, solved his problem. A lone policeman tramped into view from the west and Honeywell, crossing to the other side, accosted him.

"I don't know whether I'm lost or in the wrong block, officer," he said. "Do you know anyone along here by the name of Honeywell?"

The name was an inspiration, for he had been able for an instant to think only of "Smith," a common predicament. To ask for a person named Smith is usually to find him in every block.

The policeman had stopped. "I never heard that name 'round here," he answered good humoredly. "Are you sure it's Baker Street you want?"

"Well, I *thought* so," said Honeywell, "but maybe I'm wrong. I *thought* he lived there in the second house; but he said his name was over the bell, and I can't find any name at all."

"Up there?" asked the policeman, jerking a thumb. "Well, no, he wouldn't live *there*. That's all one house. Amos Churchill lives there. I thought everybody knew *him*."

"Oh!" said Honeywell quickly. "Then I *am* wrong, for I remember he said he lived in the next block to Amos Churchill. I'll find him now. Many thanks, officer."

"Not at all," said the bluecoat, resuming his stride; and the writer walked hurriedly away in the direction indicated.

Amos Churchill!

Good Lord! thought Honeywell, and whistled softly under his breath. "Am I going crazy?" he muttered. "Or have I uncovered something so big that it scares me?"

And quickly all that he knew or had read about Amos Churchill began to fill his mind. The man was a political power and a millionaire. Even so, he might be a crook. But the man was also a reformer! He was quoted in all the better newspapers. His fulminations against the liquor interests were part of the backbone of the Antis' crusade.

He had given thousands for better government, better police protection; to smash the crime rings and to abolish official graft.

Yet Amos Churchill lived in the second house in Baker Street, around the corner from the Blue Door. There was no law against that, to be sure; yet not ten minutes before he had seen Mademoiselle Marie Stravinsky leave the house of this same Amos Churchill—possibly in the very car in which he and Norway had been kidnaped. And Mademoiselle Stravinsky, questioned about Pemberton, had packed her things in a handbag and fled from her apartment. It was the card of Mademoiselle Stravinsky that had been found in the cab of the sleeping cabman. Her name was known to Big Ed, the doorkeeper at the gin palace.

"This thing is getting wild," asserted Honeywell, half aloud. "I'm going to do some thinking about it."

He had promised Norway that in case of trouble or of success he would telephone, and Norway was probably nervously awaiting a call. On the whole, it would be best to go straight to Norway's rooms and tell him all that had occurred. They could talk it all over and do what they decided was the thing to do—go to the police maybe, or to the state's attorney, or to the federal prohibition officer.

He stepped off the sidewalk to cross an intervening alley, and heard light footsteps behind him. The nearest street lamp, he suddenly noticed, was extinguished.

Then a stunning blow took him sidewise across the head, behind the left ear, and he dropped quietly into a pair of arms outstretched to catch him.

5

On Thursday morning Norway called his office and informed his superiors that he would not be down. He was haggard and tired, for he had sat up half the night awaiting the call from Honeywell that did not come. At length he had fallen asleep in his chair, to wake three hours later, at dawn, and call the rooms of his friend.

Perhaps, he thought, the story writer had returned late and gone directly to his bed. But there was no answer to his continued ringing, and something whispered that the worst had happened. Honeywell, too, had disappeared; he was now part of the mystery that shrouded the fate of Robert Pemberton.

At eight o'clock Norway ordered some breakfast brought up to his room by a neighboring restaurateur.

At nine o'clock he settled his hat upon his head with determination and laid his hand upon the doorknob. He would go at once to the chief of police. There would be no more fooling with underlings.

But someone was coming up the steps, wearily, and footsteps were sounding now in his own corridor. Then a light rapping sounded on his door and the handle was rattled. He flung it open, and Honeywell half fell into the room.

The amateur detective was not a pretty sight. His hair was matted and his eyes were bloodshot behind his thick lenses; his garments were stained and disordered. Norway greeted the apparition with a cry of dismay.

"It's all right, old man," said Honeywell. "It's really I; but they almost got me."

"They?" echoed Norway.

"Whoever they are—and I think I know, at last, who is behind this outrage. Don't worry about me. All I need is a bath and some breakfast, and I'll be all right again. I might do, also, with some sleep, but I don't like to waste the time. Well, maybe I've had enough." He smiled grimly. "I lay for some hours, I think, in a stinking alley."

Briefly he told his friend all that had happened, then vanished into the bathroom. Norway sat in silence until he had emerged.

"Where were you going, Norway?" asked the author. "You were about to go out as I came along."

"To the chief of police, I think."

"Not yet," said Honeywell. "By to-night we'll have all we need in the way of evidence; then we can lay it before the proper authorities. But there is still work to be done."

"What do you intend to do?"

"I'm going back to that house in Baker Street," asserted Honeywell. "I'm going to confront this Churchill and force him to tell the truth. It'll be half bluff, but I think I can put it over. If not, I'll spill the entire story in the morning newspapers."

"It's almost unbelievable, isn't it? This thing about Churchill, I mean."

"The papers won't find it so. Anything is believable that makes an eight-column scarehead. The *Morning Hawk* hates Churchill like poison; it would take a chance on *anything* about him. It isn't the best newspaper in town, but it has the biggest circulation."

Norway lighted a cigarette and seated himself. He looked with horror at the discolored bruises on his friend's face. "I think we're in for a lot of trouble, Bart," he observed, "but I'm with you in it. 'Yours to a cinder,' as we used to sign our letters when we were younger. By Jove, I'm glad to see you safely back again!"

"Meanwhile," smiled Honeywell, "can you lend me a suit of clothes and a clean shirt and collar?"

The story writer slept during part of the afternoon and went to dinner feeling vastly refreshed. It was half after seven when the two friends sallied forth to what was to be the final chapter of their misadventures.

A block from the dwelling of Amos Churchill they halted for a final word, but for the most part all plans were laid. At eight o'clock Honeywell would ascend the steps and ask for an interview with Amos Churchill. If it was denied, they would go instantly to the chief of police with the entire story. If it was granted, Norway would watch him enter the house, then patiently await the hour of nine. If by that time Honeywell had not safely emerged, Norway would follow him through the door, accompanied if possible by the friendly policeman whose schedule, as Honeywell had noted, took him past the Churchill place at nine o'clock.

"Everything clear?" asked the writer as they paused on the corner. "Okay, then! Keep out of sight, Norway, while I go forward."

"Keep your gun handy in your side pocket, Bart," whispered his friend.

"I didn't bring it," answered the other. "I have no right to carry it, and it might only get me into serious trouble. But I think Churchill will give me no difficulty. He has a reputation to maintain. He may order me out of his house, but I think there will be no violence."

He waved his hand and strode rapidly along Baker Street to the house he had come to invade. Norway saw him climb the steps and pause for a moment in the entry. Then the inner door was opened, there was a brief exchange of words, and Honeywell disappeared inside the house. Norway began to pace his little beat, back and forth, back and forth, one eye upon the place across the street. Occasionally he glanced at his watch as the time passed.

Within, a frowning butler took the card of Bartlett Honeywell to Amos Churchill, then ushered the writer into the presence. Red curtains framed the wide doorway that led to Churchill's sitting room. The furniture was expensive and of massive pattern. A yellow lamp glowed on a small table beside a deep red leather chair in which sat the man the volunteer investigator had come to see.

Amos Churchill was a man of middle age, and was very well preserved. He seemed to have great strength and vitality. He was of a somewhat saturnine cast of countenance, and, although a little mustache clothed his upper lip, his head was bald.

He looked up as Honeywell was announced and smiled a mechanical smile of welcome, the professional smile of a busy man interrupted at his herculean labors.

"Mr. Bartlett Honeywell." He repeated the name as the butler turned away, reading from the card that he held in his hand. He did not rise to greet his visitor. "I think I have not met you before, Mr. Honeywell?"

"Not before, I think," agreed Honeywell pleasantly. "I am a newspaper man, Mr. Churchill, as I informed your butler. I am a free lance, however, and am not connected with any one journal. I hope I am not intruding at an awkward hour?"

The politician smiled a hard, metallic smile.

"I am usually glad to see newspaper men," he replied somewhat cynically. "I am *used* to seeing them, at any rate. Most people are, these days. When a man has been waked from sleep a number of times, at three or four in the morning, to answer questions as to the state of his health or the amount of his embezzlement, he becomes accustomed to the activities of newspaper men."

He chuckled sardonically. Honeywell politely smiled.

"I did not come to ask you about your health," said the writer, "although I trust it is excellent; nor have I any information concerning your embezzlements. I am afraid you are going to believe me very rude, and I think I had better be frank and brief."

"That would be a good idea," agreed the politician. His ease was considerable; the story writer felt certain that Churchill was entirely sure of the reasons for the sudden visit.

Very leisurely, Honeywell began his story. He told it simply and clearly and without reticence. Everything that he had heard and seen, everything that had happened to himself and Norway, everything that between them they had inferred, he related quietly while the reformer listened. Churchill's impassive face betrayed no emotion whatever. When he had finished, the man still sat silent. The black eyebrows were slightly raised, however, as if in ironic question, and a little steely light glittered in each eye.

"I tell you everything in detail," concluded Honeywell, "because I want you to understand how completely I intend to write this story, in the event that I write it at all, for the newspapers."

Amos Churchill took a cigar from his pocket and leaned forward to light it. Then he dropped back in his big chair and blew a long streamer of smoke at the paneled ceiling. Honeywell admired his composure.

"A very remarkable tale," commented the politician at length. "I have just placed you, Mr. Honeywell. You are the Bartlett Honeywell who writes detective fictions for certain of the magazines. I have seen your name upon the covers, on the newsstands. I have not read your stories, but I am certain they are very exciting and fascinating. You have a powerful imagination. The story that you have invented, in which I am cast for the part of villain, is a really extraordinary flight of fancy. Of course, it is entirely fiction."

"You will pardon me," retorted Honeywell, reddening, "but I believe it to be entirely fact."

"I suppose you do. You would hardly have come here to-night with such a tale without believing it. Now, Mr. Honeywell, I have only this to say: I did not have to let you in here, and, having let you in, I did not have to listen to your ravings. However, it pleased me to hear what you had to say, and I think you will agree that I have been very patient and very courteous. I am going to continue to be patient and courteous. Instead of ordering my butler to throw you out into the street, I am going to ask you to leave quietly—but at once."

"You have no comment to make on what I have told you then?" asked the story writer.

"Only that which I have already made: that the whole tale is the purest fiction. I advise you to write it all out and sell it to a magazine. But in that case, be very careful to use names that are equally fictitious."

For an instant Honeywell's fingers drummed on the arm of his chair.

"Very well," he said at last, "I shall write it all out within an hour or two, and *give* it—not sell it—to the *Morning Hawk*. Whether your name is mentioned, or that of Mademoiselle Stravinsky, must be decided by the *Hawk*'s editor."

He rose to his feet.

"Just a moment, Mr. Honeywell," interposed Churchill. "Sit down again for a minute. You have just threatened me. What is more to the point, you are probably just idiot enough to put your threat into execution. And the editor of the *Hawk,* who has had his knife in me for some time, is just reckless enough to print your story. It would cost him his job, and his paper a lot of money; but the story would have been printed, and that I should not like. People believe what they read in print, and my denials would not have the full force of your accusations. I suggest that you reconsider your determination to go to the *Hawk.*"

Honeywell nodded. It was his moment of triumph. Things were coming his way in the end. It was being very suavely done, but Churchill was surrendering.

"I suggest," returned the author, "that you reconsider your decision not to speak. I suggest a compromise. I suggest that you produce Pemberton, in which case I shall at once withdraw from the affair. I can not, of course, answer for Pemberton. It will be for him to decide what steps, if any, should be taken against those who have held him prisoner." He hesitated, and then demanded starkly, "Or *can* you produce Pemberton?"

"Ignoring the implication of that question and accepting it literally, I can *not,*" replied Churchill. "I do not know the man, and I have no notion where he is. My suggestion for a reconsideration was in another connection. I suggest that you question the wisdom of the course you plan to pursue."

The level tones had become deadly, but Honeywell thought only that his victim was on the run. He again rose to his feet, glancing at his watch as he did so. They had been engaged in conversation for some time; the hour set for Norway's possible interruption was close at hand. The conversation was getting nowhere. He would better go at once to the police or the papers.

"You refuse then?" asked Churchill casually. Then, without warning, he shot forward his foot and shoved the intruder back into his chair. At the same instant his hand tugged at the drawer of a small desk that stood beside him. The drawer opened and with startled eyes Honeywell glimpsed a flash of steel within. A long revolver lay under the politician's hand. The man's face was now a savage mask of fury.

The writer leaned quickly forward. His hand was just in time to clutch the extended arm of the other and arrest its course. For a moment the two were tense in their dramatic attitudes. Then the red curtains parted and the burly butler drove into the room, an automatic pistol raised at the level of Honeywell's breast.

The latter sat back in his chair and slowly raised both hands above his head.

"Very well," he said quietly, "kill *me* as you killed Pemberton."

It was while this melodrama was at its height that Norway, backed by the ponderous policeman—an unwilling and incredible participant —ran up the steps of the house and hammered at the door.

As the sounds penetrated to the study the butler drew slowly back. He lowered his weapon slightly, still holding it ready for use, and looked inquiringly at Churchill. The hammering of Norway's fists still sounded on the glass and woodwork of the outer door.

"Your friends?" asked Churchill with a curious smile, and Honeywell nodded his head.

"And Mr. Norway—is he among them?" continued the politician. He turned to the butler. "See who is at the door, Adamson. Let them come in here."

Then Honeywell heard the front door open and close, heard hurrying footsteps in the entry and the hall, and heard the shrill voice of Arthur Norway calling his name.

The dilettante, the policeman, and the butler entered the room together. Honeywell turned and smiled.

"You are just in time to prevent another disappearance, Norway," he remarked. "Whatever this man may have been responsible for before, I now order his arrest charged with the attempted murder of Bartlett Honeywell."

The embarrassed policeman looked from Churchill to Honeywell and back again at Churchill. But Norway, after one incredulous glance at Churchill, leaped forward and grasped the politician by the hand.

"My God, Bart," he cried, "what does this mean? Have you gone crazy? *This is Pemberton!*"

A sneering smile sat upon the politician's lips.

"Yes," he observed, "at last you have found the missing Pemberton. What a damned fool I was ever to pick up with *you*, Norway."

Honeywell only looked on with unbelieving eyes.

In the silence that followed, Churchill spoke again. "Well, gentlemen," he said, "the little farce is over. I have just admitted that I was a fool. It is your turn to admit that you were even bigger fools. As I am myself Pemberton, you can hardly arrest me as my own murderer. You have, however, blundered onto certain things in my life that, I concede, would not look well in print, and I am willing to make what amends I can to you, within reason. I assure you, just the same, that not a single one of the several things you suspect about me could be proven in a court of law. I am not always a fool. I hope you take my meaning."

Then Honeywell found his voice. "Why did you do it?" he asked.

"Why did I deceive your friend Norway? Because I was an idiot, I suppose, and because *he* was drunk. I had been drinking myself, and was not eager to appear in anyone's eyes as a man who preached one thing and practiced another. The facts about Pemberton are these: he is a member of the club that Mr. Norway and I know, and was present on the occasion of the frolic. He is well known to me. For some reason, probably because we were introduced to the clever Mr. Norway at about the same instant, he confused me with Pemberton. He insisted on calling me Pemberton, and as he was a bit drunk and disorderly, I let it go at that.

"As it happens, Pemberton was leaving town on an early train, and he did not return to the club, but spent the balance of that Saturday night at a hotel. In the morning he caught his train and went about his business; I went about mine, never dreaming that I had inspired such affection in Norway that he would worry about me the next day. When he tried to reach Pemberton and failed, he became frantic, it would seem, with *this* result. I heard from several sources of his efforts to locate Pemberton, and realized that it was I whom he was trying to find. It was too late to hunt him up and confess my duplicity, I decided, and besides I imagined he would tire of the hunt and let the missing Pemberton go to the devil. Pemberton, of course, knew nothing at all about what was happening; he was actually out of the city. He is still out of the city. *I* wrote the letter you received from him, in an effort to stop your headlong career.

"Well," continued Churchill, "that's what happened. It was a mess, and it *is* a mess. The ambitious Norway enlisted *your* services, and between you you ran down a lot of things about my private life that it is most annoying to realize you know. I am talking, of course, about a certain young woman and a blue door. Oh, I admit I tried in a number of ways to discourage you, but you were too pertinacious. Silvernail failed to stop you, and so did the man who is responsible for any headache you may still have, as a result of last night's attempt."

"There are other things to be explained," suggested Honeywell, after a moment. "There was a crossing policeman who—"

"And an old cabman, I believe," interrupted Churchill quickly. "They are all susceptible of explanation, Mr. Honeywell," he added meaningly, "but need we go into everything here and now? Are you appointing yourselves defenders of the faithful, guardians of the public morals, correctors of police laxity, avengers of outraged justice? Or are you two sensible men who know when they have had enough? Who know when they are up against something bigger than they can handle alone?"

The story writer turned to the big policeman. "What do *you* make of all this?" he asked sharply.

"Hanged if I can make *anything* out of it!" answered the bewildered bluecoat. "But if Mr. Churchill says it's all right, I guess it's all right."

Honeywell flung up his hands in a gesture of surrender. "That, I suppose, would be the attitude of nine tenths of the people of Chicago," he said. "If Mr. Churchill says so, it's all right. I think I have learned a valuable lesson, Mr. Pemberton-Churchill," he concluded dryly. "My own insignificance and helplessness were never before brought home to me so clearly. But the day will come when a lot of insignificant and indignant persons will join forces to cleanse the high places of all corruption."

Amos Churchill shrugged.

"Perhaps!" he answered. "But I think you and all of us will be dead when that day arrives, Mr. Honeywell. Good luck with your stories!"

In the taxicab that took them homeward, Bartlett Honeywell swore softly to himself.

"He's right," he declared at last. "The time hasn't come. People are fools because they want to be fools; and they are fooled because they want to be fooled. Sleeping cabmen! Tired horses! Blue doors! Corrupt saints! Even if the *Hawk* printed it, it would sound like a fairy tale."

He was silent again for a time. Then he made a final remark.

"By heaven, there's one thing I can do, Norway," he grunted. "I can write it as fiction! I can make a story of it!"

He did.

This is it.

ALL THE WAY HOME

Dan J. Marlowe

Dan J. Marlowe

Some crime stories emphasize the crime; others, the story. Dan J. Marlowe's "All the Way Home" is one of the latter. Although it deals with a crime, it is also a powerful tale of tortured people, and an excellent evocation of the rural Midwest as it was between the literary era of Hamlin Garland and that of Sinclair Lewis. All of which makes it quite an accomplishment.

Marlowe claims that he writes short stories of diverse kinds as a distraction from the formularization of his "Operation" novels, which have as their protagonist Earl Drake, the ex–bank robber and deadly marksman. Drake, he points out, could never appear in "All the Way Home." Which is certainly true—and says a lot for Marlowe's versatility.

An ex-businessman, ex-politician, ex-professional gambler, Marlowe turned to writing in his forties, and since then has had twenty-four books published, as well as more than a hundred and fifty short stories. He lives in Harbor Beach, Michigan, and wrote "All the Way Home" after a visit to the state's Upper Peninsula.

"To a city boy like myself," he says, "the ruggedness of the country up there was impressive. There was a deserted lighthouse on a spit of land jutting out into the lake, and an ancient horse-drawn fire pumper in a commercial museum. I found myself writing the story in my mind during the drive home."

A.M.

ALL THE WAY HOME

The hired man drove me back to the farm from the cemetery. Becky's funeral had taken a lot out of me, although at my age I should be used to them. I came back from my father's funeral in a horse and buggy, from my mother's in an old tin lizzie, and from Becky's in a many-horsed thunderbolt. I've lived too long.

My father's farm—my farm—is on a spit of land jutting out into Lake Superior. It's a good farm. With a little help from the cows, it took care of all of us through the long years. I can't even leave it to kinfolk now. I'm the last of the Malcolms.

What still hurts me the most is knowing how Becky must have wondered why I never asked her to marry me. Especially since my mother died. Becky never let on, of course, and there was nothing I could do, or say. Not since that terrible night on Wild Swan Point so many years ago.

There used to be an old abandoned wooden lighthouse at the end of the causeway leading out to the point. It hasn't been there for a long time now, but at sunset when the west wind blows and the clouds are dark on the lake, I can sit by the kitchen window and look down the road, and once again a light seems to shine from the tiny window high up in the old lighthouse.

When I was twelve years old, the light shone there because my father had fixed up a room in the lighthouse for Miss Abby Hunter, up near the top where she wanted to be. My mother didn't like it at all when Miss Abby came back to live in our neighborhood again. Before she left, Miss Abby taught school and lived on the Brainard farm about a mile from us. I heard my mother say once after Miss Abby came to dinner at our house that some people were no better than they should be. My father heard her say it, too, and it made him angry. He told my mother later that she was a fool to believe all the gossip she heard.

We were at the supper table in our big farm kitchen when he said it. There were rusks and wild strawberry jam on the table. I wanted another rusk, but when I looked up and saw my father's face, I was afraid to ask for it. He was a big strong solid-looking man, with red cheeks and blue eyes and a temper that scared me sometimes. But his temper never scared my mother. She spoke right up to him all the time, but especially so after Miss Abby came back to live in the lighthouse.

I liked Miss Abby. She lent me books, but after my mother found out, I had to hide them. Miss Abby always looked dressed up. She was small and quick-moving and very pretty. She always wore a blue ribbon on her blond hair. When she was still teaching, she never seemed much older than the bigger kids in school.

The old lighthouse was a strange place to want to live in. It hadn't been used as a lighthouse for a long time. There wasn't much in the cobwebbed space at the bottom except a few bad-smelling battered oil drums. I never saw the room my father fixed up for Miss Abby at the top of the spiraling wooden staircase. She never invited me to see it, and I didn't know how to ask.

I came back to the farmhouse one morning after collecting the eggs in the coop and taking the cows down to the pasture by the lake, where we had a dock. My father's sailboat was always tied up at the dock during the summer. The dock was near the barn and the road, too, so I hadn't far to go. During the less busy seasons, in the spring and fall, my father used to go out on the lake with his nets and bring back whitefish, lake trout, pike, and perch.

He met me at our front gate, saying he wanted to talk to me. It made me feel important as soon as I saw he wasn't angry as he was so often those days. "Tommy," he said, "twice a week I want you to carry a pail of milk down to Miss Abby at the lighthouse. You can milk Daisy after supper, and get down and back before dark. Do it on Sunday and Wednesday nights. And let's keep it a secret, just between you and me." He put a finger to his lips, and winked at me.

It sounded fine to me. I had no brothers or sisters, and sometimes I got so lonely I welcomed the chance to talk to almost anyone. My mother was always busy in the kitchen after supper, and I was sure she wouldn't miss me. She was a tall, stout woman with black hair and snapping black eyes. She was almost pretty when she smiled, but she hardly ever smiled after Miss Abby came back to live at the lighthouse.

They argued a lot. More than once I overheard my father tell my mother that she'd better learn to control her tongue. My mother would get red in the face. Her eyes glared, and she usually left the room.

I could hardly wait to milk Daisy the first Sunday night and be on my way down to Wild Swan Point. My father had gotten me a special pail with a tight lid for the milk carrying. It didn't spill even when I ran. The sun was going down behind the lighthouse when I reached the point, and Miss Abby was sitting on a bench outside. She looked like a doll in her frilly white dress against the dirty wooden wall of the old lighthouse.

She greeted me warmly and asked me to sit down while she put the milk away. I could see that she was making a woodpile inside the big door. There was always driftwood on the shore, and I carried some inside and stacked it. Miss Abby thanked me when she came downstairs. It was almost dark when I reached home. I turned and looked back down the road and saw the high-up lighted window in the lighthouse, like a small and lonely star against the night.

The Brainards stopped by our place one Sunday afternoon in August. They had a boy a year older than me. His name was Nick, and I didn't like him. He was bigger than me, and he was always picking a fight. We sat in the front parlor, and Mrs. Brainard began talking about how queer it was for Miss Abby to come back and live in the old lighthouse when she was no longer teaching. Nick sat grinning at me from his chair across the parlor. He motioned with his head, finally, and we excused ourselves and went outside.

Nick headed for our outhouse. We had the nicest one in the area.

It was painted green, and it had a kind of small porch with mosquito netting all around it. A wild cucumber vine grew across the top. Nick stayed inside a long time, and when he came out he had a piece of chalk in his hand.

"What have you been doing with the chalk?" I asked suspiciously.

"Go in and see," he sneered.

I went inside, and one look was enough. All down one wall he'd scribbled Miss Abby's name, and my father's name, and a lot of other things. He was all doubled up laughing when I charged out the door. I got him down, and we rolled on the ground, hitting and scratching and biting.

All of a sudden I felt myself swung up into the air. "Can't you damn kids get along without fighting?" my father hollered in my ear. Nick sat up, looking scared. He glanced at the open outhouse door, then looked away. My father stared at him, set me down, and went inside. Nick jumped up and streaked it for the front gate. My father ran out in time to see him vault the fence onto the road.

"I'll make his tail smoke when I get my hands on him!" my father declared. His lips were a thin hard line. He turned to me, and I stopped rubbing the eye that Nick's elbow had banged. "Sorry, Tommy. Run to the house and get something to wash—" He broke off when my mother came around the corner of the house and walked up to us.

Nobody said anything. My mother looked at each of us in turn. Two bright red spots blazed on her pale cheeks. My father was standing between her and the open door. She started to push past him. He half raised an arm to stop her, then shrugged and lowered it. My mother went inside.

I got out of there. I knew they'd say awful things to each other. I went in the back door to the kitchen, and in the mirror above the sink I tried to see if my eye looked as bad as it felt. It was getting dark outside, and I was late with the chores. I went out to the barn and started milking the cows. After a while my father came in and sat down on a stool beside mine and went to work without saying anything. His face was grim-looking in the lantern light.

I filled the special pail for Miss Abby and left the barn. My father still hadn't said a word. I walked down the path to the road gate, and

I had just reached for the latch when my mother spoke to me from the darkness. "Where are you going?" she asked me. I nearly dropped the pail. She didn't wait for me to answer her. She took the pail away from me and carried it back to the barn.

I didn't know what to do. They didn't come out of the barn, and I knew they must be having a terrible row. I went back to the kitchen and waited for what seemed like a long time. I was hungry again, but I didn't want to be the only one eating. My mother came into the kitchen at last. She didn't speak to me. She walked as though her eyes weren't seeing anything. She passed through the kitchen and went upstairs. Outside, I could hear my father washing up at the pump, and then he walked down the path to the road.

I remembered the chalk-writing on the outhouse wall, and I wet a rag at the pump and went down to the barn for the lantern. The first step I took inside I saw the gaping stall in the lineup of placidly chewing cows. Daisy's stall was empty. Daisy was gone, and my father was gone. My stomach felt cold.

I finished up at the outhouse and then went back to the silent kitchen. I lighted the kerosene lamp and put it on the table by the window. I must have fallen asleep with my head on my arms on the table, because the sound of the parlor clock striking ten woke me up. There wasn't a sound in the house.

I went upstairs to bed, but I couldn't fall asleep again. I thought about my father and my mother, and the way it used to be before Miss Abby came. I wondered what would happen now. I wondered what my mother would do when she found out that Daisy was gone.

I didn't want to come downstairs in the morning, but I had to, finally. The big bedroom door was open when I passed it, and I thought that somehow everything might be all right. My mother was at the stove, and my father was at the table, eating, but they weren't speaking, even to me, and it wasn't all right.

I stayed away from the house all morning. In the afternoon I went out to the corncrib and got out the copy of *Wind in the Willows* that Miss Abby had lent me. I kept it hidden there so my mother wouldn't know. I went down the path to read under the big elm beside the road. The sun was shining, but clouds were forming in the west, and it was getting cooler.

I'd almost forgotten where I was when someone said, "Hey, kid!" I looked up and saw Joe Macy, the RFD mailman from Indian Bay. He was standing by our mailbox at the gate, and he had a letter in his hand. "Give this to your pa," he said to me. "It'll save me the hike to the point. He'll be glad of the chance to deliver it, no doubt."

I knew what it was even before I got up from the grass and took it from him. The letter was addressed to Miss Abby. Joe Macy grinned at me, a nasty grin. "Me, I aim to get on back home before it storms," he said.

I stood there wishing I was bigger. I'd have taken the ugly grin right off his ugly face. Over in the west the cloudbanks were much larger, and it was beginning to blow. Dust eddied in the roadside ditches. The big elm rustled loudly.

I wanted to hide the letter, but I was afraid. I put the book back in the corncrib, then carried the letter to the house. My mother was in the kitchen working the butter churn, one of my usual jobs, and my father was oiling a trap. They had their backs to each other. My father put the trap down as if he was glad he had something else to do when I handed him the letter. He looked at it, turning it over and over in his big hands.

"Where'd this come from?" he asked in a strange voice.

"Joe brought it to the gate just now," I said. "He said you could take it to Miss Abby while he got home before the storm."

"No!" my mother screamed. It was such a piercing sound that I ducked. "No, no, no! You're not going down there, Tom! Are you trying to drive me out of my mind?"

"Don't tell me what I'm not going to do, woman!" he shouted at her harshly. "Not in my own house!" He shoved the letter into his pocket. "It will keep," he said to me in a quieter tone. "I've got to get out on the lake and take my nets in before the storm tears them up."

He stamped out of the house.

My mother sank down into a chair. She began to moan and rock herself from side to side. I don't think she knew I was still there. I couldn't stand it. I went outside, too. It was almost dark, and blowing hard. Much too hard for my father to be heading out in his boat to take in his nets.

I started to run to the dock, but I stopped after I turned the corner of the barn. I could see the dock from there, and silhouetted against the lake and the low-flying clouds I could see the boat's stubby mast. My father hadn't gone out on the lake. I knew where he'd gone.

Five minutes later it was so dark I couldn't see the dock, let alone the boat. I went into the barn to get out of the wind. Daisy's empty stall reminded me of the way things were all over again. I could look down the road through a crack in the barn door left by a splintered hinge and see the light high up in the lighthouse on Wild Swan Point.

I couldn't stay in the barn, but I couldn't bear going back to the house either. The wind ripped at me out on the path. I reached the road and started to run. All along the causeway I could hear the big waves breaking against the rocks. I reached the lighthouse and sat down on the bench outside the door to catch my breath. I began to get chilled again in the fiercely gusting wind, and finally I went inside.

I couldn't find the door latch at first in the dark. The door opened easily, not creaking and groaning as it had when I was still delivering the milk. The hinges had been oiled. It was quiet inside, away from the soughing of the wind and the crashing of the waves. It was pitch-black inside, except for a single sliver of light at the top of the spiral staircase.

I felt around, trying to find something to sit on. I didn't feel like facing that wind again. I almost yelled out loud when I bumped into something big and warm. It took me a second to realize it was Daisy, tethered inside out of the storm. She butted me with her head the way she always did when she wanted to be milked. I moved away from her, afraid that she would moo.

I brushed against the railing at the foot of the stairs, and I looked up again to the crack of light at the top. I climbed the stairs silently, without really making up my mind that I intended to do it. I kept one hand on the railing, the other on the wall. I could hear Miss Abby's voice when I reached the top and stood outside the door. I could hear the wind again, that high up, but I could hear her, too.

". . . got to stop arguing with me, Tom," I could hear her saying. "You saw the letter. They can't keep the child any longer. I've got to go and get her and bring her back here with me. It's what I should do, anyway."

"No!" my father's voice exclaimed. "It's . . . it's no place for a child, Abby. Give me a few days. I'll . . . I'll think of something."

"The letter said right now, Tom." Miss Abby's voice was firm. "I'll leave tomorrow. You can think of something when I get back here."

"Good God, Abby, do you realize what you're doing to me?" My father's voice sounded like it did the time he hit his thumb with the maul. "It's impossible, I tell you! I can't—"

"You can, and you will. I've been patient long enough. Look at me, Tom. Are you saying you can't find a way? Are you telling me I should go and not come back at all?"

"No!"

Miss Abby's silvery laugh sounded after my father's hoarse exclamation. She murmured something I couldn't make out, and neither of them spoke again. The light under the edge of the door went out. I stared at the place where it had been. I felt like I did in church when the preacher talked about the end of the world: just plain scared. I crept back down the winding staircase in the pitch-black darkness and let myself out the big door at the bottom. All I could think of was what was going to become of us.

Outside it was a bit lighter. The moon showed fitfully through the racing clouds. The wind was higher than before, even, and the waves smashed solidly against the causeway. I started back to the house. I was too cold and too tired to do anything else.

I was two-thirds of the way along the causeway when I heard pebbles dislodged from the path ahead of me. I plunged down off the path on the land side without even thinking about it. I hid amidst big rocks dislodged by numerous lake storms. Above me a cloaked shadow passed by, on the way to the lighthouse. I knew it was my mother even before the moon came out again and showed me plainly. She was bent forward against the wind, and she was talking to herself. When she passed, I scrambled up onto the causeway path again and ran all the way to our house.

But when I got to the house I found I couldn't go inside. I couldn't stop thinking of my mother and father and Miss Abby at the lighthouse, and the dreadful things they'd say to each other. Nothing would ever be the same for us again.

I struggled against the wind down to the barn. I knew the animal heat of the cows always kept it warm. I took down a pitchfork and piled fresh hay in a corner of Daisy's empty stall. I stretched out in the sweet-smelling hay, and I must have fallen asleep, because it seemed like a long time later that I heard a bell ringing. At first I thought it was a dream, but then it got louder and louder.

I jumped up and ran to the barn door. The floor shook from the thunder of horses' hoofs as the four-horse team from Indian Bay skittered down the road with the old fire pumper. Its iron bell was clanging steadily.

I whirled to look at our house, but it was safely dark. I turned then toward the point, but I think I knew before I looked. Great roaring sheets of flame were blowing out of the top of the lighthouse, hundreds of feet out over the lake.

I stood there shivering. My mother had intended to kill Miss Abby, but without knowing it she had killed my father, too. She thought he was out on the lake in his boat. What would she do to herself when she found out that he wasn't?

I ran down to the dock. I threw myself flat on my stomach on the rough pine planking and clawed at the hard knots in my father's snubbing ropes at the other end of which his boat pitched violently in the black choppy water. My fingernails were broken and bleeding when I finally got the ropes untied. I had a knife in my pocket, but I couldn't leave a cut rope-end showing. The boat lurched away into the whitecaps, and I got up and hurried to the house. I was in bed when the neighbors arrived.

No one but me ever knew everything that happened on Wild Swan Point that terrible night. The lighthouse burned flat. The fire was so fierce no one could get near it. The oil drums at the bottom burned for two days. It was another day before they could sift the ashes. They found human bones mixed with Daisy's, but not many of either from a fire that fierce. The human bones were buried as Miss Abby's. It never occurred to anyone that someone else could have been inside the lighthouse.

A trawler found my father's boat on the third day. It had capsized two miles out on the lake. They towed it into our dock. My mother hadn't left the dock the whole time except for brief intervals. The lakemen told her gently that my father must have been washed overboard during the height of the storm.

My mother hired a man to help with the farm, after everything was done that had to be done. I did what I could, too. For two months my mother's eyes were sunk deeply into her head. The only person she talked to was me. Nights I could hear her praying behind her closed bedroom door.

She didn't show any sign of improvement, and I didn't know what to do. I knew she wasn't eating or sleeping much at all. I was sitting on our front steps one sunny afternoon, thinking about it all, when a man walked up our path with a battered satchel in one hand. He was leading a little girl with the other. "Mrs. Malcolm live here?" he asked me.

I nodded. I couldn't have got a word out. The girl was about three years old, with the bluest of eyes. She had a blue ribbon in her blond hair.

The man mopped his forehead before he knocked at the door. I could feel my heart beating while I waited for my mother to answer. When she did, she looked at the man inquiringly, but then she saw the little girl. My mother's features froze.

"Is Mrs. Malcolm home?" the man asked.

"I'm Mrs. Malcolm," my mother said.

"Oh, ahh—" The man was obviously taken aback. "Well, then, is the other Mrs. Malcolm here?"

"I'm the only—" my mother began, then wrenched her eyes almost forcibly from the little girl's blue eyes and blond hair. "Come inside," she said curtly to the man. They went in and my mother closed the door.

I patted the step beside me. "Come sit here," I invited the girl. "What's your name?"

"Becky." That was all she said. She sat down beside me with a tired sigh. Her little white shoes were covered with road dust, and her thin face was pinched with weariness.

"I'm Tom," I told her. Even my mother had stopped calling me Tommy.

We sat in silence then. I wasn't staring directly at Becky, but I heard her start to cry. She put her head down on her knees so I couldn't see her face. I didn't know what else to do, so I put my arm around her.

When my mother and the man came out of the house, the man was putting something into his pocket. He went down the path and up the road without saying anything, but he stopped twice to turn and look back at us. "Come along inside, dear," my mother said to Becky. She held out her hand to her. "It's time to milk the cows, Tom," she said to me in the same breath.

I knew then everything was going to be all right.

And for fifteen years it was, until my mother died of cancer. She didn't have an easy time. It almost seemed she didn't want an easy time. She never set foot inside church after that night on Wild Swan Point. She wouldn't let the preacher inside the house, either, but she sent Becky and me to Sunday school every week.

There were good years afterward, too, except I had to sit and watch Becky patiently waiting for me to ask her to marry me. I sent her away to college over her protests. She came back to the farm. My housekeeper complained for years about the waste of my money involved in the unnecessary young hired men I insisted on having on the place. Becky never seemed to see any of them in any way that mattered.

There was never an answer I could find, then or ever.

Now Becky's gone, too, and there's just me.

At least it won't be for much longer.